NEW ZIGON

THE FOUNDER'S CURSE

Book 1

By Danelle O'Donnell

"The Founder's Curse" is the first in a four-book series.

ISBN-10: 1501065629
ISBN-13: 978-1501065620

DEDICATION

To my husband, Mike, who gave me the chance to follow my dreams, and to my boys, Matt, Brian, and Jamie, who encouraged me every step of the way.

CONTENTS

PROLOGUE – 1349 A.D.

A man stood sentry in the woods; his dark gaze unwavering as he peered through the trees into a clearing. He leaned against a massive trunk with his right leg resting on a boulder, a length of rope clutched in his grip. The forest tree branches swayed in the sky above him as the fresh breeze stirred the hair around his face. Aside from the few strands of hair lifted by the gentle wind, he was absolutely still. He appeared calm from a distance, but up close one would notice his knuckles were white from the pressure of his hold on the rope, his face was unshaven and his eyes were bloodshot and strained. His tall, muscular form made a formidable silhouette as he lurked in the shadows of the trees. His stare was locked on a stream that spilled over a small waterfall before it danced around the far edge of the clearing. The beauty of the scene was lost on the man. He would not allow himself to truly see it. He would not allow himself to remember. Desperation and determination warred with each other through his body. He had no other choice left to him. He stood. He waited.

The man stiffened slightly then coiled his muscles, ready to move. The waterfall was changing. It was as if giant hands reached out and parted the water. Through the dark gap, a girl emerged. Her bright golden hair gleamed in the sun as she peered out. She hesitantly stepped forward onto a small rock, and the water fell back into place behind her. She was small of build, around thirteen years old. The glare off her white skin was nearly blinding. Her sleeveless, knee length dress of pearlescent pinks shimmered and reflected the sunlight. Her blue eyes scanned the clearing, looking for potential danger. The man held his post, silent and unseen.

Apparently satisfied with her assessment, the girl carefully picked her way out of the stream onto the grass. She let out a huge sigh as she tipped her face to the sun, soaking in its warmth before wandering through the clearing, gathering wildflowers. Her path led her closer and closer to the man's hiding spot in the woods. When she was only a few yards away, he stepped out and quietly called to her. She startled, looked at him, and froze. He started talking to her, and she pressed her lips together, shaking her head violently as she

1

backed away. He took another step towards her. She dropped her flowers, turned back to the stream, and ran. The man didn't hesitate. He started after her, preparing the coils of rope in his hands. After only a few steps, he raised a lasso over his head and threw it at the girl. His aim was true, but he didn't pull back quickly enough. The circle of rope flew over the girl's head and fell to the ground as she tried to leap out of its grasp. She was almost clear when it caught on her foot. The man jerked on the rope and it tightened around her right ankle, yanking it behind her. She hopped on her free foot, her skirt and hair swirling as she waved her hands frantically to keep her balance. The girl, her hair, and skirt all froze mid-motion. The man was closing in on her, walking the rope hand over hand, keeping the tension, but trying not to make the girl fall. It took his agitated brain a moment to recognize the curious way the girl had suddenly stopped moving. He was nearly to her when his body no longer responded to his commands. His heart thumped loudly in his chest as he helplessly watched the girl morph into stone, trapping the open-mouthed scream on her face. He felt a pinch of regret and overwhelming defeat as the transformation ran along the rope to consume him. Blackness overcame him as he was turned to stone.

The sun continued to shine down on the clearing, the stream bubbled to the side, and the breeze frolicked between the trees, grass, and wildflowers. The scene was just as it was before, only now there was an imposing statue of a man lassoing the ankle of a girl as she ran from him, frozen forever in that first moment of capture.

CHAPTER 1 – FIELD TRIP

John stood in the back of his group with his hands in his pockets and head ducked, trying his best to blend in with the wall. His class was on his school's time-honored, eighth-grade field trip, visiting the Carnegie Museum of Natural History in Pittsburgh. They had been broken into groups, each led by one of the museum's docents. John had slid his way into a group of girls in his grade who pretended he wasn't there and left him alone. He preferred it that way. They were entering the special exhibits room as another group was leaving it. His group backed into a line against the wall to let them pass. The group leaving the room included "The Crew" as John had labeled them. It was a group of wannabe jocks tagging after the rich and popular girls. Some of the girls boarded their horses at John's farm, but he couldn't name them. They had a habit of looking down their noses at him, even though he was almost a head taller. That was fine with him. The girls never stopped talking and texting, and to this day he hadn't heard them say anything but nonsensical prattle. The girls waltzed by, not sparing a glance at the "lesser," i.e. poorer, girls and ignored John. The Crew followed, throwing back their shoulders and puffing out their chests like gorillas. As they passed John, each one took the trouble to bump shoulders with him and grumble a derogatory remark. John had heard them all before.

"John Boy!"

"Farmer Brown!"

"Nice overalls, hick!"

"You smell, Amish boy. Don't they have showers where you come from?"

"Nice boots, loser!"

He almost wished they would come up with some new material. No matter how much John braced himself against the words, they cut into him, chipping away at his confidence, because they all had a thread of truth to them. He *was* wearing overalls, big heavy work boots, worked on a farm, and didn't always have time to clean up after his morning chores before school. On top of that his last name was, *sigh*, Brown. There wasn't much he could do about any of it. He had been adopted from the orphanage when he was six years old by a married couple who ran one of the few remaining working farms in the county. The couple didn't have any sons, but plenty of daughters. It took him months to learn and remember all of their names. His parents were hardworking, honest people, but they were strict and extremely old-fashioned. They weren't Amish, but they may as well be. The girls were not allowed to do the majority of the work at the farm because it was "man's work." That's where John came in. He was their free laborer. John was grateful they rescued him from the orphanage, but there was little affection between them and even less money. His father insisted on the steel-toed work boots, saying that he needed proper footwear to perform his duties on the farm. They were very nice work boots, but they were his only shoes. When he was younger, he didn't know the difference, but now that he was fourteen... well, they were the object of many taunts and jeers. He wished he had regular jeans to wear, but his father wore overalls, so, of course, they had him wear overalls. As his father got older, John's responsibilities grew, and mornings were frantic with work. If John missed the school bus, it was a six-mile walk to get to his school. Consequently, he didn't dare miss the bus. More often than not, he had to run in from the fields, grab his books, and race to the bus stop, barely having the time to knock the dirt from his boots.

Normally, John didn't react to The Crew's bullying. If he did and got caught (and it seemed he always got caught), his father would punish him. When it came to his word against the word of The Crew, school officials always sided with the well-dressed, polished boys. Today, however, John was out of his element in the huge museum, and he grew more uneasy as the day dragged on. Todd was the last of The Crew to pass him. He was the largest of the bunch and was their self-appointed leader. As Todd walked past, John stuck out his steel-toed work boot, tripping the guy. All the girls in line giggled and laughed behind their hands. Todd righted himself and whirled on John, his hands clenched into fists, his broad face turning an ugly shade of red.

The teacher was only a few steps behind them, so Todd angled his back to hide his face as he growled, "Better watch out, John Boy!" Todd caught up with his buddies, and they all turned to look at John, the menacing intention on their faces clear. John had just moved himself to the top of their hit list.

John didn't know what had come over him. His stomach tumbled uncomfortably. He had only moved his foot a mere six inches! One-on-one, John felt he could handle anyone in The Crew. His never-ending work on the farm had made him strong, and he was tall for his age. The problem was that there never was only one of them; The Crew moved in numbers. John dragged his feet more than normal and was the last of his group to shuffle into the special exhibits room.

The guide had already started her speech, standing next to a huge statue on a platform in the corner. As John joined the back of the group he caught a few words.

"Unknown origin…very old…excellent condition…very lucky to have it here…on tour…found in a hidden storage facility in Germany after World War II."

John lifted his head to get a look at the statue. A strange tickling sensation started at the top of his skull and traveled down to his shoulders. He shook his shoulders in response, but his gaze was locked on the statue. It was made up of two stone figures. There was a man holding onto a rope that was lassoed around the ankle of a girl. The girl was frozen in motion as if she was trying to turn towards her captor. She had a scream on her lips as she stood on one leg, the other leg pulled behind her by the rope. The man's face was unlined and youthful, but haggard and strained. He was over six feet tall and wore what looked like patches of leather sewn together with rawhide. It had an old European look to it, but John didn't know much about those things. The girl, however, was wearing what looked like a modern sleeveless dress that swirled about her knees, and she was barefoot. He heard the guide mention something about how the mixed styles of dress made it hard for experts to pinpoint its origin and sculptor, but he wasn't really listening. John had an inexplicable rising feeling in his chest that drew him to the statue. He wormed his way closer to the exhibit until he was standing at the velvet rope that blocked off the platform. He vaguely acknowledged that the guide had finished her story and was leading the group to the next artifact on display. John was rooted to the spot, staring at the statue, the tug in his chest growing stronger. He kept tabs on his group as they toured the room while he stayed where he was, drinking in the lifelike detail of the sculpture. When the guide led the group out of the room, John reluctantly pulled himself from the statue and joined the end of the line at the door. This was the last part of the directed tour. The class was to get a short amount of free time to roam the museum on their own before they had to get back on the buses to go home. John shook his head, trying to clear it from the strange attraction he had to the statue. He suspected The Crew would be out for him after the stunt he pulled with Todd, and he had to be on his guard.

The line stopped when he was only a few people from the door and he peered over the tops of the girls' heads to see what was the cause of the hold-up. It looked like they were waiting for an elevator. The guide and teacher were gone, as were half the girls, apparently filling up an elevator car and leaving the rest to follow as soon as the next car came along. Movement on the other side of the hallway caught his eye. It was Todd and The Crew, impatiently waiting for the crowd of girls to clear so they could get to John. John ducked his head before they saw him. He was acutely aware of the lack of teachers, or any adult for that matter. He turned around, quickly scanning the room for a way out. This was the only door. John silently cursed to himself as sweat broke out on the back of his neck. The Crew had never truly targeted him before, seeming content to throw verbal assaults at him, but he'd heard stories of others not so fortunate. They never got punished for beating anyone up; the school simply didn't believe them capable of such a thing, and it was the word of many against the word of one. His heart began beating faster every second as he frantically tried to come up with a plan on how to get out of this unharmed. The room was made up of several exhibits in glass cases on floor pedestals and larger items displayed against the walls. There was no place to hide and no other way out; he was trapped.

His gaze was pulled back to the statue. It was on a stage-like platform that was angled in the far corner. The mini-stage was a solid, boxed sort of thing, so there was no crawling under it. There was a gap between it and the corner of the room, but he didn't see any way to get there. He heard the elevator ding, signaling the arrival of another car. He was out of time. Before he could think about what he was doing, he ducked under the velvet rope, hiked himself up on the platform, and carefully stepped over the rope part of the statue connecting the girl to the man. As soon as he was clear, he dropped down into the small space between the platform and the wall. He barely made it. He heard the elevator doors close with a chime, and the hall fell silent. John felt like his heart was going to beat right out of his chest. He heard The Crew as they barreled into the room, full of pre-teen angst and self-righteous fury.

Todd shouted, "Time's up, John Boy! It's time to find out what happens when a worthless piece of farm dirt like you messes with one of us!" The other guys made grunts and other noises of support.

John thought, *What are they, apes?* He imagined them thumping their chests as they scoured the room. John was thinking of renaming them "The Ape Crew."

John held his breath as he crouched deeper in his hiding place.

"I know you're in here!" Todd shouted. "Come out, come out, wherever you are!"

Several of the goons snickered in response. John heard them shuffling about, only feet away from him. John barely breathed for risk of being discovered. Eventually, all the noises retreated and gathered in the center of the room.

Todd's lackeys took turns commenting.

"He's not here, Todd."

"There's nowhere for him to hide."

"He must have slipped into that first elevator without us seeing."

"Where else could he have gone?"

Todd made a growl of frustration, and John pictured him kicking one of the display pedestals and breaking a toe, or two. No such luck. "I'll get you, John Boy!" threatened Todd. "You can't hide from me forever! Come on, guys, let's go look upstairs where his group was heading."

As the boys left the room, John questioned their logic in threatening a room they deemed empty. He shrugged and added a mental point to the new "Ape Crew" title.

John waited in his spot as he heard the guys leave on the elevator and all became silent. He didn't move. He figured he should wait out the rest of the assigned free time and then make a beeline for the bus. Luckily, he didn't ride on the same bus as The Ape Crew. He had forgotten to wear his watch, and he couldn't see a clock from his position. His legs began to cramp, and his feet started to go numb. Finally, when he couldn't take anymore, he stood and quietly stretched his aching limbs. Blood surged back into his feet, giving him that unpleasant pins-and-needles feeling.

He silently hauled himself back up onto the platform and carefully stepped over the rope part of the statue. He got one foot free and clear, shifted his weight to that leg, and slowly lifted his other leg over the statue. He was almost over. He started congratulating himself on his quick thinking and his luck that no one caught him on an actual exhibit. He only had a few more days of school to get through until summer. If he could avoid The Ape Crew until then, they probably would forget about him over the break. In the fall they'd all be starting high school, so there would be a lot to distract them. He could always hope.

He had his other foot over, and he started to lower it down to prepare getting off the platform. At least, he thought his other foot was over the statue, but it wasn't. Later, he would wonder if it was the numbness lingering in his feet or just the sheer size of his work boots that caused the accident. Regardless, his foot caught on the rope part of the statue between the man and the girl, and he tripped.

His face went flying towards the platform and his other foot kicked back up behind him as his body went horizontal mid-fall. Between the jerking of his two feet in those darn steel-toed work boots, the rope part of the statue broke.

John heard the crack of the stone shattering as he tucked his head in his arms right before he hit the platform. He landed hard on his left shoulder and rolled to the ground just as he heard another loud CRACK. A plume of dust exploded outward and stone pieces rained down on him.

As a layer of debris settled over the room John thought, *Oh cattails!*

CHAPTER 2 – SPECIAL EXHIBIT SURPRISE

John's first thought was to get out of there as fast as possible. He raised his head and surveyed the room. Dust hung in the air, making it look like a smoke bomb had gone off. His eyes teared as he looked behind him to assess the damage. Half the statue was shattered. The man remained, his side of the rope still intact and jutting out like a pike. The girl was completely gone. Chunks of rock were strewn about her side of the platform amidst a sandbox full of stone powder. John was just about to make a run for it when he heard a small moan to the right of the exhibit. John startled, as he'd been sure no one was in the room when he made his catastrophic exit from his hiding place. *There was a witness!* John thought, his panic building. He took one step towards the door when he heard the sound again. It was so small and pitiful, the better part of him insisted he help the person even if he or she would likely turn around and report him.

At first, he didn't see anything. As he got closer, he noticed a form crumpled on the floor. It looked like a girl, but it was hard to tell, as the person was covered head to toe in dust and was all grayish-white. He caught a glimpse of long hair and what looked like a skirt as he rushed to help. He bent down in front of her and gently grabbed her shoulders to help her get up. She seemed kind of spaced out. Her pupils were so dilated, he couldn't see what color eyes she had. She was wobbly on her feet, and John feared that if he let go of her, she'd collapse right back to the floor.

John's brain started turning, realizing that if he hadn't seen the girl as he was climbing over the statue, she probably hadn't seen him. He could pretend he happened in on the scene *after* the damage occurred. Yes, he could play the dashing hero, saving the day!

He slung one of the girl's arms over his shoulder and wrapped his other arm around her waist to support her weight. He couldn't fight the instinct to flee the scene of the crime any longer, so he slowly half-carried the girl towards the door. He heard her gasp as she saw what remained of the statue. He knew he should stop and see if the girl had a concussion or was bleeding, but his nerves were too rattled so he kept walking past the elevator and around the corner to the hallway leading to the restrooms.

He gently lowered her to the floor and knelt beside her, looking her over for any signs of trauma. She was plastered with the dust from the broken statue, almost as if she purposely rubbed it over every inch of her body, but there was a curious strip of skin around her right ankle that was clean. She was wearing a sleeveless dress that came down to her knees. A thin trail of blood started at her knee and cut a track down her leg through the dirt on her skin. He noticed she wasn't wearing any shoes.

"Hey, are you okay? Is there anything I can do for you? What happened in there? Did the statue fall on you or something? Are you hurt? Other than your bloody knee, that is." As the words tumbled out of his mouth, the girl just numbly stared at him. John had no idea what to do. Even though he was comfortable talking with his numerous sisters at home, in public and in school he got rather tongue-tied talking to girls.

Her knee, he thought, *he should clean up her knee.* He jumped up and dashed into the bathroom. He grabbed the entire stack of paper towels sitting on the sink and ran them under the water. He carried the dripping mass back out into the hall and dropped down next to her. He took a few towels off the top and gently wiped at the blood on her knee. He left a clean stripe of skin in the wake of the towel. The scrape wasn't that bad and had already stopped bleeding. He didn't know what else to say or do, so he started using the towels to wipe the dust off her legs. He looked at her face as he hesitantly took her hand to clean it off. She seemed to be coming back to herself somewhat, as she calmly rested her head back against the wall. John took that as an 'okay' to continue, so he clumsily wiped off one arm and then the next. Finally, he took some clean towels and raised them to her cheek. She looked right at him as he cleaned her face, but John wasn't sure she was actually seeing him.

It had barely been a minute since the statue broke, and John's brain was slowly rebooting. A strange thought crossed his mind. The girl looked familiar, but he didn't remember seeing her walking around. The room had been so quiet before he climbed out of the corner, he'd been certain it had been empty. How did she get into the room without him seeing or hearing her? Why was she so thoroughly encased in dust? Dust had settled on his hair, shoulders and back, the parts of him that were exposed as he'd huddled on the floor, but it wasn't everywhere. Now that he thought about it, the explosion of dust when the statue fell just didn't make sense. And why wasn't she wearing any shoes? The dress she was wearing was freakishly familiar. Was what he was thinking crazy? Could it be possible? He dismissed that line of thought; he couldn't deal with it just then.

John used a few of the remaining paper towels to quickly wipe the dust off himself. Then he scooped up the used towels and tossed them in the trashcan just inside the restroom door.

He leaned down to help the girl to her feet. She wobbled slightly as she blankly looked back at him.

"Where did you come from? Who are you?" he whispered. They both jumped as several loud cracks emanated from the special exhibits room. The girl stumbled back towards the room, and John held onto her elbow to help keep her upright. They peered through the door as the cracking sounds continued. The sound was coming from the part of the statue still standing. Cracks were running from the remaining rope to the man's hands, then traveled up and down his body. John blinked as he realized there was a length of actual rope, lassoed at the end, hanging from the statue. He watched the rope fall to the ground as pieces of stone broke away, freeing it further.

The girl next to him drew in a sharp breath, and her whole body began to shake. She turned on her heel and lunged away from the room. John caught her up around the waist as she stumbled and nearly fell. She obviously wanted to get away from what was happening inside that room, and John could not agree more.

John took a chance and pushed the elevator call button. Luck finally shined on him as one of the elevators dinged open. He dragged the girl inside the car and pushed first the close door button then the button to go to the basement level. The girl stood facing him, her hands on his chest as she leaned against him, her forehead resting on her hands. She was trembling from head to toe. John awkwardly patted her back and rubbed her upper arms murmuring to her, "Shhh, it will be okay. Shhh, don't worry, I've got you."

I've got you? John thought. Why did he say that? As the elevator reached its destination and the doors opened, John wondered what the heck he was supposed to do now.

John saw a clock as they exited the elevator. He had fifteen minutes before he had to be back on the bus. He drew the girl over to a nearby bench as he collected his thoughts. She slumped against the back of the bench as if she couldn't hold herself up, but her eyes were darting back and forth. Seeing that rope hidden inside the fracturing statue could not be ignored. The girl beside him looked like the girl in the statue, was dressed the same down to her lack of shoes, was inexplicably completely encased in statue dust except that ring around her right ankle. If she had a rope tied around that ankle, it would have protected the skin from the statue dust. John pictured the statue in his mind, and yes, it was the girl's right foot that had been bound. Was she the girl from the statue?

"What's your name?" John asked. The girl made no response.

"Where do you want to go? Do you have a place to go? Are you even real?" The girl just stared at him.

Now that some of the shock was wearing off, John noticed that same pulling feeling he had when he first saw the statue was growing in his chest and was drawing him towards the girl. He couldn't help feeling like he was responsible for her somehow, that she needed him. The corridor was well-lit and much brighter than the special exhibits area. John noticed he could see the girl's eye color now. They were a clear, pale blue that got darker around the edges. His mind blanked out for a moment. *What was he doing? Oh yeah, he needed to figure out what to do with the girl.* Maybe he got knocked out when he tripped on the statue, and this was all a dream. What was he supposed to do with a statue turned to life? Should he take her to an adult official? What would he say, that he tripped on and broke a priceless ancient artifact, and this girl just came out of the stone? Yeah, right. And he could kiss his life as he knew it goodbye. He had escaped the scene of the crime undetected and had no desire to turn himself in. And who says it would help the girl? If they believed his story, would they lock her away in a government lab or something? This whole thing was crazy. He was crazy. And crazier still, he'd made up his mind what he was going to do. He was going to take the girl home with him and figure it out from there.

"Do you want to come home with me?" Again no response came from the girl.

He started to pantomime as he slowly said, "Do you (pointing at her) want to go home (he made his fingers walk away in the air) with me (pointing at himself)? The girl nodded as she first pointed to herself then pointed at John. She opened her mouth to speak, but only a rough croak came out. She swallowed hard and her hand flew to her throat as if she were in pain.

That was enough for John. He would take her back to the farm, and his sisters would help him from there. His parents didn't have to know. Heck, there were so many girls running around the place all the time, he doubted they would realize there was one more. He looked at her, assessing. He had gotten the worst of the dust off her, but she still looked somewhat grayish. Her hair was a grayish-white powdery mess, and, of course, there were her bare feet to contend with. He thought of a solution and jumped up to study the map of the museum that stood by the elevators. He located the lost and found and pulled the girl behind him as he headed in that direction.

He had the girl wait on the other side of the hall where he could keep an eye on her before he approached the lost and found desk.

"Hi!" he said to the bored-looking employee manning the station. The man was short even sitting down, and his white uniform shirt was straining at the buttons over his sizeable gut.

"Can I help you?" the man said in a monotone voice. John got the distinct impression the man suspected he was up to trouble, but had decided it wasn't worth his paycheck to actually do anything about it. The man's eyes narrowed slightly as John said, "Can I see the lost and found? I left the zipper on my backpack open by mistake this morning, and I think some of my stuff fell out. Can I check?"

The man silently deliberated, then shrugged and said, "Sure, why not, kid? This stuff just keeps piling up. They'll probably donate it soon just to clear it out." The man hefted a large bin onto the counter. John pulled it down to the floor and started rummaging through it.

Score! He came up with an old ball cap, a denim jacket that was unraveling at the cuffs, a pair of guy's sweat pants, and a mismatched pair of flip-flops. He rolled the items into a ball and returned the bin to the counter muttering his thanks as he hastily retreated back to where he'd left the girl.

He guided the girl around a corner and unrolled his finds to show her. First he held up the jean jacket. It was too big for her, but it would do the job of covering up her arms and the top of her filthy dress. He rolled up the sleeves a couple of times until her fingers just peaked out the ends of them. He buttoned the bottom two buttons for her, then he took her hands and placed them on the next button. She got the hint, and with shaking fingers she managed to continue buttoning up the jacket.

Then he looked at the sweat pants. They were too large for even him, and they smelled bad, but they had a drawstring waist that would at least hold them up. He rolled up the pant legs, holding them up to her for size. He mimed stepping into the pants and pulling them up. He held them out to the girl, and she gingerly stepped into them. She pulled the waistband up under her skirt. John shook his head and mimed tucking in his shirt. She looked at him a moment, then started to tuck the skirt of her dress into her pants. He used his hands to brush off the flip-flops the best he could. They weren't the same size or color, but one was left and one was right. He bent down and helped her slip them on her feet. Lastly, he shook out the ball cap and placed it on her head. Again he mimed instructions, this time to tuck her hair up under the cap. The cap was too large for her, but with all of her hair twisted up under it, it fit much better.

John stepped back to check the results of his efforts. She looked more like a street bum than a schoolgirl. With her rolled up sleeves and pant legs, the tucked in skirt making her sweat pants all lumpy-bumpy, and her face still smudged and hidden in the shadow of the ball cap, people would probably look away uncomfortably and ignore her.

It was almost time to leave. He led the girl out the front door of the museum. It was a dull, overcast day, but the temperature was warm. The girl had trouble walking in the flip-flops, so they took it slow. They stopped a short distance away from the buses and waited. When a large group of girls passed by them to get on John's bus, he quickly pulled the statue girl with him into the line. By the time they climbed on the bus, most people were bored with checking out who was boarding. John quickly pushed the girl into a seat a third of the way back and followed in behind her. He tipped her hat lower over her face and had her slump in the seat. John leaned forward slightly, sitting as close to her as he could, so he would block her from most people's view. She was so much smaller than he was; it wasn't very difficult.

The teacher and chaperones boarded the bus last. The teacher had a clipboard and called names, checking them off as each kid cried, "Here!" She didn't count heads or bother walking up and down the aisles. The adults sat in the front seats and turned their backs on the kids for the rest of the trip.

Once they were on the road, the girl yawned widely and leaned back against the seat, closing her eyes. John sat back and let her head rest on his shoulder as she fell asleep. It was a unique feeling having her lean against him. He felt protective and comforted at the same time. He didn't want to move and jostle her so he sat as still as possible. It took nearly an hour to get back to his school, and John was stiff from holding his position. He gently nudged the girl to wake her up. They got off the bus right in the middle of several students. Some of the kids gave him strange looks, but they always gave him strange looks, so that was nothing new.

John supported the girl by the elbow again as he walked them to the bus that would take them to his farm. This bus ride took another forty-five minutes, as he was the second to last stop. The girl fell asleep again against his shoulder. The bus dropped them off at his driveway, and as it pulled away he turned towards his home, trying to figure out the best way to sneak her in. Whatever he did, he needed to do it quickly; the girl was almost sleeping standing up. Again, John told himself he was nuthouse crazy, but that feeling in his chest drawing him to the girl overrode all those thoughts. He took her hand, and they started walking towards the farm.

CHAPTER 3 – THE FARM

The walk up his driveway was a picturesque one, with old maple trees reaching over them, providing some shade (and cover) before it opened up to a grassy yard in front of a quaint whitewash farmhouse. A large red horse barn stood to the left, and there were numerous outbuildings skirting the lawn, which sheltered various farm equipment, a few rusting cars, and his father's truck. Behind the house sat the milk house and the buildings for the cows, pigs, sheep, and chickens. It was the last week in May, and the sun was breaking its way through the cloud cover. A soft breeze carried with it the mixed sent of cow manure and the sweet smell of spring plant growth and fresh earth. John was used to the smell, but he could tell it bothered the girl, as she was alternating between pinching her nose and scrunching her face. The sight made him chuckle. Her funny expressions, on top of her gray-streaked skin, hobo clothes, and shuffling gait made quite the comic picture.

Before they left the shelter of the trees, John searched the fields, looking for his father. He finally spotted him to the right of the house, driving the tractor in the far north field. He couldn't see the pens behind the house, but the animals were quiet, so it was likely no one was out and about. No one was out front, and he didn't see any faces in the windows of the house, so he squeezed the girl's hand harder as he started to run towards the barn, dragging her behind him.

He didn't get very far. The girl couldn't run in her mismatched flip-flops, and he guessed she was too weak to run anyway. She hoarsely cried out as she stepped on a stone that had made its way between her foot and the flip-flop. The entire driveway, while worn and hard packed, was littered with dust and small stones. John quickly shushed her; he didn't want to alert anyone in the house. She pulled her hand from his to take off her flip-flop and brush off the offending rock, as well as other small pebbles and dust, before putting it back on her foot. John sighed in frustration and paced back and forth as the girl did the same thing to her other foot. He had to get her inside quickly, but how could he do that when she could barely walk? He could pick her up and carry her, but that would be awkward, and he wouldn't be able to see where he stepped; the last thing he needed was to trip and drop her. He finally thought of something. He could give her a piggyback ride like he sometimes did with his younger sisters!

Getting her on his back was a bit clumsy. He had to grab her hands over behind his shoulders and haul her up, then grab her legs to support her. He set off at a small jog towards the hay barn. He made it to the door and inside without anyone seeing them. He bent his knees and let go of her legs, and she quickly slid off his back onto her own feet. He guided her to some wooden steps on the left side of the entrance, and they began to climb. She moved more slowly the higher they went. He was worried he'd have to sling her on his back again just to get to the top. At the end of the stairs there was a small landing with a single door to enter the barn's loft.

The loft was his room. When he first came to the farm he was six years old, and he'd slept in the main house, which had four bedrooms. Mother and Father had one bedroom, he got one, and the girls had to share the other two. There were seven sisters at the time, ranging in age from Mary Margaret, who had been ten years old, to Mary Abigail, who had been only one. This arrangement worked for a couple of years, and then the twins were born. The loft in the hay barn was turned into a bedroom for him, and he'd been there ever since. It wasn't as bad as it sounds. They gave it some insulation and put up walls and the door. It already had electricity, but they had run a few extra outlets over the years. Most importantly, it had a small bathroom. That had been a big deal to install, and he'd worked extra hours on some of the neighbor's farms to earn the money for it. Father had made him do most of the tough stuff like digging and running back and forth to turn the water off and on, but it was well worth it. They had walled off the corner of the loft and put in a sink, a toilet, and a primitive shower stall. The water wasn't heated, but John didn't mind. The girls were always complaining about having to share the one bathroom in the farmhouse, and he had one all his own.

The room was very tidy; Mother and Father wouldn't have it any other way. He had a full bed with a worn hand-stitched quilt, a crate that served as both a bookcase and a nightstand, an old chest of drawers, and a beat-up table with a chair for a desk. The old, braided rug that used to be in the kitchen brightened the floor. Everything was second-hand, except for the cheapest alarm clock Wal-Mart had to offer. His family rarely came to his room, so he should be safe in hiding her here.

As soon as she saw the bed, the girl collapsed onto it and closed her eyes. John took off her flip-flops and covered her with the blanket. He doubted she would go anywhere soon; she looked like she might sleep for days. John set his backpack by the table and headed back out to do his chores.

First, he checked on the horses. They boarded four horses for some rich girls in town who came once a week with some fancy-smancy trainer for lessons. They had just been there the day before, so they weren't a concern. Then he went to bring the cows in for milking. They were lined up waiting to come in. Their utters were full and uncomfortable, and they eagerly went to their stalls to be hooked up to the milking machine. Father used to help with this, but John had been doing it all by himself for almost a year now. John had to check on and feed the other animals, then finish up the milking. He noticed his left shoulder hurt, which had taken the brunt of his fall. He shrugged it off and kept working. As he fell into his routine, he allowed his thoughts to turn back to the museum. He replayed the events over again in his mind, trying to remember what the guide had said about the statue. She had said they didn't know when it was made; just that it was very old. How did the girl get in the statue? How long had she been trapped in stone? Decades? Centuries? No wonder she was so out of it, she was waking up for the first time in years. It had been found in Germany, in a hidden storage facility. He wondered if she even spoke English. She hadn't understood anything he'd said, so probably not.

He suddenly stopped in his tracks. He had been so focused on himself and not getting caught sneaking her here, that he totally forgot the context of the statue. A man had been trying to capture her. A man *had* captured her, captured her ankle at least. And when they left that room the second time, the man's part of the statue had been falling apart. Did he emerge from the stone like the girl did? The girl had certainly been frightened at the sight of the statue cracking. If he did get out of the statue, where was he now? Would he try to come after her? Did the man get caught by the museum?

He was sure the museum had to have noticed the statue was broken by now. There had been only a half hour before closing when his school left. He would have to wait until after dinner to find out. Father and Mother watched the local and national news on their old console TV after dinner every night. They didn't have cable, so they got only three stations, maybe four on a clear day. He had so much work to do, that he rarely had time to watch TV. He usually left straight after supper to finish his chores or start his homework, but he would stay tonight to listen to the news. Today was Friday, so he had the weekend to figure out what to do with the girl when he was away at school. His thoughts strayed back to the man in the statue as he resumed his chores. He tried to imagine what it would be like to be frozen for years in stone, to be freed in such a dramatic way in a strange place, where even the language was foreign. John had been there to help the girl, but the man would be on his own.

And then there was the technology! Heck, did they even have electricity before she was frozen? The girl hadn't reacted much to the elevator, the bus and the cars, but she'd been so out of it, that he doubted much of it registered. He was amazed that she trusted him and followed him so willingly. He wondered if she felt part of that strange pull he had to her, and that is why she hadn't screamed and run from him. He shook his head, admonishing himself for his foolish behavior that day, starting with tripping Todd. If he hadn't slid his foot out that small amount of space, none of this would have happened. He hadn't even done it on purpose; it was a subconscious move. Then he'd brought the girl here. He hadn't thought beyond that. He had just been focused on sneaking her onto the farm, which, to his wonder and pride, he'd done successfully. Now he needed a plan on where to go from here.

John finished his chores in record time, then raced back to the barn to check on the girl. She was still sound asleep and hadn't moved. He cleaned up and hurried to the house for dinner. He hadn't gotten very far in his planning, other than to realize he needed help. He had to tell one of his sisters. The question was, which one should he tell? He had eleven of them in all, going from two years old to eighteen years old. In many ways he felt sorry for them. They were crammed into three bedrooms, shared a single bathroom, had to dress like freaking Amish girls, and all shared the first name *Mary*. Sometimes he thought Mother and Father were idiots. Were they ever going to stop trying for a boy? If they did have a son, where would that leave him? He was forced to wear overalls, so he didn't feel much pity for the Little-House-on-the Prairie dresses they had to wear, but the name thing was just crazy. Each had a different middle name, so they basically went by both names, at least in front of Mother and Father. Amongst themselves, they each had a nickname based off their middle name.

Mary Margaret, or Meg, was eighteen, and she was like the second mother of the household. John quickly dismissed telling her; she was strict with the rules and would run straight to Mother and Father. Mary Ann, or Annie, was seventeen, but she wasn't a good choice either. She didn't mind breaking rules, but she couldn't keep a secret to save her life and usually slipped up somehow to reveal her own misdoings. She and Meg were fastened at the hip unless there was a boy within a mile of the farm; then Annie would be on the hunt.

John decided on Mary Elizabeth, who went by Beth and was fifteen. She was the brains of the family. All the girls were home-schooled. Father didn't think girls should be exposed to the dangers of the public school system. Apparently, he didn't have the same worry where John was concerned. Meg was in charge of the home-schooling, but Beth did all the planning behind the scenes. She was good with computers, and she researched and built their lesson plans and graded the assignments. She even started taking over the bookkeeping for the farm. She was quiet and shy, but noticed everything and everyone. Even if John didn't tell her, she would probably find him out in a few days. She, if anyone, would be clever enough to figure out what to do next.

His second choice was Mary Abigail, who was nine, and went by Abby. He passed over Mary Joanna (Jo), who was fourteen, Mary Alice (Alice), who was twelve, and Mary Bernadette (Bunny), who was eleven. Abby was his favorite sister. She was sweet to the core and was the family peacemaker even though she was a thin little thing. She would have the most compassion for the statue girl. John decided to approach Beth or Abby after the news show tonight, based on which sister was available. With that decided, he ran up the front steps and into the farmhouse.

He took off his boots in the small mudroom, which led either to the kitchen or down ancient steps to the gloomy basement. He opened the glass door to the kitchen and took his place by his father's right. The table was huge and took up the whole length of the kitchen. The chair at the end by the door was Father's, and the chair at the other end, closest to the stove, was Mother's. A single long bench on each side seated the kids. Mother held Mary Grace (Gracie) in her arms. Gracie was only two and had white-blond hair like Mother. She was utterly spoiled. She refused to be potty-trained and was still in diapers. She clung to Mother, constantly running Mother ragged, but Gracie was one of the few people who could get Mother to smile. The twins had kitchen duty tonight, and while one finished setting the table, the other started to bring the food over from the stove. The twins, Mary Jane (Jane) and Mary Ellen (Ellen), were seven years old and had the same pale blond hair as Mother and Gracie. They were the only ones to receive Mother's eyes. Their eyes were such a pale blue, that sometimes they appeared absolutely colorless. They both sat down, and everyone waited for Father to come in from the living room and the evening paper. He was always the last to sit down for supper, like he was above waiting for anyone.

Father stood at the head of the table and said, "Let us pray." They all bowed their heads as they recited the Catholic before-meal prayer. With the last *Amen*, Father sat down and started helping himself to food. He passed each plate to John, where it began its circle around the table. Father believed the men did the hardest work and should get the pick of the food. All of the younger girls sat near Mother's end of the table, as Father didn't want to have to deal with them. They had meatloaf, mashed potatoes, green beans and milk. They always had milk. John guessed that Mary Joanna (Jo) cooked the meatloaf, because it was delicious and it wasn't burned. Jo was his age, fourteen, and was the girliest girl John had ever met. She excelled at most of the girly things like baking and sewing, but John often heard his sisters complain that Jo always found ways to get out of the washing and cleaning. As long as she spent her time cooking dinner for them, Father didn't care, and for once John was in agreement with him.

Father led the conversation at the table. You did not speak unless spoken to, and that included Mother. Father inquired about Mother's day then focused on John, drilling him on the status of the farm and how much work needed to be done. It was exhausting. John's mind was so wrapped up in the day's events at the museum and his statue girl, that he had a hard time focusing on the conversation. Father gave him a break and asked Meg for a status on the girls' home-schooling. As she spoke, Meg often glanced at Beth, as if needing confirmation of what she said. After sharing how the girls were doing, Meg mentioned that John had been to Pittsburgh to see the museum and wondered if the girls could go on an educational field trip.

Father almost startled at the reference to John's schooling. John suspected that Father didn't think he needed anymore schooling, to the point that Father often forgot John still went to school. Father wanted John to focus all of his time working on the farm, but Mother and the state of Pennsylvania disagreed. Father would not allow him to be home-schooled with the girls; that was too much fraternizing with the opposite sex. Father harrumphed in reply, and that was that, for now. John knew Beth would come up with a different approach to win Father over to the idea; it was just a matter of time.

They had a real treat for dessert. Jo had made a strawberry pie with the first strawberries of the season and homemade whipped cream. When they were finished, Father led them in the Catholic after-dinner prayer. The children carried their own plates to the sink, and the twins took care of Mother's and Father's as well as all of the leftover food. The family moved to the living room as the twins went to work on the dishes. Father would never spend the money for a dishwasher, not when there were so many able bodies around to do the work.

Father sat in his chair by the fireplace and resumed his perusal of the evening paper, while Mother turned on the evening news and sat with Gracie in the rocking chair by the window.

Meg, Annie, Beth, and Jo took the couch, and Meg held Mary Christine (Christie) on her lap. Christie was four and should have started home-schooling by now, but she hadn't. John thought he knew why. Christie made the most annoying wailing sound when she cried, such that the entire family did everything possible to avoid causing her to make that horrid noise. Christie had recently figured this out and was using it to her advantage. Anytime anyone mentioned schooling and her name together in the same sentence, the waterworks would come out. The tears were coming out more and more lately, John noticed, and Christie seemed to get to do whatever she pleased. John was her one exception. Christie idolized John and often tried to follow him around as he did his chores. Sometimes she tried to help him. It was hilarious to watch her struggling to muck a stall with a pitchfork three times her height! She also listened to John above everyone else. His sisters were constantly nagging at him to get Christie to do this or to stop doing that. He only stepped in when it was something where Christie could hurt herself or someone else. He didn't want to lose his influence with her from over-use. John sat cross-legged on the floor in front of the TV, and Christie jumped from Meg's hold and curled up in his lap. John wrapped her in a hug and rested his chin on her soft light brown curls as the news started. Abby sat beside him on the floor, but Alice and Bunny had retreated upstairs instead of staying for the news.

John felt like the room started spinning as the reporter started with the leading story.

"This just in… a horrific case of vandalism was reported this evening at the Carnegie Museum of Natural History. A priceless statue was pummeled to dust in the special exhibits room. The statue, entitled "The Capture," was part of a touring exhibit of historical treasures rescued from Germany after World War II." A picture of the statue showed in the upper right corner of the screen. "Museum officials noticed the damage during their closing rounds for the day. A man was found wandering the halls of the museum covered in plaster-like dust and wearing period clothing. He is now in police custody and undergoing a mental evaluation. Several schools were visiting the museum today, and our news station has learned that officials will be questioning those students to gather clues to this violent crime. Here is our exclusive interview with Erin Brandsworth, a docent at the museum, who was the last employee to have seen the statue before the vandalism occurred."

John was hardly breathing when the camera shot flipped to Ms. Brandsworth, who was his guide from their field trip. "It's just horrible!" Ms. Brandsworth said with tears in her eyes. She looked to be standing on the front steps to the museum. "The statue was completely obliterated. The biggest fragment left was no bigger than my palm."

The reporter asked her several more questions that John didn't follow. He jolted back to attention when the reporter asked if there was any security footage that would help solve the crime. Ms. Brandsworth sadly shook her head. "We don't have cameras in that room; the closest is in the hall by the elevators. When I gave my report to our security team, I found out that the camera outside the special exhibits room recorded a sound like a small explosion and stopped working within a few minutes of that. Apparently, dust from the room obscured the lens and coated the machine. The camera overheated and broke, probably from a clogged vent."

The TV switched back to the news anchorman as he reported, "There is no official word on the status of this investigation, but we have a picture of the suspect being held by the police." The screen showed a man's mug shot. It definitely looked like the hunter from the statue, his hair riddled with dust and bits of rock, and dust smeared all over his face. His eyes were half-open, and he looked like he was drunk. "If you have any information about this man, please call the number on the bottom of our screen."

And with that, he moved on to the next big news of the day, something the new mayor did, and then a drive-by shooting, before the show went to the weather forecast.

Christie, warm and content in his lap, yawned widely. Meg asked him to carry her up to bed. John whispered to Abby sitting next to him, "Can you go up and help me with her?" John internally leapt in excitement when Beth stood up and mumbled something about getting started on next week's lesson plans. The other girls stayed in the room to watch the national news and then "Jeopardy." Abby led the way up the stairs, John followed, and Beth trailed behind. When they were halfway up the stairs, John urgently whispered, "I need to talk to you both about something very important. Is there a place we can go where we won't be overheard?" His two sisters looked at him quizzically when Beth said, "We can go to my room. Meg and Annie are both downstairs and won't be up for a while."

Beth went to her room, while Abby helped John get Christie to bed. When they joined Beth in her room, she was sitting on her bed. Abby sat on another bed, and John went to stand by the desk chair, but he couldn't sit down. He began pacing back and forth, trying to figure out what to say.

Finally he stopped, faced them, and blurted out, "I need your help."

CHAPTER 4 – CONNIVANCE

Beth and Abby looked at him patiently, waiting for him to continue. He liked that about them. They let him take his time and didn't jump all over him with questions or tease him about needing help. He hoped it would stay that way during his story.

"Uh, well, you guys heard about what happened at the museum on the news?" They both nodded. "Well, that was the museum I went to on my field trip today, and that lady they interviewed, well, I was in her group." He looked down and nervously scratched the back of his head. He had Beth's complete attention, and Abby's face was beginning to show compassion for him, realizing he'd been through something that day.

"We were the last group to see the statue before it, um, broke. Actually, I was still in the room when part of it broke." Abby gasped and put her hand to her mouth, and Beth's body was stiff as she stared at him intently.

"Did you see the picture of what the statue looked like? It was of a girl running away from a man, and the man had a lasso around her ankle, like she'd just been caught. It was life-sized and was kind of angled in the corner..." he trailed off. He took a deep breath and barreled on saying, "It all started with this group of, um, jerks, who were knocking into me and giving me flack." He went on to tell them about how he'd tripped Todd, got threatened, hid behind the statue, and then broke it with his boots. He paused, not knowing how to describe the next part without sounding like a crazy person. He rolled his injured shoulder in memory of his fall. The girls had let him continue unquestioned so far, so he just let the words pour out of him. He focused it all on how he found the girl hurt on the floor and how he'd helped her. Then he started describing the things he noticed about the girl, like how she was completely covered in dust except for the band around her ankle, didn't have shoes, wore that curious dress, and how he hadn't heard or seen her before his fall. "I realized she had a lot in common with the girl in the statue." He finally sat down in the chair and paused to give them time to absorb his story. He could almost see the gears working in Beth's head as she processed everything.

Abby had moved to the very edge of the bed, practically standing. She asked, "Were you hurt? Is the girl okay? Where is she now? What did the museum people say? Wait, they don't know you were involved, do they?" Abby had this way about her that when she got excited she would stream out several sentences in a single breath, as if the words were busting to get out of her mouth. Normally, John thought it was cute, but tonight it was a bit overwhelming.

"Of course they don't know, Abby," Beth said calmly. "Otherwise, he wouldn't be here telling us. What exactly are you telling us, John? Are you saying that the girl you helped is actually the girl in the statue?"

John was pleased she'd come to this conclusion so quickly, and that she wasn't calling up the looney bin, not yet, anyway. "Yeah, I'm pretty sure it's the same girl."

"Of course it's the same girl!" exclaimed Abby. "It makes sense. Based on what John told us, I don't see any other explanation, and John has never lied to us, ever! I believe him."

Beth challenged, "It's not a matter of believing he is telling us what he thinks is the truth. What are the chances he hit his head when he fell and hallucinated the whole thing?"

"Would you like to meet her? Would that convince you it actually happened?" John asked.

"What? Where is she? Is she far from here? How can we arrange a trip off the farm to go anywhere? I'm not sure why you're trying to convince us of your story. You mentioned you need our help. What can we do to help? Are you worried you'll get caught?" Beth asked, borrowing Abby's way of spitting out questions.

"Well…," John held out the word as he stuffed his hands in his pockets and looked at his boots. "You can meet her now. She's in the loft."

"What?" Beth and Abby squealed at the same time, jumping to their feet. Then they started talking over each other, barraging him with questions. Beth quickly asked, "Why on earth would you bring her here? How did you even manage it? What were you thinking? Are you insane? This isn't some lost puppy you found; it's a human being!" At the same time, Abby asked, "Are you serious? She's here? How is she? Why did you leave her alone? Of course we'll help you take care of her! Is she hungry? Thirsty? Does she need clean clothes? Is she scared? I'll bet she's scared. I would be. Oh, imagine what she is going through!"

John hurried towards them putting his hands out, palm down, trying to shush them. "Shhhhh! You're going to bring everyone up here! Sit down, and I'll answer your questions."

The girls sat back down. Beth had a scowl on her face, and Abby was sitting on her hands trying to hold back her excitement. "First, let me tell you how I got her here." He went on to tell his story of cleaning her up, getting clothes from the lost and found, sneaking her on first one bus then another, and having to carry her piggyback to get her in the barn quickly.

"She fell straight into bed and went to sleep. I covered her up and checked on her again before dinner, and she was still sleeping, right where I left her." He left out the part about the man's side of the statue cracking open, and that he suspected the mug shot he saw on TV was the same person.

Beth asked, "Did she say anything to you? What is her name? Do you know where or *when* she came from? I'm having trouble getting my mind around this. It sounds so fanciful; how could it be real?"

"She didn't say a word. She tried once, and it seemed to hurt her throat. She didn't seem to understand me, so I don't think she speaks English. I had to act out anything I said. She was really out of it, almost like she was sleepwalking."

Abby gave him a stern look as she asked, "Did you give her anything to drink or eat? If her throat hurt, you should at least have given her some water. Honestly, John, I can't believe you got her all the way here safely, when you can't cover the basic human needs!"

John felt sick to his stomach. The girl probably *was* thirsty. He wanted to race back to her now and get her some water. He started backing towards the door.

Beth stopped him by asking, "What do you plan to do next? She can't stay in your loft indefinitely. Mother and Father would have an absolute fit if they found out. Father would give you the belt for sure if he caught a girl in your room."

John focused on the problem that had brought him to talk to them to begin with. He needed a plan. "I have absolutely no idea what to do next." John admitted. "That's actually why I wanted to talk to both of you. I need help figuring out how to help her."

Abby brought her hands together and clenched them in her lap, her face beaming with concern for the girl and pleasure that he was trusting her with such a big secret. Beth pulled her mouth into a small smirk as her eyes brightened with the challenge of a new problem to solve. "That's the first smart thing you've said all night," she said.

They quickly agreed that the first thing to do was to attend to the girl's basic needs. Beth and Abby were anxious to meet her, to see the proof of his fantastic story. Beth hurried down to the kitchen to put a small basket of food together. Abby gathered some extra clothes. John stuffed them in the front of his overalls, and then crossed his arms to hold them in place.

As John followed Amy down the steps, he could hear "Jeopardy's" thinking music playing, signaling the final round. Father looked up to see them enter the room together. "John!" Father bellowed. "What were you doing up in the girls' *bedroom*? You know that is off-limits!"

John was quick to reply, "I was putting Mary Christine to bed and Mary Abigail was helping me. Christie, ah, Mary Christine wanted to jump on the bed when we got to her room and it took a while to get her to settle down. You know how she is." John was nervous lying to Father. He prided himself on always telling the truth. He was surprised at how easily the lie came to him. He wanted to wipe his sweaty palms on his pants, but he didn't dare uncross his arms and have the extra clothes fall out. Father's scowl faded as he accepted John's story. He was probably thinking how they all avoided one of Christie's tantrums.

"Okay then, this time only. You are not to go up those stairs again without direct permission from me or Mother," Father said resignedly.

"Yes, Sir," John replied and nodded his head in compliance. The girls were allowed to call him "Father," but John had to call him "Sir," and Mother "Ma'am." He assumed he was dismissed and went into the kitchen where Beth had the basket of food ready. She was tying her shoes, and Abby was picking up hers. Father jumped to his feet this time as he demanded, "And where do you two think you're going!"

The girls jumped at the noise. They had forgotten about how adamant Father was about the girls staying inside in the evening. There was at least an hour before sunset, but Father liked to have them indoors, together. Beth was the one to come through with a lie this time, and John was impressed at how smoothly she delivered it. "John mentioned he gets hungry late at night and throughout the day on the weekends, so I made up a food basket for him. You know how hard he works, Father. You always say how important it is for a man to eat. I was just going to take the basket out to the barn for him. Mary Abigail was going with me so I wouldn't have to walk back alone."

Father gave her a small nod of approval for keeping John in top shape so he could work better. "That's fine Mary Elizabeth, but you don't need to take it to the barn. John can take it. You and Mary Abigail come back in here and forget this nonsense about going outside, when John is perfectly capable of carrying it himself," Father ordered.

"Yes, Father," Beth and Abby replied together as they put their shoes away. Beth handed the basket to John and whispered, "We'll find a way to meet her tomorrow. I'll think on it tonight and see if I can come up with a plan for her."

"Sounds good, thanks. Thanks for believing me! Both of you," John whispered back. In a normal voice John said, "Good night, Sir, good night, Ma'am," and waited for their reply before opening the door and stepping out into the evening.

CHAPTER 5 – INTRODUCTIONS

John quietly slipped into the loft with his gifts of food and clothes. The girl was still sleeping, but she'd rolled to her side facing the wall. John took the glass he kept by his bedside and filled it with water. He sat on the bed and gently shook her shoulder. "Would you like a drink? I have some water for you." *That was brilliant*, he thought. She probably didn't understand a word he said. She didn't even stir. She must be in a really deep sleep. He set the water and the food basket on the bedside table where she would see it if she woke up. He took off his boots, grabbed the one extra blanket he had, and, using his book bag as a pillow, he lay down on the braided rug to sleep.

It took him a while to fall asleep. When he did, he had crazy dreams about statues coming to life, and police arresting him. Abby watched him get thrown in jail saying, "If only you'd offered her water, John, none of this would be happening." Then he was back at the museum in a room full of statues, and Beth was talking endlessly about the science of people turning into statues. Then the statues in the room stepped off their platforms and surrounded them, their stony hands reaching for him and Beth. He started turning to stone and noticed the same thing was happening to Beth, but she never stopped talking about how amazing it was that she got to experience something like that firsthand.

He woke with a start and opened his eyes, to see the statue girl inches away from him on the floor. She had one hand over her heart and it glowed like she was covering a strong flashlight with her palm. The fingers of her other hand were lightly touching his temple and cheek. Her eyes bore into his, and all thought left him as he stared back. His head felt weird as their eyes locked. It was like his skull had been opened up, and someone was flipping through his thoughts like a Rolodex. His chest started to feel warm, and he suddenly felt very tired. He had no idea how long they stayed like that, but he grew more fatigued the longer it lasted. Soon he faded away into a dreamless sleep.

When he woke up again, the sun was shining through his single small window, and he was stiff all over. Wait a minute; the sun was shining! His alarm clock was supposed to ring half an hour before sunrise to start his chores. He sat up quickly in a panic, and the room swirled around him. He promptly lay back down. The girl appeared at his side and placed a cool hand on his forehead. "Easy now, you're going to be tired and dizzy for a while." The girl's voice was hoarse, like she hadn't used it in a while. She sat back on her heels and wrung her hands together nervously as she cleared her throat. "Sorry about that. I had to do a pretty substantial knowledge transfer, and that can really wipe you out. My name is Diana. I want to thank you for helping me." It looked like she was going to say more, but stopped when they heard someone climbing the steps outside.

Diana scooted backwards and sat in the chair by the table as the door to the loft opened. Abby poked her head inside. Her eyes widened in shock as she saw Diana sitting anxiously in the chair. Abby donned a huge smile as she stepped into the room, closing the door behind her. "You're awake! Welcome! I'm Abby. I brought you guys some breakfast; are you hungry?" Diana visibly started to relax at the warm greeting when Abby blurted, "Oh, I'm so sorry, I forgot. John said you don't speak English, so you probably didn't understand a word I just said."

"No, it's fine. Thank you, I actually *am* pretty hungry. I'm Diana. It's nice to meet you," said Diana with a small, shy smile.

Abby's mouth dropped wide open as her basket fell to the floor with a plunk. "She speaks English! John, did you know she speaks English? And her name is Diana. Did you know she had a name? Of course she has a name; I'm just being silly. Wow, it's nice to meet you, too!" Abby stopped to take a breath. "Hi!" Abby said, looking back and forth between John and Diana expectantly.

"Abby, what are you doing here? What time is it? Am I in trouble for missing morning chores?" John returned with his own string of questions as he stretched his arms over his head, trying to work out some of the kinks from sleeping on the hard floor.

Abby knelt down next to him, pulled the basket towards her, and began unpacking it as she answered calmly, "I'm here to check in on you and bring you food. It is a little after ten a.m. Beth slipped out of the house before dawn to check on you and, um, Diana. Diana was still sleeping, and you were sleeping so deeply that Beth couldn't wake you. She said she shook you, slapped your face, and pinched you, and you didn't bat an eyelash. She said that you were still breathing, so she assumed you felt sick and needed the rest. She woke me up, and the two of us got the morning chores done without Father seeing us. So the answer is no, you're not in trouble, not yet anyway," she finished with a smug look on her face.

John was bothered by the image of Beth slapping him in the face and pinching him, but he was touched they would go through so much effort to help him out.

Abby continued to throw words at John, "How do you feel? Do you feel sick? If you *are* sick, we will have to tell Mother and Father. We can't hide that. Do you think you can eat? Jo made an egg and cheese quiche this morning that's to die for. It's cold now, of course, but I'm sure it's still delicious. I have some fruit and some milk. Diana, what would you like?"

Diana waited for John to answer first. "I don't feel sick, I just feel a little dizzy and *really* tired, like I could fall back asleep at any moment. I'd love some of that egg-cheese-thing you talked about. Not too much though, I'm not very hungry," he said. He surprised himself and Abby with that confession. John was *always* hungry.

Diana said to John, "You should feel better after you eat." To Abby she said, "I'd like to have a piece of quiche, too, please, and milk would be great." She admitted, "I ate the food in the basket last night. I hope that was alright."

As Abby started getting their food ready, John pushed himself up to a sitting position, slowly this time. He rubbed his eyes and looked accusingly at the girl. Instead of answering her question, he asked one of his own, "What did you do to me? It seemed unreal, like a dream. What was with the glowy hand and all?" As soon as he said the words, he wanted to take them back. He didn't intend to sound so harsh. He noticed that she'd cleaned herself up and was wearing the clothes he'd brought the night before.

Diana flushed and looked away. She fiddled with the neck of her dress as she answered, "I had to do a knowledge transfer on you, or rather from you to me. I woke up in the middle of night and tried to remember all that happened to me after I was…freed. I started out with a small language scan, and when I realized it was a language I didn't know at all, I ended up doing a full language transfer. Transferring numbers and letters are quite straight forward as they are just facts, but many words have personalized feelings attached to them, making them harder to extract. Your mind tries to resist and that exhausts the subject, which is you. Then I did a scan of your functional memories and realized how different the world has become since…well, since *before*. I did a transfer of functional memories and some motion memories to learn how things work and how to use them, like your bathroom. Many of those had emotional memories attached to them as well, so it took some time to separate out just the part I needed, so I wouldn't fight with your natural resistance as much. Even so, the longer the transfer takes, the more energy it consumes. I'm really sorry I did that without asking, especially after you being so nice to me yesterday. It was kind of a survival instinct for me. I was surprised I had enough energy to do it, and that my Crystavis still worked." Diana took a deep breath like she was trying to settle herself. She laid her trembling hands in her lap, embarrassed by her long speech. She looked moments away from crying.

John was floored; good thing he was on the floor! He caught maybe half of what she said. He had a bunch of questions, but he pressed his lips tightly together, not wanting to say something to push her over the edge into tears. He hated when girls cried. Luckily, Abby was there to come to the rescue.

"Oh, you poor thing!" Abby said as she rushed to put a comforting arm around Diana's shoulders. "You've been through something terribly traumatic. No need to apologize to John, he'll be fine." John wasn't completely sure about that. He was still worried about the whole pulling thoughts from his mind thing, but he appreciated that Diana had apologized.

"Don't worry, you're here with us now and we'll take care of you. You just rest and build up your strength," said Abby.

Diana gave her a watery smile and nodded. An uncomfortable silence fell on the room as Diana's eyes lost their focus, and she pinched her lips together in a tight line like she was trying to stop herself from crying. John groaned internally, thinking Abby made it worse by basically giving Diana permission to fall apart. Girls! John still felt that pull in his chest that drew him to Diana, but it seemed to have faded a bit. Still, he wanted to do something to take the look of pain off her face.

John cleared his throat as he sat up straighter saying, "If you haven't figured it out already, I'm John." He lifted his hand and gave her a small wave, saying, "Hi! We're in my, um, room." Oh, he was such a nerd... or maybe not.

Diana looked at him and smiled the first true smile he'd seen on her face, as she returned a small wave of her own saying, "Hi, John."

* * *

John and Diana both dove into their breakfast, while Abby waited patiently. The quiche was fantastic, John realized, as he helped himself to seconds, and thirds. His appetite had returned. That was at least one thing back to normal. He was anxious to hear the girl's story, find out where and when she was from, and how she got in the statue to begin with. He knew she had to have been in there a long time. Oh man! He almost choked on his last bite of quiche as it just hit him, that it was probably so long ago, that her friends and family were all gone. No wonder she almost lost it when Abby said they'd take care of her. There wasn't much love lost between him and Father and Mother, but he did care for his sisters, and this life was the only one he knew. He couldn't imagine being ripped from it and thrown into another time and place all alone.

He decided to ease her into her story by starting at the end. He brushed the crumbs from his lap as he asked, "Diana, how much do you remember from the museum yesterday?"

Diana finished chewing, took a sip of milk and answered, "Not much. It kind of was a blur to me. I remember lots of dust and putting on funny smelling clothes, but mostly I remember you, John. I wasn't really aware of what was going on, it was like sleepwalking, but I remember feeling safe with you. I remember feeling like I could trust you, and you were there to help me."

Diana's cheeks grew pink as she admitted this, and John cleared his throat and shifted uncomfortably in his seat on the floor.

Diana continued, "I remember a view of the farm as you brought me here, and I remember falling into bed, and that's about it. Can you fill in the details?"

"Sure," John said, and he recounted the same story he'd given his sisters the night before. This time he embellished a bit on his gallantry and downplayed his poor choices in tripping Todd and breaking the statue.

John couldn't hold back his questions any further. "What can you tell us about the man in the statue? Who was he, and why was he trying to capture you? Did you know him?"

Diana said, "It's a very long story. I don't think I have the strength to go through it right now. I will say that I do know who he is, or rather who he *was*, and I had been forbidden to speak to him. He was trying to force me to talk with him. The problem was, that the moment he caught me in his rope, it triggered a kind of defense mechanism that turned us both to stone. I know The Founder added something to our Crystavis to keep us from talking to… *people like the man*, but I had no idea it was so hurtful." She paused and then said in a deadly, low voice, "This is all The Founder's fault. I can't believe he let this happen to me!" Diana was obviously getting upset, but this time it was anger instead of sadness that was making her hands shake as she curled them into fists. John thought her switch to anger was kind of sudden, but considering what she was going through, he guessed she was a bit on edge.

"So you *knew* the guy? He wasn't trying to hurt you; he was just trying to talk to you? Don't you think roping you like a calf was a bit extreme?" John asked.

Diana shrugged her shoulders as she replied, "Yes, I knew him. He was a friend before I wasn't allowed to talk to him anymore. He was pretty desperate over not seeing Miranda for so long. I can understand why he did it, but it was still wrong."

John cut in, "I'm getting confused. Who are these people, The Founder and Miranda? And that crysto thing, you mentioned that earlier when you talked about copying my brain over to yours. And about that, I'm sorry, but I'm not sure that I'm okay with that whole thing. It's a little creepy that you can get inside my head, and now you know all this stuff about me."

Diana was quick to apologize again, "I'm sorry I did that without asking you first. It's not like I read your mind; well, I sort of did, but I went after information, not your current thoughts. Oh, that doesn't sound good either. Let me think of how to explain it." Diana paused for a moment before she continued. "Imagine your brain is like one of your computers. Actually, it is a lot like one of your computers, but infinitely more powerful. Your computer has both short-term memory and long-term memory, right? And each file stored has a type, right? Well, I went after your long-term memory, and I was looking for specific information, non-subjective facts, like words and instructions on how things around you work. For the language, it was like pulling words without pictures, and they were just words and their definitions, not specific memories. That would be like going after a text file that was made up of just unformatted words, versus another document that has words that are formatted and pictures and even sound included. For the functional and muscle memory, those are the kinds of things your brain can perform on "autopilot," remembering the instructions without any complex analysis or decision-making. In simplistic terms, that information went from your autopilot straight to my autopilot, without any stops in-between. It was like making a photocopy without reading through it. There were ties to your emotional memories, and I did my best to block those links, so I didn't copy those over as well. I'm not sure I can explain it any better than that. Did that help?"

John said, "So you, like, took the word "sing" and what it meant, but you didn't take memories of me singing feeling happy or upset?"

"Exactly!" Diana confirmed, looking pleased that he was beginning to understand.

"Thank goodness for that! You would have run for the hills by now if you heard John *singing*," Abby teased.

John remembered her saying she copied stuff, like how to use the bathroom. He wondered what kind of emotional memory he had that was tied to that particular piece of information. John shuddered. "Can you take memories, too, if you wanted to?" John asked, ignoring Abby's jab.

Diana deflated a little. "Yes, I can, but it is much harder and takes a lot more energy. The subject basically has to remember something and relive it in his or her head, for me to take it without a tremendous amount of work."

"So you could have seen what I was dreaming but not dig out my first day of school?" John asked.

"Right," Diana said. "But I didn't see what you were dreaming. It took all of my energy just to get what I did."

John felt relieved and wary at the same time. He was tremendously happy she didn't take any of his personal thoughts, but the fact that she *could* get at what he was thinking at any particular time unnerved him. "And how are you able to do this magic? And what about those people you mentioned? You haven't told us who they are yet."

Abby jumped in, "John! Ease up on her! One thing at a time, or you'll overwhelm us all!"

John wasn't sure he was ready to hear about the magic part yet, so he asked, "Okay, why don't you tell us about the people you mentioned."

"Sounds good," Diana replied. "But just so you know, it's not magic, it's science. Okay, The Founder is the leader of our … *people*. Miranda was his daughter." Diana said *people* as if she had a hard time picking what word she wanted to use.

31

"Why weren't you allowed to talk to that man? Why hadn't he seen Miranda? Did something happen to her?" interjected Abby.

"I'll tell you both the whole story another day. It really is too long for today. The basics are that one of the people in that man's…*group* hurt The Founder's wife, so our entire populous was forbidden to talk to anyone in that man's…*group*." John noticed the word choice difficulty again over *group*. "Miranda was always breaking the rules, so her father had her under guard to make sure she didn't leave our city. It had been a couple of months since the man had last seen Miranda when he tried to capture me."

Abby seemed to want more information, but John was content with it. It sounded like one big soap opera to him, and he really didn't want more detail. "Are you sure you didn't know any English before you pulled it out of my head?" John teased with a half-smile. "I didn't even think 'populous' was in my vocabulary!"

Diana let loose a small smile, and John was pleased that he'd put it there. Abby gave him a small kick and said, "Oh, John! I'm sure you knew that word and a whole bunch of others, too. You're not a Neanderthal after all!"

"I'm jus a po' ole farm boy that haz me no smarts," John drawled. Abby rolled her eyes, and Diana let out a tiny giggle, which turned John's half smile into a whole one. "O-kay, back to buz-nezz," John continued his act, "Wha' was 'at crysto-y thingy ya talk'd 'bout? Waz 'at whut made your hand all glowy las nahte as you tippy-toed thru me brain?"

"It's called a Crystavis, and I can do more than tell you about it, I can show it to you," Diana proclaimed proudly.

Abby, who still had her arm around Diana, squealed and bounced excitedly, squeezing and jostling the other girl. Diana stepped out of Abby's grip and smiled warily. John couldn't blame her. Abby was a thin little thing, all skin and bones, but she was surprisingly strong for a nine-year-old. The two girls before him could hardly be more different. One had blond hair and blue eyes, the other brown hair and brown eyes. One was tan with hard lines, and the other was pale and soft. Jeez, what was coming over John that he was noticing and comparing things like that? One morning of skipping chores and hanging out with girls, and he was getting all sensitive and stuff.

With the distraction of Abby's squealing and bouncing, they didn't hear the creak of the steps, announcing they had company. John jumped to his feet in front of Diana to hide her from sight as the door pushed open. He must have been getting his strength back, since the room only spun a little as he did so. Abby stopped her little display abruptly, and all eyes were riveted on the opening door. When Beth's brunette head popped into sight, John and Abby let out a simultaneous sigh of relief.

Beth frowned at her brother and sister as she entered the room saying, "Boy, you two are jumpy! You both need to calm down." Beth closed the door and said, "If you act like that around the others, they will know something is up."

John sat back down on the braided rug, revealing Diana standing in front of the table. The scowl immediately fell from Beth's face as she said, "Oh, you're up."

Abby bounced over to her sister and, grabbing both of her hands, pulled her over to the table as she gushed, "Yes, Diana's up, isn't it wonderful? Her name is *Diana*, isn't that a lovely name? John was right, she didn't speak English; but now she does because she photocopied John's brain last night. She knows all about stuff like computers and showers, and you're just in time! Diana's just about to show us her crysta-thingy!"

Beth took in Abby's rant with a tentative smile and said, "Okay…"

"I'm sure that was as clear as mud, but the jist of it is that this is Diana, and she speaks English because she read my mind. She was just about to show us the amulet that let her do that. Diana, this is our sister Beth," John said helpfully.

After Diana and Beth exchanged hellos, John encouraged, "So, let's see the amulet."

"Yes, let's see this amulet," Beth agreed. John was grateful that Beth didn't ask questions about what he and Abby had just told her. He could count on an inquisition later, he was sure.

"Okay, just to warn you, pulling it out of its hiding place is a little … dramatic, so just stay calm, and I'll explain it all after I get it out," Diana said, directing the last part at Abby.

"No squealing; got it!" Abby said.

Before John's mind could come up with what "dramatic" meant, Diana put her right hand over the center of her chest, and a small ring on her hand that John didn't notice before, started to glow. A gold chain necklace popped up out of her skin like it had been inside her. The glow in the ring faded, and Diana pulled her hand away from her chest holding a pendant attached to the chain necklace.

John stood and he, Abby, and Beth all moved up to Diana to see the necklace better. It filled the center of Diana's palm and had a large brown stone in the middle, which was surrounded by different colored gems. The metal holding it together kind of swirled and wrapped around each gem. John had never seen anything like it before. Looking closer, the stone in the center wasn't really brown, it was more of a reddish brown, had veins of colors running through it, and sparkled when it caught the light. It reminded John of those rocks that looked like just rocks on the outside, but if you broke them open they sparkled. Was that quartz or something?

John took a step back to give Diana some space and said, "Whoa, did that thing just come out of your *skin*?"

Diana closed her hand over the amulet and stepped back as if embarrassed. "Yes?" she said, like she was uncertain, or just maybe unsure they would believe her answer.

Beth nearly salivated as she demanded, "Tell us how you did that!"

Abby was surprisingly quiet and still. John looked at her, and her eyes were as big as saucers, but she looked okay otherwise.

Diana pressed the amulet back to her chest, took a deep breath, and started, "I used the ring on my hand to flatten the amulet, to take the mass out of it, and store the molecular structure on my skin, in the cells of my dermis to be precise." As she was talking her ring glowed again, and the part of the necklace he could see, the chain, looked like it just sank into her skin until it disappeared. "To get it back out, I do the reverse. I push the mass back into it, so it forms shape again. There is a way to literally embed one object inside another without flattening it, where the molecules of both objects share the same space, but that's very complicated, and I can't do that yet. Very few people can." Diana made the amulet rise back out of her skin again. She settled the amulet between her collarbones over her dress and clasped her hands in front of her, nervously shifting her feet as she waited for the anticipated questions.

John could visualize flattening something and blowing it up again like a balloon, but he didn't see how that could ever be possible. The storing it in your skin part sounded kind of icky and was hard to believe as well. He looked at his two sisters to see their reactions.

Abby's jaw had dropped, leaving her mouth slightly open, and she had a dreamy look on her face, like she'd just walked into a live fairy tale. Beth was holding her chin while she stared at the necklace with her lips pressed into a straight line. The concentrated look on her face was intense, and John hoped smoke wouldn't start coming out of her ears from thinking too hard. She was only fifteen, but she was one of the smartest people John knew, mostly due to her insatiable curiosity on how all things worked.

"Can I see it?" Beth asked, as she stepped forward with her palm held out, like she wanted Diana to take off the amulet and drop it into her hand.

Diana said, "You can come here and touch it, but it doesn't leave my neck, *ever*." Diana's tone was surprisingly strong with that last declaration. Beth seemed to ignore the warning in Diana's voice as she stood in front of Diana and lifted the amulet in her hands, carefully examining it.

Honestly, John felt like his brain couldn't take any more right now. This was a lot to absorb all at one time. He could tell that the sun was nearly overhead now, and they should be showing up for lunch soon. "That was a great magic trick and all, but isn't it getting close to lunch time? We need to go to the house. I think the questions can wait for now. We need a plan for Diana over everything else. When we get back from lunch, let's focus on that."

Diana muttered under her breath, "It's science, not magic," as Abby closed her mouth and checked the sun outside the window. Abby was back to business as she said, "You're right, John, we should go now. Diana, I hope you'll be all right here until we get back? We'll bring you some lunch."

Beth reluctantly let the amulet fall back to Diana's chest as she headed for the door. "You're right, we need to figure out our next steps before we dig into everything else," Beth agreed. Abby quickly put the remains of breakfast back in the basket and took it with her out the door, saying, "Bye," and giving Diana a cheery wave.

John was the last one out. When he got to the doorway, he turned to Diana, who was still standing in the same spot, clutching her amulet and looking a little lost. "Don't worry, it will be okay. Beth's smart as a whip, and with her on our side, we're sure to figure something out. You probably already know, but don't leave the room and don't get too close to the window. We don't want anyone knowing you're here before we have a plan. So, I guess I'll see you in a little bit?" John had wanted to sound comforting, but it didn't quite come out that way.

"Alright, see you soon," Diana said before he closed the door and headed to the house for lunch.

Neither of them expected that the day would almost be over before he got back to the loft.

CHAPTER 6 – THE COOPERS

John wasn't prepared for what happened over lunch. Usually, lunch was a small matter; everyone eating quickly and getting on with their day. Today, however, Father was in a mood. As soon as they finished prayers, Father started in on John. "Where were you this morning, John?" Father asked, in that tone that let John know he was already in trouble.

"Uh, working?" John replied as he accepted the pot of soup from Father. He wished it hadn't come out sounding like a question.

"You were supposed to meet me in the north fields this morning to help pull the tractor out of that wet spot. I told you about it last night. Get your head out of the clouds, boy, and do what you're told. You're lucky I don't give you the strap for making me wait on you all morning. The north fields should have been plowed by now. Right after lunch we'll tow the tractor out. Once that's done, you're to go over to the Coopers' for the rest of the day and help them repair their border fence. Joey's not due back from college for another week, so they're one man short. We still owe them for loaning us Jay for the last shearing. I want to hear a good report the next time I see Mr. Cooper, so you head on over there real quick when we're done, and no stopping at Widow McNeally's, do you hear? And you don't leave the Coopers' until the work is done. I know you weren't born a Brown, but you've got to hold up the Brown name all the same. None of this nonsense of forgetting your duties like this morning!" Father paused in his tirade to wolf down some soup.

The Coopers owned the farm across the road. They had two sons: Joey, who was finishing his freshman year at college, and Jay, who was two years behind him. Jay was the closest thing John had to a friend, even though Jay tended to act superior most of the time. Normally, John wouldn't mind being loaned out for the day; the Coopers were good people, and John got along great with them. Mrs. Cooper made the best peanut butter cookies in the county, and she always had some made when John was coming over, because she knew they were his favorite. But today? He'd told Diana he'd be back right after lunch. From the sounds of it, he would be lucky to be back by sunset.

Father continued his lecture to John on what he expected of him, and that flowed right into Father's favorite sermon on how the path to wickedness was started through sloth, disrespect, and laziness of the mind. Apparently, John was guilty of all three by his no-show that morning.

Everyone had finished lunch, but Father continued his speech for another ten minutes. Eventually, Father stopped talking and slurped the last of his soup. Several of the girls had their hands clasped, ready to begin the after-dinner prayer, when Father surprised them all by saying as he surveyed his daughters, "You girls are going to have to help with the evening chores while John is over at the Coopers'. Mary Margaret, you help Mother with the young ones and the housework. Mary Ann and Mary Elizabeth, you two are to handle the evening milking. Mary Joanna and Mary Alice, you're to take care of the horses. Mary Bernadette and Mary Abigail, you're to feed the rest of the animals. I have to go into town for some errands, and with John at the Coopers,' everyone will have to pitch in. You are to wear work aprons and gloves, and wear your hats when you're outside. If anyone comes a-calling, don't let them see you working. The last thing I need is for the town to be gossiping about how I let my girls do men's work! Now, let us pray." Father bowed his head and led them in the after-dinner prayer. When finished, he turned and left the house, calling to John over his shoulder as he went, "I want you out to the north field in no less than five minutes!"

The girls were all in a buzz over the new instructions for the day, and Beth, Abby, and John were able to exchange quick words without anyone noticing. "You guys will take care of Diana for me, right? " John whispered. "Of course!" Abby reassured.

"Thanks, I mean it. Let her know I did mean to come back after lunch. And, guys, go easy on her. Don't ask too many questions, especially when I'm not there."

"We've got it covered," Beth whispered back. "Now get going, or for our next meal we'll all be sitting through a sermon twice as long as today's!"

"I'm going!" John said as the two girls gave him a push towards the door.

John hurriedly retrieved his work gloves and ran to meet Father out in the north fields. There was a deep patch of dense clay in that field that didn't drain well, no matter how much they tilled it. For lack of a better word, they just called it *the wet spot*. Most years, they plowed and planted around it to avoid the very thing in front of him. The tractor was well and thoroughly stuck smack in the middle of the wet clay. Luckily, they were able to tow it out. If that hadn't worked, they would've had to get the Coopers to help, and that would be downright embarrassing. John wondered what Father was thinking, driving straight through that tractor trap. It wasn't like him to make a mistake like that; he must have been seriously preoccupied. The smooth rescue must have also rescued Father's bad mood, because he let John drive the truck back to the shed.

In no time, John was walking down the drive through the arching maple trees to the Coopers' farm across the road. When John reached the end of his drive, he looked wistfully down the road at Widow McNeally's house. She had a house across the bridge on the other side of the road next to the Coopers. Her husband had passed five years back, and now she rented most of her land to the Coopers to farm. The McNeally's had three children, but they all had moved away and rarely visited. Mrs. McNeally had taken a keen interest in John right from the start when John came to live at the Brown's at age six. She was like the grandmother he never had. He stopped by whenever he could and did odd jobs to help her out. Father knew about it, and he was okay with it, as long as it didn't take away from John's chores on the farm. Father was a Christian man, and believed in taking care of "the elderly," which is how he categorized Widow McNeally. Father would not approve, however, if he knew how much time John spent in her kitchen talking and getting spoiled with baked treats. Father would certainly not approve if he knew that the widow occasionally paid John for helping out. Mrs. McNeally always offered, but John tried to turn her down every time. Every once in a while she would get her way and send John back home with a few dollars in his pocket.

John hadn't been to see the widow since last weekend. He hoped she wouldn't worry about him, as she had a tendency to do. He usually visited every Saturday and at least once during the week. John thought over whether or not he should tell Mrs. McNeally about Diana as he walked along the Coopers' driveway to their house. He wanted to tell her, but he didn't know when he would get the chance to visit next.

Mrs. Cooper met John at the door and handed him a couple of peanut butter cookies as she directed him to the edge of the property where her husband and Jay worked. The afternoon passed quickly. John worked comfortably with the Coopers, making idle chitchat and exchanging the occasional joke or jibe. Mr. Cooper was much more laid-back than Father, but was every bit as hard of a worker. With the three of them they made good progress. Mrs. Cooper brought them a light supper, and they barely paused to eat. They finished the last section of fence just as the sun dropped behind the trees.

John followed the Coopers back to their house, and they all washed up the best they could at the utility sink on the back porch. Mrs. Cooper insisted John stay for a second supper, saying the food earlier was barely a snack. John knew better than to say no to Mrs. Cooper over anything. She was a grand lady. She was beautiful at age forty-eight, and must have been gorgeous when she was young. She had this soft, knowing way about her that made her the adored queen of her small family. She didn't wear prairie dresses; she dressed like a normal human in her jeans and a T-shirt. Mr. Cooper came in and swept Mrs. Cooper into his arms. He gave her a confident kiss on the lips, making her giggle and blush. "You're filthy, Robert, put me down!" exclaimed Mrs. Cooper. She patted her shoulder-length blond hair back into place as she told the boys, "Sit down, all of you. The food is getting cold."

John loved having supper at the Coopers. Their family was so different from his own. For one thing, John didn't remember ever seeing Father kiss Mother, let alone hug her and pick her up off her feet. The Coopers were as relaxed around the table as they were working out in the field. They did say grace before dinner, but they were Methodists, so there was no sign of the cross and no after-dinner prayer. It had taken a while to get used to the way the Cooper boys and Mrs. Cooper talked whenever they wanted to. Father would scoff if he knew how they acted at dinner. John reveled in it, but still, he would only speak when spoken to; it was too ingrained in him to do otherwise. John actually forgot about Diana for a while as he enjoyed the meal. It all came crashing back down on him when Mrs. Cooper asked him, "Did you hear the news yesterday about that museum vandalism in Pittsburgh? They say the statue was pounded into dust and tiny bits of rock. I can't imagine the museum letting something like that happen right under their noses! Something about their story just doesn't add up. We're supposed to believe that no one heard anything, that the room had been empty long enough for it to happen? I wonder if there were explosives involved, and they're trying to cover it up." She tisked as she slightly shook her head. "I don't understand people sometimes." Then she looked up like she just remembered something. "John," she said, "didn't you have your field trip yesterday? Were you anywhere near the museum?"

"Yeah," Jay added, "this was the last full week of school. Isn't the eighth-grade field trip on the last Friday before summer?"

Three sets of eyes all focused on John. He nervously set his fork down and wiped his mouth as he finished chewing. Finally, he was able to answer, "Um, yeah, our field trip was yesterday."

"Well, spit it out, where did you go, dear?" asked Mrs. Cooper.

John flushed slightly at being called "dear" and mumbled while looking at his plate. "We went to the museum."

"The same museum the vandal attacked?" asked Jay.

"Yeah, the same one," John said, keeping his answers short and to the point.

"Well, don't keep us waiting, son; that kind of excitement doesn't touch us very often. Tell us everything! How close to the time the vandal attacked were you there? Did you see anything? Did the police interview you?" Mr. Cooper asked, his curiosity peaked.

"There's not much to tell," John said with a sigh. He liked being called "son" by Mr. Cooper. "I saw the statue that was ruined, before it was ruined I mean. My tour group was the last to see it before the attack, at least I think so. My group's guide was interviewed on T.V. as being the last museum employee to see the statue. I think we left on the bus before it happened, or at least before anyone found out what happened, so the police weren't involved yet. The news said they thought the police would be following up with all the schools that visited the museum yesterday, so I'm not sure what will happen Monday at school." John was getting better at lying. He heard once that for a good lie you should stick to the truth as much as possible. That seemed to be good advice.

"Does your Father know?" asked Mr. Cooper quietly.

"No."

Mr. and Mrs. Cooper exchanged a worried glance. "Well, I don't see any need to tell him. He has enough on his mind with the farm and all. I'm sure if the police want to talk to you, they'll do it at school and not come to the house. It was bad luck being in that last group. I'm sure it will all blow over quickly," Mr. Cooper reassured.

John had been fairly sure there was nothing to worry about with the museum, but he hadn't considered the fallout if the police actually did want to talk to him and Father found out. Father wouldn't care if the police were just looking for clues; he'd assume John was somehow at fault and preemptively punish him for it. The way the Coopers were acting, he guessed they were thinking the same thing. It embarrassed him that they knew Father took the strap to him. He didn't know how they found out, but somehow they did.

Jay broke the mood by saying, "You'll have to play up the whole bad boy act for the girls. They love that crap."

"Jay! Watch your language!" his mother admonished.

"I was, Mom, I was even hearing it, too," Jay teased.

"Boys!" Mrs. Cooper complained as she adjusted the napkin in her lap. "I'll bet you don't hear that kind of language coming out of your sisters' mouths at your house!"

"No, Ma'am, they save that for when they're outdoors, out of hearing range from Father and Mother," John answered with a smile on his face.

Mrs. Cooper made a "t-huh" noise as she took in a breath then released it with a giggle as she saw John's face. The conversation went back to safer topics after that. Soon, Mrs. Cooper was giving him a quick hug and sending him home with a bag of peanut butter cookies and several sandwiches for a midnight snack. Having raised two sons, Mrs. Cooper was familiar with a teenaged boy's appetite. John had overindulged at supper and couldn't imagine being hungry for a while, but he liked being fussed over. As John walked home in the dark, he felt guilty for having a good time when Diana was cooped up in the loft. At least the cookies might help make up for it. John felt sticky and dirty from working in the sun all day and couldn't wait to get cleaned up. His muscles ached in that good way after putting in a full day's work. He didn't look forward to another night of sleeping on the floor, but there was no way he'd admit that to a girl. He picked up his pace, eager to see how Diana had fared.

CHAPTER 7 – LOFTY CONVERSATIONS

Diana was alone in the loft, as he'd expected. Beth and Abby would be stuck in the house after dark. She was in bed reading a book. She looked up when John came in and gave him a warm smile. "It looks like you've had a busy day," she said, a small tease in her voice. "Beth stopped by with some food after lunch and told me what happened. I'm sorry you got into trouble."

"Um, thanks. It wasn't so bad, just a lecture over lunch. Did they bring you any supper?" John asked as he laid the sandwiches and cookies on the bedside table.

"No, they didn't get the chance," Diana said as she eagerly scooted to the edge of the bed to check out the food. She helped herself to a sandwich as she commented, "These look delicious. How'd you manage them?"

"Mrs. Cooper made them. There are cookies there, too. Save some for me if you can; they're my favorite. I'm going to clean up while you eat." John grabbed clean clothes on the way to the bathroom. He took his usual quick shower. He didn't mind the cold water, but it did nothing to help his sore muscles. He noticed a faint bruise on his left shoulder blade from falling the day before, but it didn't hurt anymore. He came out in his long PJ pants and a clean T-shirt and headed towards his makeshift bed on the floor. He was surprised to see a pillow and an extra blanket waiting for him. Upon closer inspection he discovered the "pillow" was a couple of bath towels folded inside a pillowcase, and the blanket was one of the horse blankets from the barn below. The pillow of towels would be much more comfortable than his book bag.

"Beth brought the pillow after lunch and the blanket in the evening. She didn't stay long, so we didn't get a chance to talk," Diana explained.

"So you were by yourself mostly?" John asked worriedly as he settled into his blankets. The horse blanket was clean and only had a faint smell of horse that John found comforting.

"Yes, but I was fine. I slept on and off and found a book on your desk to read," Diana answered his unspoken question. "I love reading, and I can't wait to see what people have come up with since I was … frozen," Diana trailed off. Then she brightened as she said teasingly, "Lucky for me you haven't read that many books and ruined them for me with the knowledge transfer and all."

John flushed slightly, so he turned his head away from her to hide it as he answered, "Yeah, I'm not much into reading books. There's usually no time for it. Hey, can you turn out the light now?"

She did as he asked, and he could hear her settle back into bed as his eyes adjusted to the dark. Pale moonlight filtered through his small window, keeping the room from falling into total darkness. He didn't have any coverings over the window. If the sun was up, he was up, so he never bothered trying to get a curtain or shade for it.

"I'm not sure how much I'll be around tomorrow. We all go to Mass in the morning before lunch. I have no idea what work Father will have in store for me. I could be away all day again. Sorry about that. I came up with an idea today, though. There is a widow who lives just down the road. I think she might take you in for a while to give us time to figure something out."

Diana sat up and said in a small, worried voice, "I can't stay here?"

John felt a pang of guilt in his stomach. She was all alone in this time, and the only person she knew was already trying to get rid of her. "I'd love for you to stay here, but it really isn't safe… for either of us. If my father found out, he'd throw you out on your ear, and I'd probably get the strap. You can't stay in this one room all the time, and I've got too many nebby sisters for this to go unnoticed for long. I won't abandon you or anything," John ended, trying to reassure her.

"Okay, I guess you're right," she sighed as her head hit the pillow again. "How many sisters do you have anyway?

"Eleven."

"Eleven?" Dianna squeaked. "Is that normal for this time?"

"Not really. It's only normal for backwoods farmers who have an unhealthy dose of Amish worship and who keep thinking the next one will be a boy," John said a little too harshly.

"Well, they had you didn't they? How many boys do they expect? And what do you mean by Amish worship?"

"My parents are like Amish who accept the conveniences of modern technology. They are very religious, strict and old-fashioned. Girls don't normally wear cotton print dresses, for instance, that's just my parents," John answered the easier question first. "And I'm not really their son. I was adopted."

"Oh," Diana said on a small puff of breath. "How old were you? When you were adopted I mean."

"I was six when they brought me here. Before that, I lived in an orphanage on Pittsburgh's north side. I'm fourteen now, so I've been here for eight years."

"Did you always sleep out here in the barn? I would think that would be kind of scary for a six-year-old."

"Naw, I started out in the house. There were only seven girls at the time; they split two bedrooms, and I had my own. Abby was just one year old when I moved in. Beth was seven. Jo was my age, but we don't have much in common. Jo's into all the girly stuff and thought I was too rough and uncivilized. I mostly just shadowed Father when he did the chores, helping where I could and learning the ropes. I was seven when the twins were born, Jane and Ellen. They started out in Mother and Father's room, but that didn't last very long. They moved them in with me, but Father didn't like the idea of boys and girls sharing a bedroom, so they came up with this. It took a while to get it ready, and I moved here when I was eight. I used to have to go to the house to use the bathroom, and I can't tell you how many times a night I would go over there using that excuse to avoid being out here alone. Sometimes I would curl up on the couch and fall asleep there, then get up and leave before dawn. Meg found me a couple of times. She would just wake me up and send me back here. One time Father caught me sleeping on the couch, and he got really mad. I still remember what he said. 'We didn't spend all that money building you your own room for you to just sleep on the couch! Now man up and go back to the loft!' I was more scared of Father than I was scared to stay out here by myself, so that ended that," John said, remembering his eight-year-old self. "Christie was born three years later. I think the twins wore Mother out since that was the longest Mother and Father had gone without a baby. Gracie was born two years ago. So far there's no sign there is a number twelve on the way." John was amazed at how easy it was to talk to Diana. Maybe being in the dark helped.

"Do you know why they adopted you? I don't mean to sound rude, but they were a large family already. Why would they want to add to it? Your parents don't exactly sound like the people who would do that for humanitarian reasons."

John let out a weird sound that was something between a grunt and a snort. Normally, John would have been embarrassed, but he was flooded with years of denied resentment as he said, "They needed free labor. Father doesn't want the girls to do 'men's work,' and they weren't having any luck having a boy of their own, so they adopted one. I remember them telling the orphanage that they wanted a boy who was six or seven, healthy, quiet, a hard worker, and who did as he was told. They wanted a boy who was already 'house broken' but young enough to mold into what they wanted." John was surprised by how bitter he sounded. "I mean, don't get me wrong, I'm happy to be here. This is light years better than the orphanage," John tried to back track. "I'm grateful to Mother and Father for taking me in, and I love my sisters, most of them anyway," he finished with a small smile that Diana couldn't see in the dark.

His attempt at a joke went by unnoticed. "What happens if they do have a baby boy?"

"I don't know. It would be years before a boy of theirs would be able to handle any kind of workload, and by then I'll be of age. I think it is more likely that one of my sisters will marry a farmer, and my parents will hand the farm over to him. I'm not worried about that happening any time soon. If it did, it probably would just mean less work for me. My sisters would never kick me out."

Diana was quiet as she took in his words.

"What about you?" John asked, trying to get the focus of the conversation off him. "Did you have a big family where you come from?"

"No, I am…I mean I *was* an only child," Diana said with a small hitch in her voice as she changed to the past tense.

"Oh *cattails*, Diana, I'm sorry. It's got be hard for you, losing everything like you did. I shouldn't have brought it up."

Diana sniffed and said in a small voice, "No, it's okay. I think it is good for me to talk about it. I feel like I'm in a dream, and I'm waiting to wake up. Talking may help me accept that this is real, and that I can't go back."

It was John's turn to be quiet. He waited for her to continue at her own pace.

"I was an only child, and I have to admit I was rather spoiled in all things but one. My parents expected a lot of me; they expected me to be the best at everything. It was a lot of pressure, but I think the pressure I put on myself was even greater," Diana began.

"I lived in a very contained community, which felt almost like living with extended family. I didn't get along too well with the other kids though; I related better to adults. My best friend was a grownup named Miranda. She was my unofficial mentor. I spent as much free time with her as I could, learning as much as I could. She would often take me to the outside to work. She was so patient with me, and she spoke to me as an equal. She had one friend, Mirabelle, who was kind of like a maid to her family and who went with us a lot of the time. Miranda shared most everything with us, and we kept her secrets. Miranda always made me feel special by confiding in me and spending so much time with me. She was kind of like a princess to our community, which made her time with me even more precious."

Diana quieted, deep in thought.

"*Miranda*, that sounds familiar. Did you mention her before?"

"Yes, I think I did," Diana sighed. "She was who Michael was trying to see."

"Michael?"

"Michael is the man who lassoed me. He hadn't seen Miranda in a couple of months and was desperate, and before you ask, he was desperate because he and Miranda were secretly married. That was one of the secrets Miranda shared with just me and Mirabelle," Diana said almost defensively. "I'm sure Michael wouldn't have hurt me," she said uncertainly. "I'm pretty sure, that is. It was very unlike him to try to restrain me so forcefully."

John wasn't sure what to think about this *Michael*. His instincts and his gut were telling him two different things, if that were even possible. His instincts made him feel a possessive protectiveness over Diana that saw Michael as a threat, since he'd basically attacked her with the rope. In his gut was a deep, settling feeling of calm when he thought of the man. He hadn't known it was there before, because there were too many other things and feelings going on. It felt like trust, which was weird because he didn't know the guy. Usually, it took a long time for someone to earn his trust.

"Oh my gosh!" Diana interrupted his thoughts as she sat up and put her hand over her mouth. "I'm starting to remember things from that day Michael caught me. He stepped out of the woods and called my name. He said he needed to talk to me and not to run away again. I started to back away from him and turned to run, and he shouted after me that I didn't understand, that he needed to see Miranda, that she was pregnant."

"She was pregnant," Diana whispered to herself. "Oh, Miranda! Michael! They never got to see each other again. Michael was going to be a father, and his child lived and died years ago. That's so sad! I wonder where Michael is now. Did he get freed from the statue, too?" Diana turned to ask John.

"I think so. Do you remember his half of the statue started to crack and fall apart as we left? I think I saw him on the news the other night. I didn't get a chance to see the news today."

"He was on the *news*? What happened to him? Do you know where he is?"

"Yeah, the news said that he was found wandering the museum covered in dust like you were. The police had him in custody, and they were giving him a mental evaluation. That's all I know."

"Oh, poor Michael! He has no one to help him! I hope wherever he is, they have someone who can speak Italian to him; otherwise, he will be so lost! I have to help him. Miranda would never forgive me if I let something happen to her Michael!" Diana said, clearly upset.

"Whoa, slow down there," John tried to calm her. "Michael is a grownup and can take care of himself, I'm sure. If the police have him, we know that he's safe and getting fed. Let's worry about you first, okay? We need to get you a place to stay other than this room, remember?"

Diana rubbed her eyes and sighed, "I guess you're right; he's at least safe for now. Once we get me settled though, I want to find and talk to him."

"Okay," John agreed, even though he wasn't sure he could do anything to help her get to Michael.

"You said Michael speaks Italian? Is that where you're from?"

"That's where Michael is from. I'm from New Zigon," Diana said with a hint of pride in her voice.

"New Zigon? I've never heard of that before. Is it a place near Italy?"

"It's not really anywhere," Diana said vaguely. "It's in a Lacunavim, which is a special place hidden within the folds of reality."

"Say what?" asked John, totally confused.

Diana sighed. "I can't really explain it, because I never really understood it myself. I know that it is connected tightly to this world, because we can cross back and forth easily, but I never got to study the science of it to learn how it works. I would have learned though, if I had stayed."

"How do you get there?"

"You use a Crystavis to walk through a waterfall," Diana answered as if it was a simple thing.

"Say what?" John repeated. "Am I asleep, or did you just say you use that amulet of yours to walk through a waterfall into another world?"

"A Lacunavim isn't another world; it is more like an in-between place. It is a contained space, encircled, like under a dome. It is really pretty. The 'dome' is partly luminescent and shimmers in pinks, blues, and reds. My mother said it is like being inside the womb of the universe."

John shivered and shook his head at that last bit of imagery. Honestly, didn't Diana know there were some words you just don't say around boys, like *womb*? John shivered again at the thought.

"Can we go there? Do you think some of your people might still be living there?" John asked her hesitantly. It sounded like a place he couldn't get to, and, even though he'd only known Diana for barely two days, he didn't like the thought of not seeing her ever again.

"I've thought of that," Diana admitted. "We can go there, but I'm a bit scared to find out what's happened after all this time. We need a waterfall that's at least a couple of feet taller than we are."

"Tall waterfall; got it. I can't think of one off the top of my mind, but my sisters might know. They get to go exploring a bit more than I do. How much time has gone by anyway? Do you know how much time you spent as a statue?" John finally asked the question he was most curious about.

"It's been over six hundred and fifty years," Diana answered in a pained voice.

They were both silent for a long time, and John felt his body start to relax into the floor and knew he probably wouldn't be able to fight off sleep much longer. He said as much aloud, "We'd better get some sleep. We're going to need it for tomorrow. I'll see Widow McNeally at church, and I'll see if I can get her to ask my father to let Beth and me come over to help her. Then Beth can stay in the loft, and you can walk with me with a hat on your head, so everyone will think you're Beth."

"Okay. Good night, John," Diana said.

"Good night." John was happy with his plan and was sure that Beth and Mrs. McNeally would go along with it. Knowing that he was close to finding a place for Diana, he allowed his mind to relax with his body and soon fell asleep.

CHAPTER 8 – MASS MANIPULATIONS

The next morning John's alarm clock went off as it should, half an hour before sunrise. Diana lifted her head from the pillow, her eyes still glued shut with sleep. "It's okay, go back to sleep," John told her softly. Diana obediently flopped back down onto the pillow and was out like a light. She didn't budge as John moved about the room gathering his things before he went into the bathroom to get changed. She was still sound asleep when he came out, put on his boots, and left.

John's morning chores were similar to his evening chores. There was the morning milking, feeding the various animals, letting them out to pasture, and mucking stalls. He had a few things to do in the milk house, and then he was back in the loft taking a shower and getting dressed into his church clothes. His dress clothes consisted of a pair of khaki pants that matched his boots, a button-down white dress shirt, a brown tie and matching belt. He used the small mirror over the sink to comb his wet, dark blond hair to the side with a straight part. His hair was almost brown now at the roots, but he spent so much time in the sun it was bleached blond on top. The shirt was getting a bit tight across his chest and shoulders, and the pants were a couple of inches too short. They still covered the tops of his boots, so it really didn't matter. He was only allowed to wear these clothes to church and nowhere else. He would've liked to wear them to school once in a while. He didn't think he looked half-bad. He flexed his muscles and studied the effect in the mirror. Joey, the older Cooper boy, bragged that he picked up a full-grown cow once. He had selected one of their newly born calves and picked it up several times a day. He continued to do this as the calf grew. He claimed the calf was a full-grown cow and he could still pick it up before he finally stopped. John thought Joey was full of cow pies, but he knew Joey was crazy strong; you could tell just by looking at him. As John inspected his muscles, he considered trying the same thing out on one of their calves later on that day.

When John stepped out of the bathroom, Diana was up and making the bed. She had already picked up the bedding on the floor. The light was shining in the window, making her long blond hair glow like she had a halo.

When she looked up at him and smiled, her pupils almost disappeared in the bright light, and her blue eyes looked enormous and clear as a lake on a sunny day. Then he noticed she was still in her nightgown, so he quickly turned away to give her some privacy. The nightgown was probably more modest than the dress she'd been wearing, but he was too well-trained by his parents to think of it as anything other than forbidden sleepwear.

"Good morning!" Diana said cheerily. "You look really nice. Are you going to church soon?"

"Yeah, in a little bit. We'll have a brunch when we get back. I'll make sure you get something to eat," John replied while staring at the wall with his hands shoved nervously into his pockets.

Diana looked at him and then at the spot on the blank wall that seemed to have his attention and back again. "Find something interesting on the wall?" she asked, puzzled by his behavior.

John turned his head towards her then snapped it back to the wall. "Nah, it's just that you're not *dressed* yet. I'm trying to be a gentleman here," John said defensively.

"Not dressed?" Diana scoffed. "This nightie is bigger than the dress you gave me!" John stood resolutely staring at the wall. Diana huffed, "Oh, alright. I'll get changed. Please don't leave before I come back out."

While she changed, John took a brush to his boots. He just finished when Diana emerged from the bathroom wearing the dress they had given her.

"Better?" Diana asked with a hint of mockery in her voice.

"Yeah, um, yes," John stuttered. He had to find a place for her to stay soon. Having a girl in his room was unsteadying him. "I was thinking, the whole family goes to church, so there won't be anyone around here for about an hour and a half, maybe two hours after we leave. You could have a quick look around the place if you like. Just don't go close enough to the road for anyone to spot you, and if you go in the house, don't leave any evidence that you were in there, okay?"

"Oh, that would be nice. I'd love to stretch my legs and get some fresh air," Diana said as she moved to the window to look outside.

"Just be careful," John emphasized. "If all goes well, you might be able to stay at Mrs. McNeally's starting today, so you won't have to hide out for much longer. I'd better get going. See you soon!" John said with a wave as he headed downstairs.

"See you soon!" Diana called back.

Father had the pickup truck parked in front of the house, and he was checking the oil while the girls poured out of the house. Meg was first, and she had the two designated blankets with her that were spread out in the truck bed every Sunday. John quickened his pace to help her lay them out, then took his place at the end by the tailgate and helped his sisters up into the truck.

Mother came out with Gracie in her arms and Annie had Christie in tow.

As soon as Christie saw him, she broke away from Annie and squealed, "Jon-Jon!" in her high-pitched voice that made everyone within a six-foot radius wince. Christie stopped at the back of the truck, bouncing on her toes and waving her chubby little hands as high as she could towards John. Annie caught up to her and lifted her into John's waiting arms. John set Christie down on her feet next to him where she caught his leg in a death grip as John helped the rest of his sisters up into the truck.

Father slammed the hood down, apparently satisfied with the engine, and climbed into the driver's seat. Mother was already there with Gracie on her lap. They never had a car seat for any of the kids, and John was surprised they hadn't gotten into trouble for it. Of course the only time the little ones were in the truck was either for Sunday Mass or to see the doctor, and Father never drove over twenty miles an hour. John wondered if Father had bribed the sheriff to look the other way.

John closed the tailgate and joined his sisters sitting on the floor of the truck, gripping the truck bed wall with one arm and securing the other one tightly around Christie. Father inched the truck along the driveway, trying not to kick up too much gravel or dust. Once they made it out to the main road, it was smooth sailing all the way into town.

They arrived at the church a respectable twenty minutes before Mass started. They were one of the first ones there every week, and they filled up an entire pew three rows from the front. Father sat on the inside aisle with Mother next to him. Then sat Gracie, Meg, Jane, Annie, Ellen, Beth, then Jo, Alice, Bunny, and Abby. John sat at the other end of the pew by the wall with Christie between him and Abby. Christie was content sitting under John's arm, fiddling with her prayer beads that Mother had given her. All of the girls had them, but the only ones he saw out were in the younger one's hands. Gracie was sucking on hers, and Jane and Ellen looked like they were trying to see who could play cat's cradle with them first. They didn't get very far before Annie stopped them. It didn't take the family long to figure out that those two needed to be separated in church. John didn't envy Annie her referee position between the twins.

John felt a familiar pat on his shoulder as Mrs. McNeally took the seat directly behind him. She knelt on the kneeler and whispered in John's ear, "I missed you yesterday. Is everything all right?"

John turned his head towards the wall and whispered back, "Yes, I'm fine. I need to talk to you after Mass, okay?"

"Sure, John. I'll talk to you then."

John was impatient for the service to be over. The wait before Mass was interminable, and the readers seemed to walk to and from the podium slower than ever before. It was as if they knew John wanted to rush things, and they were trying to teach him a lesson by moving punishingly slow. They stood, they prayed, they knelt, they stood, they sang, they shook hands, they had communion, and finally sang the recessional song. Christie just sat in the pew the entire time, refusing to stand, kneel, or participate in any way. It said something about the abrasive quality of her wail that she was able to get away with acting like that. He saw Mother glancing over at her several times behind the other girls, as they were standing and Christie was sitting. Mother looked simultaneously disappointed and defeated as she inspected Christie's bad behavior. John didn't try coaxing Christie into submission; he had too much on his mind that morning.

At the end of the service, they were slow to leave. Mother and Father stood talking with other parishioners, and the girls patiently waited. John turned around to Mrs. McNeally and reached out, offering another handshake. She took his hand warmly in both of hers, and her worn face crinkled cheerfully around her eyes as she smiled at John and said, "John, you always look so handsome in your church clothes. I swear you grew an inch since last Sunday! What did you want to talk to me about, dear?"

John leaned closer to her and said, "I can't really go into it here. Can you tell my father that you need my help and Beth's help this afternoon? It would be a huge favor, and I can tell you everything when I get to your house."

Mrs. McNeally still had John's hand grasped firmly in hers, as her smile got impossibly bigger. "Oh, so mysterious, my boy! An old, lonely woman like me needs all the entertainment she can get out of life. I'll be on pins and needles until you stop over." She glanced over to Beth. "You've never asked to bring one of your sisters with you before. Oh, this is going to be a lively afternoon! You just leave your father to me!" Mrs. McNeally proclaimed as she hung her purse securely from her left elbow and kicked up the kneeler that was still sitting on the floor. Mrs. McNeally's pew was almost empty, and she stooped her shoulders as she turned and shuffled her way over to John's father.

"Thomas!" Mrs. McNeally called out in a voice loud enough to turn several heads their way. John couldn't stop the smile that started working its way onto his face. Oh, Mrs. McNeally was a hoot. He'd seen her jog out to the mailbox, as light on her feet as someone half her age. He thought she was laying on the little old lady act a bit heavily. John noticed that she dressed the part, too, whenever she went into town. He wasn't always sure why she did that, but it certainly seemed to work towards his advantage today.

Father saw the turned heads and got a caged look on his face. Father didn't like making a scene in public, and even less so in church. He'd probably give in to Mrs. McNeally's request just to quiet her down. Yes, Mrs. McNeally knew what she was doing.

"Thomas! There you are, Thomas! How did you enjoy the service? I thought it was just lovely, but these old bones just creak and complain from sitting on this hard bench for so long. I swear my feet swelled to twice their size in just the one hour!" Mrs. McNeally lamented, her voice fractionally softer than before, but still at a head-turning volume.

John saw Father pale a bit as he addressed Mrs. McNeally. John couldn't hear what Father said from where he stood. It was some nice pleasantries he was sure. Father was nothing if not polite to everyone in town. People respected him for it, and John took note. It was one quality of Father's that John wished to emulate. Mrs. McNeally continued her act, "Thomas, I need some help this afternoon. Now, now, before you start making excuses, I don't need you specifically. You could send young John over, and I'm sure he'll do just fine. Oh, and I need some help with my computer. My kids are all good with that stuff, but when they try to explain it to me over the phone, I get completely lost. The darn thing won't print, and it keeps locking up on me. Can you send Mary Elizabeth over with John right after lunch? You are such a good Christian man, Thomas, helping out this poor old widow in her time of need!" She added a pitiful little pat on Father's arm at that last bit. She had raised her voice substantially when praising Father. John watched as heads turned once again, but this time sending nods of approval towards Father.

Father noticed and smiled as he covered Mrs. McNeally's wrinkled spotted hand with his own large calloused one. "Of course, Widow McNeally. I'll send the kids over right after brunch. Keep them for long as you need them."

John almost laughed aloud as Mrs. McNeally pulled her hand from under Father's and patted Father warmly on the cheek saying, "That's a good boy, Thomas. May the Lord in heaven shine down on your generous heart." With that, she turned towards the exit, gave John a conspiratorial wink, and began her shuffle out of the church. John could learn a lot from Mrs. McNeally on how to handle people. He couldn't wait to introduce her to Diana.

CHAPTER 9 – MRS. MCNEALLY'S HOUSE

John was practically bouncing on his seat during brunch. He tried to play innocent when Father announced that John and Mary Elizabeth were to change out of their church clothes and head straight over to Mrs. McNeally's after brunch. They all had heard the exchange between Father and Mrs. McNeally at church, but no one knew what was going on. Beth and Abby both gave him sharp, inquiring looks, but John kept his face even, not giving anything away. He couldn't help smiling though, while he polished off the last of his food, remembering the way Mrs. McNeally had shuffled triumphantly out of church. He wiped the smile off his face as he saw Beth staring at him with her eyebrow raised.

John went straight outside after the meal, and Beth and Abby rushed out to catch him.

Beth grabbed hold of John's right forearm. "What's going on? Why am I going to Mrs. McNeally's? Does this have something to do with Diana? You're up to something, I can tell," she asked as John walked away from the house.

"Why does Beth get to go and not me?" Abby whined, pulling hard on John's other arm.

When they were far enough away from the house not to be overheard, John used their grips on his arms to spin both girls around in front of him. "No one's going with me to Mrs. McNeally's, nobody except Diana that is," John hissed at them. He tried to tamp down his excitement and in a softer tone said, "I want to see if Mrs. McNeally will take Diana in for a while. I don't think she should stay in the loft any longer than she has to. We'll be found out for sure if we don't get her out of there."

"But then why did you get her to ask for me?" Beth questioned. "Unless…" Beth was thinking fast, "you want a reason for having a girl leave with you for Mrs. McNeally's house."

John gave his older sister a mischievous smile. "That's exactly why. Would you hang out in the loft while I take her over? Wear something you think Diana could fit into and bring an extra set of clothes for yourself. Then come to the loft, and bring the biggest hat you have. You two can switch clothes, and you can put your feet up on my bed and read all afternoon if you like, while Diana and I head over to Mrs. McNeally's."

"That's brilliant, John!" Abby exclaimed.

"Not too bad, little brother," Beth admitted. "Sounds like a day off for me! I'll go get changed." And with that she hurried back to the house.

"Can I come, too?" Abby begged. "I don't want to miss out on anything! Surely, you can think of an excuse to bring me along, too! If not, I'll be cooped up all day in the stuffy living room practicing boring needlepoint, or, ick, darning Father's socks!"

John looked down at her pleading face and thought for a moment. "Okay, here's what you do. Go catch up with Beth, and have her tell Meg that she wants you to watch how she fixes Mrs. McNeally's computer, like it's a lesson for you. Then Meg and Beth can go to Mother and ask the same thing. If Mother suggests it to Father, he won't say no."

"Ooo, John, I never knew you could be so devious!" Abby exclaimed as she went up on her tiptoes to give John a quick kiss on the cheek before she ran full speed after Beth.

John continued on to the barn with a light bounce in his step. Things were going to work out; he just knew it.

When John got to the loft and saw Diana propped on the bed reading the book again, he smacked himself on the forehead. "*Cattails*, I forgot to bring you lunch! I've been so focused on getting you over to Mrs. McNeally's that I forgot to sneak out food. I'm sorry!"

Diana's welcoming smile didn't break as she said back, "Don't worry, I ate the rest of the peanut butter cookies!"

"I guess I deserved that," John admitted sheepishly as he ran his hand over the hair on the back of his head. "Beth and maybe Abby will be here soon, so I've got to get changed," John said as he grabbed a pair of clean overalls and a work shirt and headed for the bathroom.

"So what's the plan?" asked Diana through the closed bathroom door. John told her as he quickly changed. He had just stepped out and was retying his boots when Beth and Abby breezed into the room.

"I'm coming with you!" Abby squealed as she bounced and clapped her hands excitedly. "Your plan worked like a charm, John. I told you it was brilliant!"

John flushed slightly and jammed his hands in his pockets as he peeked at Diana to see if she'd heard Abby's compliment. He couldn't tell, as Beth was in the process of dragging Diana to the bathroom to change. Soon they were ready to leave. Beth looked like she was in heaven, stretched out on his bed with her shoes kicked off and a ring of books around her. Beth had the foresight to have Diana bring her own clothes with her in the event she wasn't coming back, so John and Abby could return Beth's things. If anyone saw them coming back one girl short, they'd make something up about Beth walking home on her own.

Diana and Abby dawned big straw hats, and they set out under the bright May sun to Mrs. McNeally's house.

Mrs. McNeally was waiting for them on her front porch peeling some potatoes. Abby danced up the steps first, practically singing as she greeted the widow. Mrs. McNeally said, "Abby, child, what a nice surprise. I certainly wasn't expecting you today," as she pulled the girl into a warm hug and gave her a kiss on the cheek. John was next up the steps and Mrs. McNeally didn't hesitate to grab his face in her hands and pull it down to plant a kiss on each cheek. "There's my boy, you had me worried yesterday when you didn't stop by," she clucked at John as she affectionately pinched his cheek. "And Beth, dear, it's been a while…" Mrs. McNeally paused when she got a good look at Diana. "But it hasn't been so long that I'd forget Beth has brown hair and brown eyes!" She looked accusingly at John before turning back and holding out her arms to welcome Diana to her. "So who is this angel you bring to see me instead?"

As Diana stepped towards Mrs. McNeally and grasped her outstretched hands, something loosened inside John's chest. He wouldn't admit even to himself that he'd been nervous about how Mrs. McNeally would react to Diana. He needn't have worried.

Mrs. McNeally pulled the surprised Diana in for a quick hug. "Just lovely, absolutely lovely," Mrs. McNeally declared as she pulled back and gently held Diana's face, turning it left and then right to get a good look. "You remind me so much of my Jennifer at your age," she sighed, the longing for her daughter evident on her face. "Well, come inside, children, the day isn't getting any younger, and Lord knows, neither am I."

They followed her inside to the kitchen where two plates waited for them, one of egg and chicken sandwiches and the other of cookies. Diana, John noticed guiltily, immediately grabbed a sandwich. Mrs. McNeally poured each of them a large glass of lemonade and then joined them at the table. "Now, John Christopher Brown, put me out of my misery and tell me what is going on!" she demanded.

John got the introductions out of the way by saying, "First, let me introduce you to my new friend, Diana. Diana, this is Mrs. McNeally." John cleared his throat and asked, "So, Mrs. McNeally, when was the last time you watched the news?" John dived into his story. He was a bit nervous with Diana and Abby listening, because he knew he left some things purposely out on each of their versions, but he decided to hold nothing back with Mrs. McNeally. Diana's face tightened with concern when she heard all of the details about Todd and The Crew. He even went into detail about how foolish The Crew acted when looking for him, and how he newly dubbed them "The Ape Crew." That got a smile out of Mrs. McNeally, as he knew it would. He'd been telling her stories about The Crew for years. Mrs. McNeally's face was animated as she listened to the story, but she didn't interrupt him. Abby's face contorted with worry when John told about the man breaking out of the statue and seeing him on the news. He then asked Diana to tell about Michael and Miranda and what had caused Michael to go after her. Abby's concern shifted quickly from worry over Diana's safety, to worry over where Michael was and what he was going through. Abby had such a soft, generous heart.

John could see Diana was getting upset talking about Michael, so he took over the storytelling again. He told about the knowledge transfers Diana performed and tried his best to describe Diana's amulet and how it worked. He told them about New Zigon and its waterfall doors. He told them that they wanted to go to New Zigon to see what had happened there while Diana had been trapped in the statue. John ended by asking Mrs. McNeally if she wanted to see Diana's amulet. Diana put her hand on her chest, her ring already glowing in preparation.

Mrs. McNeally, whose face had stilled when John mentioned the knowledge transfer, caught sight of Diana's glowing ring and said briskly, "Just hold that thought for a moment, child." She got up from the table and turned to the kitchen counter. She opened a cupboard showing a short row of neatly placed cereal and grabbed a box of Wheaties. She opened it and pulled out a silver flask, which she unscrewed, tipped to her lips, and quickly downed several large gulps. She set the box on the counter and sat back down, still clutching the flask. "Go on then, dearie, what are you waiting for?" she asked.

Diana's ring glowed as she made the amulet rise up out of her skin. Mrs. McNeally's jaw nearly hit the table. John's had already been there since the moment Mrs. McNeally had pulled out the flask. Mrs. McNeally snapped out of it first. She took one more swig from the flask, screwed the cap back on, and returned the flask to its hiding spot in the cereal cupboard. By the time she returned to the table, the gleam was back in her eye, and she resolutely took charge of the situation.

"Okay now, children, the first thing we are going to do, is that Diana needs to move in here with me immediately. We can't have her sleeping out in that loft, and, John, your back is going to be in a twist if you spend any more nights sleeping on a hard floor. Next, we need to find a waterfall tall enough to get you back to your New Zigon place and see if your folk are still there. Third, John, I'm going to give you the cell phone my kids bought me; the useless thing is around here somewhere. If the police want to question you on Monday, you call me immediately, and I'll drive out there and insist I sit with you when they do. And most of all, don't say a word of this to anyone. Not *anyone*," she reiterated.

John jumped up from his chair, nearly knocking it over as he moved to wrap his long arms around Mrs. McNeally in an awkward hug. "You're the best, Mrs. M, do you know that? You're the best!" John said using his pet name for her.

"I agree!" Abby sang as she noisily pushed her chair back and hugged Mrs. McNeally over top of John's hug.

"Oh, children! You warm up this old woman's heart!" Mrs. McNeally said with watery eyes as she patted John and Abby on the head in an attempt to return the hug.

Diana sat in her chair, beaming at the happy scene in front of her.

* * *

They stayed talking around Mrs. McNeally's kitchen table well into the afternoon. They polished off all of the sandwiches and cookies along with the entire pitcher of lemonade. They worked out a simple story to explain Diana's presence. She was Mrs. McNeally's grandniece coming to visit for the summer. "I'll put you in Jennifer's old room," decided Mrs. McNeally. "There actually should be some bins of clothes in the bottom of her closet from when she was in high school. I boxed them up years ago and meant to give them to the Salvation Army, but never got around to it. My kids are always telling me to clear things out of here, but in this case it is a good thing I didn't." Mrs. McNeally leaned back in her chair and folded her hands over her stomach contentedly. "It'll be so nice to have some new life in this old farmhouse. I've been here by myself for far too long." She paused before turning to John and saying, "We'll need a reason to get you over here every day. Thursday is your last day of school, right? Hmm...," she tapped a gnarled finger to her lips as she thought. "I have an unfortunate sewage leak in the basement. I ordered a part for it, but it won't be here until Friday. You'll have to stop by every day to carry buckets of dirty water out of the basement to dump out back, and I'll need you all day Friday to do the repair. Yes, Thomas will love that. The more unpleasant the job, the stronger the lesson to take care of the elderly. I'll phone him after supper," she finished with a surprisingly evil glint in her eye.

"Mrs. M, you're too much! I almost lost it at church this morning with that little show you put on. I've never seen Father look so trapped before," John said chuckling.

"Oh, men like your father are easy to handle. You play to their fears and their pride, and they'll flip over for you like a June bug on a hot skillet," Mrs. McNeally shared smugly. "Did I ever tell you the time I tried to get Mr. McNeally to move the horse paddock so I could have more room for my vegetable garden?" Mrs. McNeally regaled them of how she used every trick in her book to no avail. She tried cajoling, pleading, blackmailing him in public, and even served peanut butter and jelly for dinner every night for two weeks. Mr. McNeally remained stalwart. Mrs. McNeally had all but given up, when one weekend she returned from an overnight visit with her mother to find a brand new plot of earth plowed and fenced in to the side of the house, ready for planting. "He told me that I could use the existing vegetable garden to grow those posies I loved so much, and he hoped this would put an end to my incessant womanly conniving, and if he ever saw another peanut butter and jelly sandwich it would be a day too soon." Tears filled the crinkles around her eyes as she smiled lovingly at the memory. "He got a three course meal, roast beef, steak, pork ribs, chicken pot pie, you name it, for over a month!" She dabbed at her eyes with a napkin saying, "Lord knows I miss that man!"

"Let's talk about something else," she said, shaking off the memories and turning her clever gaze to Diana. "How about you explain to us how that magic amulet of yours works."

"It's not magic, it's *science*," Diana breathed like it was a worn-out mantra. "It is difficult to explain all at once, but I'll try my best."

Diana took a deep breath and began, "You've watched Star Wars and know about *The Force* mentioned in the movie?" As they nodded their confirmation she continued, "Well, Mr. Lucas was onto something, but he didn't get the whole gist of it. There is a power that connects us, but it is not limited to, nor generated by life. It just is. We call it the 'Pleovis,' which means 'filling power.' The Pleovis is what fills in the spaces between…everything. John, from your memories I see that you've learned about protons, neutrons, and electrons, and even quarks. The Pleovis is what is between each of those things. It is what gives an item mass. It holds things together, pulls them apart, moves them and stops them. It is constantly changing. Sometimes it circles around molecules, binding them together, and sometimes it vibrates like when it supports an electric current, or hums like when it transmits light energy. Sometimes, it stays still and acts like both a filler and a glue. It has a song of its own, dancing around and through everything in the universe. Are you with me so far?"

"So this *plē-ō-vis* is a dancing glue version of The Force?" John asked.

Mrs. McNeally smiled fondly at him. "Always a way with words, this one," she teased.

Diana sighed, slightly frustrated. "The only other way I can think to describe it, is to compare it to the air around us. The air between us is always there but behaves differently all the time. Sometimes, it is hot and still. Sometimes, it swirls crazily around us, and, sometimes, it is abrasive and cold as in winter. It can be pushed through instruments to make music, and sounds and smells can be carried on the wind. The Pleovis works similar to that, but it flows between every atom in your body. It actually is way more complex, more like a symphony than a single tune, but I'm trying to simplify this as much as I can."

"So you somehow used the Pleovis to read John's mind? I thought your amulet is what let you do it," Abby interjected.

"I was getting to that," said Diana patiently. "Every living being has an impact on the Pleovis. Your brain activity causes waves in the Pleovis. We call this impact a person's Visity. Some people have called it an aura.

Visualize tossing a pebble into a pond and creating ripples. It is an unconscious impact, but you do feel its effects. That's why moods can affect other people. If your Visity is causing the Pleovis to move in a pattern, that pattern can be 'felt' by people around you. If you don't have tight control of your own mind, it will contour to the way the Pleovis is moving. An unprotected mind is open to patterns in the Pleovis, and a negative or positive emotional pattern can cause a negative or positive response in your brain."

"Thoughts and memories are basically energy pulses in the brain carried over the Pleovis. I tapped into that and used the Pleovis to replicate the same pulses into my brain. It's sort of my specialty where I come from. Not everyone can do it," she said with a hint of pride.

"So where does the amulet come in?" asked John, impatient to get the full picture.

"Just wait, I'll get to that," said Diana calmly. "Everyone in New Zigon is able to direct their Visity, to project it. We study and train how to move our Visity in different patterns to get the Pleovis to do what we want. Some of the first things we learn are how to make it emulate negative or positive emotions and how to block ourselves from movements in the Pleovis that would impact us in a bad way. These are simple patterns that any Zigonian can do without a Crystavis."

"Can you do it to us?" John asked hesitantly.

"Yes, show us how it works!" Abby vehemently agreed.

"Okay, I'll do the negative one first," Diana said as she concentrated, eager to show off her skills. The skin around her eyes tightened slightly. Suddenly, John felt utterly depressed. This whole situation was one big mess. He couldn't help Diana, and he certainly couldn't help her get back to New Zigon. A hornet's nest of trouble was waiting for him at school tomorrow. He wished he could play sick, but that would never go over at home. He looked at Mrs. McNeally and saw that all the light had gone out of her eyes, and her shoulders hung dejectedly. When he looked at Abby, he almost didn't recognize her. Her eyes were flat, and her face was contorted into a frown. She was hunched over, curling in upon herself.

Diana saw the change in everyone and said, "Okay, get ready for the positive."

The skin around her eyes did that tiny scrunchy thing again, and, suddenly, John felt like he could float out of his chair and touch the ceiling. All was right in the world. This situation would all work out, and the mess at the museum would soon be forgotten. This summer was starting out great with a new friend and all the excitement surrounding her. A spot of sunlight from the window was shining on his arm where it lay on the table. John turned over his hand as if he could catch the golden light in his palm. As it warmed his skin, peace and contentment settled over him. He looked at Abby and Mrs. McNeally, and they both had happy, content looks on their faces. Diana's face relaxed and John realized she'd stopped whatever it was that she'd been doing, because his prior worries started working their way back into his thoughts.

"How was that?" Diana asked tentatively.

"Wow, first I felt like life was nothing but never-ending, meaningless work, and there was no hope, and then, suddenly, I felt like I was on top of the world!" Abby volunteered with astonishment in her voice. "That was freaky. Have you done this to us before now?"

"Oh, no! This is the first time I've even tried it since I was freed from the statue," Diana said defensively.

"That seems like a handy little trick," Mrs. McNeally commented. "People tend to be much more pliable when they are in a good mood."

"The effects don't last that long after I stop. Sometimes the mood sticks and sometimes it doesn't. People with susceptible minds will pick up the pattern of the emotion and start to emulate it themselves, keeping the emotion going. Others will slowly go back to their original mode with a subtle slant in the direction I led them. That's why I started with the negative; so I could leave you with the positive," Diana explained. "The pattern sunlight creates is similar to part of the pattern for positive thinking. That's why most people are happier when the sun is shining. Only a few patterns affect mood."

"So where does the amulet come in?" asked John again.

"Okay, okay, Mr. Impatient! Several types of crystals and gems can be structured to create patterns in the Pleovis, much like a musical instrument. Once a crystal or gem has been structured to perform a particular task, we call it a Crystavis. It means 'power crystal.' I could structure a crystal to generate the pattern for positive thoughts, turning it into a Crystavis. Then to create that projection, I only need to push my Visity through the Crystavis to create the pattern. It makes it much easier on the mind."

"Could anyone use one of your crystals?" asked Mrs. McNeally. "Could I use one to bend someone to a positive mood?"

"It doesn't work that way. Only the people of New Zigon are able to direct their Visity. Our DNA is different from yours, and we use a part of the brain that's dormant in most humans. Also, each person's Visity has its own Signature, and every Crystavis is made with that in mind. A Crystavis can be made or altered to accept more than one Signature. You can also make it generic so anyone can use it, but the more generic the entry into the Crystavis, the less effective the result. It's like blowing air at the large end of a funnel versus blowing directly into a tube. The Primary Crystavis are the only exception."

"The tradition in New Zigon is for a student to learn how to project a certain pattern, and once that's perfected they make their own Crystavis. A mentor or expert guides them through the process of making the Crystavis so there are no mistakes. It is a very sensitive process. It's like if by singing a song and getting one note off key, you might turn someone's skin green instead of getting rid of their pimples."

"The stone in the center is a type of Pollampium. That means it is a power amplifier. It will amplify a person's projection. I have one in my ring, too," Diana said as she held out her right hand to show them her ring more clearly. "There is a tiny Crystavis set in the ring's Pollampium. This Crystavis is structured to flatten an object or restore mass to a flattened object. It's what I used to take out my Crystavis amulet and put it away. A Crystavis usually glows whenever Pleovis is being pushed through it."

Mrs. McNeally stood up and gathered the empty plates and glasses on the table to take them over to the sink. As she worked she said, "Well, that's more information than this old brain of mine can take in at a time. Let's stop here and pick up later."

* * *

John turned and waved for the third time as he and Abby headed towards the road. Mrs. McNeally had an arm around Diana, tucking her protectively into her side as they both stood on the porch watching them leave.

"She'll be fine, John," Abby reassured.

"I know, it just feels like I'm abandoning her," John said with a sigh. They didn't talk the rest of the way home. John could hardly take in all that they had learned that afternoon. Beth was sleeping peacefully when they got back to the loft, her hand on a book that was open over her stomach. Abby promised to tell Beth everything later. John wondered how well that was going to go. He wasn't sure he could relay what they had learned without getting things utterly mixed up.

John did his chores and sat through an uneventful supper. Mrs. McNeally called after dinner, as expected. Father told John to stop by the Widow's every day after school, and on Friday he was to go over after morning chores. He said that Mrs. McNeally thought it might take all weekend to fix her sewage problem, and that she'd arranged for Jay Cooper to come over and cover his chores while he was gone. John could hardly believe his ears. He wondered how Mrs. McNeally had managed that! Even more so, he wondered what she said to Father to get him to accept the help without any protest.

John headed back to his loft at bedtime. Diana had only spent two nights there, but tonight it seemed especially empty without her. He welcomed getting his bed back, however, and didn't have any trouble falling asleep.

On Monday morning John made sure he had time to clean up after chores before going to school. He had Mrs. McNeally's phone in his pocket, and he kept checking that it was still there. It was comforting to know she was only a phone call away.

John didn't see any of The Ape Crew all morning or even at lunch, which was odd. It wasn't until the period right after lunch that anything happened.

The principal came in the classroom and called out a list of people to come with him. He named all the girls in the room who had been in John's group at the museum. John sat frozen in his seat, staring down at his desk, the blue lines on his open notebook starting to blur where the sweat from his hands seeped into the paper.

"I'll have them back in no time," the principal told his teacher. "The police want to question them about the museum incident last Friday, to find out if they saw anything, no matter how small." He ushered the girls out into the hallway and closed the door behind them.

John's head snapped up in disbelief. Why hadn't they called his name? John cursed his forgetfulness as he realized he'd snuck into their group, that on paper he was supposed to be in a different one. What did this mean? If they found out he joined that group without permission, would that automatically make him look suspicious? Would the girls in the group rat him out?

The girls were back in half an hour. The teacher was letting the class get a start on their homework, so there was quite the buzz as the girls sat back down. John eased his chair subtly to the right and leaned further to pick up on the conversation of a ring of girls who had pulled their chairs together.

"They just wanted to check if we saw anything out of the ordinary," said one girl, her voice high with excitement over the attention. "They had a video showing everyone leaving the room. Mrs. Brandsworth, our guide, told the police that when she led our group into the room it had been completely empty, so they picked up the security tape from that point on. They had us call out as each one of us showed up on the video to make sure all of us left the room."

"Did you find out anything about what happened?" someone asked.

The girl, gaining confidence in her turn in the spotlight, leaned forward conspiratorially as she said, "When we went into the conference room for questioning, guess who was sitting in the hall?" She paused for dramatic effect. "Todd Scottsdale and his friends! I heard the secretary gossiping with a teacher's aide that the video showed them going into the room after our group left, and they were in there a while. They were the last ones in the room before the camera shut down. Apparently, the cops have been questioning Todd and his gang all day because their stories don't match up!" The girls appreciatively tittered at the gossip and started talking over one another.

John had heard enough. He couldn't wipe off the stupid grin that suddenly split his face. The Ape Crew was apparently on the cops' suspect list! They couldn't confess to going after him without landing themselves in more trouble. Ha! Fortune was smiling on him. If the cops only checked the video from the point his group started leaving the room, they would have seen nothing to connect him to being there. The girls seemed too caught up in the excitement of it all to remember his tagging along. He had forgotten about the security video problem. He suspected that it was more than just dust that caused the camera by the elevators to overheat. Breaking the statue had to have made a massive impact on the Pleovis, and who knew what that would do to electronics.

John glided through the rest of the school day. On the way out to his bus he spotted a line of black luxury cars with a whole entourage of men in suits heading into the school. He bet The Ape Crew was "lawyering up." Oh, this was too good to be true!

John raced straight from the bus to Mrs. McNeally's house. He found his friends sitting on the porch swing, drinking iced tea. Diana was sweaty and smeared with dirt. She saw him noticing and broke into a proud smile. "I was helping Mrs. McNeally with her vegetable garden all day," she bragged.

Mrs. McNeally poured him a tall glass of iced tea as he pulled up a porch chair and told them what happened at school. John returned the borrowed cell phone, and Mrs. McNeally chuckled, "It's about time those boys got caught with their meaty paws in the cookie jar. I'll bet their daddies aren't too happy with them!"

Mrs. McNeally and Diana decided to drive around the next few days, checking out local streams and creeks for a suitable waterfall to get to New Zigon. Diana and John would travel there on Friday morning, but Mrs. McNeally would stay "on this side" to do damage control. Mrs. McNeally had cleared John's schedule for him through Saturday night for the trip.

"About that, Mrs. M," John challenged, "How in the world did you work all that out with Jay covering for me and getting Father to take the help without complaining? I know you have your ways, but this one goes down in the record books!"

Mrs. McNeally's eyes twinkled out of their nest of merry wrinkles on her face. "Oh that? That was nothing. I talked to Jay Cooper first and mentioned how I was going to be pulling you from your duties, then commented on how pretty Annie looked in church that day. He practically tripped over himself offering to stop by and help out. Then I talked to Mrs. Cooper and told her how proud she should be, raising such a generous young man. I asked her when was the last time she'd talked to Mrs. Brown, and she said it had been a while. I gave her the idea that it would be downright Christian of her to visit Mrs. Brown while Jay was helping with the chores, that it would do Mrs. Brown a world of good to get some adult company. When I spoke to your father, I told him that Mrs. Cooper had planned on stopping by, and Jay would help out while she visited. I don't think he heard anything past 'Mrs. Cooper will be visiting'. You know he and Mrs. Cooper used to date back in the day. I think he still sees Mrs. Cooper as the one who got away. No disrespect to your mother of course; she won the annual county fair beauty pageant three years in a row before marrying your father. She was quite the catch herself!"

John stared at Mrs. McNeally, stupefied. "First of all, *ewe*, don't talk about Father dating, and second, *ewe*, he and Mrs. Cooper? Ugh! I'll never get that image out of my head!" John said as he shivered in horror. "And third, I had no idea about the depth of your powers of manipulation! For all I know, you've been playing me like a harp to do your beck and call all these years!"

Mrs. McNeally tisked, "Now, John, dearest, I would never have to do anything like that to you! You are so generous with your time and help me out with anything I need. Why put all that effort into it, when all I have to do is ask and you say 'yes?'" Mrs. McNeally's smile was adoring as she gently teased John.

"Oh, and Wheaties Cereal? Mrs. M, what's up with that?" John called her on her surprising behavior the previous day.

Mrs. McNeally had the grace to look slightly ashamed. "You can't blame a woman of my age to not indulge in a little liquid courage now and then, especially with that fairy tale you threw in my face yesterday."

"But *Wheaties*, Mrs. M?" John pressed.

Mrs. McNeally smiled at his persistence. "It's the safest hiding place I could think of. Who would pick Wheaties with Frosted Flakes sitting right beside it? Oh, my pistol is in there, too, but forget I told you that!"

John almost spit out a mouthful of iced tea over that declaration.

After sharing some more lighthearted banter, John stood up to leave.

"Just hold on a minute, dearie, I have something for you," Mrs. McNeally said as she disappeared into the house. She came back out with a small mason jar that had some murky liquid in the bottom of it. She walked right up to John and splashed its mysterious contents all over his pant leg.

John jumped back, nearly falling down the steps yowling, "Cattails, Mrs. M! What did you go and do that for? What was that?" Then John got a whiff of it and complained, "What is that *smell?*"

Mrs. McNeally innocently said, "Your father thinks you're over here emptying out buckets of leaking sewage. He'd be suspicious if you didn't spill a little on yourself." She bit her lip to hide back her smile as she raced back into the house, all signs of her hunched shuffle left behind in the dust.

Diana covered her mouth to stifle her laugh as she followed Mrs. McNeally inside. "You'd better get home and start your chores, John. Oh, and you might want to take a shower before supper. You kind of stink!"

John heard Diana and Mrs. McNeally burst out laughing somewhere inside the house, and he kicked at the dirt the whole way home. He'd probably laugh at it later, but he was too grossed out to find it funny. He made sure to run into Father during chores so the "evidence" wouldn't be for nothing. It worked. Father actually gave him a pitying clasp on the shoulder as he told him he was proud of him for helping their elderly neighbor. That made it almost worth getting sewage thrown on him.

CHAPTER 10 – THROUGH THE WATERFALL

The next three days sped by for John. School was wrapping up for the year, so there wasn't any homework, and it was all about turning things in, cleaning out lockers, and learning what to expect from high school in the fall. There was no sign of The Ape Crew. He suspected their parents pulled them out of school to keep a low profile.

He stopped by Mrs. McNeally's each day, and it became a game to see if they could mark him with "evidence" of their cover story. They almost got the slip on him on Thursday, but he managed to get away just in time. They had found the requisite waterfall where a stream fell over a small bluff into the local creek. It was close to the borough park so it was easy access, but far enough away from prying eyes. Abby and Beth were both disappointed that they couldn't go. Beth made him promise to bring a notepad and paper and write everything down so he wouldn't forget a single detail. He promised to bring it, but he didn't say anything about actually writing in it.

John had trouble sleeping Thursday night. He woke up before his alarm clock and started his chores early. He showered and changed, then headed over to Mrs. McNeally's in the dim morning light. They were up and waiting for him with eggs and pancakes on the stove. John ate, but he barely tasted his food. Mrs. McNeally and Diana had two stuffed backpacks ready for them by the front door. They were filled with flashlights, extra batteries, a blanket, jacket, water and food.

Diana had changed into the dress she'd been wearing as a statue. It reminded him of the dresses the bridesmaids wore in a cousin's wedding; all kinds of pinks and shiny, but hers was soft and flexible instead of stiff. He noticed she was wearing the sneakers Mrs. McNeally had found for her.

"I see you got your dress cleaned up. It looks nice," John said, then flushed.

"Thanks," Diana said with a flush of her own. "It was a gift from my friend Miranda. It's made out of a special material they have in Zigon. Miranda's father had just showed her how to build it. It's amazing. It's strong and unbreakable like body armor, but looks and feels like regular fabric. It modifies my body temperature, too. It's the first of its kind in New Zigon.

All the other kids were so jealous," Diana drifted off. "Thanks," she mumbled again as if she wanted to take back that lengthy description she just threw out at him.

"Cool," John said and left it at that.

They all climbed into the front seat of Mrs. McNeally's truck. Mrs. McNeally had the bench seat pulled so close to the dash that John could barely fit. He felt like his knees were pushed back to his ears. He noticed that she also sat on a pillow to be able to see over the dashboard. "Why are we taking this thing, Mrs. M? This truck doesn't really, um, fit you," John said as delicately as he could.

"This is Arthur's truck, and I don't have the heart to get rid of it. It's the only vehicle I have that's both four-wheel-drive and road-worthy," Mrs. McNeally responded nonplussed. "The drive down to the creek can get a little messy."

John was thankful it was a short ride. Every bump in the road made the dashboard jolt into his shins. Diana sat buckled in the middle of the seat, deep in thought. He was nervous about this trip; he could only imagine what she was feeling.

When they got to the creek, Mrs. McNeally parked the truck. Diana and John hopped out, swinging the backpacks up over their shoulders.

"Wait, don't move!" ordered Mrs. McNeally. They both looked up at her, startled, only to have a flash go off in their eyes. "Smile!" she said belatedly.

"Mrs. M!" John whined like a little kid.

"I feel like my babies are going off on their first date. I have to take pictures. Oh, sugar, the flash was forced on. Wait a minute... there!" Mrs. McNeally did something with her camera then started snapping more pictures. John slapped his hand over his face as Diana turned away, blushing. *Click. Click.*

"Okay, *enough*," John declared as he snatched the camera out of Mrs. McNeally's hands and took a few quick reciprocating pictures of her before tossing it on the truck seat, out of her immediate reach.

"What are you just standing around for, we've got things to do, places to go," Mrs. McNeally unfairly chastised as she shooed them towards the creek. "Let's get a move on!"

"I thought you weren't coming with us," John asked as he noticed Mrs. McNeally following them.

"I'm not. Do you think I'm going to just sit in the truck and miss you turning a waterfall into a portal to another world and disappearing into it?"

"It's not really another world, it's a . . . " Diana started to correct her until John motioned her to just let it go.

It was a beautiful morning with the sun dancing off the creek water and birds singing all around them. John attempted to calm himself by taking it all in, but was too excited to really focus on anything other than his imaginings of what New Zigon would look like.

"The waterfall is just around that curve," Diana said slightly out of breath as she pointed ahead.

They rounded the bend in the creek and the waterfall was right in front of them.

Click.

John and Diana jumped and spun on Mrs. McNeally. She was taking pictures with her phone and had a triumphant smile on her face. "Gotcha!" she gloated.

Diana stopped to take off her shoes and socks while John just stared at the Widow, amazed that she'd figured out the camera on the phone.

"To get to the waterfall we have to get into the creek first," Diana explained when John shook himself from his trance and gave her a questioning look. He followed suit, and they stuffed their shoes into their backpacks. John rolled up the legs of his overalls.

Diana pulled out her amulet and carefully stepped into the creek. The water barely came up to her knees. John looked at the waterfall and while high, it didn't look like a lot of water to him. He could see the rock wall of the bluff right through it.

"You're sure this is going to work?" John asked. "This looks more like a trickle of water than a true waterfall."

"It'll work," Diana said with a waiver in her voice.

"You're not really building confidence here," John quipped.

Diana, not realizing he was teasing, answered, "It has more to do with the height of the waterfall than the amount of water. The water has to freefall straight down and not hit the earth behind it. The energy of the falling water and the pattern it makes in the Pleovis is what…"

"I trust you. No need to go into detail," John cut her off. He wasn't in the mood for a science lesson. "Let's get this show rolling."

"I think you have to get your feet wet first," Mrs. McNeally said as she gave him a playful push into the creek. The first rock John stepped on was covered in creek slime, and he nearly fell.

"Hey! Watch it!" John snapped.

"Go on! Be careful, most of the rocks are slippery," Mrs. McNeally said, her whole face glowing with excitement. John was grateful for the levity she was trying to bring and took comfort from her solid presence. "I'll be by the truck for the next few hours. Oh, I almost forgot; take this with you," she said as she handed John a cell phone.

"Where'd this come from?" John asked. It wasn't the one Mrs. McNeally had lent him on Monday.

"It's a burner cell I bought this week. The man at Wal-Mart helped me set it up. It will bring me peace of mind knowing you have it. If I'm not here when you get back, you can call me," Mrs. McNeally said like it was no big deal.

John shoved it deep into his pocket and said, "Thanks. I doubt they get a signal in New Zigon though."

"Call me when you get back, silly. If the truck's not here, that means I went home to watch my soaps."

John knew that she was joking around again. He doubted she would leave the spot before they came back. He'd noticed she'd packed some food and a bag of stuff for her wait out in the truck.

He joined Diana in front of the waterfall. Her amulet glowed in her left hand. She held out her right hand to him and he took it, his heart racing with anticipation.

The falling water began to part like a curtain on a stage, as if giant hands had split the world in two and were peeling back the edges. The space that opened up was dark, and the damp mist from the waterfall hid the floor from sight.

Diana smiled and confidently stepped into the hole she'd created, pulling John with her. With a fleeting glance back at Mrs. McNeally, who looked a bit shaken but still smiled encouragingly, he followed Diana into the darkness.

CHAPTER 11 – LACUNAVIM

Once John had passed all the way through the waterfall, the split behind them closed, and they were left standing in complete darkness. John could feel Diana's hand trembling in his. "Are you okay?" he asked her softly. He knew she wasn't okay, but he couldn't think of anything better to say.

Diana took a deep, shuddering breath then said, "I'm scared, John. I have no idea what we'll find."

"Well, there's only one way to find out," John said with more confidence than he actually felt. He gave Diana's hand a small squeeze to urge her on. He didn't want her to know, but he thought he might break into a full-out panic attack if they didn't get out of this dark nothingness soon.

The glow of Diana's amulet broke through the pitch black, and a rift started opening in front of them, letting in more light. The light reflected off their persons, but nothing else. It was like they were standing in mid-air with the vastness of a starless outer space around them.

Diana led him through the opening, and once they both had cleared it, it disappeared behind them. The first sensation to hit John was the noise. He felt a damp spray on his back and he looked over his shoulder and saw a massive fall of water. It sounded like Niagara Falls was visiting and had brought extended family. They were standing at the end of a small platform edged with a railing to his right. The railing continued in front of them, but there wasn't one to protect them from the raging waters from which they had just emerged. To Diana's left, there was a walkway leading away from the falls along the cliff wall. He carefully stepped forward and looked over the railing, wanting to move away from the waterfall.

The view took his breath away. They were high up – *very* high up in the air. The falling water thundered and crashed into a small pool far below. There was a dull, reddish glow emanating from a dome that curved over them, and a city spread out below them. A stream cut through the city from the roiling foam of the waterfall, straight to the edge of the dome. There were little homes and streets neatly laid out on either side of the stream that stopped about a hundred yards away from the edge of the dome. The houses had mostly rounded roofs made out of a smooth material that varied in color between white, coral, or pink, or any of the shades in-between. They looked like huge goose bumps all over the floor of the cavernous space.

His gaze panned right, and he noticed another stream, the source of which he could not determine. It looked like it came from somewhere around the edge of the cliff, like there was another side to the waterfall. There were more houses filling the space between them and the dome edge.

His left hand started to hurt. He looked down and realized Diana was squeezing it for all she was worth. He looked at her face, and she had her free hand covering her mouth while tears were silently leaking out of her eyes. He had been secure in a place of wonder at his first glimpse at New Zigon, but her reaction was bringing his senses to a state of alarm.

"What's wrong?" he asked her worriedly.

Diana breathed in a hiccupping sob and said, "They're gone. They're all gone. New Zigon is dying."

"Huh?" John said stupidly. He wasn't sure he heard her correctly over the sound of the water. Then he followed her gaze back down to the buildings below and saw the problem. There were no people out in the streets and no lights on in any of the houses. The city was deserted. "No one's here," he said loud enough to be heard.

"And the Lacunavim is dying. It should be much brighter than this."

"Hey," he shook her arm playfully through their joined hands. "We just got here. Let's look around a little. Maybe there are people in other parts of this place."

Diana bit her lip and nodded, her gaze still on the abandoned landscape below. She shivered once from head to toe before she looked at John and gave him a weak smile. Then she turned to her left and pulled him across the walkway.

The walkway wasn't very long. There was a door-like opening into the rock wall on their left, and a little further down the walkway, steps were carved into the side of the cliff. Diana walked right past the doorway and tugged him onto the steps to put on their shoes before heading up. John got dizzy just looking at the size of the rock staircase. It seemed to take them to the top of the cliff where the waterfall started. They climbed and climbed. John's legs began to burn with the workout. He could tell Diana was getting tired. She kept pausing on a step here and there to take several deep breaths and shake out a leg or two. John just looked at the step right in front of him to keep his dizziness at bay and said several quick prayers of thanks that there was a railing. The way they were holding hands, he was on the outside edge of the steps. Their hands had grown sweaty, but neither of them let go, needing the reassurance of the other's presence.

When they reached the top, they passed between two large decorative pillars out onto a large, round, open space, edged with a low wall interrupted by pillars similar to the ones they had just walked through. They looked to be made out of some type of marble. Other than being a bit dusty, they seemed brand-new. To their left was an impressive building that reminded him of those Greek buildings, like the Parthenon, with its soaring columns and wide steps. The back of it disappeared into the cliff. The building and the rock were organically intertwined, and John fancied the structure grew out of the rock, or the rock was growing up over the building.

Upon closer inspection, the open circle was actually a tiered pit, like a sunken amphitheater. The floor of the open space was covered with specially cut tiles to form a circular pattern with a design in the center. On each tier, a row of stone benches followed the curve of the wall. The stone was a soft pink color, but it could have actually been white with the rose color coming from the dome's light. It was beautiful.

Diana pulled him as she walked down into the center of the pit and then climbed back up the tiers to the wall exactly opposite of the building. "This was the Scholar's Circle. They used to have lectures and debates here," Diana said as they wove their way through the skirt of benches to lean against the wall and peer out.

They stood there for countless moments, absorbing the view. They were twice as high as before and could see the entire perimeter of the enclosed space. The floor under the dome was flat with this single cliff rising straight up out of the ground, having just the one ridge upon which they were standing. It was like a huge finger poking into the center of the dome, sticking about a third of the way through to the other side. Beneath their feet was the top of the waterfall. John could see the water rushing out below him to begin its quick journey to the ground.

This must be a second waterfall, John thought, because they were facing a different direction. John pulled his hand out of Diana's grip and walked around the edge of the wall as it curved left, covering the ground quickly with his long strides. His suspicions were confirmed as he found the waterfall they had entered through. He turned around and strode back to Diana, passed her, and continued the circuit to the other side where he found a third waterfall. It was as if the water couldn't make up its mind which side it wanted to fall down, so it picked all three. He imagined the view from below was equally impressive.

John walked back to Diana and put his arm around her shoulders, wanting to comfort her as he returned to studying the landscape. The city continued throughout the cavern with streams leading from each waterfall to disappear under the dome. He couldn't tell where the water went when it met the dome. A small pool encircled the bottom of the cliff to catch the falling water. There were two fairy-tale bridges crossing over the water to the base of the cliff between the waterfalls. John noticed the buildings nearest to them were taller, and a lot of them were square instead of round. He pointed it out to Diana.

"Those taller square buildings aren't residences. They are community buildings like libraries, schools, development centers, some storage facilities, things like that. In the very center of the dome there's a town square of sorts. It is more like a town circle. "

"Something seems like it is missing," John thought aloud. "Other than people and lights, I mean." *Cattails*, thought John, *open mouth, insert foot.* It seemed like everything he said was wrong, but then Diana leaned into him like she was having trouble supporting herself. John tightened his grip around her shoulders, thinking he might try to say the wrong thing more often, then chastised himself for the shallow thought.

He focused back on the city and it came to him. "Hey, why aren't there any trees? I don't see anything green down there, no grass, no flowers, nothing!"

"I know," sighed Diana. That's why I was always so eager to get out of the Lacunavim, to see a real blue sky, smell the fresh air, and look at flowers and trees. Actually, the day Michael caught me, I was sneaking out against the rules to get some time outside."

"What's in the building behind us?"

"That's our city's capital. Our leader, The Founder, lived there, as well as many of the Crystavis masters. It is where the Primary Crystavis are stored along with our Summas Stone. The Summas Stone is the largest piece of Zigonite on earth. It is the heart of this city, and I'm guessing something's happened to it. It would explain why there's hardly any light." Diana thought for a moment then stepped away from John and grabbed his hand again, pulling him towards the building saying, "That's where I want to go next. I want to look in the repository to see what happened. Then we can go to the archives and see if something is documented there."

Diana took them deep into the building. It was too dark to see much of anything. John wanted to stop and pull out his flashlight, but Diana was in a rush and seemed to know where she was going. They climbed a massive staircase with heavily decorated railings up one floor. Then they moved to a dimly lit side stairwell and up three more floors. John had no idea the building was this tall from looking at it outside. The stairwell ended in front of a set of double doors, and John noticed there was a large, square hole in the roof overhead. The glow from the walls of the dome is what had given them enough light to see by.

With no hesitation, Diana pushed through the double doors into a rectangular space that opened to a massive, round room. John was noticing a theme; round houses, round courtyard, and now a round room. The ceiling of the round room had a huge, circular opening in it, allowing the dome's light to softly fill the space. As they passed through the doorway, John felt a small tightening in his chest, like the air had just gotten heavier somehow. He looked back to watch little pinpoints of light in the doorframe wink out. Diana reflexively put her hand on her amulet, but if she felt anything different, she didn't acknowledge it. She was completely focused on what lay in front of them. In the center of the round room was a grand, circular platform, which had pillars reaching to the lip of the opening in the ceiling. A pedestal stood in front of each pillar. In the center of the stage-like area was what looked like an altar holding a small stand. The pedestals each had a display apparatus that looked like it was supposed to support something, like one of those Chinese eggs or something irregularly shaped, but they were all empty. The stand in the center was empty as well. Several steps radiated down from the platform to the floor, like tiers on a cake. There was a wide amount of walking room between the platform steps and the continuous wall of the room.

They crossed the span of the first room, which reminded John of a vestibule at church. Diana stopped at the entrance into the round room and froze. "They're…they're all gone! How could that be possible?" Diana took the discovery better than she did finding the empty city, as if she'd almost expected it.

"Do you think they just up and moved somewhere else and took everything with them?"

"Maybe…" Diana considered.

Diana squealed as they heard the doors to the room bang open. John spun around, fists clenched, as he positioned himself between Diana and the door.

In the doorway stood a tall, slight person, dressed in a light-colored, loose robe outfit. The light coming from the stairwell put the person's face in shadow, but John could see wisps of hair floating around the silhouette of the person's head. The figure seemed to stare at them for a heart-pounding moment before turning to inspect the doorway. Tiny dots of lights popped into existence along the frame, softly illuminating the person's face. It was a woman, but it was the oldest woman John had ever seen in his life.

She was all skin, bones, and wrinkles. Her hair was pure white, pulled back behind her head with small bits escaping and sticking out all over. Her face was sunken, and her eyes kind of bugged out of her skull, but there was nothing old about the sharp, surveying look she gave them. The woman stepped into the chamber and moved to a side table John hadn't noticed before. She picked up a candle and lit it, turning her back on them briefly. John spun slightly to give Diana a quick look. She had moved so close to him, that he almost decked her with his elbow. Diana put her hand on the dangerous appendage and peered around him to study the woman. She seemed excited but wary. One thing she wasn't, was afraid. John allowed himself to breathe again. The woman turned to them, candle in hand, and took a few steps forward so barely five yards separated them.

"How did you manage to get in here?" the old woman asked sternly.

"We, um, walked in," John answered, standing taller and straighter to emanate an air of confidence he'd seen Father do a million times.

"But you shouldn't have been able to get through the doorway. The Reactive Crystavis inlaid in the frame should have blocked your entrance, unless…" the old lady narrowed her eyes at them. "Step out where I can see you, girl!"

Diana switched her grip to John's right hand as she moved to stand next to him.

The old woman, eyes still narrowed, closed in on them and stuck her candle in front of Diana's face. John was getting ready to pull Diana back before she got her eyebrows singed, but the woman jerked back from them, her eyes wide with disbelief like she'd seen a ghost. The old woman raised a trembling hand to her mouth as she whispered to herself, "No, it couldn't be…" Making her voice a bit louder she asked, "Diana?"

"Yes?" Diana answered tentatively.

"Diana! It is you! You've been released and come back to us! Oh, glorious motherland, The Founder will be so pleased to see you!" the old woman rejoiced as she put one bony arm around Diana to give her a welcoming embrace.

"The Founder? He's here? I don't understand… and sorry, but how do you know me?" Diana puzzled.

The old woman gave a hoarse chuckle and said, "I suppose you wouldn't recognize me. I was only eight years old when you last saw me. I'm Gina."

"Gina? Mirabelle's daughter? How is that even possible? I thought the regeneration Crystavis was lost with Lady Aberlene and all the Primary Crystavis are gone!" Diana said with astonishment.

"True, true, but you know The Founder can project in all twelve avenues without a Crystavis. I'm the only one he has left, so he keeps me going. I haven't had an eternal youth like Lady Aberlene's Crystavis could have given me, but I'm here, so I'm not complaining," said Gina a little sadly.

"You must tell me what happened here! Where did everyone go? Why is it just you and The Founder? Is he still like he was, when I… *left?* What happened to the repository? Why is the Lacunavim dying?" the questions poured out of Diana's mouth.

"Well, that's a story now, isn't it? We'll need to sit down for this one," Gina said as she led them back to the table that had held the candle. John saw there were several chairs against the wall near the table and let go of Diana's hand to pull three of them over so they could sit. Diana took off her backpack and pulled out a few bottles of water and a Tupperware of nuts as she sat across from Gina.

John sat between them as Gina made herself comfortable before starting her story.

"First, you must introduce me to your handsome escort," insisted Gina.

Both John and Diana blushed as Diana answered, "This is my friend John. He is the one who freed me from the statue." Gina had set the candle in a sconce on the table, and he hoped it was too dark for either of his companions to notice the depth of his blush at being called handsome. Girls, even ones older than time itself, rarely noticed him.

"Interesting…" Gina drawled, as she looked John over from head to toe. "You must tell me the details."

"You go first," Diana negotiated.

"How far back do I need to go?"

"Why don't you start with Lady Aberlene's disappearance, and the reactive projection The Founder put on all of us," suggested Diana.

"Sure, here it goes… once upon a time…" Gina said with a smile and a youthful giggle, "There was a king and a queen of a small peaceful kingdom tucked into a magical place called a Lacunavim."

"The king and queen were truly in love and had been for centuries. The king was the son of the first and only Zigonian to reach Earth. The king was a wizard, who found a way to change Earth humans to be a race more like him, so they could practice his magic. He found the love of his life in Lady Aberlene, and he changed her and made her his queen. The king filled his kingdom with handpicked human wizards who were pure of heart. The king changed them to share his magic, and New Zigon was born."

"You're going back a bit far aren't you? Diana complained. "We'll be here for days!"

"Nah, this is good!" John spoke up. "Please keep going," he encouraged.

"Overruled, Diana, sorry," Gina said before resuming the story. "The king taught his lovely queen and loyal subjects his magic and encouraged them to study it and learn more about it on their own. Lady Aberlene specialized in life magic. She created a magic amulet, which enabled her to remain young and beautiful by her husband's side for centuries, since the king, being a true Zigonian descendant, aged very slowly.

And so they lived, their small community of wizards blossoming over the years into a dazzling city. After hundreds of years of waiting, the king and queen had a child, New Zigon's first princess. The princess was as beautiful as her mother and as talented as both her parents put together. The princess was not happy in New Zigon, however, and escaped to earth to mingle with human creatures as often as she could. The inevitable happened; the Princess fell in love with one of the unenlightened creatures, and not just anyone. Her human was cousin to one of the largest and most powerful landowners in the country. The princess and her beloved married in secret, as the king and queen would surely never approve. When her mate's cousin learned of New Zigon, he grew greedy and hatched a plan. The princess finally told her mother about her clandestine marriage, and the queen went out into the world to meet her daughter's husband. Only she didn't meet her daughter's beloved, she met his cousin instead. The cousin had planned this all along. He knew of the queen's magic amulet, and he held her captive and tortured her until she made one just for him.

Once he got what he wanted, the evil cousin killed the queen. The king almost died when he heard his queen was gone. He became a broken man and forbade his subjects to leave their safe Lacunavim, ordering them to *never* talk to human creatures again. Realizing the greed of humans, the king wanted to safeguard his people from the queen's fate. He created a very special protection spell. He summoned his entire kingdom and hid the spell in each of their magic amulets.

To protect the princess, he put her under lock and key to keep her from ever leaving the Lacunavim again.

But the king did not understand the love the princess shared with her human, even though it was so like the love he had for his queen. The princess's mate went mad looking for her and constantly sought out the princess's smallest friend, who was able to sneak past the king's guard to visit Earth. The princess's little friend ran from the human every time, until he finally cornered her. He begged the girl to let him know of his princess, for not only were they married, they were with child. When the girl ran again, the desperate primate captured her to force her to talk. This triggered the king's protection spell, which turned both the girl and the human to stone. The girl was protected from being tortured or killed, but was protected from living as well.

The princess escaped and found her human and little friend frozen in stone. The king refused to break the spell, and the princess hated him for it. When her baby was born, the princess punished the king by not letting him meet his only grandchild. For two years the princess tried to break the spell, borrowing the city's magic crystals one by one, but nothing worked. Then one day the princess and her son disappeared with all of the city's most magical crystals, including the king's prized magic stone. They were never seen or heard from again.

With the magic crystals and the magic stone gone, and with only a broken king to guide them, New Zigon fell apart. The city was abandoned, and without the king's magic stone to energize it, the Lacunavim began to die as well.

All was lost, until one day, six and a half centuries later, the princess's little friend was freed from her stone prison by a handsome knight, who rescued her and returned her to her home in New Zigon. The princess's little friend had a piece of the king's magic stone and used it to save the Lacunavim and restore the city to its former glory, and they all lived happily ever after. The end."

"Say what now?" John asked. "Diana is supposed to save this place? How?"

Diana hadn't gotten to the same point yet. "I think I understood most of your code words, and it's not magic, it's *science*!" Diana reminded. "You're saying that The Founder refused to reverse the projection that turned Michael and me to stone, and no one else could get us out? How can that be? Surely the Primary Morphing Crystavis could have removed the stone. Or the Mass Primary could flatten the stone layer, freeing us!"

"I'm sure Miranda tried that and more," Gina postulated. "The Founder had created a looping impenetrable pattern in the Pleovis that surrounded you and Michael. There was no way to manipulate the Pleovis trapped inside that pattern."

"Then how in the world did John free me?" Diana asked while staring at John with wide, questioning eyes.

"Hey, don't look at me! I just learned about the Pleovis a few days ago." John retorted. "And I'm not even a New Zigon person, so I can't move the Pleovis, at least, not on purpose!"

"You said everyone abandoned New Zigon?" Diana asked. "How long before that happened?"

"It took a while," Gina said sadly. "Many were unquestioningly loyal to The Founder. It took for the next generations to come of age, people who hadn't experienced New Zigon in its full glory, for the unrest to find its majority. About fifty years after Miranda disappeared with our treasures, the first wave of citizens left to live on earth."

"Now it is your turn to tell me your story about how you were freed," Gina said eagerly.

John shifted uncomfortably in his seat, not knowing where to start. Diana solved the problem by telling the story herself. She began with John hiding behind the statue, leaving out The Ape Crew's part. She told about how he broke the rope piece of the statue. "John said there was an initial cracking sound, then, a moment later, a larger one accompanied by a poof of dust. John helped me out of there, and on our way out, Michael's side of the statue started to break. We didn't have time to help him. He's with the human authorities now." John was surprised that she didn't say how they had run away from Michael because Diana had been scared and John had thought he was a threat.

"I was extremely tired for the next twelve hours or so and slept through most of it. When I woke up I did a knowledge transfer from John to pick up the language and customs," Diana admitted.

"Wait a second here," John stopped her. "How come Diana didn't know any English, but Gina is speaking it just fine?"

"Oh, I'm not speaking English," Gina said mysteriously. At John's dumbfounded look she clarified, "It is one of the reactive projections placed on the entire Lacunavim. It maps the feelings of the words into your appropriate language memory. Marvelous, isn't it?"

"What is a reactive projection? You two keep mentioning it," John asked, bypassing Gina's explanation for later consideration.

"It's when the Pleovis moves in a type of holding pattern, waiting for a certain pattern to initiate the desired Pleovis manipulation. It's like encasing one pattern inside another. Once the one on the outside recognizes its trigger, it releases the pattern on the inside. The more complex projections use this concept over and over just like an 'If…then' statement in programming," Diana explained patiently.

"They call it The Founder's Curse you know," Gina said.

"What do you mean?" asked Diana.

"The reactive projection that turned you to stone; after a while people called it The Founder's Curse." Diana was quiet, then nodded her head slightly as if she agreed with the description.

"Do you have any New Zigon blood in you, John?" Gina asked abruptly.

"I don't think so. I was adopted, so I don't know who my real parents were."

"Is there any way of tracking down your parents?" Gina pushed.

"No. I asked the orphanage once. Apparently, I was just dropped off at their front door when I was around three years old. The only thing they got out of me was that my first name was John. They had to guess my age and make up a birthday for me. I was adopted when I was six. I don't remember anything before the orphanage; I was too young."

Diana looked at him compassionately as Gina said, "That's too bad. It is odd that The Founder's own daughter couldn't break the statue after trying for over two years, yet you broke it with your boots."

"Did she ever try kicking it or smashing it with a hammer?" John asked.

"I have no way of knowing," Gina replied. "This will be a challenge to figure out. Did you feel anything when you broke the statue?"

"Yes, I felt my shoulder slam into the platform," John said sarcastically.

"You know that's not what I meant, young man," Gina scolded.

John took a moment to sift through his memories. "I don't *remember* feeling anything while it was happening. That doesn't mean nothing happened, just that I was too much in shock to register it. Before it happened, I felt this strange pull in my chest drawing me to the statue. I felt it afterwards towards Diana, but it faded after a couple of days."

Diana's cheeks turned pink as she admitted, "You felt it, too? I was afraid to ask. I think that pull is what made me trust you so quickly. If not for that, I'd probably be in police custody with Michael right now."

John jumped in his chair when Gina pressed a bony hand to his chest. Her Crystavis was glowing. "You don't have a flattened Crystavis stored on your dermis. Curious."

John leaned away from her invading touch, and Gina pulled her hand back.

"A normal human cannot get in here. The reactive projections embedded in the doorframe only let a person with New Zigon blood through. You must have some New Zigon blood in you, no matter how small."

"Huh," said John, eloquent as usual.

"Seriously? I guess with New Zigon abandoned, there could be lost New Zigon blood being passed through the generations on earth," Diana said, looking the happiest she had since entering the Lacunavim. She reached out and squeezed John's forearm. "Isn't this wonderful news? It means I can start training you on how to project your Visity!"

"You mean I can do all the stuff you can do?" John asked Diana incredulously.

Gina choked a little. "Well, I doubt you can do *all* the things she can do, but you might be able to do some. Our Diana here has the highest pottitude score ever taken. She scored higher in the Mind Crystavis Avenue than even The Founder."

Diana took her hand back and started fiddling with her fingers on the table, not meeting John's gaze. "What does that mean?" he asked.

"It means," Gina scoffed, "that Diana could eventually master every avenue in Crystavis study, and one day could be as powerful as The Founder himself!"

"I don't know about *that*," said Diana modestly.

"So you're like some kind of child prodigy?"

"I'm not sure I like being called a child, but I was treated as a prodigy. Remember I told you how I related better with adults? Well, kids my own age didn't like being around me, especially in lessons, because I would learn so much faster than they would. I quickly moved on to train with Crystavis Masters here in the capital building, so I wasn't even living in the city with them anymore. That's why I spent so much time with Miranda. She was my teacher, my mentor, and my friend. Gina, you said she and her child just disappeared a few years after I was frozen. Did anyone go look for her? Did she leave anything behind that gave information on where she was going?" Suddenly Diana's face brightened. "John, just think, you could be a long lost descendent of hers! You have to be descended from someone in New Zigon!"

"So if I'm descended from a princess, does that make me a prince?" John asked with half a smile.

"Miranda wasn't really a princess, John. I just called her that in my story to make it easier to tell," Gina pointed out.

"Oh, I knew that! I was only trying to see if I could get Diana to call me Prince John!" John elbowed Diana, eliciting a scowl.

"To answer your question, Diana, yes and no," Gina said. "My mother looked for her for several years before she dropped the search. Once you were gone, my mother was Miranda's only confidant. She left a few things with her that I think you'll find very interesting."

"Can I see them?" Diana asked excitedly.

"Be patient, all in good time. First, I want to see if you can help the Lacunavim," Gina deflected. "If you couldn't tell, it's not doing very well. Once the Summas Stone was taken, it no longer had the power to perform the many tasks of maintaining life here. The fading illumination is just one sign of its decline."

"What do you expect Diana to do? She's just one girl, and she just got out of that statue after being trapped for hundreds of years," John said protectively. He didn't like the idea of this skeleton of a woman expecting something out of Diana. If anything, Diana is the one who should be helped. "There's hardly anyone left here. Why bother?"

"Why bother? Why bother you ask? Just look around you, child! This place has stood for a thousand years and has housed an entire race of people. Those people are still out there, mingling with humans; humans who would suck the marrow out of our bones if it would help them achieve money or power!" Gina nearly shouted. She started to cough, the strain of her outburst too much for her aged vocal chords.

John was still irate, not knowing what the old woman was going to ask of Diana. Wild thoughts of Gina stealing all of Diana's youth or cutting her wrists over a goblet to fuel some blood spell had his mind racing and his body on high alert. This woman was only eight years old when Diana knew her. With the hardships she'd been through, not to mention looking after a crotchety old king for a few hundred years, he doubted she was anything like the girl Diana once knew.

"Calm down, John, I have an idea of what she is suggesting," Diana said, trying to smooth his nerves. She wrapped her fingers around his as she said to Gina, "You want my Pollampium to fuel the Lacunavim, don't you."

Gina's whole body relaxed at the words. "Yes, child, you have one of the few pieces of Zigonite known to us. It is not as big as the Summas Stone, but it still is one of the most powerful pieces of Pollampium in existence."

"What about The Founder's Zigonite? Why aren't you using that?" Diana asked with some suspicion as her grip on his fingers tightened. John's unease jumped right back to the forefront as he looked from Diana back to Gina. He felt like saying, "Yeah, what about that?" but he stayed quiet. He had no idea what Gina was asking of Diana. It sounded like she needed a piece of Diana's amulet. But if Diana had to take her amulet apart, what would that mean for her?

Gina's shoulders tensed; not a good sign. "He is not willing to use it to save New Zigon. I think he is hoping that when it dies, it will take him with it," she admitted sadly.

"Why should I give up my only Pollampium when The Founder isn't willing to lift a finger? What did New Zigon do for me during those hundreds of years I was imprisoned in stone? The Founder turned his back on me, and I have a new appreciation for Miranda's hatred of him!" Diana threw back at Gina. *You go, girl,* John thought as he turned his head back to Gina. He felt like he was at a tennis match.

Gina leaned forward and folded her hands on the table, striking a relaxed pose as she said in a comforting voice, "Oh, child, I'm not asking you to give up your Pollampium! I just want to see if it would help and give the Lacunavim a little energy boost, buy us a little time to figure out something better. Can we at least give it a try to see if it is even an option?"

Diana sighed as she let go of John's hand and pushed her chair away from the table. She leaned back, looking a little resigned. "I guess it won't hurt to see if it will even work before we argue over it," she conceded.

"Can you explain to me what you're talking about with Pollampium, the Summas Stone, and Zigonite?" John asked, thinking to calm the situation a bit with a shift in the topic of conversation. He also hoped to put off Gina's test to give Diana time to think it over first.

Gina jumped at the question. "The Founder's father was the first and only person from Zigon to ever make it to earth."

"You mentioned that in your story," John commented.

"That's right!" Gina gave him a wrinkled smile. "I'm glad you were listening. He brought precious stones from Zigon, stones that don't exist on earth. They make the best Pollampium there is. Quartz is the second best, but it doesn't compare to Zigonite. There were several stones. We called the largest the Summas Stone. It was bigger than an ostrich egg," Gina held out her skeletal hands to form an oval shape about ten inches long and six inches high. "It sat in the center of the repository over there," she pointed at the round room they had been about to enter when Gina found them. "It sat on the altar where the Lacunavim could tap into it."

"But there were several of these Zigon rocks, and Diana has one of them? If there were so few, why would she have one?" John asked, trying not to sound accusing.

"There were a couple dozen of them ranging in size from a chicken egg to a marble. The biggest ones went to The Founder, Lady Aberlene, and Miranda. Each Crystavis master was given one marble-sized. The rest were stored in an alcove of the repository and were available to support study and research. When Diana took her pottitude test, Miranda convinced The Founder that Diana should be given the largest available one to help her reach her full potential. If you've seen her amulet, you know it is quite sizeable."

"What happened to all of the other pieces?" John wondered aloud.

"Well, The Founder has his of course, Lady Aberlene's was lost when she was taken, Miranda took hers, the Masters each kept theirs when they left, and the ones in the repository were looted when the city was abandoned," Gina counted off her fingers. "And Miranda stole the Summas Stone, as I've already said."

Diana stood up resolutely. "We might as well get this test over with, so we don't waste time talking in circles."

"Yes, let's see if it works," Gina agreed.

John didn't feel comfortable with the glint he saw in Gina's eyes. "Are you sure about this?" John bent down and whispered in Diana's ear as he walked next to her into the circular room.

"No, but she won't stop pushing it until we at least try," Diana whispered back.

"I don't trust her."

"What's not to trust? She stayed here to help The Founder when everyone else left. That says something."

"Exactly," John said through gritted teeth.

They entered the circular room, which John assumed was the repository. He and Diana took their time by starting a slow circuit around the room, not moving to step up onto the round platform. They passed several alcoves John hadn't been able to see from the doorway. He couldn't make out what they contained, and he wanted to stop and explore. Diana noticed. "You can take a closer look around if you want, while I do this test," she offered.

A glint of gold caught John's eye in the last alcove, and he distractedly agreed, "Yeah, sure. I'll be there in a sec."

With a small smile, Diana shook her head at his back. She took a deep breath then joined Gina on the platform. John could hear them talking in the background as he reached the alcove. He found a gold crown waiting on a dusty pillow. There was a small mirror behind it on the wall. John couldn't resist. He picked up the crown and placed it on his head. His first hint that something was off, was that the crown instantly warmed up. He had a hard time seeing his reflection in the dark, but then the alcove started to light up, and he admired the ornate object on his head. He imagined himself sitting on a throne giving out orders to the masses, and having guests come and drop treasures at his feet. Then his brain jumped back to reality. He could see his reflection better because the crown was lighting up like a Christmas tree. His stomach flipped as he panicked over doing something wrong and getting caught. He whipped the crown off his head to examine it. It had become so hot that it nearly burned his fingers. It had tiny gems embedded around its entire circumference. All of them were softly glowing, fading back to darkness before his eyes. He quickly put it back on its cushion and decided it was time to join Diana and Gina.

As he approached the platform, he realized that Diana and Gina were arguing. Diana had her necklace visible and was gripping the amulet in her fist. Gina was gesticulating animatedly, waving and pointing between the amulet in Diana's hand and the altar. Diana reluctantly lifted the amulet's chain up over her head and moved to place it on the center of the altar.

"No, Diana!" John yelled as he raced towards her, taking the steps in two bounds. "Don't take it . . . " Diana dropped it on the table just as he made it to the platform, ". . . off," he finished lamely, realizing he was too late as the entire room erupted with light.

John kept moving towards Diana as his eyes adjusted. He placed himself between Diana and Gina, wrapping and arm protectively around Diana's shoulders. He glared at Gina, who was clapping her hands together with glee. It sounded more like clinking than a clap, as she didn't have much flesh on her palms.

John was still blinking as he checked out how the light transformed the room. It was as if the light was coming from within the floor, the walls, and the columns, from the room itself. It was dazzlingly white and almost burned his eyes. He watched as a beam of light emanated from the altar and rose up through the opening in the ceiling to shine on the Lacunavim. John watched, stunned, as the piece of dome the light touched changed before his eyes. It went from a ruddy bluish-red to a sparkling pink that reminded him of Diana's Zigon dress. The pink started to seep out from the illuminated spot and expand slowly over the surface of the dome.

"It's working, it's working!" Gina squealed excitedly.

"Yeah, it works," John said darkly. "The test is over," he declared as he reached to get Diana's amulet back for her.

"No!" Gina shouted as she reached out a claw-like hand at him, the other around her glowing amulet, which was suddenly visible around her neck. John felt like a cement wall rammed into him as he was thrown back from the table. He skidded on the floor almost to the edge of the platform towards the door.

Pride filled him as he watched Diana seize the opportunity while Gina was still focused on him, to shove the old woman onto her backside with one hand and scoop up her amulet with the other. Gina tried to grab at Diana's ankles as Diana started for John.

Diana stopped and spun on Gina. "If you grab me, we'll both turn to stone, and then where would you be!" Diana said angrily. "John, time to go home!" she shouted as she reached down for John's arm, apparently willing to drag him out the door if needed.

"Diana, don't turn your back on the only home you've ever known!" Gina screeched. "Your homeland needs you!"

"You can't keep my amulet, and you shouldn't have hurt John!" Diana spun back again to confront Gina.

"I'll do more than just push him if you don't put your amulet back on the altar!" Gina threatened.

Diana's response was to help John to his feet and move to get off the platform. John and Diana jumped and turned to look as Gina made an inhuman wail that almost split their eardrums. Gina had her hand reaching towards one of the alcoves, the glow of her amulet giving them an x-ray view of her other hand. Gina flicked her fingers from the alcove towards them as her scream stopped, like a conductor wrapping up the last note of concert.

John felt himself getting pushed again, but this time it was Diana pushing him aside as she stepped in front of him. Suddenly, Diana was lifted off her feet and slammed backwards into him, pushing them both down the steps of the platform onto the floor. The room started to dim again as John fell on his back a second time, but now he had the added weight of Diana landing on top of him. All the breath whooshed out of his lungs, and he struggled to breathe. The items in his backpack both cushioned his fall and dug into him painfully. Diana wasn't moving. John slid out from under her and was able to get some precious air back into his lungs. Diana looked like she was unconscious. John scooped her up in his arms and started for the stairwell. He heard something hit the wall an inch from his head. He descended the steps as fast as he could without tripping, retracing their path to get out of the building. When he made it outside, Diana stirred in his arms as she groggily said, "Put me down, I can walk."

John gratefully set her on her feet and wrapped a steadying arm around her. He did *not* want to carry her down the steps on the side of the cliff.

"You'll be back!" Gina shouted over their heads. They both turned to look up and see her standing on a high balcony of the building. "I have a Crystavis you'll want, Diana; one specially coded for you and left in my mother's care by Miranda!"

"It's time to go," John said as he ushered Diana through the circular courtyard, heading for the cliff-side steps. "We need to regroup with Mrs. M and come back with a plan."

Diana was silent as she let John lead her down the steps to the waterfall. She put her amulet back around her neck and used it to open the portal to take them home.

It was late afternoon when they stepped back into the creek. They hadn't stopped to take their shoes off, and John felt the cold water rush over the tops of his boots to soak his socks. He was already in a state of shock, so it didn't faze him when he saw Mrs. McNeally sitting at the side of the creek with a washboard between her knees, a spoon in each hand. She alternately dragged the spoons across the ridges of the board and banged them like drum sticks. It wasn't very loud, but it was an obnoxious sound.

At the sight of them, Mrs. McNeally jumped to her feet, dropping her strange instrument as she stood at the water's edge, ushering them nearer with her hands. "Good Lord Almighty, you two are a sight for sore eyes! Come here, dearies; get out of that cold water."

John still had ahold of Diana as she collapsed against him. "Ouch," she said softly. John scooped her up into his arms again and splashed them out of the creek. He put her back on her feet, and Diana nearly toppled into Mrs. McNeally's arms.

"John, help me get her to the truck," Mrs. McNeally ordered crisply. She pulled Diana's left arm over her shoulder to help support her weight, making Diana cry out in pain. Mrs. McNeally nearly dropped her, she was so surprised and upset over hurting Diana.

John picked Diana up again and started for the truck, the water sloshing around inside his boots. "Mrs. M, can you go get the truck started?" he asked. Mrs. McNeally picked up the purse she'd set on the bank and jogged to the truck, getting her keys out as she went. "Mrs. M, you left your…spoons," John huffed as he carefully picked his way over branches and stones.

"Never mind that, just get her over here," said Mrs. McNeally, opening the passenger door.

John's overworked mind dully thought that if things continued like this, he wouldn't have to go find a calf to pick up every day. Diana was giving his arms a real workout. He was smart enough though, to never, ever say anything like that out loud.

Diana was carefully holding her left side. She winced several times sliding into the truck. They buckled up, and Mrs. McNeally peeled out of the park. "Should we go home or to the hospital?" Mrs. McNeally asked.

"She doesn't have insurance or a social security number," John said thinking it through. "I don't think a hospital would be a good idea."

"Take me home," Diana requested. "I just need to catch my breath, and I can use my Crystavis to heal myself. I think I have a bruised rib."

"What in the world happened in there?" Mrs. McNeally demanded.

"I was sort of shot," Diana said simply.

"Shot?" John and Mrs. McNeally exclaimed at the same time.

"Gina flung some kind of projectile at you, John. It would have killed you. My dress is like armor, remember? Whatever it was bounced off me, but left a nasty bruise, I think."

John was stunned. He remembered Diana pushing in front of him, then getting slammed back into him. She did that to protect him. He reached over and took Diana's hand, giving it a gentle squeeze. "Thank you," was all he could think of to say.

John kept ahold of her hand the rest of the short trip back to Mrs. McNeally's house. Mrs. McNeally drove right into her front yard and stopped the truck with the passenger door as close to the front steps as she could get. John got out and turned to help Diana. "Do you think you can walk?"

"Yes, I think so," Diana said weakly.

John wrapped an arm around Diana, supporting her under her elbow, trying not to hurt her.

"Put her on the davenport," Mrs. McNeally instructed. At John's confused look she said exasperatedly, "the *couch*, John. Put her on the couch."

John let Diana lean against him as he helped her up the steps, through the kitchen, and onto the sofa in the living room. Diana lay on her back, taking up the length of the sofa. John put a throw pillow under her head as Mrs. McNeally took off Diana's wet shoes and covered her with a blanket. Mrs. McNeally smoothed the hair away from Diana's forehead and in a motherly tone asked, "Can I get you anything, dearie?"

"Water, please. And I think I'll need something to eat after I'm done," Diana said, already covering her amulet with her left hand. The now-familiar glow shone as Diana closed her eyes. It didn't last very long. Some of the stress melted off Diana's face when she was done.

"Was that it?" asked John.

"No, that just took the edge off the pain," Diana answered with her eyes still closed. "I have to do this in steps and rest in between. Healing yourself is harder than healing someone else; it takes a lot of energy."

Mrs. McNeally returned with a glass of water, cheese and carrots. Diana lifted her head and gratefully downed almost half the glass before helping herself to the snack. She took her time but eventually laid back, eyes closed, and worked to heal herself again. When she was done she swung herself into a sitting position.

"Better now?" Mrs. McNeally asked.

"I'll need one more round, and I'll be as good as new," Diana said as she sipped her water and nibbled on the food. John, who had been sitting on the coffee table in front of her, joined her on the couch as Mrs. McNeally sat in her La-Z-boy recliner.

"One of you'd better start talking," Mrs. McNeally said with equal parts concern and impatience in her voice.

John took up the tale to give Diana a chance to rest and did his best to describe their experience. He remembered Gina's fairy-tale version of history almost down to the last word. He left out the part about him accidentally setting off the golden crown, and he wasn't gentle in his description of Gina. "She was like a walking bag of bones, Mrs. M; it was almost hard to look at her. Her eyes were all watery and bugged out of her head. I was so grossed out when she put her zombie hand on my chest, looking for a Crystavis. What made it even freakier was the look in her eyes. There was no confusion or Alzheimer's there. She might have been a bit evil-crazy, but she wasn't crazy-crazy."

"John, she isn't evil," Diana said defensively.

"Diana, she tried to *kill* me! She was younger than you are when you saw her last. She's had a lot of time to change, like several hundred years. She may have been your friend before, but she sure isn't anymore," John said angrily. He felt bad when he saw Diana's face fall, but she needed to accept the truth of the situation. He decided to bring up the one thing that had made her smile when they were there. "Guess what, Mrs. M! Apparently, I've got some New Zigon blood in me. Gina said I wouldn't have been able to enter the repository if I didn't. Diana says she can train me to do some of her magic!"

Diana perked up at that. "Quit saying it's magic! For the last time, it's *science*," Diana corrected irritably. *That seems to be a pet peeve for Diana,* John thought as he smiled. He tucked that one away in his pocket for future use. He had a whole mental file folder of little things to get his sisters riled up, and he was starting a list for Diana.

Out of everything John had said so far, this revelation got the biggest reaction out of Mrs. McNeally. She seemed both proud and worried. "I always knew you were a special one, John Christopher Brown, but this? Good Lord, have mercy. Don't go off and hurt yourself, and don't go off and leave all of us mere *humans* behind!" she said making the sign of the cross.

They both sat in silence as they watched Diana heal herself one more time. When she was done, Diana let her head fall onto the back of the couch and took a deep breath, eyes closed. She looked exhausted. As John's adrenaline continued to wear off, he realized he was completely tuckered-out as well. "I still have lots of questions for you, Diana, because I don't understand a lot about what happened, but I think the most important thing is for us to figure out what to do next," John said.

Mrs. McNeally looked assessingly back and forth between Diana and John. "I think that can wait for now," Mrs. McNeally said with authority. "You two need to rest. John, you can spend the night here in Bobby's old room. I'm going to order some pizza, and we'll have a movie party to give your minds a break." Mrs. McNeally went over to her TV cabinet and opened the doors to reveal a very new-looking flat screen TV before she started rooting around in a drawer.

"Mrs. M!" John said excitedly. "When did you get a flat screen, and why have you been hiding it from me?"

Mrs. McNeally kept her attention on the drawer as she answered, "My oldest, Paul, bought it for me. I told him I didn't need it, but the kids are always buying me expensive things. I keep telling them I want more of their time instead of these fancy gifts, but they don't listen." Her face was turned away so John couldn't see her expression, but he could hear the pain in her voice. "Ah-ha!" Mrs. McNeally said triumphantly. "They left a bunch of movies when they were here last Christmas. Do you want to watch *Avatar*, *Iron Man*, *Thor*, *Captain America*, or *The Avengers*?"

They ended up watching *Captain America*, and after they had pizza, Mrs. McNeally made them popcorn. John couldn't remember the last time he felt so lazy. It was like a vacation for him. They didn't talk about New Zigon the rest of the night. After the movie they headed for bed, knowing they would have a lot to talk about the following morning.

CHAPTER 12 – INSANE PLANS

When John woke, the sky was a mix of brilliant pinks and oranges as the sun reappeared to light their world for another day. John had to remind himself that *they* were spinning around the sun and not the other way around. The thought made him feel very small.

As John made his way towards the bathroom, he could hear Mrs. McNeally rattling around in the kitchen. John reveled in taking a hot shower and lingered much longer than he normally did. When he got back to his borrowed bedroom, the bed was already made, and there was a clean set of clothes waiting for him on top of the blankets. There was a navy blue T-shirt and a well-worn pair of jeans with a belt. Jeans! John raced to try them on, and they were a little big for him, but the belt took care of it. John thundered down the stairs and found Mrs. McNeally and Diana in the kitchen. He hitched his thumbs in his pockets and casually leaned against the frame. Mrs. McNeally noticed him first.

"Well, look at you! Don't you look dashing! I found some of Bobby's old clothes that I thought might fit you. It appears I was right," Mrs. McNeally said, beaming at him. She set a huge plate of bacon and eggs on the table and ushered him into a seat. Diana smiled at him and wished him a good morning. John practically inhaled his breakfast, getting second and third helpings.

John thought he'd get the conversation started as he asked with an amused glint in his eyes, "Mrs. M, what was with the washboard and spoons yesterday?"

"Oh that," Mrs. McNeally said with a shrug. "People kept coming by, and I had to figure out a way to keep them away. We couldn't have you walking out of that waterfall in front of a bunch of folk, now could we?"

John waited, but she didn't continue. "So, you decided to become a one woman band?" he prompted.

Mrs. McNeally rolled her eyes like she couldn't believe she had to explain herself. "I had to figure out a way to keep people away without arousing suspicion or starting a fight. I got some funny looks, but it worked. Nobody wanted me as their background musical accoutrement, would you?"

Diana gave Mrs. McNeally a strange look that John couldn't interpret. He chuckled and said, "You're going to get yourself a reputation Mrs. M. People are going to think you're losing your mind. Watch out, a social worker might be showing up any day now to take you away."

"I'd like to see them try!" Mrs. McNeally said with flint in her eyes. "Besides, it's always best to keep people guessing."

Diana took her plate over to the sink and said, "I guess we should talk about what happened yesterday. I'm not even sure where to start. It's just starting to sink in that Gina tried to hurt us."

"What did she mean when she said she had a Crystavis from Miranda for you?" John asked.

"I'm not sure, but I'm guessing it is an encoded Crystavis that holds a message for me," Diana said as she sat back down. "Crystavis can be used to store information which can be encrypted. It sounds like Miranda left a message for me with Mirabelle that's coded only for my Visity Signature. It may help us find out where Miranda went when she disappeared. We have to go back for it," Diana said eagerly.

John clasped his hands together on the table and leaned forward towards Diana. He felt sick to his stomach over what he was about to say, but it had to be said. "Diana, I don't mean to sound harsh, but why should we ever go back? Whatever happened to Miranda happened hundreds of years ago. I know she was your friend, and I'd be curious, too, if I were you, but is it worth the risk of confronting Gina? New Zigon was empty. There's nothing there for you anymore," he finished softly. He looked at her intently, waiting for her reaction. She stared back at him, a square of sunlight from the window hitting her face and lighting up the blue of her eyes.

Her eyes flicked back and forth between his as she processed his words. In a shaky voice she said, "But it's my home..."

"Do you want to go back there to live?" John asked her gently. "There's no one there. Your friends and family are gone."

Diana's face crumpled, making John feel like a jerk. Still, he stood his ground, wanting her to think this through. It scared him when she got hurt yesterday, and he didn't want either of them to have to talk to Gina again.

"But, I can't just turn my back on New Zigon," Diana started to protest.

Mrs. McNeally went to stand behind Diana, putting her hands supportively on Diana's shoulders. "I know this must be incredibly hard for you, dearie, but John is right. I'm not sure I want to let you go back there after what happened to you yesterday."

"But, where am I supposed to go?" Diana said in a small, childlike voice.

Mrs. McNeally squeezed Diana's shoulders and shook her slightly. "You, dearie, are going to stay here with me for as long as you need, don't you worry about that."

Diana's resolve wilted against the dual assault. She patted one of Mrs. McNeally's hands and looked up at her with a grateful smile. "Let me think about it. It probably would be a good idea to stay away for a while to let Gina cool down." Diana clasped her hands on the table, mirroring John's position. She stared at her hands for several quiet moments. When she looked up again, her eyes gleamed with determination. "I think it's time to go find and help Michael."

When John and Mrs. McNeally didn't say anything, she pleaded her case. "I know you both think I'm crazy for wanting to help him, but he really is a friend. We were pushed into that horrible situation by The Founder's rules, and Michael was desperate. You never saw him and Miranda together. It was kind of gross how much they were in love. Michael was this large, powerful man who turned to complete jelly around her. It was like one was not complete without the other. I kept Miranda company after her father put her under house arrest, and she was miserable. She was grieving over both her mother and not being able to see Michael. Miranda was my best friend. I owe it to her to help Michael. Michael is just a regular human, even though he has been exposed to New Zigon's ways for years. When he was freed from the statue, he was all alone with no one to help him, in a strange place, where he didn't even understand the language. Now he is probably in some prison or mental health institution. I can't just leave him to that kind of fate. It's not fair, and after all he has gone through and lost, it just isn't right." Diana finished her impassioned speech and looked between John and Mrs. McNeally trying to gauge their reactions, desperately wanting their support.

Mrs. McNeally sat down at the table next to Diana and covered Diana's small, soft hands with her spotted, wrinkled ones. "We'll see what we can do, dearie, but don't get your hopes up. We're not even sure where he is now."

"But we can find out, can't we?" Diana asked, undaunted.

"I'm sure we can," John said giving her a reassuring smile. He had no idea how they were going to do that, but between going back to New Zigon and finding Michael, he'd pick the latter ten times out of ten.

They decided the news would be their best source of information. Mrs. McNeally went to get the newspapers from the last week. She sorted through the stack, dismissing classified, sports, and advertising inserts, making a substantial pile for them to review in the middle of the table. They each grabbed a small stack and began reading.

John hated to read. He didn't want to overlook anything by accident, so he did his best as he scanned the articles and tried not to let them just blur before his eyes. They clipped all relevant articles and had a little more than a handful when they were done. They found out that Michael had been taken into police custody as the primary suspect in the museum vandalism, awaiting felony charges. Officials reported that Michael would not say anything intelligible, and they were not able to communicate with him. Michael had been evaluated to see if he was competent to stand trial, and they suspected he was 'mentally challenged.' He had a competency hearing scheduled for Tuesday morning. If found incompetent, he would be transferred to West Penn Psych Center.

They argued over what to do. Diana wanted to go see him in prison and give him a knowledge transfer so he could speak English. Mrs. McNeally and John disagreed, assuming that Michael would be deemed incompetent to stand trial as-is. They reasoned that it would be easier to get him out of a mental health facility than it would be to try to break him out of prison. Diana conceded, so they started brainstorming a plan.

"Should we try to fake getting him released, or should we just try to sneak him out?" John wondered.

"Whatever we do, I have to be the one to see him first; he doesn't know either of you," Diana said as if expecting an argument.

"I agree, but you will *not* be doing this on your own. So what do you think, trick or sneak?" John asked with a quirky smile, trying to be clever.

Diana drummed her fingers against the kitchen table. "Faking a release could be difficult. We'd have to have a person requesting the release, either someone impersonating an official or someone we put under a sort of mind control. It might be easier to sneak him out, but then would they be looking for him afterwards?"

Mrs. McNeally chimed in, "We'd want to get him out in a way that would close his case, so they won't search for him."

"What kind of things can you do with your Crystavis, Diana? Maybe that would help us come up with a plan," John suggested.

"There are lots of things I can do with it," Diana answered with a mysterious smile. "It would be faster to think of what we want to have happen, and then figure out a way to do it."

"What if we faked his death?" John threw out. "If there was a way we could make it look like he died, then we could get his body out of the morgue. If they thought he was dead, they would close the case against him and not look for him."

"That has possibilities," said Mrs. McNeally. Mrs. McNeally and John both looked at Diana expectantly. "Can that amulet of yours make a person look like they've died?" Mrs. McNeally asked.

"I'm sure I can figure something out," Diana said confidently. "I'd have to go by myself though, unless John can learn how to make himself invisible."

Diana said she could create a pattern in the Pleovis to "lock" Michael's image from a single second, so it would look like he wasn't breathing. She'd have to be able to touch him to make it happen, and she'd have to stay with him as they moved him so she could keep freeze-framing his image. She said she had the capability of making herself or another object invisible. "Light is carried on the Pleovis. I can make the Pleovis carrying light to detour around an object instead of bouncing off it. It actually is one of the easier patterns to perform, which is why I think John might be able to learn it in time." She said that as long as she could touch Michael, she could block the sound from his heartbeat as well as block other vital checks so that he appeared to be dead.

She said she had the ability to alter a person's memory, but she had to be able to touch the person to do it, and the bigger the alteration, the higher the difficulty. She suggested making an aide or intern think they had sent the body off to the funeral home to be cremated. She could make Michael invisible for a short period of time and walk him out the front door.

They had an outline of a plan by lunchtime. Mrs. McNeally would drive Diana to West Penn Psych on Sunday afternoon, before Michael was transferred there, and gather information about the layout of the place, schedules, and policies for dealing with the deceased. Diana would look around while invisible and "borrow" a couple of uniforms that she and John could wear, so if their invisibility projection waivered, they wouldn't draw as much attention.

Diana wanted to start training John immediately, so after lunch they spent time in Mrs. McNeally's barn, out of view from the road.

John was excited about their first lesson, until he found out that Diana wanted him to just lie back in the hay with his eyes closed and "feel the Force." Well, that's not what she said, but it seemed to John that pretty much summed it up.

Diana launched into a long speech about breathing in and out, holding your breath, and visualizing different things. She went into excruciating detail that John couldn't follow.

"You want me to do what?" John asked, totally confused.

"Just do what I say," Diana said with no small amount of exasperation.

"Breathe in. Stop. Hold it. Breathe out, all the way. Stop. Hold it. Breathe in. Stop. Hold it. Breathe out, all the way. Stop. Hold it. Breath in," Diana instructed. "Keep breathing like that, where you stop for a moment after breathing in and stop for a moment after you breathe out."

John breathed in and out several times, stopping like Diana had said.

"Now, as you breathe in and out, imagine a cartoon of Superman using his super breath. When you breathe out, there is a stream of air blowing away from your face in swirly lines. When you breathe back in, imagine sucking that back into you, building up like a dam," Diana told him, then waited for him to breathe a few times. "Can you picture it? Can you picture your breath shooting away from you like a dragon breathing fire?"

"Yeah, I think so," John answered, wondering how this breathing was going to help him. "Dragon's fire breath; got it."

"Well, it doesn't have to be *fire* breath, just air," Diana said as she watched him breathe a few more times. "Now, next time you breathe in, hold it and use your mind to push the air like you were imagining your breath had done."

Nothing happened as John did as she said. "Is something supposed to happen?"

"You should create a small breeze," Diana told him. "Try it again. Imagine your thoughts are a fishing rod, and you need to cast them out in front of you."

John did as she said and just about jumped out of his skin when Diana let out a surprised scream. He opened his eyes to see small licks of fire die out far above him. Diana was leaning against one of the barn beams several feet back from where she'd been standing. Her face was flushed, and she had a hand over her heart as if to calm it, or, *duh*, John thought, hold her amulet, which John could now see between her fingers.

"What happened?" he asked.

"You just created a flame of fire ten feet tall!" she said in awe. "I told you not to envision fire! We are in a very flammable barn, genius!"

"I made fire? That's so cool!" He tried flinging his thoughts out again to create more fire, but nothing happened. He tried several times, but not even a spark ignited. "Why can't I do it again?" he complained.

"You're not really concentrating, you're too riled up," Diana said. "You must have a strong affinity for the light and energy avenues to project fire on your first try, I mean your second try," Diana said with a smirk. "I was hoping for just a soft breeze."

Just then, Mrs. McNeally came running into the barn, a worried look on her face. She stopped and bent over with her hands on her knees, trying to catch her breath. "Is everything…okay?" she gasped. She looked at Diana leaning against a beam and John lying on his back in a small pile of hay on the floor. "Am I going senile, or did I just hear a scream?" she asked angrily.

Diana pushed off the beam and started walking towards Mrs. McNeally saying, "You did, that was me. I'm so sorry, I couldn't help it. John projected a huge burst of fire, and I was standing a bit too close."

John sat straight up and asked, "I didn't burn you did I?"

"No, I'm fine," Diana said dismissively.

Mrs. McNeally gave each of them a long, hard look before straightening up and taking in a deep breath. "You two are going to give me a heart attack. No more screaming!" she demanded. "And if you're going to play with fire, take it outside!" With that warning she turned on her heel and headed back out of the barn.

Diana walked over to John and held out a hand to help him up. He didn't really need help, but he accepted it to be polite. She held his hand in both of hers and was literally bouncing on her toes, her face beaming with excitement. "You have no idea how big this is! Making a small breeze is one of the simpler projections, because a strong visualization can make your mind project almost sub-consciously. To create *fire* from visualization is really unusual." She squeezed his hand. "That's how The Founder and Miranda can project in all twelve avenues of Crystavis study without a Crystavis; they visualize! You just might have some original Zigon blood in your veins after all!"

"You mean Miranda could be my great-great-great-great-grandmother or something?" John asked incredulously.

"Yes! You could be a Prince John after all," she teased.

John liked the sound of that. It didn't seem quite real to him, because he didn't actually see himself create the flames. Diana let go of him and nearly skipped over to where she'd left some things on a hay bale when they first came into the barn. She came back with a large hand mirror.

"I didn't think we'd get to this today, but I brought it just in case," she said breathlessly. "We're going to have you try the first step towards projecting invisibility. If my guess is right, you should be able to pick it up by visualizing instead of having to learn and replicate the intricate patterns to project."

"I hope you're right," John said, looking at the mirror skeptically. "I don't like the sound of 'learn' and 'intricate' said in the same sentence at the beginning of summer."

"John, this isn't a joke! We're working to get Michael, who might be your great-great-great-great-grandfather!" Diana chastised.

John thought it highly unlikely he was related to Michael, but he didn't argue. He put on his best studious look and asked, "What do you want me to do?"

"We are going to work on bending light," Diana said as she walked over to a patch of sunlight that was spilling onto the floor from the open door. She knelt down and held the mirror so it stood perpendicular to the ground. She placed it in the path of the sunlight, and the mirror dutifully reflected the light, making its own small spotlight on the dirt floor. "Sit across from me; far enough away to see the mirror's reflected spot of light." Once John was in place she continued, "I'm going to talk you through some visualization exercises. The goal is to change how the light reflects off the mirror and make the reflected spot of light move."

"Oh, that's all," John joked.

"John!" Diana reprimanded. "Be serious! We want you to learn how to be invisible, which is making the light flow around you instead of bouncing off you. The first step is to move the light's reflection." They tried several things that didn't work, like bending the angle of the light forcibly, envisioning a tool that would *push* the angle open wider, and trying to pull the light out of the mirror at a different angle. Finally, Diana had him mentally follow the path of the light through the door and bounce off the mirror several times, then try adjusting the bounce just a bit. This made the patch of reflected light move ever so slightly.

"Yes! I did it!" John shouted.

"Wait a minute, I think my hand holding the mirror just wobbled a bit," Diana said as she looked around them for something. She found a couple of empty flowerpots, and used them to prop up the mirror. "There! Now try it again. If the light moves this time, we'll know for sure that it was you."

John tried again. He had to mentally follow the path of the light three times before he could change the angle of the reflection. When he did, Diana let out a whoop of success.

Their shouting brought Mrs. McNeally back to the barn, but this time she walked in at a normal pace. The widow just shook her head mildly as the young teenagers showed her what John had accomplished before telling them to come inside for supper.

* * *

They talked about their plan over dinner. Diana and Mrs. McNeally would be going to Pittsburgh the next day after church. Mrs. McNeally had called the mental institution that afternoon and found out that there were daily visiting hours from one to five o'clock. Mrs. McNeally planned on hanging out in a lobby or waiting room while Diana went on her invisible spy mission. If Diana got caught, she would plead ignorance, saying that she got lost, and that her great aunt was waiting for her.

John was to continue practicing his projection to bend light. Mrs. McNeally gave him a little makeup mirror that was smaller than his palm. Diana wanted him to continue bending the light further and further, until he could bend it around the mirror as if the mirror weren't even there. Once he could do that, he was to put down the mirror and try the same thing with just his hand. John was determined to figure it out so he could go with Diana when they went after Michael.

The next obstacle was how to get the results of the competency hearing and find out if and when Michael would be transferred. If Michael hadn't even said a word since his arrest, they were fairly confident he would be found incompetent and transferred to the mental facility. Mrs. McNeally decided to go downtown on Tuesday and see if she could sit in on the hearing or overhear something outside the courtroom. It was too risky to have Diana be seen in town. They all doubted anyone would connect her to the broken statue, but they didn't want to take any chances. John realized that Diana could make herself invisible and go with Mrs. McNeally, but Diana didn't bring it up. He had the feeling that Mrs. M wanted to make that particular trip on her own; Diana must have sensed that, too. They were planning the rescue for Wednesday and would change plans if the transfer happened later in the week.

Mrs. McNeally came up with a story to get John out of farm work on Wednesday so he could go on the rescue mission with them. She would corner John's Father at Mass, as she'd done the previous Sunday. Diana was going with Mrs. McNeally to church so she could be formally introduced to the entire Brown family. John was looking forward to watching Mrs. McNeally in action again.

After dinner, John changed back into his overalls and headed home, trying to evaluate the warring emotions inside of him. Mainly, he was worried; worried about Diana and Mrs. McNeally going to Pittsburgh without him, worried how he would get through the day not knowing what was going on, worried about learning the invisibility trick, and worried about the whole darn thing. He also felt trapped, that he would be stuck on the farm until Wednesday and kept in the dark on what was happening. He felt excited about learning to project his Visity and what that would ultimately mean for him. He also felt scared. He was nervous over meeting Michael, but he couldn't explain why. Maybe he was worried he would lose Diana to him, since Michael came from her past.

Thankfully, John didn't have any trouble falling asleep that night and performed his chores with new vigor the next morning after having such a nice break from them. He took extra care getting ready for Church and repeated the weekly ritual of helping his sisters into the truck.

Christie had snuck several rubber bands to church. John didn't realize that she had some around each wrist and each ankle and in both of her skirt pockets and even had a few extra on her two short braids. Every time John looked down at her during Mass, she had another one out and was either trying to make noise with it or was trying to shoot it at someone. He confiscated each one and soon had quite the collection in his pocket. Christie was her usual obstinate self. She sat in the pew through the whole service, refusing to stand or kneel at the appropriate times. John's patience had worn thin over the rubber bands, and as they stood to pray the Our Father, John picked Christie up and held her to force her to behave. Throughout the prayer he looked straight into his little sister's face, encouraging her to join along, which she did. At least, she tried to. She got the last couple of words for each phrase, and her toddler voice rang out so high and sweet, John forgot his irritation with her and held her through the rest of service, including carrying her up to Communion with him. Christie was beaming with the attention and even tried to sing the Recessional Song.

John hadn't seen Mrs. McNeally during Mass and was getting worried that she and Diana hadn't made it. After Mass, his family stayed in their pew while Father talked as per their usual. Christie was getting heavy in John's arms, but he was afraid if he put her down now she would start fussing. He was pulling his necktie out of her hands when Mrs. McNeally tapped him on the arm. Diana was standing behind her wearing what he assumed were more of Mrs. McNeally's daughter's clothes. She had on a simple flower dress that wasn't quite "Little House on the Prairie", but close. He guessed this was intentional.

"Showtime," Mrs. McNeally said with a wink as she took Diana's arm, leaning heavily on it. Diana "helped" Mrs. McNeally down the empty pew to the center aisle where John's father stood in conversation with several other men.

"Thomas! You-who, Thomas!" Mrs. McNeally warbled loudly, waving a small, old-fashioned hanky in her free hand. Just like the week before, Father got a caged look, but he seemed to resign himself to it much quicker than last time. Again, John could not hear what Father said. Mrs. McNeally flourished her handkerchief as she said, "Thomas, this is my grandniece, Diana. She is going to be staying with me through the summer to help me out. These old bones just don't get around like they used to. I'd be indebted to you if your girls could take her under their wing and keep her company from time to time. The poor thing will go daft with just this poor old widow to keep her company. She's such an angel, listening to me go on and on about my arthritis and the bone spur on my foot and my aching back…, oh, sorry, I'm going off-course! I won't bother you with such things in the House of the Lord. I want to ask if I can send her over when I run out of things for her to do. She could help your girls out and learn a thing or two about what is expected from proper young ladies on a farm."

John couldn't tell if Father was pleased Mrs. McNeally just complimented his daughters or annoyed that she was dragging him into another scene. Either way, he appeared to comply as he said something, nodded, then stretched out a hand to take in the row of his girls. Diana kept her head respectfully bowed throughout the entire conversation, but John saw her peek up to give Beth and Abby small smiles of greeting.

Mrs. McNeally started to pat her brow with her hanky and leaned even more heavily into Diana. She kept this up as she continued, "Like I said, I'd be indebted to you. I apologize, Thomas, but I must ask to borrow your boy one more time this week. I've been meaning to clear out the shed since Arthur passed and just haven't gotten around to it. I made an appointment at this recycling place in Pittsburgh that will take a lot of the junk laying around. I'd like John to help me load the truck, then ride into town with me to help unload it. It shouldn't take him from his chores. And make sure he brings his work gloves; a lot of the scrap pieces are rough around the edges."

Father asked her a question to which she said, "Wednesday."

Mrs. McNeally gave her parting address, "Thank you ever so much, Thomas. You are so kind to help out an old woman during the end of her days. Every morning I thank the Good Lord for allowing me one more day on this beautiful earth. It's having generous, Christian neighbors such as yourself that make living in this decrepit old body bearable." She patted Father's arm, giving him a generous swipe with the handkerchief in the process. She pulled her hand back to sneeze loudly into the hanky. Father visibly cringed. "Enjoy your day," Mrs. McNeally sniffed as she pulled Diana into the aisle and leaned on her all the way out the door. Diana, head still bowed, gave John a sideways look that just about cracked his composure. He could see Diana study his sisters as she left with Mrs. McNeally, her smile growing when she looked back at John holding Christie.

* * *

John was ready to crawl out of his skin by the end of the day. He hadn't heard from Diana or Mrs. McNeally, and he was certain something had gone wrong. It didn't help that his sisters wanted to chatter on endlessly about Diana. Beth and Abby seemed to be doing a pretty good job of pretending like they hadn't met Diana before. In the middle of the afternoon, Beth and Abby found him practicing his projection out in one of the fields and got him to bring them up-to-date on all that had happened. They both looked incredibly jealous over his newfound ability to project. Beth made him painstakingly describe every step Diana had taken him through, and he could tell she was trying to do them herself.

Finally, just before supper, Diana came over with two strawberry rhubarb pies from Mrs. McNeally. She went inside the house and didn't come back out. When John went in for supper, Diana was sitting at the table chatting happily with every single one of his sisters except for Gracie, who was in the living room with Mother. Apparently, Diana was staying for supper.

John had a hard time concentrating during supper with Diana there. He guessed he was afraid what his family would think of Diana, and what Diana would think of his family. Father welcomed Diana to the table but didn't ask her any questions. It was a quiet dinner, and it went by quickly. The pies Diana brought over were delicious, and Father told Diana to thank Mrs. McNeally for them. After dinner, Father told John to walk Diana back to Mrs. McNeally's, as it was getting late.

Perfect! John thought. Beth and Abby dallied and looked as if they wanted to go with them, but Father called them into the living room. John held the door open for Diana, and he followed her out of the house.

They didn't speak until they hit the rows of maple trees. "So am I to die of curiosity, or are you going to tell me what happened today?" John blurted out.

Diana laughed at him as she told him, "It went better than expected. I snagged us a couple of uniforms as well as a magnetic badge to open the doors. I found the daily schedule for the 'residents' and wandered around getting familiar with the layout. I found the room in the basement where they put the deceased before they are sent to the funeral home. We can take him out of there."

"So, we have to get to his room unseen, make him look like he died, get someone to find him and take him to the basement, then you make him invisible, and we walk him outside. Sounds simple enough."

"How's your projection practice coming along? How far can you get the light to bend?"

"I can make it bend as far as possible without going behind the mirror," John answered. He was frustrated he couldn't get it to move around the mirror.

"That's wonderful, John! Now you have to visualize the light curving around the mirror. First you bend the angle of the reflection, and then you have to make it curve around so it can go behind you."

John scratched the back of his head. "Okay, I'll give it a try." When they reached Mrs. M's yard, he stopped and asked, "Hey! Why didn't you offer to go invisible the first time I brought you to Mrs. M's? We went through all that trouble with the hats and the clothes, and you could have just made yourself invisible! What gives?"

Diana looked down at her feet, and John could have sworn she was blushing. "I was too shy, and I didn't want to freak you guys out."

John thought about it and guessed that maybe she was right. If he'd seen her go invisible before hearing the big explanation, he may have turned and run. "I guess that makes sense."

John went inside with Diana to see Mrs. McNeally before heading home. "You be careful tomorrow, Mrs. M. You don't want anyone to think you're connected to Michael, or you'll be questioned. If Michael hasn't talked, they probably don't even have his name," John advised.

"Don't you worry about me, dearie, I can figure things out. Diana, why don't you head over to the Brown's tomorrow while I'm gone? There's no sense in you staying by yourself all day."

Once back in his loft, John practiced bending the light from his desk lamp. He tried to visualize the light curving in every way he could think of, but nothing worked. He went to bed frustrated and soon fell into a restless sleep.

He dreamed he was in a funhouse mirror room. He had to make a laser beam bounce from one mirror to the next, hitting every single mirror. He had to keep starting over, because when he got to the second mirror, he lost hold of the laser beam from the first mirror. Then a Jedi was trying to skewer him with a light saber, and he had to bend the light in the light saber, so it wouldn't touch him. Then he was dressed like a clown riding a unicycle with several spotlights on him. He had to make the spotlights bend around him, or he would get burned. Then the dream would loop back to the funhouse. Each time the dream looped, he had a harder time making the light bend. After a few cycles of this, Diana appeared at the funhouse wearing her Zigon dress. She moved backwards in slow motion into the position of her statue. It was weird seeing her skirt and hair move from a standstill into a swirl then freeze. As soon as she completed the pose, she turned to stone right in front of him.

"No!" John screamed and tried to reach for her, but he couldn't move his feet. Then her reflection replicated through every mirror in the room. John felt a warm breath on his neck as someone whispered, "Can you feel it, John? Can you feel your Visity move the Pleovis? You have to feel it, or you will not be able to protect yourself." He finally was able to move his feet, and he started searching for Diana but kept hitting mirrors. The voice at his ear said, "Use the Pleovis to protect yourself. You must protect yourself." The dream morphed from one crazy situation to another, all of them requiring him to bend light to save himself. Statue Diana made continual appearances as did the voice at his ear. He could never turn around to see who was talking. The tickle on his neck startled him every time, but for some reason the voice didn't scare him, much. The longer the dream went on, the worse his ability to bend light became, and he was getting burned and cut at every turn. He was exhausted when his alarm clock woke him up the next day. The dream wounds had been so realistic; he half expected them to still be there. A quick check verified there were no actual cuts or burns. The dream's message had seared its way into his memory, despite his attempts to shake it off.

CHAPTER 13 – FARMING FOLLY

John started off the day with his morning chores. His dream kept running through his mind, the disembodied warnings challenging him. He was a bit freaked out about the thought that he might need to protect himself. He decided to try to move beyond just visualization to see if he could feel his Visity, or projection, or Pleovis, or anything. After he finished his chores and ate breakfast, he had some rare free time for himself. He took his pocket mirror and walked to a copse of trees edging one of the many streams that cut through the farm. He sat with his back to a tree where spots of sunlight filtered through the branches. He held his mirror in his palm under one such ray of light and worked on bending the reflected beam. It took him several tries, mentally tracing the path of the light from between the rustling leaves above, down to his mirror, then bouncing out again, before he got it to work. He could make the light reflection move, but he couldn't keep it there; it returned back to its normal trajectory as soon as his mental path reached the end of its run and returned back up to the treetops. It was perfect weather, the temperature not too hot and not too cold. The breeze lazily rustled the leaves and branches as birds tweeted and whistled. John breathed in the beautiful day, trying to relax as he repeated the task over and over again. He closed his eyes, still continuing the mental exercise. As he let his brain grow fuzzy, dropping all thoughts except the path of the light, he noticed his thought pattern changed subtly. He still followed the path of the light, but where it hit the mirror, it corkscrewed away at the angle he wanted instead of just flowing in straight lines.

John tried focusing just on that corkscrew movement, and, when he opened his eyes the light reflection was steady at the unnatural angle. John imagined the corkscrew curving around his hand, and to his incredulous delight, the light started to follow. Within seconds, the light was hitting the mirror, any sign of refracted light gone, and the spot of sunlight continued below his hand as if his hand and the mirror weren't even there. John put the mirror down and tried the same thing with just his hand, and it worked. John nearly whooped with joy. He raced back to the house to find Beth or Abby to show them his new trick. He found them alone in the vegetable garden next to the house. Abby was thrilled, but Beth didn't give much of a reaction. If John didn't know any better, he'd say she was jealous, but that's one emotion he'd never seen on Beth before, so he wasn't sure. Meg came by to check the girls' progress, so John left them to it.

At lunch, Father told John to hook up the brush hog to the tractor and clear out the northwest pasture on the far end of the property. The tractor wouldn't start, so he had to do some tinkering to get it running. He had black grease over his hands and was sweating profusely when Diana stepped into the building where he was working. John tried not to be embarrassed; farm work was messy. He couldn't help it, however, when he looked down at himself then looked at Diana leaning on the inside of the doorframe all clean and fresh and pretty. Pretty? Did he really think she was pretty? Looking at her with her golden hair lit from behind by the sun, her blue eyes and a smile on her face just for him, he thought, *yeah, she's pretty.*

He shook himself out of his train of thought as he realized he'd just been standing there, staring at her without saying anything. He grabbed a rag and tried to wipe off his hands as he walked over to her.

"Hi," Diana said shyly.

"Hi," John said back. After a few more awkward moments of just standing there, John said, "Hey, I um, got the light to bend around my hand." He held out his hand in the light, making a shadow on the dusty stone floor. Then he made the light warp around his hand so his shadow disappeared.

Diana's eyes widened as she stared at his missing shadow. "You did it," she said looking up to him in awe. "You did it all on your own. I was going to walk you through several more steps, but you figured it out all by yourself. John, that's amazing!" The enthusiasm started to build within Diana as she talked, to the point she was almost bouncing at her last statement. She took a step towards him and looked like she wanted to hug him, but after noticing how dirty he was, she came to her senses in time and stepped back.

"Can you tell me how you did it? There are several ways to approach it, and I'm curious to see which one you found."

"I was mentally following the light as you told me and was making it bend. When I closed my eyes and relaxed, I noticed the light moving in a corkscrew as it changed course. I started working on just that part, the corkscrew, and, wah-la! No shadow," John explained as he made his shadow appear and disappear again.

Diana smiled up at him and shook her head back and forth in disbelief. "That's amazing, John! You weren't seeing the light corkscrew; you were seeing the Pleovis moving! Usually, new students have to meditate hours and hours to see the Pleovis!"

"But I only saw that one little part, and wait… my eyes were shut, so how did I 'see' it?" John asked, confused. He started to rub the hair on the back of his head then stopped himself as he remembered the grease on his hands.

"You were changing the Pleovis, and disruptions are easier to see. In time, I'm guessing you'll be able to pick up more. You don't *see* the Pleovis in the traditional sense; it is more like you intuit it, and your brain translates the sensations as a kind of internal sight," Diana explained, her smile still strong.

"The next things to learn are how to keep the pattern going without your having to focus on it every second, and how to make it work all over your body from every angle," Diana continued. "To keep it going, you have to snap back your Visity in a single point, then surge it forward to surround your projection, and release it. To make it work all over your body, you have to make a mental suit of armor made up of millions of corkscrews like you did with your hand. It's like…"

"Sorry, Diana," John reluctantly cut her off mid-sentence. "I have to get back to work. I need to cut the brush in the northwest pasture. Can you stick around until after, so we can talk some more?"

Diana visibly deflated as she replied, "Sure, I'll go see what your sisters are up to."

John self-consciously went back to work on the tractor. After a few minutes, Diana left. John wondered why he felt so guilty. He was guilty if he brushed off his farm duties and guilty if he didn't focus on the New Zigon stuff. He couldn't win. He tried starting up the tractor one more time, and it choked into life. *Finally!* John thought as he went to task getting the brush hog hooked up. He didn't dare shut the tractor off for fear it wouldn't start again.

John drove the tractor out to the northwest pasture and hopped down to get the brush hog set to go. As he worked, he wondered why Father had left this land fallow this year. It was surrounded by fields of their various cash crops, and they didn't have electrical fencing out this far to bring the cows to pasture. There was a utility road along the far side at the property's border that went all the way to the main road, which made this plot a little unique. John couldn't puzzle it out and just let his mind wander. He'd made four passes along the field when he spotted Diana walking with Alice and Bunny, heading his way. John wondered how she got grouped in with those two. Alice and Bunny were close in age, Bunny being eleven and Alice twelve. They both had blond hair, although Alice's was much lighter. The three of them walking together made quite a picture as they made their way along one of the split rail fences. With the sun lighting up their different shades of blond hair, the gentle breeze blowing it away from their faces, and the picturesque farmland scenery behind them, it made John's heart settle soundly for a moment. As John continued his slow back and forth passes across the pasture, he wondered what Diana thought of Alice and Bunny. Those two were close friends, and you rarely saw one without the other, unless, of course, Bunny went wandering. Bunny had a bright, cheerful personality, but sometimes John would swear her brain got detached or something. She had the shortest attention span of anyone he knew and had the hardest time with her school lessons out of all the girls. She loved to wander around the farm in a daydream, which often got her lost. Recently, Alice seemed to be Bunny's self-appointed watcher, and Bunny hadn't wandered off on her own in months.

Alice was a troublemaker. She was high-energy and loved physical activity. John bet she would be fantastic at sports if she went to a real school. Without adequate outlets, her energy often was channeled into mischief. Somehow, she always seemed to get away with things. She would use Bunny as an excuse for exploring off the farm, and she often pinned blame for other things on the twins. The twins were only seven, but John had the feeling they were starting to catch on to Alice's set-up jobs. The fact that Alice looked like an angel with her pale blond hair, fair complexion, and hazel eyes, helped her to talk her way out of things more often than not.

John worried that Alice might pull Diana into some harebrained scheme and get her into trouble. He was finishing another pass as the girls reached the fence enclosing the pasture. All three climbed on it and sat on the top rail to watch him. He turned, driving away from them on the other side of the pasture along the opposite fence. Trees grew along almost every fence line where it was difficult to mow, and the trees shading this side of the field provided a welcome reprieve from the sun.

John twisted backwards in his seat to give the girls a smile and a wave. He called out to them, "I'm almost done!" Maybe if he'd kept both hands on the wheel, the accident wouldn't have happened. If he hadn't turned around like a fool for so long, it definitely wouldn't have happened. As the girls returned his wave and were making gestures in an attempt to communicate over the roar of the tractor, a branch caught John right across his back and he was thrown from his seat. Off the tractor. Onto the ground. In front of the oncoming brush hog.

As he fell, besides thinking, *Oh, crap!* John remembered Father saying, "Even though these blades aren't sharp, each one is several inches thick, and when they are spinning at 150 mph, you'd better not be anywhere near them."

Well, he was about to be very, very near those blades. John hit the ground, barely missing the back wheel of the tractor. His head and shoulders were clear of the brush hog's path, but the other half of him wasn't. He had one, maybe two seconds before the brush hog would run him over. Time seemed to freeze for John in that moment. He wondered, "Where are the scenes from my whole life that are supposed to be flashing before my eyes?" Surprisingly, the only memory that came to him was one from his nightmare last night. He remembered the voice saying, "Use the Pleovis to protect yourself. You must protect yourself!"

He didn't know if it was instinct driving him, or adrenaline, or something else buried deep down inside, but he felt like his mind exploded in all directions, leaving his head empty and dizzy. His chest grew warm like his heart was overheating. He should have closed his eyes, but it was like watching a train wreck, a train wreck that…didn't happen. It felt surreal as he watched the brush hog roll over him, *over* being the operative word. It was as if there was an invisible ramp lying on top of him. He watched as the one wheel, still spinning, rose up over his body and lowered back to the ground on his other side, the deadly blades never reaching him.

The cut ground cover was another matter. After the brush hog passed, it tossed up a blanket of twigs, grass, and weeds that draped over his invisible body armor. John let out the breath he didn't know he was holding, and the space between him and the cuttings disappeared, allowing the vegetation to fall the rest of the way, covering him. John laid his head back in the newly cut field and heard the tractor sputter and die now that his foot was no longer on the gas pedal. As the sound of the tractor and spinning brush hog died, a new sound took its place. Screaming. Blood curdling, think-someone-is-going-to-die, screaming.

CHAPTER 14 – REPERCUSSIONS

Which is what John should be right now, dead, or at least he should be much, much shorter than he was a few moments ago. He was giddy with shock and relief, and his brain was making bad jokes!

The screams were closing in on him fast, and he heard his name being called. With a groan he rolled out of the path the brush hog had taken, the cuttings coming with him, sticking to his sweaty skin and clothes.

In a moment he had a sister on each side and Diana peering down at him overtop the girls' heads. Alice and Bunny were sobbing and calling out his name, their faces red from screaming and running across the wide field. Diana's face was drained of all color, and she looked like she was going to be sick. John lifted his head and moved to sit up. Both his sisters pushed him back down, a bit roughly he thought, given the situation.

Alice was saying, "John! Just lay still, John, it will be okay. We're here, you're not alone. Oh, God, help us!"

John realized dully that they thought the mower had got him, as well it should have! The cuttings completely covered his lower body, so they couldn't see the lack of damage. John wasn't sure what happened, but he did know he shouldn't tell his sisters the truth. So he added another lie to his list of sins.

"Hey, hey now," he said trying to be reassuring, but his voice came out hoarse. "I'm okay, just a little banged up from the fall. I must have landed clear of the brush hog. It didn't get me."

At that admission Bunny doubled her tears and wrapped her arms around his neck, sobbing on his shoulder. Alice turned and pushed all the cuttings off him like she wouldn't believe it unless she saw it with her own eyes. Once she verified his legs hadn't been turned into hamburger, she hugged him and started crying on his chest. Diana, he saw, was looking from him to the spot where he'd been moments before, a slight frown on her face. She walked over to where he originally fell, amulet out and in hand. John felt something float over and through him. It was almost like a mini shock wave, and it came from Diana's direction. He tried to look at what she was doing, but Alice was in the way.

John was overwhelmed at his sisters' reaction. He hadn't known they cared so much about him. He tried to reverse the situation and think of how he would feel if one of them was run over by the brush hog right in front of him. His throat got tight, and his eyes burned at the thought. He managed to pull his arms out and put one around each of his sisters and hugged them tight.

Bunny started squeezing his neck a little too hard. "Bunny My Honey," John said using her childhood nickname, "I can't breathe. Let up a bit." Both girls pulled back, sat on their knees, and tried to stifle their sobs.

"John, don't scare us like that! That could have *killed* you. You are so lucky you fell clear of that thing," Alice reprimanded. She swatted him hard on the shoulder. "Shame on you! You should have known better and watched where you were going!"

"I'm (hiccup) so glad (hiccup) you're okay," Bunny said through her drying tears.

"Can you help me sit up?" John asked. He wasn't comfortable with the unexpected attention. He felt more than a little light-headed and very tired as Bunny and Alice each grabbed an arm. Diana stood back a few paces, looking anxiously out towards the farmhouse. She was alternating between twisting her hands and rubbing them on her jeans. John's mind went off on a tangent as he thought she should know better than to wear anything other than a dress when coming over here. Father wouldn't approve.

"John," Diana worried, "Someone's coming on a horse. I think it's your father."

John looked over his shoulder towards the farmhouse, and sure enough, he saw Father riding one of their boarded horses towards them, and he did *not* look happy. John scrabbled to his feet and nearly fell over. He put an arm around each sister for support. His father reined in the horse and surveyed the situation. He was riding bareback with just a bridle on the horse. One of the buckles wasn't tucked in completely as if it had been done in haste. He wondered how Father got up on the horse without a saddle and with his bad knees. Father was always a bit scary when he was angry, and from his position up on the horse looking down at them, he looked absolutely formidable.

"What's going on here?" Father demanded. "I heard screaming."

"I was mowing the pasture with the brush hog and…" John started.

"And there was a low branch on one of the trees that knocked John off the tractor. Bunny, Diana, and I were walking by when it happened. We're the ones you heard screaming," Alice broke in to explain. John gave her a grateful squeeze on her shoulder.

Father's eyes momentarily widened before they narrowed in scrutiny. "You look to be in one piece. You hurt, boy?" Father asked with a pointed nod at John.

"N…no, Sir," John answered weakly. He sounded like a wimp to his own ears.

"You girls okay?" Father asked. Both girls nodded.

Father looked beyond them to the tractor and the brush hog attached behind it. "Tractor looks okay. You able to finish out here?" Father gruffly asked John.

John pinched his lips into a straight line, wanting to say yes, needing to say yes, but another wave of dizziness and fatigue washed over him. He didn't trust himself to get back on the tractor. "I'm sorry, sir, but I can't finish today," John said honestly. "I don't trust myself to drive right now. I could hurt myself for real or damage the equipment."

Father snorted. "Ha! At least you're smart enough to admit that!" Father finally spotted Diana standing a few feet back. His frown deepened as he looked back to John. "What were you doing, or what *weren't* you doing to get hit with a branch like that? That is sloppy work, John, very sloppy. You should know better than to *ever* take your eyes off the path!" Father's voice was getting louder and deeper with every word. "You should know better!" Father repeated, his stare drilling straight through John, making him feel six years old again. Father dismounted, his knees buckling just a bit as he hit the ground. Father quickly straightened himself and marched over to Diana. His six-foot-three-inch wiry frame towered over her as she stood frozen like a scared rabbit in front of him. He put his hands on his hips and stared down angrily at her. "What are you doing here?" Father demanded, his voice a menacing growl.

Diana visibly blanched, and her answer came out like a little child's, but she held her ground and didn't step back. "I came over to spend time with your daughters, Sir. Y . . . you invited me at supper the other day, remember?"

Father took a small step backwards, giving Diana a little more space. "Of course I remember, do you think I'm stupid?" Father said, annoyed. "What I meant was, what are you doing out *here,* in this particular field?"

"Alice, Bunny, and I were out walking. They were giving me a tour. We saw John working and we decided…" Diana paused as she saw both Alice and Bunny making frantic motions from behind their father, waving their hands and mouthing, "Noooo!" Diana seemed to pick up on the hint that they shouldn't admit to stopping to watch John. "I mean we walked along the other side of that fence over there," Diana helpfully pointed, "thinking if we stayed out of the field, we wouldn't disturb John's work."

Father stared at Diana for nearly a full minute. It seemed like one of the longest minutes in John's life. Father's scowl deepened further as he crossed his arms and bent forward a little so he was nearly face-to-face with Diana. "You didn't happen to stop when you got here, did you?" Father asked in a low, deceivingly calm voice. "Before you answer, don't lie to me, missy. I saw you girls sitting on the fence clear from the house."

"Y..yes," Diana squeaked. "We took a break from our walk and sat on the fence to see John work. I'd never seen a mower like that before."

"Let's get one thing straight," Father said, standing tall. "If you want the privilege of learning from my girls, you're going to have to follow some rules. First, you must dress like a proper young lady, no more jeans. Second, you're not to interfere with anyone's chores on this property. If I ever catch you gabbing with one of the girls when there's work to be done, or batting your eyelashes at my boy, I'll turn you out on your ear so fast, you won't know what hit you. Do I make myself clear?"

"Batting my eye…," Diana started, confused.

"DID I MAKE MYSELF CLEAR?" Father roared.

"Yes, sir," Diana said, head bowed.

"Good. Your visit's over for today. Go home," Father ordered, back to his normal tone of voice. Diana didn't say another word as she started walking away. She didn't look back. Father turned to face his children. He put his hands on his hips and stared at them, looking them up and down then locking eyes with them, each in turn. He occasionally looked over to the tractor then back to them. He seemed to grow more agitated as the minutes passed. John and the girls knew better than to speak out of turn. Father paced back and forth several times. The only sounds were the crunch of vegetation under Father's boots, some birds off in the distance, and the occasional pop or crack from Father's knees. He stopped short and wheeled on them.

"This is NEVER going to happen again, do you hear me?" Father nearly shouted, startling them.

"Yes, sir," the three said in unison.

"I nearly lost ten years of my life when you girls started screaming." Father paused, staring at the tractor. "Do you have any idea how lucky you were today, boy?" Father returned his gaze to John. "You could have been…" he choked off.

John's heart rose. Did Father actually care about him? He knew he cared that he was healthy and strong so he could do his chores, but did he care about him as a son?

"If you'd gotten yourself maimed or killed today, where would that leave the family? Where would that leave the farm? Eight years, *eight years* I've been training you to take care of this place. You're finally a strong young man and bam, in a few seconds it could have all been for nothing."

John's heart fell as Father's words sank in.

Father started pacing again. "You were incredibly irresponsible today, John. I've warned you enough times about the dangers of towing machinery with the tractor. People *die* from the kind of mistake you made. Farming can be dangerous work. Apparently, you haven't learned this lesson." Father stopped with his back to them as he said, "After dinner tonight, meet me at the horse coral. Twenty straps."

John meekly said, "Yes, sir." Twenty straps were more than he'd ever had before. Father must be beyond angry. John trembled from head to toe in anticipation of the punishment.

"And you girls," Father said sternly as he whirled back to look at them. Bunny and Alice both took a step back as they took in a simultaneous deep breath. "You are old enough to know not to do *anything* to distract someone driving a tractor. You hold some of the blame in this."

John still had an arm around his sisters' shoulders. He gave them each a gentle squeeze and pulled them in closer to him. They were both trembling but seemed to be strengthened by his small show of support.

"As your punishment…" Father waited ten full seconds before continuing, "You are to be on dish duty for two weeks, and you're going to muck out the horse stalls every day for a month."

John felt both girls move their upper body backwards as they got whiplash from Father's verdict and punishment. John couldn't believe Alice had the guts to talk back as she said, "But, Father, mucking out stalls is men's work. We can't…"

"You can, and you will!" Father said sternly, brooking no further argument. "Now," Father said in a back-to-business tone, "You girls take John and the horse back. John, you can rest until evening chores. I'll finish the field. Go on, go," he said, shooing them away with his hands.

John took the horse's bridle as they headed back. He was still uncertain on his feet and thought the horse would provide more support than either or both of his sisters. Besides, it looked much better to come in off the field leading a horse than hobbling back supported by two small girls.

"John, I'm so sorry," Alice whispered when they were about halfway to the house.

"Me, too," agreed Bunny.

"Twenty straps, that's …," Alice couldn't finish her thought. John couldn't come up with words for it either.

"Don't worry about it. Nothing happened. There's nothing to apologize for," John insisted.

"Twenty straps isn't *nothing*," Alice argued.

John didn't have a response for that. They made it back in the barn, and surprisingly, the girls each gave him a quick hug before running for the house. John sighed. He guessed he would have company soon, once they spread the news. He was thankful there wasn't a saddle on the horse. He didn't think he would have the strength to lift it off if there were. He picked up the brush and started working the horse's coat. He wished there was someone else to do this; he felt so tired. If he had any energy left, he would have jumped out of his skin at the touch on his forearm. Diana was standing right next to him, a concerned look on her face. "How do you feel?" she asked, giving his arm a small squeeze before letting go.

"Okay, I guess," he answered without much conviction. At her querulous look he said, "Dizzy and tired. I feel dizzy and tired, like my entire head blew up, and there's not much left."

"Do you realize what happened out there?" she asked gently. "Besides you almost *dying*?" She roughly whispered.

"I was incredibly careless?" John said sarcastically.

"John, I think you know what I'm talking about. That mower went right over you, but you're not hurt. I was so scared, my mind just froze. All I did was run, following your sisters. I didn't help at all," Diana finished miserably.

"Don't worry about it. I fell clear, it didn't get me," John answered automatically, keeping to his lie, although he didn't know why. This was Diana he was talking to after all.

"John," she said undeterred. "You did something. Even if I hadn't felt the ripples in the Pleovis, I saw the place where you'd fallen. The brush wasn't cut there, like the mower hopped over a spot."

John froze mid-brush and looked at her with wide, startled eyes. "Don't worry," she soothed, "I took care of it. I used my Crystavis to cut that spot so it looked like the rest of the field."

John put his other hand on the horse's flank and bowed his head for a moment, trying to pull himself together. "I thought I felt something, like maybe a small shock wave."

It was Diana's turn to widen her eyes. Her face turned contemplative. "I guess I kind of predicted that would happen, that you'd begin feeling impacts to the Pleovis. I can feel them, too, you know. That's how I know something big happened out there in the field."

John didn't lift his head as he responded numbly, "Yeah, something big happened. I should be dead right now, but…"

Diana waited, but he couldn't continue. She put her hand on his arm again and gave it a little push to turn him towards her. "John, you used the Pleovis to save yourself. I can't believe you have enough energy to still be standing. It took a tremendous amount of strength to lift up the weight of the mower like you did." Diana gave him a tender smile. "It was pretty amazing."

John finally lifted his head to look at her. He drew a little strength from her comforting presence and decided to let it all out. "I had no idea what I was doing. One second, I'm on the tractor, the next thing I know, I'm hitting the ground and have seconds before the brush hog would run me over. Then that dream voice came to me, and I just reacted. I didn't realize what I had done until I saw those blades go over me like on an invisible ramp. I don't think I could do it again, it was sort of a reflex."

Diana searched his eyes, like she was looking for something. "Dream?" she questioned.

"Yeah," John said in a shuttering breath. "More like a nightmare. I kept getting in situations where I had to bend light to save myself from something, over and over. Each time it got harder to do. You were there. You were frozen in that statue, and there was this voice in my ear saying…" John took a breath to make sure he got the wording right. "It said, 'Use the Pleovis to protect yourself. You must protect yourself.' It said something about feeling the Pleovis, too."

"John," Diana said as she took a small step towards him. "I know we joked about this before, but I really think you have some original Zigon blood in you. There's no other way to explain how you did what you did. Intuitive or not, what you did was definitely *not* a beginner level projection."

John froze at her words. "That means," Diana continued, "that you're a descendent of The Founder, either through Miranda or someone else if he had any more children while I was frozen." She paused, gauging his reaction. "There's a strong chance you could be related to Michael, too."

John didn't have time to say anything. He heard several people calling his name as they approached the barn. His sisters were coming. "Diana, you'd better go before Father sees you," he said quickly. "We'll talk tomorrow."

"Okay," Diana conceded. "Make sure you get lots to eat and get some rest. Maybe one of your sisters can finish this for you," she said gesturing at the horse. She gave him a small smile saying, "Watch and learn…" She didn't even pull out her Crystavis; she just disappeared.

John stood slack-jawed as the barn's back door opened and shut on its own. *Wow*, he thought, *I'm going to be able to do that? The possibilities!* John thought of how many times at school he tried to make himself invisible to avoid the constant teasing. If he figured out how to do that, and Diana seemed confident that he would, the whole school could be his playground! As his sisters poured through the barn's big front doors, John's conscience battled with thoughts of pranking The Crew. His sisters were all there except for Gracie. Meg and Annie reached him first. Meg gave him a swift, fierce hug. Then she pulled back, still holding his shoulders. She looked him up and down, as if to ensure herself that he wasn't harmed. She shook him forcefully a few times.

"What were you thinking, John Christopher?" Meg yelled at him. "You know better than to let yourself be thrown from the tractor!"

Annie pushed Meg's arms out of the way as she gave him a quick hug. Annie moved to his left and laid an arm around his shoulders, shaking and squeezing him into her side so they were both facing Meg. "No lectures, Meg. Can't you see how rattled he is?" Annie said.

Beth and Jo approached him next. Beth's eyes were furrowed in concern as she searched his face. She stood on his right and put a hand on his upper arm as if she wanted to touch him to make sure he was there, but afraid to at the same time. "I'm glad you're okay," she said softly. Jo grabbed ahold of his left hand and sniffled, "Oh, John! You must be more careful! Farm work can be so dangerous! You are our brother, and we don't want anything bad to happen to you!" John squeezed her hand back and was trying to say something when Alice and Bunny hit him. Bunny came in under his left arm, hugging him around the waist. Alice wormed her way between him and Beth on his right side, giving him an equally tight hug around his stomach. Neither said anything, but their eyes were tear-bright and their mouths were pressed into tight lines. They looked to still be in shock. The twins, Jane and Ellen, each grabbed a leg and held on.

Abby came last, holding Christie in her arms. Abby had tears leaking down her cheeks, and Christie was looking at him with saucer eyes. Christie lunged for his neck, and he grabbed her with his right arm since Jo still had ahold of his left. Abby came with her and tried to hug him around Christie. Meg, not to be left out, stepped into the huddle and put her hand on his shoulder. John stood for a moment in shocked silence. He couldn't remember ever feeling so much love and caring in his life. He loved his sisters, but they rarely showed affection, except for Christie and sometimes the twins. Every day was business as usual, eating meals together but not talking, sometimes watching evening TV with little to no conversation, occasionally getting together during rare free time. It wasn't always like that; when he first came to the farm, the older girls mothered him, and the younger ones looked up to him. They played together often, but as John grew older, moved to the loft, and took on more responsibilities, they saw each other less and less.

John basked in the warmth of his sister cocoon for a full minute before he began to feel awkward, and heat began to flush his neck and color his face. He cleared his throat loudly and said, "Um, I love you, too?" Some giggled at that, and several arms tightened their grips on him. Through the open barn door, John spotted Father walking out of the tractor shed towards the house. Father saw him with the girls huddled around him and almost did a double take. John thought he would come to the door and yell at them, but instead a strange look fleeted across his father's face. Immediately, Father's expression hardened as he continued on to the house. John's stomach lurched at the thought of the punishment waiting for him after supper.

John cleared his throat once more and said placatingly, "Ladies, ladies, don't worry now, I'm not going anywhere. You might want to go somewhere else though, soon. This horse here is due to let out some nasty gas, and we are standing within the impact zone." John knew it was a lame, crude joke, but he had to break this sad, teary-eyed mood before he did something embarrassing and emotional.

His comment earned him a near simultaneous, "Eww, John!" as his sisters released him and stepped back. Little Christie was pinching her nose in anticipation, one tiny arm still wrapped around his neck.

Abby asked, "How are you doing, John?"

"I'm a little sore from the fall, and I'm *really* tired," John admitted as he bent down and picked up the horse brush, which he'd dropped during the sister-onslaught.

"Let me take care of this for you," Abby offered, snatching the brush from John's hand. "Go get some rest before dinner."

Beth offered, "I can do the afternoon milking for you."

"I can feed the animals," Annie said.

"It sounds like everything is covered," Meg declared. "Now march yourself up those steps and have yourself a lie-down."

John did as he was told and trudged to his room to find his bed. He fell asleep the second his head hit the pillow. It seemed like he'd barely closed his eyes when Beth was shaking him roughly awake. "It's time for dinner," she said. "You'd better wash up a bit. You look like you were rolling around in the field."

The mood at dinner was a somber one. Father didn't talk much, other than to announce to the family John's near miss that day, and Alice and Bunny's part in it. Mother dropped her fork, and it clattered as it hit the table. John stared at his plate as Father gave a short lecture on the seriousness and safety issues of dangerous farm equipment. To his horror, Father announced their punishments. By the sound of several intakes of breath, John guessed Alice and Bunny hadn't shared that part of the story. John pushed the food around his plate before forcing it all down. He didn't want to upset Father further by wasting food.

After dinner Mother approached John, holding Gracie on her hip. She put a hand on his shoulder, giving it a squeeze. "I'm glad you're okay," she said simply as she stared at him, searching his face. "That was a serious error in judgment you made today. You know that kind of mistake cannot go unpunished." John nodded, not sure how to handle the sympathy in her eyes. Mother moved her hand to John's cheek, giving it a gentle pat before turning away. John headed to the horse paddock as Father went into the living room and picked up his unfinished newspaper. John sat on the fence and tried to clear his mind. This was always part of the punishment. Father would make him wait there so he'd plenty of time to think about what he did wrong as his anxiety over the pending strapping grew.

Finally, Father left the house and went into the horse barn to get the strap used solely for this purpose. Father met him at the part of the paddock that was hidden from both the house and the road. As John jumped off the fence, Father said gruffly, "You know what to do." When John didn't move, Father's voice rose in anger as he said, "drop those pants, and hands on the railing."

John was mortified. He hadn't had the strap in almost two years. He felt way too old to be dropping his drawers like that, but he complied. Father delivered his punishment quickly and efficiently. The hits from the strap lit his bum on fire, but they never broke the skin. John grunted but resisted crying or screaming. He winced as he hooked his overalls back on his shoulders, gritting his teeth. He understood the severe consequences that could have happened from his fall today, and the pain he was feeling would guarantee he would never divert his eyes even an inch while driving the tractor from now on. He also knew he would have trouble sitting down for several days.

To his complete astonishment, Father grasped him by the shoulder and said, "You were very lucky today, John," as he gently shook him. "We all were," he said so quietly, John wondered if he'd imagined it. John made it back to his room, and, when he closed the door behind him, he finally let the tears fall. He slept on his stomach that night.

CHAPTER 15 – DEMENTED DIVERSION

Tuesday was a difficult day for John. He was basically going through the motions with his chores, his mind constantly on their plan for the next day or wondering what Mrs. McNeally would learn at the courthouse. John felt awful. He was still dizzy and tired from the day before, and his bruised rear end was painfully uncomfortable. He wished he knew how to heal himself, like Diana had done. Father showed some unexpected compassion in having his sisters deliver his meals to him in the loft. This way John could eat standing up. He didn't think he could bear sitting through a meal.

John was just finishing his supper, standing at his desk, when he heard a knock on his door. He muffled out a "Come in," while he still had food in his mouth. The door opened and closed of its own accord, and then Diana materialized right in front of him. John nearly choked on his last bite of food.

"Sorry," Diana said, "I didn't mean to scare you. It's just that I didn't want anyone to see me, and I thought you'd want to find out what happened at the hearing today."

"No problem," John said as he pounded his chest. "So…?"

"So…, he was found mentally incompetent to stand trial and is going to be transferred to West Penn Psych tomorrow morning."

"So we're going tomorrow then."

"Yes," Diana said on a huge exhale of breath. "How's your invisibility practice been going?"

"Not all that great," John said, looking at his boots. "I can make my shadow completely disappear, but that's it." He had been practicing off and on all day, but with his nerves on edge he didn't get very far.

"Let's work on it then," Diana said as she stepped further into the room. She gave him the direction again to imagine making an entire suit of the corkscrew pattern around his body, starting with just his hand and arm. John got increasingly discouraged as he couldn't get what Diana was talking about.

"How about I show you what it is supposed to look like," Diana said. She reached out and grabbed his hand. "I'm going to make your hand and arm invisible. Watch for the impact my projection has on the Pleovis."

John watched intently as Diana made his hand disappear up to his elbow.

He could pick up the Pleovis moving, but he couldn't actually describe how he was seeing it. It didn't have any color, yet he sensed the movement. It looked like he had a spiraling, twisting gauntlet wrapping in every direction around his arm and hand.

"See if you can make the rest of your arm invisible," Diana suggested. This was something he could actually do. Once the pattern was started, it wasn't too hard to make it grow up his arm.

After working for a full hour, John was able to make himself invisible, but only if Diana started it for him by making his hand invisible first. He couldn't get the projection going on his own. Diana decided that it was probably good enough, and that he needed to work on making a projection stick. "You can continue maintaining the projection directly, but it takes a lot more power, and if your concentration slips, the projection will drop," Diana told him.

She told him to think of snapping back his Visity into a single point, then surging it forward to surround his projection, then release it. After that didn't work, she told him to think of it like throwing a fishing line, to whip it back then throw it forward, releasing the wheel to let it fly. John got it to work for a bit, but he could only lock his projection for five minutes or so before it dissipated.

It was getting late, and John was tired and frustrated. "I'm not getting any better, Diana. You may as well go home. Big day tomorrow and all."

"Don't be down, John, you're doing great! You're trying to learn something in a couple of days that would normally take months. Seriously, you're making amazing progress!"

John started pacing as he rubbed his hand on the back of his head. "But I don't have a month. I need to know how to do this *tomorrow*!"

"We'll have the uniforms, so if your projection breaks, you won't stand out. I can help you with the invisibility projection. The only time I really need you to take it up on your own is when we get to Michael, and I have to make it look like he died. It *will* work," Diana said confidently.

John stopped his pacing to give her a dubious look. "I can't do anymore tonight. I guess I'll see you tomorrow after breakfast at Mrs. M's?"

"Okay," Diana said, taking the hint. "I'll see you tomorrow." She disappeared, making herself invisible. "Good night," her voice floated through the air before the door shut behind her.

"Good night," John said to the now empty room.

* * *

The next morning John walked over to Mrs. McNeally's as prearranged. When he got there, he expected they would be heading straight into the city, but Mrs. McNeally had different ideas. She had the truck backed up to one of her many out-buildings. "Where are your work gloves?" she asked him.

"I didn't think you were serious about that."

She huffed as she grabbed a pair of work gloves for each of them before walking to the truck saying, "I was telling your father the truth about cleaning out this junk and taking it to Pittsburgh. We're doing that first. So let's get to work!"

John thought to himself, *should've known*, as he put on the proffered gloves and started hauling dirty, rusty scrap pieces onto the truck bed. He ended up doing almost all of the work. Mrs. McNeally directed them as to what needed to go, and Diana delicately picked her way through the clutter, moving smaller items out of the way. When John asked her if she could just magic all of the junk into the truck, she rolled her eyes and hissed between her teeth, "It's not magic, it's…"

"Science, I know," John interrupted. "So, can you *science* all this stuff into the truck?"

"I could, but I need to save my energy for our trip into town," she said evasively, ignoring his jibe.

When they couldn't fit another single piece into the truck, Mrs. McNeally had them cover it with a tightly secured tarp to prevent pieces from flying out when they were on the highway. By then John and Diana were dirty and sweaty. John was getting anxious as it was already 8:30 in the morning. They cleaned up and changed into the stolen uniforms, wearing a normal shirt and saving the bright white shirts for when they arrived at the institute. John was worried that his clunky work boots would give him away, but Diana reasoned out that if he did actually show himself, it would only be for a short time, and people probably wouldn't be looking at his feet. Piling into the truck, Diana got into the middle again, and John eased himself onto the passenger side. He swallowed back his wince as he sat down. He tried to hold himself up off the seat just an inch or so to avoid the worst of the pain. The way Mrs. McNeally had the bench seat so close to the dash, it actually made it easier for him. He used his knees to brace himself between the dash and the seat back. He reckoned Mrs. McNeally hit every single pothole on that country road, regardless of which lane it was in. Somehow he managed to hide his discomfort from the two females. It was a long ride into Pittsburgh. Mrs. McNeally stopped somewhere on the North Side to dump the scrap metal. John got out to "stretch his legs" but luckily there were enough guys there that he didn't have to help unload the truck. He and Diana donned their uniform shirts, and by the time they got back on the road, it was after 10:30 a.m.

John was miserable. He had a hard time keeping his bum off the seat, and every time he waivered, he wanted to cry out with the pain. On top of that, he was terribly nervous about this rescue plan. When they talked it through in the safety of Mrs. McNeally's kitchen, it sounded so simple, but as they approached the huge West Penn Psych facility, he wondered what in the world they had been thinking. Diana grabbed his hand, and they both went invisible before pulling into the parking lot. Mrs. McNeally gave them a sideways glance then patted their faces awkwardly with her hand as she drove. "Just checking," she said cheerfully as she parked the truck.

"Okay, let's go over the plan real quick," said Mrs. McNeally. "I'm going to come around and open your door like I need to get something, and you two will slip out. I'll hobble my way into the building, and you can follow me through the doors. I'll hang out in the lobby as your backup. You find Michael, fake his death, and follow him down to the morgue. John will come get me, and I'll drive around and pick you up."

John was glad they couldn't see the worried look on his face as he said, "No problem. We'll be in and out." Famous last words.

John and Diana held hands as they followed Mrs. McNeally. They could 'see' each other by the corkscrew ripples they created in the Pleovis, but by holding hands, Diana could help John keep up the invisibility projection. He didn't say so, but it helped him maintain a semblance of calm as well. Mrs. McNeally took her good old time making her way into the building, and John was ready to jump out of his skin by the time she sat down in the lobby. Diana led the way to a set of locked double doors. Diana had stolen a keycard but didn't want to use it where people were watching, so they waited until an employee opened the door and slipped through before it closed. John's mind wandered, wondering how she'd managed to get a keycard. He'd have to remember to ask her later.

They came upon a nurse's station, and Diana left him to hurry behind the desk and snoop around. She rejoined John and whispered in his ear, "He got here earlier this morning, and he's already been processed. They have lunch in the cafeteria at 11:45, which is in twenty-five minutes. I say we get him there, where lots of people can witness his 'dying."

They walked to the main set of elevator banks, and, blessedly, it was deserted. Diana pushed the call button and whispered, "The cafeteria is on the second floor. There should be signs as soon as we get off the elevator."

Their luck continued as the first elevator was empty. Diana pressed the second floor button as they boarded. John wanted to hold Diana's hand again, but for some reason, he was paralyzingly shy over it. The doors were almost shut when a hand was thrust daringly between the closing jaws, triggering the doors to reopen and allowing several employees to flood into the elevator. John scurried to one corner as Diana moved to the other. Once they were all in, they heard someone call, "Hold the door!" Another employee pushing a patient in a wheelchair backed them both into the car. The other passengers crowded in closer to make room. John was afraid to breathe as he flattened himself tighter into the corner. Luckily, no one pressed too close. "Tenth floor, please," asked the newcomer. Finally, the doors closed and the elevator lifted them up to the second floor. Several of the employees were disembarking, and the guy with the wheelchair patient pushed out of the elevator to make room for people to exit. John saw Diana's rippled outline slip out of the elevator with the crowd. The person blocking

John didn't move. John managed to wriggle out from behind him, just as the guy with the wheelchair patient rolled back onto the elevator car, blocking his exit. The doors shut and he was being lifted up higher into the facility, leaving Diana behind on the second floor.

No problem, thought John. *I'll just ride the elevator out until I can get to the second floor.* It was a good plan in theory. Unfortunately, his elevator suddenly became very popular. They frequently went to the second floor, but no matter where John positioned himself, he couldn't get out of the car without bumping into someone. He was struggling to hold onto his invisibility projection as it was, and he didn't know if he could maintain it if someone touched him. After a while the walls seemed to close in on him, and John feared he would start to hyperventilate. He couldn't take anymore of the crowded elevator and got off on the relatively empty eighth floor, deciding it would be easier to take the stairs. He saw a sign pointing right that said STAIRS, so he headed that direction. He must have missed the next sign, because he'd entered a patient sitting room of sorts. There were elderly people dressed in hospital gowns, pajama's and robes, sitting around on couches, chairs, and in wheelchairs. Most stared off into space while others watched TV.

John turned to leave when a voice rang out, "I see you, Zigonian!" John froze, unsure of what to do. The voice entreated, "Please come. Come here. Don't worry, no one can see you. *But I can see you!*" The person nearly sang the last part. John realized it was a woman. He turned and scanned the room. A little old lady sat in a chair at a table by the far window. She was waving and motioning him towards her. "*I can see you*," she lilted. "Come here and talk to me. Come on now, don't be shy. Surely you can spare an old fellow citizen a few moments of your time?" When John didn't move, she continued her coaxing, "Come now, I won't bite. I don't even have a Crystavis. You get over here before I have to get up and come to you. Don't be rude now by making me walk all the way over there!"

"Claire, clam up. No more *Zigon* babbling. We are sick to death hearing about your fairy tales and magic nonsense," said a bald, burly old man planted in front of one of the TV's, holding a remote control.

"Don't mind him, he's just jealous he can't see you!" retorted the woman, who was apparently named Claire.

Twisting to face Claire, the man grumbled, "Jealous of your stupid rantings? Woman, you're crazy if you think anyone is jealous of your personal la-la land!"

A thin, gray-haired man sharing the couch with the grumbler said, "If you're not going to watch the television, hand over the remote, you old toad." The bald man apparently decided that keeping dominion over the remote was more important than heckling Claire, since he turned back to the TV and didn't say another word.

John's curiosity got the better of him, and he started making his way towards the back window and Claire. John knew it was a mad diversion, but he just sighed and added it to his rapidly filling crazy train. Claire beamed at him out of her old, wizened face as he approached. She continued to wave him towards her the entire time. When he reached her, she motioned him to sit down. John opted to lean against the window frame, as sitting was definitely out for the day, and maybe even the rest of the week.

Claire didn't seem offended at his refusal to sit. "Well?" she asked, her whole face lit up with expectation and delight.

"Well what?" John whispered.

"Well, tell me who you are. How old are you? Where did you come from? Who are your parents?"

"My name is John, I'm fourteen, I live on a farm north of the city, and I don't know who my parents were. I was adopted." The information just spilled out of his mouth. John wanted to slap himself. He didn't want to give this little bird of a woman any details about himself, so why did he say all that? "Who are you? What's *your* story?" he asked quietly. *Better to turn the table on her*, he thought. Why was he even having a conversation with her in the first place? He needed to find the stairs and get back to Diana. He glanced at a clock on the wall and found it was 11:30 a.m. He had lost ten whole minutes on his elevator ride. John pushed himself off the window frame with the intention of heading towards the door when Claire started speaking.

"My name is Claire. I am one hundred and eighty-nine years old. I am descended from one of the greatest Crystavis Masters of Magnetism of all time. I studied the science of the Magnetism Avenue for the first one hundred years of my life, and spent the last eighty-odd years trying to find a student who wanted to learn. I thought I'd found that student in Rachel, my seventh-great-granddaughter. I gave her my Crystavis a couple of years ago to begin her training, but her parents upped and moved the same week. Without it, I ended up here." The smile on her face dimmed as she said, "They hardly visit anymore. Can't say that I blame them; I wouldn't want to come to this place for visits."

John thought she was off on her age by oh, about a hundred years, yet he couldn't stop himself from asking, "Why are you here instead of with them?"

Claire sighed and tried to tug the sleeves of her robe over her wrists. Her hands and wrists were bulging with arthritis. "They're on a quest and constantly traveling. Can't drag an old woman like me all around the world. I've already been anyway, around the world that is. With my arthritis I'm sometimes lucky to walk the length of the hall." Claire looked down at her hands as she folded them and refolded them.

"I don't understand; this is a psych facility. You don't seem crazy to me." Well, she did seem crazy as she called him over, but now that he was talking to her, she seemed fine.

"Aww, you're a sweet boy," Claire said smiling. John nearly jumped out of his boots when she suddenly shouted over her shoulder, "Hear that, Stuart? My friend here thinks I'm not crazy!" *Okay*...John thought that maybe he'd spoken too soon.

Stuart didn't even turn to look at her. He just waved his hand dismissively over his head at her from his position on the couch. His gray-haired companion looked at Claire then returned his gaze to the TV.

John decided it was time to leave. He shouldn't have stayed in the first place. "I've got to run, Ms. Claire, ma'am. I really shouldn't be in here," he said as he started for the door.

"No! Wait!" Claire shouted as she jumped out of her seat. The chair leg grabbed her foot as she tried to move out from the table, and she let out a small squeal of distress as she started falling towards the floor.

Without thinking, John reached out and grabbed her. "Be careful, Claire. Don't hurt yourself!" he softly chastised her, hoping no one could hear him.

The gray-haired man on the couch stood up, looking alarmed. "I'm okay, no worries. It was a little stumble, that's all," Claire said, waving him away. Claire settled her waving hand on John's chest to push herself upright. When she touched him she gasped. "Such power," she murmured, transfixed. "I've never felt so much...it's different somehow...I wonder..." Frowning in concentration, she flattened her hand over his heart, almost pushing at him, and she brought up her other hand and laid it on the first one like she was about to give him CPR. Where she touched him, he burned. His chest was so hot under her hands, he thought he was about to go up in flames.

"What the..." John stuttered as he took a half-step back. Claire grabbed his wrist and reached up to cup his cheek with the other hand.

"Oh my, I am so sorry. I shouldn't have done that. I'm sorry, *so* sorry. Please don't be mad at me! You must come and see me again. It is so lonely here. Let me at least see your face before you go."

John tried to pull his hand back, but Claire had a surprisingly strong grip. He heard one patient scream, then another. He looked down at his hand. His hand; he could see his hand! Where Claire touched him, his invisibility suit seemed to melt away. So, if that were the case, with her other hand on his cheek...

One lady in a wheelchair started banging her fists on her forehead. "I see a head. I see a head. I see a floating head. A floating head. Hee-hee-hee, that could be a song!" The lady then started singing those words over and over again to her own private tune.

John broke away from Claire and ran from the room. He fixed the holes in his invisibility armor in the hallway. Those poor people, they just saw a hand and part of a head float out the door. He was going to do penance for this; it was so wrong. The whole room was in an uproar. John moved aside as two attendants rushed past. John ran back the way he'd come, found the stairwell he'd bypassed before, and ran down the steps as fast as his legs would take him.

CHAPTER 16 – CAFETERIA CHAOS

John didn't run into anyone in the stairwell, and he was dizzy and breathing heavily by the time he reached the second floor. He hugged the walls and followed signs to get back to the elevator bank. Diana was nowhere in sight. John paused as he caught his breath and organized his thoughts. She probably waited for a while then went to the cafeteria to go on with the plan. He followed the signs again, this time to the cafeteria.

It was 11:48 a.m., and there was a constant flow of people leaving the cafeteria, patients and attendants alike. John waited for a break then slipped inside. There must have been another entrance because there was a line of patients along the far wall holding empty trays. The line was being closely monitored by several attendants. He noticed that while the people in the room where he found Claire were all elderly, the patients here were much younger and scarier. They were all men, and several of them looked like they should be in prison instead of a mental institute. They even wore prison-orange scrubs, while the patients leaving all wore grays and blues. It wasn't too difficult to figure out Michael had been grouped with the criminally insane. Looking around, John spotted two security guards by the lunch line and two more standing by the door through which he just entered.

John hastily moved away from the door and the guards, finding a spot against the wall to stand where he wouldn't be bumped.

He scanned the line. He didn't see Michael, but he did spot Diana's blurred outline against the wall a few feet from where the lunch line exited the kitchen. He wished he could see her face. He inched his way closer, hugging the wall. A trickle of sweat ran down his spine. It was unpleasantly warm in the room, and his nerves were through the roof after the incident with Claire. He was about ten feet from Diana when her blurred outline raised an arm and waved. Good, she'd seen him.

He decided to stay put for the moment. He guessed Diana was waiting for Michael to come out of the kitchen line. Sure enough, after a very long five minutes, Michael exited the kitchen with lunch on his tray. Diana immediately stepped in behind him and followed Michael as he sat at an empty table. John edged his way over to them.

Diana greeted him, whispering, "Nice of you to join us."

"Hey," John hissed back, "I couldn't get out of that elevator without bumping someone and…"

"I'm just teasing you," Diana interrupted him. "I'm a little nervous here, and getting separated wasn't part of the plan."

"Well, I'm here now." John watched Michael as he ate the unappetizing food. His eyes were unfocused, and it looked like he was running on autopilot. "What's wrong with him?"

"I think he's pretty doped up," Diana speculated. "It looks like a lot of them are. I'm glad we came to get him right away, before the drugs have time to mess with him. Some of these guys seem edgy. It's creepy; I don't like it."

"So now you make him faint or something?" John asked. With all of the noise in the cafeteria, he wasn't too worried about being overheard.

"Let's wait for more people to sit down first," Diana said. He noticed the attendants that had been monitoring the lunch line had started roaming through the tables. "As soon as one of those lunch monitors comes close would be a good time, so they can see him."

"What exactly are you going to do?" John asked her, but she didn't have time to answer.

"Here comes one of them. Stay close, but not too close," Diana said, the tension in her voice obvious. She made a wild grab for his hand and put it on her shoulder. He guessed she just needed the physical reassurance he was with her while she focused on Michael. John saw her outline move to put a hand on Michael's broad shoulder, close to his neck. Michael didn't react. John gave Diana a supportive squeeze and waited. As soon as the approaching attendant was within five feet of their table, Michael slammed both hands down on the tabletop, making John and everyone else in the vicinity jump. Michael stiffened in his chair and started shaking all over like he was going into an epileptic fit. John felt Diana shift slightly to maintain her hold on Michael.

The other patients at the table quickly pushed back away from him as the attendant rushed to Michael's side. Michael's eyes rolled into the back of his head and his convulsions increased. The attendant fluttered his hands over Michael, but didn't seem to have any idea what to do. The attendant suddenly stood up and called to the guard by the door, "Get a medic in here, we've got a guy seizing!" The attendant put his hands on Michael's shoulders to keep him from falling off the seat. Michael's entire body stiffened painfully to a straight line then collapsed down into the chair. The attendant struggled to keep Michael from falling.

From that point things happened quickly. Two male medics rushed in and took over. They eased Michael to the floor, and after checking for vitals, started CPR. John moved with Diana as she positioned herself at Michael's head. When one of the medics pulled out a defibrillator, John heard Diana grit out, "Darn it!" John had been watching things play out in a state of shock, but hearing Diana swear made his stomach rise through his throat. "John, I need your help!" Diana whispered urgently.

"How... what can I do?"

"I need your strength. Push your Visity into my amulet, quickly!"

John lifted his other hand so he was gripping both of her shoulders and tried his best to do as she asked. He couldn't see her amulet, but he imagined where it was and pushed everything he had towards it. A phantom of Claire's rheumatic hands burned through his chest. Diana shuddered slightly, as just then the medic lowered the paddles to Michael's chest and shouted, "Clear!"

To John everything looked like how it happens on TV. They tried resuscitating Michael several times to no avail. Finally, one of the medics called time of death, and they started packing up their equipment. There was a bang across the room as another two medics raced in with a stretcher and more medical gear. A crowd of patients had surrounded them, so the newcomers had some difficulty getting to Michael and the other medics. They collapsed the stretcher to the floor. It took all four medics to heave Michael onto it. One of them got out a sheet while the others expanded the stretcher's legs to regular height. They spread the sheet between them and covered Michael's body.

John felt Diana twist away from him and climb underneath the stretcher. He saw she had one hand snaked under the sheet to touch Michael's head.

The noise from the other patients had steadily increased throughout the ordeal. As the medics were trying to push the stretcher out of the room, it rapidly moved to pure chaos.

The patients started shouting hysterical comments like, "They killed him!" "It's the food, they've poisoned it!" and "No one is safe; they are going to kill us all!"

John was trying to stand up when someone bumped him, and he fell onto his bruised butt. He let out a small cry of pain that went unnoticed in all of the tumult. John scrambled to his feet as fast as he could with patients jostling him as they pressed in towards the stretcher. In moments, he was separated from Diana and Michael. Patients were shouting and shoving, and many of them were tall and brawny. He heard the stretcher get knocked over, and his heart skipped several beats. Thoughts of Diana and Michael being trampled flashed through his mind. He tried to muscle his way towards the stretcher and got several elbows to his ribs and stomach for his efforts. When someone grabbed him by his collar and nearly lifted him off his feet, he realized that he'd dropped his invisibility projection. He was hauled face-to-face with a bear of a man whose bald head was covered with tattoos. The man shook him several times, shouting straight in his face, "You all are murderers, murderers! It's you or us!" John felt the man's spittle spray over his face as he roared, then watched in horror as the man cocked his arm back for a punch. John turned and lurched away, but the punch still connected with the side of his head. If he'd taken the punch straight on, John would have been knocked unconscious. Even so, being clipped with the tail end of the punch sent his brains reeling as he fell to his knees. He thought he heard Diana scream his name, but with the ringing sound in his ears, he couldn't tell.

With that one punch, the chaos morphed into a riot. Patients were punching medics, attendants, and each other. John crawled under one of the tables to avoid being stepped on. He saw the wavering outline of Diana doing the same thing under a table closer to the exit.

Both of the cafeteria doors were suddenly flooded with a mix of security officers and large, muscular attendants. Nurses followed with an arsenal of syringes. The employees started hauling patients one by one from the brawl and holding them steady as a nurse shot them up with what must be sedatives or tranquilizers. As the shots took hold, the institute's employees lowered each patient to the floor. John risked getting trampled to make his way to Diana. He lowered his head and shoulders like a football player and forced his way to her before any of the employees spotted him. He threw himself under Diana's table and grabbed her arm, using her invisibility projection to jump-start his own.

John changed his grip to hold her hand as they waited out the bedlam around them. Patients were felled by the nurses' needles, and the room gradually settled down. John noticed several patients huddled against the outside walls, trying to avoid the violence. Employees ushered them out of the cafeteria, likely back to their rooms. John frantically looked for Michael and the stretcher. As the employees cut a path through the crowd, John finally spotted the upturned stretcher lying on the floor close to the wall. Four medics righted the gurney then lifted Michael back onto it and covered him again with the sheet. Michael had been tossed between the stretcher and the wall, so thankfully was out of reach of the commotion. As soon as the medics had Michael situated, two of them pushed him quickly out of the room.

Diana and John rushed out from under the table to follow, but it was difficult weaving their way over the drugged patients slumped on the floor. By the time they got to the hallway, the medics and Michael were gone.

CHAPTER 17 – MORGUE MISHAP

Diana didn't hesitate. She pulled John along with her down a hall and said, "They must be taking him to the morgue in the basement. We can catch up with them there." When they got to the elevator bank, John steered her towards the stairs instead.

"We can't afford to be separated again," he explained as he hustled her into the stairwell. They only had to go down three floors. Diana led them confidently to a metal door marked 'MORGUE' that was slowly closing on air-compressed springs. John quickly rammed his steel-toed boot into the opening. As he slowly pushed the door back open, they could hear voices. John craned his ears as the men spoke.

"Good timing today, Greg. I've got another one for you; still warm in fact."

"That so? There's nearly a full load today." There was a pause followed by the clicks of a keyboard. "This one's young."

"Yeah, from what I hear he just seized up during lunch and fell over dead. He just got here today. You should have seen the cafeteria; it was a complete madhouse. I wouldn't be surprised if we get another sent down here. Those oranges are messed up man; they give me the creeps."

"What did this one do?"

"Let me see here..." John heard more typing. "Ahh, this is the guy who vandalized that museum piece a while back. It says he was found wandering the place covered in dust and debris from the statue. He wouldn't talk, and it looks like there were several incidents in detainment where he fought with officers and other prisoners, babbling nonsense. Apparently, he inflicted several injuries. He's a big son of a gun. I can see why the boys in blue wanted him processed so quickly and off their hands."

John had the door open enough for Diana and him to slip through. John went to duck down behind an examination table, when he remembered he was invisible. He recovered quickly and hoped Diana didn't see his flub. He still couldn't see her face with the invisibility projection, but he knew something was up, because she was squeezing his hand so tightly it hurt. He looked into the room just in time to see two men zip Michael into a body bag.

He jumped when the door was banged open by a large man pushing an empty gurney.

"Last one is loaded for you, Greg; you're good to go," the man said as he entered the room. The man gave the gurney a shove and sent it rolling right in Diana's and John's direction before he turned to saunter over to the men zipping Michael up.

Diana made a little squeak that couldn't be heard over the rattle of the gurney heading right at them. On instinct, John dashed under the exam table, dragging Diana with him. One wheel of the gurney hit his boot before he could tuck it under the table, and the stretcher jumped and banged wildly. The men had been talking, but stopped at the noise and looked over in their direction. Not seeing anything abnormal, they resumed their conversation.

"We've got one more to load up, Drew. It just came down from the cafeteria. Poor sucker just got signed in today. I think that's the shortest visit we've ever had here. He didn't even get to sleep in our triple-A, Diamond-Class beds." The man snorted at his own joke.

"Just came down, eh?" said the newcomer, Drew. "You got his papers through already? That was fast." As he spoke, Drew returned to the front of the room and grabbed his errant gurney.

The other hospital employee cleared his throat nervously before saying, "Well, we can catch up on that stuff later, can't we? Greg won't be back for two weeks, and I don't want to hang out with a corpse all that time. It's bad enough I got assigned here until they fill this awful position. Greg, my man, you know I'm good for it. Take this guy now, and I'll have all the paperwork to you by the end of the day. Help me out here, buddy."

The guy who must be Greg snorted as he helped line up the empty gurney next to Michael's prone form. "It's no skin off my nose. What are they going to do, fire me? Good luck finding someone willing to haul dead bodies around for minimum wage."

The men grunted as they moved Michael to the gurney. "Man, this guy's a giant," commented Drew. "I think it will take both of us to load him up. As soon as you're ready, Greg, we'll head out together."

"Will this one fit in your oven?"

"Oh, yeah. You should see some of the bodies that come through, a few are huge. The director's going to have me burning all day."

John's temper, already running thin, boiled over at the men's disrespectful behavior. Sweat dotted his forehead and he was still trying to calm his breathing from the race down the steps. He clenched his fists and held his tongue, the desire to hit something almost overwhelming as he waited for an opportunity to get to Michael.

The men chuckled as Greg signed some papers on a clipboard, and he and Drew pushed Michael out of the room. John tugged Diana as he quickly got to his feet and rushed to catch the door before it closed. The men were several yards ahead of them when they got to the hall. John stayed back as they tailed them, so he could talk to Diana.

"What are we going to do?" Diana said dismally. "They're taking Michael to the funeral home, and they're cremating everyone from this institute today! Of course, that may not even matter. I'm not sure Michael will be able to breathe in that body bag!"

John's blood was pulsing through his ears as he was trying to calm down enough to think.

"One of us has to go with them, and the other one stay here to get Mrs. M to drive to the funeral home," John finally decided.

"I think I should go with Michael," Diana offered.

"Then I'll stay and get Mrs. McNeally," John finished out. "You should try to ride wherever they put Michael and unzip him as soon as possible. Do we have to worry about him waking up?"

"Not for a while yet," Diana replied. They walked in silence, picking up their pace to close the gap between them and the men. They turned a corner, and John felt a fresh breeze hit his face. Double doors were propped wide open to the outside at the end of the hallway. A large van was backed into the doorway, not allowing room for anyone to get in without climbing through the vehicle. The inside of the van had three shelves lining each of the sidewalls, with a stretcher on the floor between them. All six shelves held a body bag. They crept as close as they dared.

"How are we going to get past them? Any ideas?" John asked Diana. "I think you need to get in the van before they load him. They might shut the doors as soon as he is inside."

"You're probably right," Diana said, her voice surprisingly calm. "Don't worry, I've got this." She gave his hand a quick squeeze then crept forward. The men had stopped, blocking the doorway. Diana crouched down and crawled under the gurney. The men kept on talking. Drew was gesticulating wildly as he told some story or another. When Diana was almost out from under the gurney, Drew laid his hand on the gurney and shook it to emphasize a point he was making. John could swear he heard a stifled squeal, but the men didn't seem to notice.

John watched Diana's blurry outline hitch up into the van and climb the metal racks on the right side to crouch on the top one. John's heart was beating out of his chest. Eww! Didn't Diana realize she was practically sitting on a dead body? The funeral home guy, Greg, kept checking his watch as Drew went on talking. Even John couldn't follow what Drew was saying. It was something about the strip district, dancing, and girls. John wished the guy would just shut up. Michael needed to get unzipped before he suffocated. Finally, Greg moved to the van and started pulling the stretcher from the floor, all the while still listening to Drew. Drew kept talking as the men worked to transfer Michael to the van's stretcher.

"Are you going to need help unloading?" Drew asked Greg. Greg started pushing the stretcher back into the van, its legs collapsing as it made contact with the rear bumper. It was just the right height, and since it was on wheels, it rolled straight in. Greg quickly jumped in the back of the van and said, "Nah, I'll just keep him on the stretcher. We have a way of rolling them off to go in the oven." Greg scurried deep into the van and opened a small door, which revealed the front seat. John suspected he was trying to avoid Drew starting another story.

"Okay, have a good one!" Drew said as he shut and latched the van doors.

"Thanks, you, too" John faintly heard Greg say back. The vehicle's engine roared to life, and it pulled away with Michael and an invisible Diana stowed away inside. John barely saw 'Winston's Family Funeral Home" on the side of the van before Drew closed the institute's doors.

John followed Drew back to the morgue. As they approached the familiar metal door, it opened and the other worker stepped out. "Hey, Brad," Drew called to the man, "You headin' to lunch?"

Brad locked the doors and answered, "Yep, let's go."

Excellent! John thought. *If they lead me to the elevators, I can find my way from there.* John perked up as he overheard the men talking about Michael.

"I wonder what they'll do with this guy's stuff. It was sent over with him. Gary said there's some wickedly old things in there that may be worth something. I just might stop by the patient storage after my shift today and check it out."

"Drew! You could lose your job over stuff like that! Don't be stupid, man."

"Who's going to know? Are you going to tell? I'll be in and out in a flash. I'll snag a keycard from the nurses' station, and since Mr. John Doe just got here today, his stuff will be close to the door."

The men walked quietly for a few moments.

"I'll even let you in on the cut if there's anything worthwhile in there. The stuff will just get donated somewhere; the guy's got no family, so what's the harm?" Drew pushed.

Brad relented, "Okay, man, I won't say anything. Just be careful. If you get caught, you're on your own."

"It's a deal!" said Drew as they reached the elevators.

John headed for the stairs again. He was *not* risking another elevator ride. He made his way to the first floor lobby and saw Mrs. McNeally sitting on the end of a sofa, knitting something.

John rushed over and dropped like a rock into the seat next to her. Mrs. McNeally gasped at the movement and dropped her knitting.

"Oh, I'm so sorry, Mrs. M, I forgot I'm invisible," John apologized quickly. He brought her up on the main points of what had happened.

"So now we find out where this Winston Funeral Home is, help Diana to get Michael, and head for home?" Mrs. McNeally asked.

"Well…," John hesitated.

"Good Lord Almighty! Child, just spit it out! We don't have time for mumbling," Mrs. McNeally said sternly.

"I think I should go get Michael's things before we leave," John blurted out.

Mrs. McNeally closed her eyes and laid her head back on the couch. She took several deep breaths before saying, "and why, pray tell, should we do that?" The way she was acting, it was as if *she* were the one who had run up and down flights of stairs and had lived through a riot of criminally insane guys!

"What if he had something from New Zigon? We can't let that get away. Besides, it might help Michael adjust if he has some of his own things with him. He's lost a lot, remember." John didn't know where this sudden compassion came from. "And there's a guy planning to steal his stuff later today."

Mrs. McNeally lifted her head and looked right at him, even though he was invisible. It was freaky. "All right, John. I've decided to just 'go with the flow' as you young people say. What do we need to do?"

"First, we need to find out where the patient storage is located."

John went up to the receptionists' desk in the lobby, looking at everything he could without moving objects. Unfortunately, they didn't include patient storage on the public maps.

As a middle-aged nurse walked in and greeted the receptionist, the receptionist quickly stood up, returned the 'hello' and asked, "Evelyn, would you mind covering the desk for just a few minutes? I really need to use the restrooms."

The nurse, Evelyn, looked at her watch, "Sure. I'm a bit early today. But if you're longer than five minutes, I have to leave to start my shift on time."

"Oh, perfect! Thank you!" said the receptionist as she grabbed her purse and ran out.

John came up with an idea, one needing Mrs. McNeally's acting skills.

He rushed to tell Mrs. McNeally his plan. She gave him a twinkling smile saying, "It's nice to see you loosen up a bit, John. Let's go."

Mrs. McNeally pulled out her handkerchief, furiously rubbed her eyes until they were red, then stood up and ambled over to the receptionists' desk.

"May I help you?" Nurse Evelyn asked.

"Oh, I certainly hope so!" Mrs. McNeally said with a snuffle. "My dear brother Andrew passed here a few days ago…" Mrs. McNeally dabbed her eyes with her hanky and sniffed.

"I'm sorry, but I don't normally work the desk. I'm just filling in for a few moments. The regular receptionist should be back soon. You could ask her. She has a pretty good memory of who comes in and out of here."

Mrs. McNeally gave Nurse Evelyn a hard stare as she said in a clipped voice, "Passed as in *died*, not as in passing by."

"Oh! I'm so sorry! What can I do to help?" Nurse Evelyn's face turned beet red as she fumbled to cover up her mistake.

Mrs. McNeally was back on form as she nearly wailed, "The institute called yesterday and told me he'd died. He was all alone when it happened. It took hours before someone came into his room to check on him." Mrs. McNeally stopped to sniff and blow her nose. "They told me I could come and pick up his belongings from a locker, or storage bin, or something?"

"Oh, you must mean the patient storage room. That's on the basement level. Turn left off the elevator. It's the third door on your left," the nurse said helpfully. Then she flushed slightly as she said, "I think there's a protocol for releasing belongings to family. Will you wait until the receptionist gets back to make sure we follow procedure?"

"Oh, no problem, dearie, you've been most helpful." Mrs. McNeally shuffled away from the desk to a seat near the front door.

"As soon as the nurse turns her head, leave!" John instructed. "I'll meet you at the truck."

"Be quick about it, John," Mrs. McNeally worried, "I don't like the idea of our Diana riding in a van with a bunch of corpses all by herself."

"I'm with you there," John fervently agreed. He gave Mrs. McNeally a quick pat on the shoulder and raced for the stairs.

For once, things went his way. John got to the patient storage room without any problems. No one was at the desk, and he quickly found a keycard marked "Guest" that let him in the room. He found several large kitchen bags on a table by the door, and one had 'John Doe' and today's date written on it. He was going to just grab the bag and go, but thinking it through, he didn't want to raise any suspicions by the thing completely disappearing. He scavenged the room and found a spare bag along with a bin full of clothes and junk marked 'Donate.' He dumped Michael's bag straight into the spare bag, not bothering to look at its contents. He couldn't help noticing the two huge swords and scabbards, however. Yikes! It scared John a bit to think of what kind of action those swords had been through. The medic had been right; fourteenth-century swords would be worth a lot of money. Then John went to the Donate bin and picked out items to fill Michael's bag. He did his best to find a full set of clothes Michael's size and some old junk that would pass as vintage. *That will have to do,* he thought.

Before opening the door to leave, he glanced down at himself, or rather through himself, to the floor. Later he would think about how cool it was; now he had to hurry. He mentally punched himself several times, as he realized Michael's bag was *visible*. *Way to stay on top of things, chump,* he thought to himself. *You nearly walked out of here with a floating bag hanging over your shoulder!* It took him several tries, but eventually John was able to extend his invisibility projection to cover the bag as well. He had to keep a solid grip on it, or the projection slipped.

Finally, John retraced his steps back to the lobby and left the building. He climbed into Mrs. McNeally's truck with a sigh of relief, despite the stagnant, sun-warmed interior.

Mrs. McNeally started the truck up and said, "Heavens to Betsy, that took you long enough! Keep that invisibility thing going; we'll probably need it. Now, where are we heading?"

John let out a little groan. He was more than ready to drop his projection, but if he did, he wouldn't be able to start it again unless he reached Diana. "We're going to Winston's Family Funeral Parlor," John answered.

"And where is that?"

John lifted his shoulders in a shrug that Mrs. McNeally couldn't see and said, "I don't know."

Mrs. McNeally sighed heavily as she leaned her forehead against the steering wheel. "You don't know," she repeated. "Okay, let me think about this for a minute." Mrs. McNeally sat, forehead still pressed against the steering wheel. There was no sound over the thrum of the truck's engine. "We need a phone book," she finally said. "Problem is, where do you find one in this day and age?" When she finally lifted her head, the imprint of the steering wheel was stuck to her forehead. "I saw a display with all kinds of advertising cards in the lobby. It had morbid stuff like coffins and funeral homes. There might be one for Winston's there. Was the receptionist back at the desk when you went through? I don't want that nurse to see me and start asking questions."

"Yeah, I'm pretty sure she was back. It's been longer than five minutes, and that was how long the nurse said she could cover."

Mrs. McNeally shut off the truck and hopped out. "Aren't you coming?" she tossed over her shoulder at John. John had to hustle to catch up. He thought, *boy, Mrs. M could really move when she wanted to.* As soon as they were in sight of the people in the lobby, Mrs. McNeally slowed to her shuffling crawl. It drove John nuts.

"We don't have time for your shuffling act. Let's go!" he scowled.

"Hush now!" Mrs. McNeally scolded. "I'm going for the advertisements. You check the receptionist for a phone book, okay?"

John nodded. Mrs. McNeally huffed, "OKAY?"

"Okay!" John answered, just realizing she couldn't see his nod.

"Hush now!" Mrs. McNeally repeated.

Exasperated, John said, "But you just asked . . . "

"Hush!" Mrs. McNeally said sternly. John gave up and clamped his mouth shut, looking around as he baby-stepped his way behind Mrs. McNeally.

John saw two men exit a black SUV, which they left in a no-parking zone. They were richly dressed, wearing dark dress suits and sunglasses. *Figures!* John thought. *They probably won't even get a ticket. If that were me, I'd have a ticket before I even made it to the front door.* The two businessmen walked briskly to the hospital doors, but they couldn't politely get past Mrs. McNeally. John sympathized with them, watching them shift their weight from foot to foot, as they were forced to follow the Widow's snail pace. As soon as they cleared the door, they hastily skirted around Mrs. McNeally and headed straight to the reception desk.

Mrs. McNeally shuffled to the display of advertising cards and pamphlets. "You'd better not still be walking next to me! Get going!" she hissed in a low voice. John didn't say anything; he just followed the businessmen to the desk and slipped behind it. He found the yellow pages on a shelf below the phone. He knelt in front of it, thinking for a moment. Could he slide it to the floor and flip to the page he needed without being seen? He could make the book invisible, but then *he* couldn't see it either. He decided to just take the book. He placed his hand on it and worked on extending his invisibility projection again. Once the book was no longer visible, he grabbed it and stood up. A few words from the businessmen's conversation drifted to his ears. He heard "John Doe" and "family." He froze in place and listened. They'd been talking for a while, and he'd missed all of the important information. "Let me call the relations department," said the receptionist. She punched an electronic tune of buttons.

"Hi, Betty? This is Laura from reception. *(pause)* I have two gentlemen here inquiring about a John Doe that was brought in by police today. They say they recognized his picture on the news and are here representing the family who want to claim him." *(pause)* "Who did you say you were representing?" the receptionist asked the men.

When they answered, "Lord Vito Dragotta," the receptionist nearly dropped the phone. "They say they are representing Lord Vito Dragotta," the receptionist said into the phone in a shaking voice.

John had heard enough. He ran to Mrs. McNeally, who was still scanning over the display of advertisements. He grabbed her under her elbow and whispered urgently in her ear, "I've got the phone book. There's trouble. We have to leave, *now*. I'll explain in the truck, but we've got to move fast."

Mrs. McNeally didn't comment, as she turned sharply and power-walked to the door. They raced to the truck and didn't look back. John pulled his invisibility projection off the phone book and flipped through it until he found the funeral home they were looking for. He read off the address to Mrs. McNeally, and she said, "That's not too far from here. Now tell me what the emergency is; you have me worried."

"Did you see those business men that came in behind us? They were asking about Michael! They said they represented Michael's family and wanted to 'claim' him. When they told the receptionist whom they represented, she just about had a heart attack, she looked so scared. It won't take them long to track down what happened, and they'll head to the funeral home next."

Mrs. McNeally's hands tightened on the steering wheel as she floored the gas pedal.

John tightened his seat belt as Mrs. McNeally raced her truck around turns and through back streets. They found the place and pulled into the parking lot. As they rounded the house, they saw the Winston van back away from a service entry into a parking spot. Greg jumped out and headed back inside the building.

"You follow that guy, and I'll pull up to that service door. Get Michael and you can load him straight into the back," Mrs. McNeally decided. John jumped out of the truck and hurried after Greg.

The room the service door opened to was painfully bright, white, clinical, and smelled of antiseptic and other chemicals. There were five lumpy body bags lined up on stretchers. John heard a low roaring noise coming from an open door and went to investigate.

He stepped into the next room just in time to see a door closing along the right wall at the far end, dampening the roaring sound that had drawn him there. The room was plain and narrow, furnished with a few simple folding chairs and had a third door on its other side. A window spanned the length of the right wall up to the door. The space was illuminated by harsh florescent light pouring from the adjoining room through the window. John saw Greg on the other side of the glass. John walked past the window to the door and slowly tried the knob. It was locked. John went back to the window to watch Greg, wondering what he should do next. The adjoining room had the same over-lit clinical feel as the one holding all the body bags. A conveyor belt that was about table height ran along the opposite wall. It had a control panel at one end, and the other end led to a square door in a huge machine. The machine had a foggy rectangular glass panel on the side facing him, showing a compartment roughly four feet high and eight feet long. The compartment was empty except for an eerie red glow coming from the seams in the corners.

Greg pulled a stretcher out of a corner beyond John's vantage point. The stretcher was slightly higher than the conveyor belt and had a body bag on it. Greg unzipped the bag completely and revealed the corpse inside. It was an older man with a beard, cold and blue in death, and he was…naked. Eww. John tried not to look. Greg didn't seem to be bothered by the dead guy's nudity. He walked to the end of the stretcher, pulled a toe tag off the deceased and secured it in a clipboard, which he placed on a small table by the control panel. Greg positioned the stretcher so it was tucked lengthwise against the conveyor belt, the man's gross feet facing the door to what John realized was a cremation chamber. Greg grabbed one side of the body bag and pulled it, so the body slid closer to him. Then he lifted the bag until the body rolled onto its front, landing half on the conveyor. A little maneuvering and Greg flipped the body again, so it was on its back on the belt.

Now at the control panel, Greg wrote on the clipboard, typed into a computer, and did some system checks. A push of a button caused the chamber door to slide straight up like a garage door. Greg pulled a lever and pushed a green button large enough for John to see from where he was standing, bringing the conveyor belt to life. John watched transfixed, all thoughts of Diana and Michael momentarily purged from his mind as the belt propelled the body through the door and into the chamber. The little door slid shut, and Greg stepped away from the controls to watch. The roaring sound increased as the light in the chamber became steadily brighter. With a large whoosh, the entire chamber burst into brilliant flames, encasing the dead body and hiding it from sight. John's vision blurred as he let the blazing light mesmerize him. He was so distracted, that he didn't pay attention to Greg moving about the room. By the time he snapped out of his haze, the chamber had darkened to a ruby glow, and Greg already had another body positioned on the conveyor belt.

This body wasn't naked; it was dressed in bright orange scrubs. When Greg moved to take shoes off the corpse's feet, John saw that it wasn't a corpse at all. It was Michael.

CHAPTER 18 – FLAMES

John's heart dropped right through his feet to the floor. "Noooo!" he tried to scream, but his voice came out in a hoarse choke. He pounded his fists on the window, but the glass must have been really thick or the noise of the furnace too loud, because Greg didn't hear him. John rushed to the door and tried it again, but it was still locked. "No, no, no, no, no!" John chanted as he wrenched wildly at the door handle. He went back to the window and saw Greg checking out Michael's clothes. He could tell the moment Greg decided to not bother removing them. When Greg walked to the control panel, John spun to scan the room for anything that would help him. He grabbed one of the metal folding chairs and swung it with all his might at the glass. The vibration of the impact shot deep in his arms all the way up to his shoulders, but there wasn't even a crack in the window. John dropped the chair and screamed, "Diana! Where are you? I need help!"

John stared helplessly through the thick glass as Greg opened the chamber door and started the conveyor belt. John's heart was surging within his ribcage while his head spun trying to absorb what was happening in front of him. He banged on the window again, screaming, "No! He's not dead! He's not dead! STOP!"

Greg moved to push the stretcher out of the way, when he suddenly screamed and jumped, stumbling backwards before he fell on his butt. Greg scrambled to his feet, shoved the empty stretcher out of his way, and crashed through the locked door into John's room. He disappeared out the third door, screaming uncontrollably. John didn't waste a second. He grabbed the door before it closed and launched himself into the cremation room. Michael's body was more than halfway into the chamber and was moving fast. Michael's body suddenly stopped with his shoulders at the chamber entrance. One of Michael's long arms was hanging over the side of the conveyor belt, and it had prevented him from going all the way into the chamber, but not for long. Later, John would realize that Michael had flung his arm out right in front of Greg, throwing the poor man into hysterics. The tug of the belt was slowly moving Michael forward, moving his arm up over his head as he went. John jumped up onto the belt and tried dragging Michael out of the chamber, but the man was large, and the moving belt was working against him. He had to walk his feet backwards on the belt, because there was nowhere else to stand. He had no leverage. He tried grabbing Michael's shirt, but it just rucked up his body. He grabbed him under the armpits and heaved. He gained an inch or two, only to have the belt eat up his progress when he repositioned his feet.

The door to the chamber slid down like a guillotine, but when it met Michael's chest, it reversed course and opened again; probably a safety mechanism. John braced one foot against the wall of the machine and pulled with all his might, lifting his other foot off the moving belt as he arched his back and used his own weight to move Michael's body. It worked, sort of. He planted his other foot on the wall, horizontally straddling the door. He managed to pull the large man out of the chamber as far as he could reach, but it only freed him down to his waist. John couldn't reposition his hold on Michael without losing it altogether. John screamed as he continued pulling, not making any progress, but at least holding him steady. The chamber door tried to shut again, dutifully retreating when it hit Michael's stomach. John could feel sweat dripping down his face and neck, soaking into his shirt. Between the heat from the furnace and the burning of his exhausted muscles, John felt like he was going to faint.

As his muscles began to shake from the effort, John screamed at himself, "Think! Think! There has to be a way!"

When the chamber door tried to shut again unsuccessfully, an idea came to him. It wasn't a solution, but it would buy him time. He adjusted his grip on Michael as he shifted his weight to rely on his right foot. With his left hand, he awkwardly untied the lace on his left boot, still braced against the wall. Somewhere along the way he'd dropped his invisibility projection, allowing him to see what he was doing. He pulled the laces out of the eyelets, freeing a longer stretch of the laces. Now came the tricky part. Shifting his weight even further to the right, he managed to bang and shake the boot nearly off his foot. He made a grab for the hanging laces and yanked the boot onto Michael's chest. Using his teeth and his left hand, he tied the very ends of the laces together. There was a small gauge on the wall next to the chamber door that was encased in a block of protective plastic. John waited for the door to try to close again before he made his move. John let go of Michael, who promptly slipped all the way inside the chamber. John fell back onto the conveyor belt without Michael's counterweight to hold him up. Before the belt scraped his backside too much, he rolled onto the floor, never losing sight of that small plastic protection box. He looped the tied laces around the box and fed the boot onto the conveyor belt. Anchored in place by the laces, the boot bounced on the belt directly under the chamber door. The door tried closing again but retreated when it met the boot. John ran to the control panel at the end of the machine, searching wildly for some kind of stop button. He pushed the large green button Greg had used to start everything, but nothing happened. When he raised the lever next to it, the conveyor belt slowed to a stop, then started running in the opposite direction, away from the chamber. John's boot was pulled away from the machine just as the chamber door tried to close once more. John threw himself towards the chamber and barely got his fingers under the door in time to make it retract.

Michael's one arm was straight above his head, and John was able to reach his hand to pull him out. It was much easier to move him when the conveyor belt wasn't working against him. Once he got Michael's shoulders out, the conveyor belt did the rest of the work. When Michael's feet cleared the door, John rolled the man's large frame off the belt and onto the floor. John ended up falling to the floor with him, his own chest cushioning Michael's head, knocking the breath from his lungs. The chamber door shut completely, and the conveyer belt stopped.

As it had before, the compartment glowed hotter as the roar of the furnace grew. The large 'whoosh' sound preceded the explosion of light and flames inside the chamber.

John gently moved Michael's heavy head (who knew a head could weigh so much!) off his chest to the floor. With the weight lifted, he dragged in a ragged breath. Michael let out a low groan but didn't move. John closed his eyes and didn't bother watching the flames surge through their hypnotic dance.

CHAPTER 19 – MAJOR MOJO

John must have blacked out for a few minutes, because the next thing he knew, a soft but calloused hand was smoothing his sweaty hair from his face. He heard someone gently calling his name, bringing him back to the present. He opened his eyes to see Mrs. McNeally bending over him, his head pillowed in her lap.

"Ah, there's my boy," she crooned. She helped him sit up, and he gazed about the room. Diana was there, and she had a cut on her forehead that left dried trails of blood down her cheek. She was holding a glowing amulet, and Michael's body was floating through the air to land on the same stretcher on which he'd arrived.

"Come on now, up you go," Mrs. McNeally encouraged, helping him to his feet. He noticed his left boot was back on his foot, securely tied. "We need to leave," she said.

John took a few stiff steps towards the door as Diana went over to the control panel and studied some clipboards. Her amulet glowed briefly before she turned back and started pushing the stretcher. John quickly regained his footing, and Mrs. McNeally moved to help Diana push Michael out the door. As they passed through the viewing room, John straightened the chair he'd thrown to the floor, returning it to where he thought it had been when he first saw it. They moved quietly through the room with all the body bags, and John noticed the service door was open. Mrs. McNeally's truck was backed up to it with the tailgate down, the sun glaring off the truck's metal. John shielded his eyes until they adjusted; there hadn't been any outdoor windows in the viewing room or the crematorium, and his weary mind had envisioned it was nighttime.

Luckily, Michael's stretcher was collapsible, and they were able to push it onto the truck bed, folding the legs under it. Diana climbed onto the back of the truck, and Mrs. McNeally handed her a knitted afghan she kept in the truck cab. Diana wrapped it over Michael and used the straps already on the stretcher to tie both him and the blanket down. Mrs. McNeally pulled out a pile of bungee cord tie-downs and handed them to John, then gave him a gentle push towards the truck. John handed half of them to Diana, and they worked quickly to secure the stretcher to hooks on the floor of the truck bed. Mrs. McNeally got out the tarp that had covered the scrap metal, and they used it as a flat cover for the bed of the truck, making sure there was enough air circulation for Michael. John continually glanced around the vacant parking lot, giving thanks and praise that no one was around to see what they were doing. They climbed into the truck's cabin, and Mrs. McNeally headed for home. John was so tired; he didn't even register the pain in his backside from sitting down.

John couldn't believe it was still light outside. It felt like they left the farm two days ago instead of just that morning. He was shocked when he found out it was barely three in the afternoon. John turned to Diana and asked, "Are you okay? Where were you? What happened?"

Diana grimaced as she said, "It seems our *friend*, Greg, is not a very good driver. He slammed to a stop so hard, I'm surprised the air bags didn't release. I was standing over Michael at the time, and had just got his bag unzipped down to his mouth when I was thrown across the van. I hit my head hard enough to knock me out. Apparently, Greg's wild turns around corners rolled me under one of the cots on the wall, at least that's where I woke up."

They drove a little over a block when the businessmen's black SUV passed them. John watched them in the mirror to see the vehicle turn into the funeral home's parking lot. John told Diana about seeing them at the institute.

"What are they going to find at that funeral parlor? Did you guys see Greg?" he asked.

"They are going to find exactly what we wanted people to find. The funeral home has records showing Michael's body was cremated, both on a clipboard and in the computer. Greg had filled most everything out; I just had to copy the signature at the bottom." John didn't bother asking how she did that.

"We found Greg sitting on the front steps, smoking a cigarette. He was pretty shaken up. He was mumbling something like 'knew it would happen one day' and how he'd finally lost it. It was easy to walk up to him invisible and do a small memory adjustment. He saw Michael move his arm, and it completely freaked him out. I just had to erase that part and plant a memory of him first watching the cremation happen, like he'd watched thousands of times before, then walking out front for a smoke. I added a suggestion to stay out there a while, to give us a chance to get you and Michael out." Diana finished her story with a small, satisfied smile on her lips.

"How come Michael moved? I thought you made him go to sleep."

"I did, make him fall asleep that is, but it only lasts about an hour before slowly wearing off. I was able to reinforce the sleep suggestion on the van, but that was a while ago. Another ten minutes and he would have fully woken up. We'll have to stop in an hour, so I can reinforce it again."

"How long are we going to keep him asleep?" John asked.

"Not too long I think. Let's get him home and go from there."

"John, dear, can you tell us what happened to you and Michael in that room?" Mrs. McNeally asked. John took a deep breath and told them. He was too exhausted to embellish the story or soften any part of it. He recounted it the best he could, just as it happened. "And when I woke up, you two were there," he finished.

Diana looked at him, her eyes as big as saucers. "You saved his life," she said softly. "Thank you."

Mrs. McNeally cleared her throat and said in a tight voice, "You do us all proud, John Christopher. You're one in a million."

John appreciated their praise, but he felt more like a million kinds of hurt. He laid his head back on the headrest and fell asleep for the rest of the ride home, not even waking when they stopped for Diana to do her sleep-thing on Michael.

When they arrived at Mrs. McNeally's house, she drove the truck around back. To John's surprise, she parked in front of her old rooming house. Back when the McNeally's actively farmed the property, they kept on hired hands and boarded them here. It was a simple rectangular building with a cement floor and a boiler and steam pipe system for heat. There were four bedrooms on each end, separated by a common room and rudimentary bathroom facilities. Mrs. McNeally kept the structure maintained, but the rooms were simplistic, each holding an old metal camp bed and a musty, canvas-covered mattress. It would give a Boy Scout cabin a run for its money.

"Why are you putting him here, Mrs. M? You've got plenty of room in the house," John asked as they all worked to remove the tarp and bungee cords from the back.

"It's one thing to take a lovely, innocent young girl into your home," said Mrs. McNeally, matter-of-factly. "It's quite another to invite a large, strange man whom you've never met. He'll be just fine out here. Diana and I have been working to fix it up."

They rolled Michael's stretcher off the truck and into the building, the stretcher conveniently unfolding as it left the truck. John grabbed Michael's bag of belongings, then lagged behind, feeling a blush rise up his neck in tandem with his rising shame. He'd asked an awful lot from Mrs. McNeally since the museum field trip. She'd risen to every task, plus more. He never thought how she would feel about taking Michael in, just that she did. He hung his head to hide his face as he scuffed his toe into the dirt.

Mrs. McNeally came out and wrapped an arm around him. Almost as if she could read his mind, she said, "Don't worry your handsome head over this one more second. I'm happy to have the company, and if this man is as noble as Diana says he is, he'll prefer being out here, too." She gave John a little push and followed him into the building.

A single, naked bulb on the ceiling illuminated the common room. Diana had gone down the left hall and was inside the first door on the right, trying to pull the stretcher inside the room. John stepped forward to help, and they managed to wedge it through the tight angle. Diana was wearing her amulet 'out,' he noticed. The room had been transformed. It had curtains over the single window, the walls looked freshly painted, and there was a real bed and mattress instead of the camp cot. There was even a bedside table with a lamp on it and a fan whirred by the door, pushing the afternoon heat into a paltry breeze.

John dropped Michael's bag of belongings on the floor with a clank and asked, "We got him here; now what do we do?"

Diana didn't say anything as she unstrapped Michael and removed the blanket. When she got to his bare feet she gasped, then covered her face with her hands and started to cry.

Mrs. McNeally, who had been standing in the doorway, pushed into the room and gathered Diana in her arms saying, "Hush now, child. We're home. Everything is going to be all right. What is it that brought these tears?" Diana didn't say anything; she just pointed with one hand to Michael's feet then pulled her hand back to cover her face again, like she was afraid to look.

As if pulled by the same string, Mrs. McNeally and John leaned closer to see what the fuss was about. When he saw it, John nearly heaved his stomach. He was lucky he hadn't eaten lunch, because it would've been all over the floor now by now. "Good Lord Almighty! The saints be with us," whispered Mrs. McNeally, as she took a step back and made the sign of the cross.

Michael's feet had been burned. Burned seemed too mild of a word to describe them. His heels took the worst of it; they looked like raw meat that melted into angry blackened and cracked skin on his ankles and calves. The bottom parts of his pant legs were missing, and the remaining fabric was edged in seared black. The rest of his skin was a shiny, deep red color, with small blisters starting to appear.

'Dumb, dumb, dumb!" John screamed at himself. He should have thought of this right away. That cremation chamber would have been scorching hot, and Michael's bare feet were in there a long time during John's fumbling rescue.

Mrs. McNeally snapped out of it first. She still had one arm around Diana, and she shook her head gently, saying, "Now, now, dry those tears, dearie. We'll all face this together. We can either take him to the hospital, or you can do your magic tricks on him." Mrs. McNeally wiggled the fingers of her free hand when she said 'magic'. When Diana looked up at her, Mrs. McNeally smiled and said, "So sorry, I mean *science*!"

Diana smiled through her tears, and then wiped her face with the back of her hand. Straightening, she said, "Okay," in a 'let's get down to business' voice. "No hospitals! I have some healing to do, and he needs a knowledge transfer. Because this will take a huge amount of energy, I'll have to do it in steps. I think it best if he doesn't wake up until I'm done. Healing first, plan later." Diana didn't wait for a response before she clutched her glowing amulet, closed her eyes, and held her free hand above Michael's ravaged feet.

John watched in amazement as the redness lessened and the cracks began to close on Michael's ruined flesh.

"John, help me again! Push your Visity at me."

John moved to stand behind Diana and put his hands on her shoulders like before. He imagined all the force he could muster, and pushed it at Diana's amulet. John's chest grew pleasantly warm as Diana let out a small huff as if she'd been hit on the back. The rate of the healing dramatically increased and red skin emerged to cover Michael's heels. The cracks were all closed, leaving no traces behind, and the blisters were gone. Finally, the redness started to pale until it was a healthy pink color. The hand Diana held over Michael's feet was trembling. Mrs. McNeally grabbed it and eased it to Diana's side, saying, "That's enough for now, dearie."

Both John and Diana were shaking. John felt like his knees were about to buckle at any moment. With his hands still on Diana's shoulders, he moved them to the bed, and they both sat down. John let go of Diana and fell back with a tired moan. Then he groaned in pain at the pressure on his butt and rolled to his side. Diana scooted to the top of the bed and lay down on her side facing John, pulling her knees up to her chest. "You've got some major mojo going on there, John," she said as she closed her eyes.

"Huh?" was his response, his neck and face getting very warm all of a sudden.

"Your Visity," Diana said, and then yawned. "It's very strong. I wanted to say something at the institute, but with everything going on, I forgot."

"Oh," John said, deflating, then reddening again. "That's cool."

Diana opened her eyes and looked at him from only a few feet away. "Yes, it's very cool."

Every thought and worry flew out of John's head as he stared at her baby blue eyes. He was transfixed by how the color turned to navy at the outer edge. He never really thought about eyes before. Her irises were actually made up of several shades of blue, giving the effect of a starburst of crisp, complex mountain ranges. He blinked and shook his head. Whoa, that was enough of that girly stuff. He was looking forward to having Michael wake up for some 'manly' company.

Mrs. McNeally covered Michael back up with the afghan. "You two look washed out. Diana, can you do that sleep thing on Michael again? I don't want him to wake up before we're ready."

Diana yawned again, and as she reached inside her pants pocket she said, "I don't think I can, sorry. We could use these though." She pulled out three capped syringes that John immediately recognized. They were the ones the nurses used to subdue the patients during the riot.

"How'd you get those?" he asked her.

"Five finger discount," she answered sleepily. "I figured they might come in handy with Michael, or help us out of a tight situation."

Mrs. McNeally took them from Diana, saying, "We'll just keep an eye on him. I don't think we should use these; we don't know what's in them. I'll put them somewhere safe."

"Wheaties?" John asked with a half-smile.

"I shouldn't have shown you that," Mrs. McNeally said, tisking.

"Too late!" John teased.

"I'm going to put these away. Don't move until I get back," Mrs. McNeally instructed as she bustled out of the room.

"No problem," John said groggily, raising a hand half-heartedly in acknowledgement before letting it drop like a rock back to the bed. He barely registered Diana dragging herself towards Michael, amulet glowing, before falling asleep.

* * *

"John…"

Someone was shaking John's shoulder. He tried to open his eyes, but his eyelids weren't cooperating.

"John, sorry, dearie, but you need to get up."

John recognized Mrs. McNeally's voice and groaned.

"John! Wake up!" Mrs. McNeally said as she shook him harder.

"What? I'm moving," John mumbled as he wiped the sleep from his eyes. He slowly sat up and took in his surroundings. The day's events came flooding back to him as he saw Michael motionless on the stretcher. Diana was fast asleep at the head of the bed. The sun was coming through the window, low and soft, but still bright. John jumped to his feet. "I've got to go. I've got chores!" John said, wide-awake now. "How long was I asleep?"

"Not very long; you still have plenty of time to do your chores before supper. Come to the kitchen before you go and have a bite to eat," she said, leading the way out of the room. John stretched and yawned as he followed her. When he stepped outside he told Mrs. McNeally, "I've got to go. I don't have time to eat." Right then, his traitorous stomach let out a loud growl.

Mrs. McNeally huffed, saying, "It appears your stomach disagrees. No arguments now, you need to eat something. You missed lunch, and Diana said using your 'powers' wears you out. You need something solid in your belly to get through your chores. You are coming inside!" Her tirade accompanied them all the way to her back door.

John obligingly sat at the kitchen table and inhaled two ham sandwiches, a banana, six cookies, and two glasses of milk. Mrs. McNeally pressed him with an apple for the walk home. On his way out, after thanking her profusely, Mrs. McNeally grabbed his face and pulled it down to give him a motherly kiss on the forehead. He surprised her by wrapping her up in a big hug as he thanked her once more. Mrs. McNeally hugged him back. After giving him a fierce squeeze, she pulled back and gently pushed him towards the steps.

She swiped the back of her hand across her eyes as she said in a choked voice, "Get out of here now, you. Think nothing of it; it's what family does for each other." She shooed him again as he hopped down the steps and took off for home in a light jog. He smiled at the idea that Mrs. McNeally thought of him as family.

John was a little late for dinner. Surprisingly, they had waited for him. Mother and all the girls were at the table, and as soon as John walked in, Father joined them. John tried to hide his discomfort as he sat on the hard wooden bench. After prayers, Father was quiet as he ate. This was the first time John had seen Father since getting the strap, and the silence was tense. Finally, Father asked Mother about her day, then asked Meg about the home-schooling. It wasn't until they were eating dessert that Father said anything to John. Eyes on his plate and between bites, Father asked, "How did today go with Mrs. McNeally?"

"Fine. Everything went fine."

"What was she getting rid of?"

"We filled her truck with mostly scrap metal and old parts."

"And that place in Pittsburgh, they just took it all? Did she get any money for it?"

"I'm not sure, but I can ask her the next time I see her."

Father hmph'd and took another bite. "Did she feed you?"

"Yeah, I mean, yes, Sir, she fed me when we got back," John answered, grateful Mrs. McNeally had forced him to eat.

Father nodded, apparently satisfied, and they finished their dinner without further conversation.

John went into the living room after dinner for the news. He was hoping to talk to Abby or Beth. He hadn't told them about the true reason for going to the city, because he didn't want them to worry. Now that he was back, he really wanted to talk about it with someone.

John stood leaning against the fireplace to spare his back end. Christie tried her best to get him to sit down so she could have his lap, but John resisted. Fortunately, Christie didn't throw a fit. Instead, she settled for sitting on John's feet, facing the TV and banging her head back onto his legs over and over. As the news started, she got up and pulled John's legs away from the wall and a couple feet apart, so she could spin and weave around them like they were monkey bars. John barely noticed. He was trying to think of a way to get Abby or Beth alone, when something on the news caught his attention.

"Channel 6 News brings you this breaking story; the primary suspect in the Carnegie Museum vandalism is now dead. After being judged mentally incompetent to stand trial in a court hearing yesterday, the suspect, still unidentified, was transferred to West Penn Psych Institute this morning. Insiders report that there was a violent riot in the cafeteria where several patients and West Penn Psych personnel were injured. Witnesses saw the suspect's dead body extracted from the cafeteria during the brawl. Channel 6 reporter Alexis Drummond has the story."

The mug shot of Michael had been displayed in the upper corner while the reporter spoke. Now the screen showed Alexis Drummond with a microphone, standing outdoors.

"This is Alexis Drummond, reporting live outside the West Penn Psych Institute. There are many unanswered questions about what transpired here today, but Channel 6 News can tell you this… (She holds up a piece of paper blowing in a mild wind.) The Institute has confirmed that the suspect, identified as John Doe, was admitted this morning and died only a few hours later. Time of death is reported to be at 12:19 p.m. due to natural causes. The Institute refused to comment on the riot and will not substantiate if John Doe died during or before the riot occurred. There will be no autopsy to confirm cause of death. Channel 6 can exclusively report, that the body of the deceased has already been cremated."

The screen split so Alexis was on the right and the news anchor on the left.

"That seems a bit rushed. Can you tell us more about what happened?" the news anchor asked helpfully.

"Our sources say that it was a mistake and the result of coincidental timing. Our witness was unwilling to go on camera, so we are blurring his face and altering his voice to protect his identity."

The screen switched to a shot of a microphone being shoved into someone's blurred face. The mystery person began speaking, and his voice sounded deep and electronic.

"I was there, I saw it. The patients were going insane! More insane than usual, that is." The person laughed at his own joke. "The group in the cafeteria at the time was classified as being high-risk for violence. They were punching and fighting anyone they could get their hands on. This one buddy of mine had a huge shiner and split lip!" The witness was obviously getting excited over his story.

"What about the suspect John Doe? What can you tell us about his death and premature cremation?" the reporter asked to get back on topic.

"John Doe, yeah, he was one scary-looking dude. He was tall, over six feet, and muscles everywhere. I hear he just dropped over dead. The body was brought down to the building's morgue. Our contracted funeral home just happened to be onsite to deal with our unclaimed dead, and John Doe was sent with the rest for cremation before his paperwork was processed."

"So the sudden cremation was caused by human error?" asked the reporter.

The witness was silent for a moment, and then simply said, "Yes."

The screen went back to the live shot of the on-site reporter. "There you have it, folks. Stay tuned for updates on this developing story. This is Alexis Drummond, reporting live for Channel 6 News. Back to you, Bob."

"West Penn Psyche Institute would not comment on today's events, but Channel 6 News was able to get confirmation from Winston's Family Funeral Home, who performed the cremation."

The news anchor turned a page over on his desk and then said, "Today the mayor made new friends as he visited…"

John tuned out the rest of the broadcast. One corner of his lips lifted into a sly half-smile. Even with all the problems, their plan had worked.

After the news was over, he walked up to Beth and asked, "Can you help me put some food together? I'd like to take something to eat to my room."

Father glanced over, gave a curt nod, and went back to watching TV.

"I'll help!" said Abby quickly as she followed them to the kitchen. They all stood in front of the refrigerator, out of sight from the living room. Alice and Bunny were just finishing the dishes. As soon as they left, Abby couldn't hold back any longer. "What happened? Is Diana all right?"

"Diana's fine, and before you ask, I'm fine and Mrs. McNeally is fine. Did you catch that report on the news about Michael?" John asked them in a hurried whisper.

As both girls nodded solemnly, Beth said, "I'm so sorry to hear about Michael. I hope Diana isn't too upset."

"Michael's not dead," John dropped the news and waited for its impact.

Abby squeaked, "What?" and they had to shush her. Beth raised an eyebrow and said, "Explain."

"When I went into Pittsburgh today with Mrs. McNeally, Diana came with us. After we dropped off the scrap metal, we went and rescued Michael," John explained quickly. "He's in Mrs. McNeally's old rooming house. He was doped up at the institute, and Diana was making him sleep until we got him here. He should be waking up tonight."

"Beth, 'Jeopardy' is about to start," called Meg from the living room.

"I'll have to tell you the rest tomorrow. I'm hoping I can go to Mrs. M's house after morning chores. Father didn't give me any special jobs at dinner, so I should have some free time before lunch," John said as Beth quickly rummaged through the fridge and put an apple and a cheese stick in a brown lunch bag for him.

Back in the loft, John paced as he thought over all that had happened that day. He was hoping Diana would stop by with an update, but she never came. Eventually, he gave up and went to sleep.

CHAPTER 20 – A FOURTEENTH-CENTURY WARRIOR

The next morning, John still hadn't heard from Diana. After morning chores, he headed straight for Mrs. McNeally's house. Mrs. McNeally was there by herself. After exchanging "good mornings" with each other, John sat at the table where a tall stack of blueberry pancakes waited for him. John tore into the food, despite having already eaten breakfast. "Where is everyone?" he asked between bites. "What happened with Michael last night?"

Mrs. McNeally pulled out a chair and sat with him at the table. "He woke up yesterday evening. Diana talked with him most of the night. He took the whole situation pretty hard. I can't say that I blame him."

The back door slammed, announcing Diana's arrival. She joined them at the table and grabbed a pancake. She started picking at it without butter or syrup, eating it in small bites. John thought that she needed to learn how to eat, as he dragged half a pancake through a small lake of syrup on his plate before stuffing the whole thing in his mouth. Mrs. McNeally promptly passed him a napkin.

"You look awful," he said to Diana before he could censor his tongue.

Diana gave him an affronted look. Sighing, she said, "I hardly slept last night, and I also did that knowledge transfer to Michael."

"How is he?" John asked, frustrated that he was out of the loop.

"He's not doing so well," Diana said as she picked at the pancake. "He's heartbroken over losing Miranda and his child. He doesn't even know if it was a boy or a girl," she said sadly.

"Can I meet him?" John asked hopefully.

Diana and Mrs. McNeally exchanged a look he couldn't interpret. "He's not really up for company," Diana said hesitantly. "Mrs. M has only seen him for a few minutes here and there. He's talking to me because he knows me, but I don't think he wants to see anyone else right now."

"What did he say happened to him?" John asked, looking for any bit of information at this point.

"About what we expected," Diana sighed again. "He was freed from the statue but was really dazed and tired. His mind was in a fog when police took him into custody, and he slept most of that first day. He realized that he didn't understand the language, so he refused to talk. He didn't go into details, but I'm guessing the police were pretty rough on him. The guards harassed him a lot because he wouldn't speak. After a few days he hit back and got sent to solitary confinement. The guards left him alone after that, although people in suits kept trying to interview him. He heard someone speaking Italian in the jail, but he said it was different than his Italian, and the guy who was speaking it wasn't anyone he wanted to get to know.

"When do you think he'll be ready to meet people?" John asked.

"Maybe tomorrow?" said Diana. "He's sleeping now, and I'm going to take a nap, too."

John looked down to his nearly empty plate and pushed the remaining food around dejectedly. What was the matter with him? Of course the guy was upset. He wouldn't want to trade places with him for anything. Michael also didn't know John from Adam. It just was that after all the things he went through to save Michael yesterday, he felt that he should at least meet the guy.

Mrs. McNeally put a comforting hand over his and said, "You'll get to meet him tomorrow; he won't be going anywhere soon. Come back tomorrow morning after chores, and we'll see how he is doing, okay?"

John pushed back from the table and took his plate over to the sink. "Alright, I guess I'll see you tomorrow then," he said with a half-hearted wave as he slouched out of the house and headed home.

Beth and Abby found him and coaxed him into a walk so he could tell them about his adventures the day before. He readily agreed; it was Thursday, and the rich girls would be there soon with their trainer for their riding lessons. He managed to miss them the week before by heading over to Mrs. McNeally's house to empty the imaginary buckets of leaking sewage. The walk cheered him significantly, as he was able to tell his sisters about Claire, the riot, and how he saved Michael from being cremated. Beth was duly impressed by his problem-solving capability under stress.

"Using your boot to keep the door open, John, that was very clever," Beth said approvingly. To Beth there was no higher compliment than to praise one's intellect.

"John, you're a hero!" Abby proclaimed loudly, skipping and hopping in her exuberance.

The rest of the day was uneventful. John worked on starting the invisibility projection during his free time, but just couldn't get it. By supper he was tired and drained. After dinner John followed everyone into the living room. His back end was feeling much better, so he sat on the floor. Christie was too wound up to sit in his lap. She took advantage of his being at her level and wrapped her soft toddler arms around his neck. Then she proceeded to try to jump on his head and shoulders, nearly strangling him in the process. She showed no signs of slowing down after five minutes, so John grabbed her with one of his long arms and pulled her into his lap. There she played with his hands, trying to make them clap, then folding and unfolding each finger into a fist. John wasn't paying much attention to her. He wanted to see if there was any more news on Michael. He didn't have to wait long; it was the leading story of the night.

"We bring you updates to the bizarre circumstances surrounding yesterday's death of the Museum vandal suspect."

"As we exclusively reported, the primary suspect in the violent and costly vandalism at the Carnegie Museum of Natural History died of natural causes within hours of being transferred to West Penn Psych Institute yesterday. Mistakes made at the Institute caused the body to be immediately cremated, ruling out the chance to do an autopsy. Since our report released, several eyewitnesses have contacted the station with further information. Alexis Drummond has the story."

The screen switched to Alexis standing somewhere downtown. "That's right, Bob; Channel 6 News has exclusive interviews from people who were at West Penn Psych yesterday. Our sources asked that we not reveal their identity due to the sensitive nature of this story. Here is what they had to say."

A woman with her face blurred and her voice altered said, "I was in the cafeteria after the riot. There were large men in prison-orange covering the floor, and several attendants and guards were bloodied and bruised. It messed up the schedule for the whole afternoon. The cafeteria was closed for hours, so meals had to be delivered individually."

"Why were those patients dressed in orange?" asked the reporter before shoving the mic back at Ms. Blurry.

"Patients dressed in orange are either criminally insane or incompetent to stand trial, like that John Doe."

The screen flipped to a man, also blurred and speaking in a mechanical voice. "The whole place was crazy that day. There was the riot in the cafeteria, but there also was a huge commotion in one of the common rooms just before lunch."

"Can you tell us about it?"

"The common room was full of elderly dementia patients. Several of them started screaming, and then they *all* were screaming. The odd thing was, everyone hallucinated the same thing."

"What did they see, or think they saw?"

"Part of a face and a disembodied hand floating in the air."

"What do the doctors say, can they explain it?"

"Their best guess is that they all watched the same TV show and got it mixed up with reality. Still, I thought it was weird."

The camera returned to Alexis. "When asked if the police would launch an investigation over these suspicious circumstances, the Chief of Police said there was not enough information to substantiate one at this point in time."

"To add to the intrigue surrounding this story, we received the following video, taken from a cell phone by someone in the West Penn Psych lobby yesterday afternoon around 1:30 p.m."

The screen switched to an amateur video of a middle-aged woman sitting on a chair in the institute's lobby, the building's doors directly behind her.

"Smile Mom!" came a cheery voice.

"Put that away before I take it away," was the weary response. In the background you could see Mrs. McNeally shuffling inside and the two businessmen in suits impatiently walking around her to get to the reception desk.

"Well, hello! What do we have here?" said the narrator, moving the phone from the woman to the businessmen. "I'm going to get closer. Those guys are hot!"

"Sit back down, we'll be called any moment now," said the mother.

The video wobbled as the owner of the phone walked to the desk. She got there in time to see the receptionist pick up the phone and begin the same conversation John had overheard. When the men said they were representing Lord Vito Dragotta, the person recording the video took in a sharp breath. A moment later, the screen was jerked roughly away, and you could hear the mother's voice saying, "They called us. It's time to go see Grandma," before the video ended.

The TV screen went back to Alexis. The video had passed over the spot John had been standing, and it looked like nothing was there. John thought it was freaky.

"Yes, you heard correctly. Lord Vito Dragotta, one of the richest men in the world, is somehow connected with this mysterious John Doe. Representatives of Mr. Dragotta refused to comment."

The screen split to show Alexis on the right and the anchorman on the left. The anchorman asked, "Will the police question Lord Vito Dragotta?"

"They probably will; however, Mr. Dragotta rarely visits Pittsburgh. We expect a formal statement to be made by the Dragotta representatives very soon."

"Thank you, Alexis," said the anchorman before the view of the reporter disappeared. "And remember, you heard it here first on Channel 6 News," the anchorman said straight into the camera. Music started playing, the station's cue that they were cutting to a commercial.

John wasn't sure what to think about the newscast. One thing he did know was that he was going to ask Michael about Lord Vito Dragotta.

* * *

The next morning John headed over to Mrs. McNeally's, just as he'd done the day before. Also like the day before, Mrs. McNeally was waiting for him in the kitchen with a big stack of pancakes. Today they had chocolate chips in them. John momentarily forgot his purpose, as he dowsed his stack in butter and syrup and dug in. Mrs. McNeally watched him with amusement. "When you come up for air, we can talk about Michael," she teased.

"Mm hmm nm," John intoned with his mouth full. John swallowed a huge gob and said, "How is he? Can I meet him today?"

"Finish your food first," Mrs. McNeally instructed. "That should take about all of two minutes."

John cleaned his plate with the last bite of pancake in under a minute. "Well?" he asked impatiently.

"He's a little bit more put together today. He actually talked with me for a while this morning. Diana's told him about you and your part in his 'liberation,' and he wants to meet you."

John jumped up from the table like a kid at Christmas and was to the door when Mrs. McNeally chided, "Plate!" He whirled back around and took his dishes to the sink, taking care to rinse his plate. It didn't take much as he'd all but licked it clean. Then he ran out of the house.

Once in the yard, he forced himself to slow down. Seriously, why was he so geared up to meet this guy? He couldn't explain it even to himself. Did he want a thank you for getting him out of the looney bin? No, that wasn't it. He did that more for Diana than for Michael. Was it just that he was this cool Italian muscle man that was centuries old? That was part of it. He couldn't give a name to the rest of the reason. It was kind of a combination of wanting to know a piece of Diana's past, sympathy for what Michael had to be going through, and guilt for getting Diana out of the museum but leaving Michael there. He rushed into the rooming house, being careful not to slam the door. No one was there. His heart skipped a beat, fearing something was wrong. He stepped back outside and scanned the yard. He saw Diana leaving the chicken coup with a basket, heading for the house. He jogged up to her and asked, "Hey, do you know where Michael is?"

Diana shifted her heavy basket from one arm to the other. "Hi John! How are you? I'm fine, thanks for asking."

John fell into place beside her and lifted the basket from her hands. "Hi, Diana, how are you? You're fine? That's great. Have you noticed what a beautiful day it is today?" John said mockingly, but he relaxed a bit at the jesting and gave her a half smile.

Diana wiped some sweat from her brow before she smiled back at him. John noticed she had several chicken feathers stuck in her hair and on her clothes. He held the basket with one hand and grabbed at the fluff in her hair with the other as they continued walking.

Diana instantly put both hands up to her hair and ducked away from him. "What? What's wrong with my hair?" she said in a high voice.

John laughed as he held up a downy feather, "You have some stuff in your hair. I don't know a lot about girl fashion, but I don't think chicken feathers are in style."

Diana swatted the feather out of his hand and dragged her fingers frantically through her hair. "Did I get them? Did I get them all?"

"Almost. There's a couple left. Put your hands down and let me see," John said, laughing. Diana lowered her arms while they both continued to walk slowly towards the house. John grabbed two more feathers from her hair and let the wind take them. Unable to resist, he grabbed a lock of her hair hanging over her shoulder and gave it a teasing tug. "All better. Now you just need to brush off your clothes."

Diana looked down at herself and gave a small, surprised wail before she started laughing. "I asked Mrs. M what I could do to help today, and she sent me to get the eggs. She didn't warn me about the feathers, and she certainly didn't warn me about that nasty old rooster!"

John laughed with her, trying to imagine her facing down the ancient, territorial rooster that was still hanging on to life by a thread. After their laughter died down, he said, "So, did you see Michael?"

"Oh, sorry, John, he's in the barn chopping wood. He was getting stir-crazy in the rooming house, and I don't blame him. Mrs. M thought it best if he worked out of sight of her 'nosy neighbors.' Here, give me my eggs back." She made a grab for the basket, but John held it out of her reach.

"Nuh-uh, I'll carry this. You brush off those feathers. Those carry lots of germs you know." Diana squealed and began brushing off her clothes as if she had ants crawling all over her. John laughed again. "I'm just joking, there's hardly any left." Diana gave him a sour look that made John laugh louder. They were at the back steps to the house by then, and John carried the heavy basket into the kitchen for her.

Mrs. McNeally lifted a critical eyebrow at him and said, "Weren't you all hell's bells to see Michael? What are you doing back here?" Then she noticed the basket of eggs and beamed at Diana. She exclaimed, "Well done, child! Well done!" as she turned and took the eggs to the sink.

"See ya later, Mrs. M, Diana," John said as he ran back out of the house and towards the barn. His teasing banter with Diana had settled his nerves, but as he got closer to the barn and heard the thwack of an axe hitting wood, his heart sped up. The barn doors were opened slightly, and Michael was standing in the middle of the floor wearing the boots and leather pants he wore when trapped inside the statue. He wasn't wearing a shirt, and John took a mental step back, even though outwardly he didn't alter his pace. The guy on the news was right; Michael was huge. He had muscles in places John didn't know there were supposed to be muscles. The chopping block had been moved into the barn, and Michael was working his way methodically through a stack of wood. John watched as Michael placed a big piece of wood on the block, swung the axe up and over his shoulder, then split the wood in a single, perfectly aimed slice of the blade. John tried hard not to flinch but wasn't sure if he was successful. The pancakes in his stomach churned with his unease.

When Michael moved to pile the newly split wood, he noticed John. The big man dusted off his hands and grabbed a small rag to wipe his face as he cautiously studied him. John sucked up some courage, took a step forward, hand out, and said, "Hi, I'm John Brown. I live at the farm across the road."

Michael took his hand and gave him a single, firm shake as he said in a deep, measured voice, "Nice to meet you, John. I am Lord Michael Dragotta di Florence." John looked him straight in the eyes as they shook hands, just as he was taught. When his hand returned to his side, he was at a loss for words.

Michael moved over to a couple of bales of hay and sat down, motioning for John to join him. John sat, trying not to look as meek and scared on the outside as he did on the inside next to this powerful man... who was a *lord* for crying out loud. Somehow, Diana failed to mention that. Maybe she had, but he forgot.

"I hear I owe a good part of my present freedom to you, young sir, for getting me out of that ... institution." He said the last word like it tasted foul on his tongue.

"You're welcome," John said, adding, "Sir." He wasn't sure how you were supposed to address a lord.

"And I learn as well, that you are solely responsible for freeing Diana and me from our centuries' long stony imprisonment," Michael continued, his expression unreadable.

"Y-yes, Sir," John stuttered.

"I appreciate all you have done for me, and even more so, am grateful for the assistance you have given little Diana," Michael said formally.

In answer John blurted, "Diana isn't so little. She's about the same age as me, and if she is little, then you're calling me little, and besides, Diana can do some incredible things with her Crystavis, none of which are little." John was amazed at himself for speaking out like that, and he held his breath to see what Michael's reaction would be.

To his surprise, Michael's face slightly softened. "No, I suppose you are right, the magic Diana performs with her Crystavis is anything but little."

"Don't let her hear you calling it magic. I think that's a pet peeve of hers. She prefers to call it *science*," John said, relaxing a bit in the commonality they found in their respect for Diana.

"So she does," Michael agreed. Michael sighed as a look of sadness and a fatigue of life took over his face. "I suppose you are curious about how I came to be...here," he said, spreading out his hands, gesturing to the entire barn.

"Yes, I do. I mean yes, I am. I am curious. Diana told me you weren't trying to hurt her, that you were trying to force her to talk to you. Oh, and she didn't tell me you were anything special, like a *lord*." John internally winced at his choice of words.

Michael didn't seem to notice. "Yes, I had tried approaching her on multiple occasions to find out what had happened to my wife and why she had not returned in two months' time. Besides my Miranda, the only Zigonians I had met were Diana and Miranda's maid, Mirabelle. Diana is the only one who ever ventured out of that unnatural Zigon rift in the universe after Miranda's disappearance. She has filled me in on what happened leading up to that fateful day. What she hasn't been able to explain is why you were able to break our stone bonds, when my Miranda could not after years of trying."

"I have no idea," claimed John honestly. "Diana did say I have some Zigon blood in me. She's been teaching me how to do stuff, to *project*. I did something really strong by instinct the other day, and she said she suspected that I might have not New Zigon blood, but original Zigon blood in my family history. We'll never know though. I'm an orphan the Browns adopted, and I have no idea who my real parents are."

"Fascinating," Michael considered as he looked off into space and rubbed his prickly chin. Michael had a couple days of growth on his beard. His long blond and brown hair was tied back with a small leather cord.

"So…you're a lord? Does that mean you're like royalty or something?"

Michael gave John his full attention again as he answered. "Yes I am a lord, but my cousin, Lord Vito, is, I mean *was*, on the ruling council of the city-state Florence. We were not royalty, but we were landowners and successful merchants, and quite wealthy I might add. I still am confused as to why Miranda's parents would not approve our match, even with the differences of New Zigon."

"Wait, so Lord Vito Dragotta is your cousin?" spluttered John.

"He was my cousin, yes."

"I'm not so sure he's a *was*. Diana said that Lord Vito tortured and killed Lady Aberlene to get a Life Crystavis. He could have been regenerating himself for years. And there was a Lord Vito Dragotta looking for you at the institute. We barely got there in time."

"Hmmm," Michael said pensively as he looked down at his large, clasped hands. "Lord Vito and I did not always see things the same way," Michael admitted. "His main concerns were in politics and making money. I led and trained our warriors to defend our land. He used stealth and trickery to achieve his objectives. I lived by truth, loyalty, and honor. Actually, I am not sure we saw anything the same way."

Michael let out a weary sigh and dropped his head. "I fear this whole debacle is my fault. I trusted Lord Vito with Miranda's secret. I encouraged Miranda to take him into confidence against her better judgment. I did not realize the depth of his fixation on New Zigon power. He questioned Miranda for hours on how her power worked, what she could do, what she couldn't do, and the strengths of the individuals in New Zigon. What has come to be known as the Black Plague was sweeping Europe at the time, and

Lord Vito was terrified. I should have guessed that he would be planning some deception to obtain New Zigon power to protect himself. It appears he not only protected himself from the Black Plague, but from death itself."

"You couldn't have known," John said as a pitiful attempt at comfort. "Whatever Lord Vito did was his own fault and not yours."

"Logic tells me that is true, but it is small comfort against all I have lost," Michael said quietly. An agonized look consumed his face, and John felt extremely uncomfortable.

"Well, I have to go home and get back to work. It's nice to meet you, Sir," John said hesitantly as he stood.

Michael nodded at him, and John escaped the barn and the despair that was radiating off Michael in waves so thick, he could almost taste it. A few paces outside of the barn he could hear the thwack of the axe as Michael resumed splitting wood. John once again marveled at Mrs. McNeally's insight into people. She had known that a man like him, a warrior he'd called himself, would need something physical to help him deal with his emotions. Guys, emotions, and sharing? Those words didn't belong together in a sentence. Working up a sweat, hitting, and breaking things? Mrs. McNeally was a genius.

CHAPTER 21 – BONDING TIME

John went back to the farm, and the day was almost a repeat of the one before. He had lunch, went for a walk with Beth and Abby, and practiced trying to project invisibility on his own. He understood now why Diana and Mrs. McNeally had been hesitant to let him meet Michael. The man was… broken inside. John had a feeling Michael would pull himself together eventually, but he'd felt uncomfortably useless in the face of all that pain. Diana had taken things remarkably well when compared with Michael. Either Diana wasn't that close to her family, or she was a stronger person than he'd given her credit for. He suspected the latter.

The next day was Saturday, and Father kept John busy with work from sunup to sundown. Diana came over to the loft after dinner and insisted they practice his projection. This time he was able to start his own invisibility projection by just looking at Diana's projection without touching it. He still couldn't do it on his own without her there, but it was progress. Diana continually told him how great he was doing, but it didn't ease his frustration. She was really impressed with the way he'd extended his projection over other objects, like the phone book and Michael's bag of possessions at the institute. She had him practice that extension over various things in the loft, like a book or shoe, and worked all the way up to larger things like his table and bed before she finally left. In the few seconds between when John's head hit the pillow that night and when he fell asleep, he realized that Diana was not only a slave driver, but a perfectionist, too. He wasn't so sure he liked that about her at the moment.

Church on Sunday morning was uneventful until Mrs. McNeally shuffled over and played on Father's character like a master. She talked him into letting John come over to her house to work on a project from Monday morning through Tuesday evening. John wondered if Father would start leaving the church right after Mass to avoid being cornered again. Father didn't seem too happy about this arrangement and worked John to the bone the rest of the day to make up for the time he would be away. John fell asleep that night before Diana had a chance to come over and drill him with more practicing. He was curious about what they had in mind for the next two days, and he had all kinds of wild dreams about it. First, he dreamt Michael was training him to be a warrior and fight with a sword, then he and Diana were moving tractors with their minds. One dream had him, Mrs. McNeally, Diana, and Michael sitting around Mrs. McNeally's kitchen table. They were eating chocolate chip pancakes, but they were all floating four feet off the floor, table and chairs included.

The next morning after chores, dreams forgotten, John was sitting at Mrs. McNeally's kitchen table eating Belgian Waffles with strawberries, when he got the first inkling of their plan. Bonding time. A shudder went down his spine. They wanted him and Diana to take Michael on a hike and then a picnic. Apparently, they had two days' worth of activities lined up.

"But I thought he wasn't supposed to show his face around here?" John asked, trying to argue against it.

"He won't exactly be showing his face, John," said Mrs. McNeally, steadfast in her plan. "You'll be staying on the property, going through the leased sections to the glade on the east border of the farm. You may be seen by the neighbors, but they are going to have to see him eventually if he is going to be staying here any length of time."

"What does Diana think about this?"

"She thinks it is a wonderful idea, as do I, it being my idea and all!" she joked. "Now go meet Diana and Michael. They should be waiting for you in the barn."

John did as he was told, trying to change his attitude about the day. Internally, he always put up walls when he was forced to socialize. He tried to calm down, reminding himself that he'd be spending most of the day with Diana, and she was his friend. Michael made him a bit nervous, but with Diana there as a buffer, everything would be fine, right? John adjusted the pack Mrs. McNeally had given him for their lunch and went into the barn. He stopped short at the sight that greeted him.

Michael and Diana were playing some kind of game, and they were both winded and laughing hard. The transformation on Michael was astounding. The severe edge was gone for the moment, and he was dressed in regular clothes… boots, jeans, T-shirt, and ball cap. It looked like he'd cut his hair, too. John watched them chase each other for a few moments before stepping towards them, clearing his throat. "Hi guys! I guess we're going on a hike today? Nice clothes, Michael, sir."

"Just call me 'Michael' please. Mrs. McNeally went to a thrift store yesterday. These clothes are different from what I am used to, but they are growing on me." Michael closed the distance between them and held out his hand for John to shake. This shake was a little less stiff than the last one had been. "Shall we go?" Michael asked.

John took a quick look at Diana, also in jeans and a T-shirt, her hair pulled back in a ponytail. John felt out of place in his overalls. Maybe he should check out the thrift store. Why didn't he ever think of that before? A thought hit him looking at Diana. He and Michael had golden skin that tanned in the sun, but she looked white as a sheet. "Diana, I think you should go see Mrs. McNeally for some sunscreen."

"That's a great idea," Diana said brightly. "I normally use a projection or just heal myself afterwards, but why waste the energy, right? Be right back!"

Once she left, John awkwardly adjusted the pack on his back and looked around the barn for ideas on what to say. "It looked like a fun game," he finally commented.

Michael took off his ball cap and swiped a hand through his hair before putting it back on. "I suppose."

"How long have you known each other?"

Michael sat down on a hay bale and answered, "I met Diana nearly four years ago." He paused for a moment, and then corrected himself. "Four years before the statue caged us, that is."

John felt responsible for the sadness that drifted across Michael's face, but most conversations would eventually bring up something from the past. Since the damage was already done, he may as well push forward. It was easier to talk to Michael when he was sitting down and John was standing. Having that bit of height advantage boosted his courage. "You two seem to be pretty close. Did you get to spend much time with her before...?"

Michael sighed, "Yes, I did. She was nine when I met her. That was around the age she started increasing her training, and Miranda took her to this little meadow on my land to practice. I ran across them one day when out riding, and kept running across them, more by intention than coincidence. Miranda was a spitfire, not at all like the females of my time. When I first met them, I asked if they realized they were trespassing. Miranda defended their presence so ardently, she convinced me it was my privilege for them to be on my lands. She did not know at the time how true those words were." Michael's face had lost his sadness and was almost smiling at the memory. This was more information than John had been looking for, but there was no way he would interrupt.

"They would always stop their practicing whenever I came by, and I never saw them leave or arrive. I could not figure out where they had come from. One day, I rode to the meadow and they were not there. I was about to leave when I saw them come out of the waterfall at the far end of the clearing." Michael chuckled. "I nearly lost my mount, I was so unsettled. I confronted her and accused her of witchcraft. I was in anguish that this beautiful woman that I was beginning to care for, could be capable of such atrocities. She sent Diana back through the waterfall, then came running at me like a demon. I was so stunned, I did not realize I was dismounting on the opposite side of the horse from her. She kept apologizing for allowing me to see how they got there. She continually tried to slip around the front of my horse to get close, and I kept maneuvering the mare to keep her between us. I am sure it appeared quite comical."

Michael was really smiling now, and John took off his pack and sat on a hay bale, settling in for the story.

"She finally managed to duck under the horse's head. She came at me trying to touch my face with her hand. I backed away from her until I hit a tree. When she reached for my face, I grabbed her wrist. When she raised her other hand, I grabbed that wrist as well. I spun us so she was the one against the tree, and I… we…"

John swore the warrior started to blush. "You what?" asked John, intrigued.

Michael cleared his throat and looked away. "We discussed the matter."

That seemed to be all Michael was going to say, so John prompted, "And?"

"And she decided to trust me to keep her secret. She had been trying to touch my face to wipe my memory. After that, I spent a lot of time in that meadow. They let me witness their lessons, and I learned about New Zigon, Crystavis, and the things they could do. I courted Miranda in earnest, and within a year she accepted my proposal to wed. When I took her to my keep to introduce her to my family, she slipped up once in front of Lord Vito without her realizing it. She found herself doing that several times. Now I suspect he had set small traps for her that encouraged her to use her power where he could witness it. If he had confronted us right away, Miranda would have done a simple memory wipe. As it was, Lord Vito could be quite the charmer when he put his mind to it, and he wanted to know all about New Zigon. I backed Lord Vito and encouraged Miranda to trust him. I was blinded by our blood connection and did not see the depths of his flaws."

"We married within the year. She convinced me that her parents would not approve, and she did not want to tell them. She would spend half her time with me at the keep and the other half in New Zigon to keep up the pretense."

Michael stopped talking, but it seemed he was reliving many memories as he sat there. John watched as the remembered happiness turned to grief over the loss of making more memories with his wife.

After a while John decided to prompt him, "You were going to tell me about you and Diana?"

"Oh, yes. My apologies, I went rather off topic. Diana, yes. She was like the little sister I never had. Miranda treated her as a sister as well, yet they shared no blood between them. Anyone Miranda loved so unconditionally could not be anything other than very dear to me. We spent a lot of time together in that meadow, and the three of us became a family long before Miranda and I actually married."

"I think of you as family, too. I'm sorry I doubted you after the whole lassoing-and-turning-into-stone thing," said Diana, who had just returned from the house.

Michael stood and said in a choked, vulnerable voice, "Diana, I am so sorry for scaring you like that with the rope. I have no idea what I was thinking. You would not talk to me, and I had not seen Miranda in months. With her being with child, I was so anxious…"

Diana ran up to him and gave him a big hug around the waist. Her head barely came up to his chest. "I'm sorry, too! Let's just forget about it, okay?"

Michael returned the hug, saying, "I doubt either of us will forget what happened, but perhaps we can move past it."

"Sounds good to me," Diana said, her voice muffled into Michael's T-shirt.

John quietly left to give them some privacy.

* * *

The two soon joined him outside, and Michael immediately stripped John of the pack. "Hey," John said, startled. "Um, I can carry that." Michael just gave him a smile like one would give to a small child. To John it said, "Don't be ridiculous, you are just a boy and taking care of things is beyond your years." The fragile bond they made in the barn slipped a bit. John didn't say anything else about it, but he sulked for a while, like the little boy Michael had painted him to be.

It was a beautiful day, the clear blue sky reflecting in Diana's eyes. She nearly skipped as they made their way along the cleared path between two fields. Maybe she was skipping just to keep up. Michael was walking with an easy stride, but his legs were so long, a single step was worth at least three of Diana's. John had to hustle every so often to keep up as well. Finally, Diana stopped slightly out of breath in front of Michael and yelled at him. "Michael! This is supposed to be a relaxing walk, not a run! I can't keep up with you!"

Michael snapped out of the haze he'd been in since they started. John knew the beautiful day had gone unnoticed by Michael. "I'm sorry, Diana. I will slow down, but let us stop for a moment; you seem out of breath," Michael said, moving to stand under a tree along the path.

John was grateful Diana spoke up. He would have just kept suffering rather than admit any form of weakness. John found his own tree, and let the surrounding nature calm him. They were just about to continue their walk, when two sharp CRACKs filled the air. They all turned back to the house.

"What was that?" Diana asked hesitantly.

CRACK!

"That sounds like…" John said.

CRACK!

"Gunfire!" John said as he sprinted back towards the house.

* * *

John had only one thought as he ran: Mrs. McNeally. Michael quickly surpassed him with his longer legs. Then Diana sped past both of them, her amulet glowing brightly in her hand and her feet not touching the ground. It looked like she was flying!

"Diana!" John yelled in both wonderment and reproach.

"Diana! No! Wait for me! Stop! Diana!" Michael continued to roar as Diana moved beyond their sight. Michael increased his efforts and soon was almost a field's length ahead of John. John didn't have the endurance for this kind of running, and his boots weren't helping. He slowed to a walk, clutching the cramp in his side, but soon went back to running as his fear of what happened to Mrs. McNeally overtook him.

By the time the farm came into view, the few minutes of running seemed like an eternity to John. First he noticed a shiny black SUV parked behind the barn out of sight from the road. Then he saw Jay Cooper running towards the house from the left and his father driving the tractor towards the house from across the road. He got there well ahead of Jay and Father. No one else was in sight; he figured they must all be in the house. John tried to get his ragged breathing under control. His heart was racing both in fear and from the run.

Some instinct told him not to enter the house. He moved to stand under the open kitchen window.

"You'll do exactly as I told you, or I shoot the girl!" he heard someone snarl. "And don't play the old and helpless act with us again! We know better now, and won't make the same mistake twice. Now go to the door and get rid of them!"

He heard Diana sniff and let out a small whimper. "Don't worry, Diana, everything will be all right. I'll be right back," Mrs. McNeally said in a comforting voice, but John could hear the undertones of worry.

"Everything *won't* be all right until you go to the door and get rid of your neighbors!" the man growled.

John heard overlapping shouts from Jay and Father calling Mrs. McNeally's name. Mrs. McNeally went to stand on the front porch. "I'm all right!" she called out. "Everything is fine! No need to worry!" John crept around the house until he was closer to the front door and out of Jay's line of site. Ducking behind a bush, he heard Jay thunder up the steps.

"Mrs. M! I heard gunshots! What happened? Is everyone okay?" Jay said between gasps as he tried to catch his breath after his impressive run. Father wasn't far behind. He left the tractor running a ways from the house and walked the rest of the distance.

"Edna, what happened? Where's John?" his father demanded.

Mrs. McNeally tried to assuage them, repeating, "I'm all right, no need to worry! John's fine. He's checking on something for me in the far fields."

"What about the gunshots? What happened?" Father persisted.

162

"Oh, silly old me," Mrs. McNeally said chuckling at herself. "I was cleaning and came across Arthur's old pistol. I was feeling sentimental, remembering all the target practice he did with the thing, and I went outside and took a couple of practice shots myself, that's all. I'm sorry I didn't warn you. I have to say though, I'm quite touched that you would so swiftly come to my rescue should anything happen!"

"Mrs. M, of course we'll come when there's trouble. Warn us next time. Better yet, don't be firing a gun in the first place!" Jay ranted.

"I agree with the boy," said Father. "You have no business firing a gun unnecessarily. Enjoy the rest of your day."

John peeked through the branches to see Father head back home. With the way Father held himself and the irritation in his voice, John guessed he was angry at the interruption and the lost time.

"You scared me Mrs. M! Please don't do that again!"

John heard soft thudding sounds, and he imagined Mrs. McNeally giving Jay a hug and thumping him on the back.

"Oh, don't you worry about me. Go on now; I've taken enough of your day."

John heard Jay call his mother on a cell phone, reporting that everything was all right. John managed to catch Mrs. M's eye after Jay left. She gave him a warning look and a sharp shake of her head before going back inside. Unsure what to do, he returned to the spot under the kitchen window.

"Well done, lady. You're quite the little actress, aren't you, you old bird."

"What do you want with us?" Mrs. McNeally demanded.

"We don't want anything from you; Lord Vito wants something from *him*," the intruder said, followed by a sick-sounding thud.

John very carefully peeked up over the lip of the windowsill and saw Michael lying unconscious on the floor and two men dressed in suits. They were the same two businessmen from the hospital. One had Mrs. McNeally by the arm and had a gun shoved in her back. The other had Diana backed into a corner and had his gun aimed at her.

"Please, don't kick him again!" Diana cried. "What are you going to do?"

"We have a message for you to give Michael. Lord Vito wants him to get the Primary Life Crystavis."

"Why does he want that? He has the one Lady Aberlene made for him *over six centuries ago*. Apparently, it works well enough," Diana argued.

"Lord Vito has his reasons; it is not for us to question," was the only reply given.

"How is he supposed to do that? The Primary Crystavis have been missing for centuries! What makes you think Michael can find it, and what makes you think he will do this for you anyway?" Diana pushed, her voice growing louder.

"He can find it," the man pointing a gun at Diana said, "because it was his wife who stole it."

"And he will do it for us," continued the man holding Mrs. McNeally, "if he ever wants to see Grandma here again."

"What?"

The man guarding Diana took a card out of his coat pocket and threw it on the table. "Call the number on the card when you have news. If we don't hear from you in twenty-four hours, there will be a little less of Grannie to return to you."

The kitchen turned to bedlam as Mrs. McNeally struggled and shouted insults, while Diana screamed for them to stop. John wanted to race into the kitchen to help, but knew he couldn't go up against two guns. He gritted his teeth and clenched his fists, frantically trying to think of a way to help. If he could turn invisible, he could sneak up behind one of the men. John tried to start the projection, but with his blood racing and fear consuming him, he couldn't even do the projection to hide his shadow.

He heard a loud *thunk*, and Mrs. McNeally stopped yelling and Diana's scream grew impossibly louder. He peered over the sill just in time to see one of the men backhand Diana across the face. She was thrown backwards into the wall before she slid to the floor cupping her cheek. Mrs. McNeally was slumped in the other man's grip, and she had fresh blood dampening her hair. John's stomach clenched as he realized the goon had probably butted her on the head with his gun.

John bolted to his feet, ready to storm into the house, but he paused at the back corner when he heard the screen door slam shut. Both men were racing towards and behind the barn to get to their vehicle. One of them had Mrs. McNeally thrown over his shoulder like a sack of potatoes. John's heart tore in two at the helplessness of the situation. Now that the men were out of the house, he could call the police, but they still had Mrs. McNeally, and they could kill her if he made the wrong move. John raced into the house, calling Diana's and Michael's names.

Amulet out, Diana had her free hand over Michael's head. Tears were streaming down her face. John went to kneel beside her, wondering if he should lend her his power again. The amulet's glow died, and Diana dropped her hand only to turn and throw her arms around John. John held onto her, thankful that she was there and unharmed.

"They took her, John. They took Mrs. M!" Diana said between hiccupping sobs.

"I know," John said roughly as he heard the SUV peel out of the driveway.

Michael groaned and moved on the floor. Diana broke their hug to check on him.

"What happened to him?" John asked.

"They hit him on the head with their gun and kicked him several times."

Michael sat up slowly, holding his head. John noticed blood drying on Michael's forehead. John wetted some paper towels at the sink then handed them to Michael. When John noticed the bright red mark on Diana's cheek from getting backhanded, he said, "Diana, why don't you heal your face. It looks pretty nasty. I can lend you some power if you need it."

"Thanks, John. It *is* kind of throbbing." Diana held her amulet and closed her eyes. John put his hand on her shoulder and envisioned sending her amulet his strength. He got that same warm glowing feeling in his chest as the other times. He watched in amazement as the red mark dissolved before his eyes. Michael stood and helped Diana to her feet. John stood as well, and in silent agreement they all sat around the kitchen table.

"What happened?" Michael said, looking directly at Diana.

"They took Mrs. McNeally and said we had to give them the Primary Life Crystavis to get her back." She fingered the card the man left. "They said we have twenty-four hours to give them an update or they'll hurt her." Fresh tears spilled from Diana's eyes, but otherwise she kept her composure.

Michael snatched the card from Diana's hands, and John leaned over to look at it. It was Lord Vito Dragotta's personal business card. There was one phone number and an address that was in Pennsylvania, but John didn't recognize the town. Michael balled his other fist and was clenching his jaw. John was surprised he didn't tear the card to pieces.

"Can you fill me in on what happened from the beginning?" John asked Diana. "I got here ahead of my father and Jay. I was outside the window, listening."

Michael slammed a fist on the table, making John and Diana jump. "You were *here* and you *just listened* as you hid like a coward? You did not do anything to help?" Michael bellowed.

John pushed back his chair as he stood up. "What was I supposed to do? Walk through the door and get knocked out like you did?"

"You had the advantage of knowing the situation you were walking into. You could have taken them by surprise!"

"And why didn't you know what the situation was before *you* walked in, huh? You didn't help anyone by bursting blindly through that door. So what if I could have surprised them. What next? They would take an extra second or two before they shot me?"

Michael stood up and loomed over him as he said, "That is not the point. The point is that you did not even *try!*"

"Stop it!" Diana screamed, now standing, too. "Stop it, both of you!" she said in a slightly calmer voice. "Everyone take a deep breath and sit down so we can talk. This is not helping Mrs. M!" John was reeling from Michael's sudden attack as they grudgingly sat down. He was already beating himself up; he didn't need Michael adding to his guilt.

"John is right," Diana said as she put a comforting hand over Michael's large fist. "Those men were dangerous. They threatened to hurt Mrs. McNeally if I tried using my amulet. They said if my hand went anywhere near my necklace, that they would … cut Mrs. M." Diana gulped. "When I got here, one of them had wrestled Mrs. McNeally to the floor and was knocking her gun away. I don't know who did the shooting, but no one was hit. The other guy pointed his gun at me from the moment I opened the door. They started their threats before I could think of what to do. They knew not to touch me and trigger The Founder's Curse. They just cornered me with the gun and stood on opposite sides of the room so I couldn't easily project to both of them at the same time. I was trapped, but not physically captured. They knew there was a fine line between the two, and they knew how to walk it."

John tried to process what she said. It made sense that Lord Vito would know all about how to handle New Zigon power. The fact that he knew the limits of The Founder's Curse was unsettling. John wondered how he'd figured it out.

"Did they say how they found us?" Michael asked with laser-like focus.

"Yes, I asked them. They said the second newscast, where the station reported the floating hand and face being seen by the dementia patients, is what made Lord Vito suspect that something was up. It took them a while, but after checking all the security tapes they saw Mrs. McNeally getting in and out of her truck."

"So?" John asked, wondering how that could have led Lord Vito's men here.

"They said they saw the passenger's door open and close on its own. Three times," Diana said, not looking at John.

John thought he was going to be sick. He didn't even think about opening the truck's door when he was invisible. Mrs. McNeally hadn't thought of it either he realized, trying to make himself feel better. Luckily, Michael didn't seem to make the association that John was to blame.

"Then Michael nearly tore the door down, they knocked him out, and then the bad guys made Mrs. M deal with Jay and Mr. Brown." Diana turned to Michael. "Then they passed on the message from Lord Vito to you, that you have to get the Primary life Crystavis, and you have to call this number within twenty-four hours," Diana said tapping the business card.

"No need to wait twenty-four hours, I am calling now!" Michael declared as he went to pick up the corded phone hanging on the kitchen wall. John and Diana waited tensely. A few moments after dialing, Michael slammed the phone back on the wall with so much force, John feared it would break. "It went to voicemail. Lord Vito left a message just for me, saying not to bother calling until I had something useful to share," Michael explained at Diana's quizzical look.

Michael started to pace as Diana and John sat. Diana stared at John, watching for his reaction when she said, "We have to go back to New Zigon and talk to Gina."

"Gina?" Michael asked. "That is not…"

"Mirabelle's daughter? Yes it is," Diana confirmed.

"She's so old, she looks like a walking skeleton, but she's dangerous," John added.

"Dangerous?" Michael asked as if the idea were crazy. "That little slip of a girl? I have a hard time believing that."

"So did I, Michael, but she's lived through six and a half centuries since then. She used the Pleovis to throw John through the air and shot something at me that was as bad as a bullet."

"She shot you with something?" Michael asked, all protective concern.

"Yes, but John carried me out of there, and I was able to heal myself once we got home," Diana said, giving John a look that made his stomach flip a little.

"Hmph," Michael said, falling short of his usual eloquence. John saw the warrior give him a begrudging look that was far from approving. John wondered what he'd done to get on the guy's "unworthy" list.

"Why did she attack you? I thought you told me New Zigon was all but deserted?" Michael asked, attention fully on Diana again.

"She wants the Pollampium in Diana's amulet, because it is the biggest piece of Zigonite she has a chance of getting her bony claws on," John jumped in before Diana could answer. "She wants to use it to power up the Lacunavim before it dies."

"Let the bloody place die. You cannot afford to give up your amulet, you need it to defend yourself," said Michael.

"I agree," said John. Michael did give him a small nod at that.

"Why do you say we should go see her?" Michael asked.

"Because she has a Crystavis encoded with a message from Miranda to me," Diana said softly.

Michael froze like he was devoid of all emotion. "Did you just say…?"

"She has a message for me from Miranda. It may contain a hint as to where she put the Primary Crystavis she stole."

Michael's face went completely white before turning an angry red. Michael turned and gave them his back as he said in a strained voice, "There is a message from my wife, and you did not tell me because…?"

Diana didn't seem fazed by Michael's reaction. "I didn't tell you, because I thought it was too dangerous to confront Gina, and I doubted she would give it to us anyway."

"Well, we have to go now to save Mrs. M, don't we? Unless Michael has an idea of where Miranda may have hid all of the stolen Crystavis?" John said.

Michael still wouldn't turn to face them when he said dejectedly, "No, I have no idea where she might have stowed them. The only place I can think of is my castle, but I doubt she would risk running into Lord Vito, knowing what he did to her mother."

John inched his chair closer to Diana. "What are you thinking?" he said to her. "You said you doubted she would give it to us; do you have a plan? She wasn't exactly all warm and cuddly when we left."

"I'm thinking of giving her what she wants, my Pollampium."

"You can't do that!" John insisted. "You can't lose your amulet!"

"I agree," said Michael facing them once again. "Think of something else."

"Listen guys, I didn't say I would *give* her my amulet. I was thinking more that I would put my amulet on the central podium in the repository for a period of time, like maybe an hour or so, with the promise of more time after we get Mrs. M back."

"But we can't trust her!" John said, getting worried. "What's to stop her from attacking us again?"

"I can protect us if I'm prepared," Diana insisted.

"But once you let go of your amulet, you'll be helpless!"

"That's why we won't let her in the repository while I'm doing it."

"I don't like it," John said, frustrated.

"Can you think of a better plan?" Diana challenged.

After a long pause, John muttered, "No."

"I mean other than Michael over here trying to charm the encoded Crystavis from her, I think striking a deal with her is our best chance." Michael gave her a confused look.

"What, like you don't know?" Diana chided. "Eight-year-old Gina had a huge crush on you!"

"But I barely saw her once!" Michael said, aghast. "We never even spoke!"

"Apparently, you made an impression," Diana continued to push her teasing. "She talked about you all the time, and wanted every detail when she knew we had seen you."

Michael resumed his pacing, a confused scowl now on his face.

"Well, good or bad, it seems we have a plan," John said standing. "Where's the pack you took from me?" he asked Michael.

"What does that matter?" Michael asked, annoyed.

"Where is it?" John pressed.

"I dropped it a few feet from the house," Michael answered dismissively.

John rushed out of the house and came back with the pack. He opened it up and started setting out its contents on the table. Diana watched him in confusion.

"John, wha…?" she started.

"We don't have much time! We need to go confront Gina immediately. Diana, you should eat to get your strength up after healing Michael. Then I think we should go." What he didn't say was that he was trying to actually *do* something, to help in a tangible way.

No one argued with him as they ate the food Mrs. McNeally had prepared for them. John barely tasted it and had to force it down. They talked very little. Afterwards, John cleaned up as Diana disappeared, returning with the backpacks they took on their first trip to New Zigon. Diana went through the cupboards and threw in some granola bars and other snacks, and pulled some water from the fridge.

John thought it was a good idea to be prepared, but at the same time he wondered how long Diana expected they would be there.

They all walked out to the truck, and Michael said, "Get in children, I am driving," as he twirled the keys.

His comment bugged John. "Do you even know how to drive?"

"Yes, Diana gave me the instruction in her knowledge transfer," Michael answered confidently.

John couldn't help himself, "Well, since that knowledge originally came from *my* brain, we have the same experience. Maybe I should drive!"

Michael just snorted and said, "Get in the truck," as he climbed behind the wheel. Diana sat in the middle again, giving Michael directions to get to the waterfall they had used before. Michael ground the gears several times but otherwise managed. They all took off their shoes and waded into the creek to stand in front of the falling water, Diana in the middle. John felt the spraying mist cool his face as Diana asked, "Ready?" Not getting an answer, she took a deep breath, clutched her amulet, and said, "Okay then, ready or not, here we come!"

CHAPTER 22 – GETTING THE MESSAGE

The water parted before them, revealing a black pit. Diana led them into the darkness. The slit behind them closed like dropping curtains, and John tried not to panic as he waited for Diana to make the opening to enter New Zigon.

John had been prepared for the platform in front of the raging waterfall, but instead they stepped into a dark space that he could only describe as a cave. Water fell behind them, but it was a fraction of the waterfall he'd been expecting. The only light was from Diana's amulet. As soon as they were all through and the rift closed, Diana went for her pack, emerging with her flashlight. After a moment, John snapped out of his disorientation and followed suit. John flicked his light around the room and confirmed his first impression. They were in some sort of cave with an opening on the far side.

"Where are we?" John whispered.

"We're in New Zigon," Diana whispered back as she zipped up her pack and slung it over her back. Then she looked at him with a twinkle of the flashlight's beam reflecting in her eyes. "What, did you think I'd take us in at the same place where Gina will be looking for us? Give me *some* credit!"

"So where *are* we?" John repeated as he put his boots back on.

"We're inside the cliff, behind the waterfall. Didn't you wonder how I snuck out so often when the whole place was under lock-down? Those platforms suspended halfway up the falls are not a place you can easily sneak through, in case you didn't notice. Miranda showed me this spot. She never said, but I think she tunneled it herself to have her own private portal."

Michael had been silent through this exchange, taking in his surroundings as he put on his boots. "Where do we go from here?" he asked Diana.

"We go to the repository. The reactive projections in the entrance will be like ringing a doorbell. There is only one way into the room, so Gina can't sneak up on us. We can also block her out of the room while I put my amulet on the podium."

"Let us go then, we have no time to waste," Michael said as he took John's flashlight right out of his hands and directed Diana to lead. Just as John was about to say something, Michael said, "I shall go last and shine the beam ahead of your feet, so we both can see."

John bit his tongue and grudgingly agreed with the logic, following Diana out of the cave. Still, Michael could have asked for the flashlight instead of just possessing it like he was making the calls. Being the only adult, did that automatically put Michael in charge? John felt he had more at stake here since he had known Mrs. McNeally first, and that should count for something. He was touched that Diana had grown so attached to her in such a short time, but he questioned Michael's motives. Was Michael worried for Mrs. McNeally because he cared about her as a person, or just because an injustice was done to his host? John couldn't figure the guy out. Sometimes he came across as a gentle giant, like when he was joking with Diana. The rest of the time he seemed to swing between anger, grief, and disinterest.

John tried to swallow his resentment and put himself in Michael's shoes. The man certainly had lost a lot. Michael was a fourteenth-century warrior and landowner. He was probably a big shot in his time, and people did what he said without question. He likely took what he wanted and physically fought his way through confrontations. What was it Michael had said? That he lived by truth, loyalty, and honor? Nowhere in that self-proclamation did he say he was *nice*. John felt like he was constantly under judgment, and it made him nervous, like Michael hadn't made up his mind whether or not John was worthy of being Diana's friend.

The thought that Michael may keep him from Diana made him queasy. Diana was quickly becoming one of the best friends he'd ever had. Since meeting her, things had changed for him, building his confidence. Helping her and learning how to project made him feel special in ways he never had before. Falling off the tractor had opened his eyes to how much he cared about his sisters, and even more so, how much they cared about him. Between his sisters and Mrs. McNeally he felt... loved. He knew Mother and Father cared about him, but he didn't know how deep that ran. Mother seemed barely aware of her surroundings, and she focused so much on Gracie, John sometimes wondered if she remembered her other daughters. *That was mean*, he told himself; of course Mother wouldn't forget her daughters. It was more like... like she figured they didn't need her. Father was so hard to figure out. He rarely showed physical affection to anyone and didn't seem to like children in general. He wouldn't have much to do with his daughters until they could carry on a conversation and behave themselves. Father was strict, but he wasn't mean-hearted. John knew Father would be there for him if he got into trouble; he would be punished for it later, but Father would help him first.

John lost this newfound confidence around Michael. Why did Michael's opinion of him seem to matter so much? If he could shut down that feeling, then maybe he wouldn't react so strongly to Michael's mood shifts and everything would run smoother. He had to remember that the man was broken with grief and he should cut the guy some slack.

These scrutinies and more ran through John's head during the long, silent march to the repository. It really bugged John that he couldn't shut these thoughts out of his head. Never in his life had he spent so much effort thinking about other people and their motivations. He blamed it on spending so much time lately around girls.

Diana led them through tunnels that curved and slanted upwards, up spiral staircases, and through random caves. It was like a maze down there under the rock. Finally, they came to a dead end where Diana used her amulet to open a hidden door. They went down a short hallway, and John recognized they were in the stairwell that led to the repository.

"Cool secret passage," John whispered.

Diana just looked at him with her finger to her lips to shush him. They must have been below the main level of the building, because they had to go up six flights of stairs this time. About halfway up, Michael and Diana shut off the flashlights. John hoped Michael would return his, but no such luck.

When they reached the top of the stairs, even Michael was a bit winded. John had a terrible side cramp and was out of breath, but he tried to man-up as much as he could. Diana had no qualms about showing a weakness apparently, as she bent over clutching her side while taking ragged breaths. She finally calmed down and opened the double doors to the outer chamber of the repository. Diana and John went through, but when Michael tried to walk through the door, it was as if he hit a cement wall. He bounced back clutching his nose, gritting out, "Diana?"

"Oh, sorry, Michael! I forgot you can't get through the door. You have to have Zigon blood to pass."

At that, Michael straightened and stared at John assessingly. "So you really are a descendent of someone from New Zigon."

"Actually I think…" Diana started to say when a voice behind her made her jump.

"Well, well, well," Gina said gleefully, rubbing her skeletal hands together. "You've come back, how nice."

Diana took John's hand, pulling him to her side as she positioned them to block Michael from Gina's sight. "You said you had an encoded Crystavis for me from Miranda?" Diana asked as she stood straight, chin held high.

"Yes, I do," Gina crooned as she stepped closer.

John noticed both Gina and Diana had their amulets out, and they were both glowing. Some fight was going on that John couldn't see. John tried sending Diana his power to help tip the scales in their favor. John's chest warmed as he watched the glow of Diana's amulet more than double in intensity. Gina took several faltering steps backwards.

"My, my, child, I knew you were good at projecting, but I had no idea you had so much power," Gina said bitterly. John watched as Gina looked down at Diana's and his joined hands then back and forth between them, obviously trying to figure something out.

"Unless…" Gina drawled, "You are getting some … *help*."

The way she said 'help' made it sound like a dirty word. John almost dropped Diana's hand out of embarrassment, but he didn't. Instead, he gave Diana's hand a small squeeze of support.

"You may have caught me off guard last time, Gina, but this time I'm prepared. You can't fight me and win," Diana said with confidence.

"Maybe not, but I have something you want!" Gina sang wickedly.

"And I'm willing to give you something in return," Diana said placidly.

"Rrrreally, you're going to give me your Pollampium?" Gina asked excitedly as her hands twisted in front of her like claws, ready to take what she wanted. It made John imagine her slouching a bit more with green skin saying, 'I'll get you my pretty and your little dog, too!' Was he the little dog in this scenario? *Focus!* He mentally yelled at himself. *You've got to stay sharp to help Diana!*

"Of course I'm not going to *give* it to you, but I'm willing to have it charge the Lacunavim for an hour now, and more in a couple of days. You have my word," Diana said, chin even higher as if challenging Gina to doubt the sincerity of her words. John finally noticed that even though the room was still dark, it was much lighter than last time. Those few minutes on the podium during their first visit had made a difference. He wondered what an hour would do. Gina apparently had the same thought, because she jumped on the chance.

"I want six hours from your Pollampium by the end of the week," Gina shot back. John could see the greed in her eyes.

She probably wished she'd demanded more time when Diana immediately said, "Done!"

Gina began to pace back and forth, slightly stooped over and wringing her hands, the poster child for evil witches everywhere. "I have your word that you'll use your Pollampium to charge the Lacunavim for one hour now, and for five more hours within the next seven days?"

"Yes, you have my word," Diana repeated.

"How do I know you'll keep your word?" Gina said as she stopped abruptly and faced them.

"You doubt my word?" Diana said, obviously offended.

"Better to be safe than sorry!" Gina chuckled as her amulet glowed and pen and paper appeared in her hand. "I want this in writing!"

Gina was so focused on getting what she wanted, that she didn't notice Michael standing just outside the door. Gina went over to the same table they'd sat around last time, sat down with her back to Michael, and wrote the simple contract. Gina added a clause that if Diana failed to meet the deadline for the promised five hours, she would owe double the time every week she was late. Diana didn't seem to like it, but allowed it anyway. John guessed Diana was confident it would never get that far.

"Now we must seal the deal," Gina said excitedly. Their amulets once again glowed, and Diana and Gina each took a turn pressing their thumb to the bottom of the paper. Gina snatched up the contract, folded it, and tucked it somewhere inside her robes.

"Let's get that hour started. Go on, get up there," Gina instructed, trying to shoo Diana towards the platform in the middle of the circular room.

"Two problems with that, I am afraid. For one thing, you will not be in the room during that hour, and for another, we want to see the encoded Crystavis before we do anything," Michael said in his deep voice from the stairwell, startling Gina so badly, John hoped she would collapse into a pile of bones right in front of them.

Gina turned around slowly, disbelievingly. "Michael?" she squeaked.

Michael made an imposing silhouette, backlit by the opening over the stairwell. He was standing guard, filling out almost the entire doorway, from his wide shoulders down to his narrow hips and firmly planted feet. John imagined him in armor and a sword. The thought made him shiver. He would never want to be on the wrong side of this man.

"Gina," Michael nodded. "I would say it is nice to see you, but I cannot; not in light of how you treated Diana the last time she was here."

"Oh that, I just got a little over-excited and wasn't thinking straight," Gina said light-heartedly. "I was so happy to see her, truly I was. I hugged her right away, didn't I, Diana, love?"

"That was before you shot me with something," Diana accused.

"But… I wasn't trying to hit *you*," Gina whined, "I was aiming for that *boy*."

"Nonetheless, Gina, I expected more out of you," Michael said in his most condescending tone.

Gina seemed to fold under his glare. "I'll give the encoded Crystavis to you, Michael, but no one reads it until the hour is up," Gina negotiated.

"And you have to leave the room," insisted Michael.

Gina's papery face broke into a huge smile. John thought her skin might actually rip. "Michael, you can keep me company downstairs while we wait." Gina dug through a tiny pouch at her waist and emerged with a small purple crystal. She walked up to Michael and pulled at one of his crossed arms then opened his hand. She placed the crystal in his palm and closed his fingers over it, cradling his fist between her wasted hands. Michael didn't seem to react. John would have yanked his hand immediately from the old hag's touch. Gina, smiling up at Michael, snaked a hand around his arm and moved to head downstairs.

"We'll be right below you, one level down. I'll be able to feel when the Lacunavim is charging, so don't try to cheat on the time! One hour!" Gina warned.

After they were out of sight, Diana, amulet shining, went to the doorway and skimmed her hand about an inch away from its surface as she outlined the frame. The little crystals embedded in the wall twinkled as her hand passed over them.

John waited until she was finished before asking, "What was that about?"

"I just reprogrammed the door to only let you, me, and Michael through," she said as if it was no big deal. "You can look around again if you like, while I get this started," Diana offered.

Since no one but Michael could come into the room with them, John relaxed a bit and took her suggestion. He started around the outer wall, checking out the alcoves.

Diana climbed the steps to the platform, and when she reached the altar-like table, she stopped and lifted her amulet chain over her head. Holding the amulet over the podium she asked, "Do you have a watch?"

John turned and nodded saying, "Yeah, want me to time it?"

"Yes, please," Diana answered. John looked at his dime store watch. It was very plain and didn't even have a second's hand, but it told the time, and that was all John cared about.

"I'm ready," John called out.

"Start…now!" Diana said as she placed her amulet on the podium. Nothing happened at first. Then a slow, warm glow began to build, extending the shadows in the room.

The room itself started glowing, just like last time, only today it was a comfortable shine, nowhere near the blinding light from the previous visit.

Diana took a step away from the altar, concern and confusion on her face. A shaft of light shone from the altar through the roof's opening to the dome of the Lacunavim. It was more like the beam of a flashlight than the brilliant beacon it had been before. The dome overhead started to heal, but at a much slower pace.

"That's odd," Diana began. "Did I do something wrong? Is something missing?" She bit her fingernail as she paced a short path, thinking hard. She stopped and looked at John. "Maybe…," she thought aloud. "John," she called to him from the platform. "Last time we were here, did you maybe give me a power boost unintentionally?"

John turned to face her fully and considered. "I don't remember doing anything on purpose, but my focus *was* on you and your amulet."

Diana walked towards him to the edge of the platform. It was weird having to look *up* at her for a change. "You protected yourself from that farm machine without really knowing what you were doing. Maybe something similar happened here."

"What makes you say that?" he asked, even though he'd already guessed.

"Because…look, it's not the same," she said gesturing to the altar.

"Well, no harm in trying a power boost. Usually, I have to touch you though."

Diana held out her hand to him. "Let's give it a try."

John started mentally building his energy, having it ready in his fingertips so that the moment he stepped on the platform and grabbed her hand, he let the energy flow. The effect was instantaneous. The light in the room was immediately brighter, nearly white like before, but still slightly dimmer than the first time.

"Well, I guess that answers that question," Diana said wryly. She tugged him to the altar.

"I'm not sure how long I can keep this up," John admitted. Diana sat down cross-legged and leaned against the altar, still holding his hand. John sat down next to her and stretched his feet out. His muscles seemed to soak into the floor. He had been too riled up to pay attention to how tired his body was. He had that huge run from the fields to Mrs. McNeally's house and the long hike up the steps to get here from the cave, so it was no wonder he was exhausted.

Diana yawned hugely, and John couldn't stop himself from joining her. "Crazy day," Diana commented tiredly. John's thoughts immediately swung back to Mrs. McNeally.

"I wonder where they took her. I hope they are treating her okay," John said, the pain evident in his voice.

"I'm sure they won't do anything to hurt her. She's going to be fine," Diana tried to comfort him, but her words sounded empty. She yawned again, and he followed suit.

"So…tired," Diana said. She surprised him by switching her hands. His right hand had been holding her left, but now he held her right. She lifted his arm up and scooted under it and up against him, wrapping his arm around her shoulders before she rested her head on his chest. She looked up at him sleepily and asked, "This okay?"

John swallowed hard and acknowledged, "Hmm-Hmm." Diana rested her head on him again, and by the slow, even pace of her breathing, he realized she was asleep. John tried to stay awake, he really did, but there were too many things working against him. Constantly diverting his power, his body slowly melting into the ground, the heat building in his chest, and the warmth that was Diana curled into his side, finally wore him down. He fell asleep, head resting against the altar at his back.

He was suddenly yanked awake, literally, as Michael grabbed him by his overalls straps and lifted him to his feet. "Whoa, Diana!" John yelled, reaching for Diana to catch her before her head hit the floor. Michael shoved him and caught Diana just in time, bringing her up gently to her feet.

Michael spun on John and in a loud voice asked, "What do you think you were doing? Anyone could have walked in here and killed you both without an ounce of resistance. This is not the time for a *nap*," he growled.

Here we go again, John thought.

Diana tugged on Michael's arm trying to get him to back down. "Really Michael, we were perfectly safe. I changed the reactive projection on the door so only you, me, and John can go through."

Michael looked sternly at Diana, "That is… pretty clever actually." Michael's eyes shifted to John as if to say he wasn't off the hook just yet. "I guess that explains…" Michael gestured towards the doorway, where a furious Gina was kicking and hitting the invisible barrier with everything she had.

Diana giggled, and John couldn't hold back his smile. Michael pulled the purple Crystavis out of his pocket and handed it to Diana. "Do you want to listen to it here or when we get back to the house?"

"I'm not sure. I don't want Gina to hear or see any of it, which means wait for home, but if Gina is playing a trick on us and gave us the wrong Crystavis, I don't want to have to travel all the way back here."

John didn't miss the fact that Diana said "home" whereas Michael said "house." "Why don't we listen in here, maybe on the other side of the platform? Since Gina can't get past the door, we know we won't be disturbed. How does this thing work, anyway? Do you see the message in your mind, or is it projected where we can see it, too?"

"I can do it either way."

"Can you throw up a shield or something that will block the light and the sound so Gina won't see or hear anything?" John asked.

After thinking a moment Diana nodded and said, "Yes, I think that will work." She grabbed her amulet from the pedestal, and they all walked off the platform to the side of the room opposite from the doorway. The light from within the platform and pillars didn't fade right away, just like last time. It started fading as John started down the steps from the platform and was gone by the time they reached the floor. He almost tripped as a thought came to him.

"You okay?" asked Diana.

"Yeah, fine. Still waking up, I guess," John lied. Michael gave him a derogatory look, but John decided to ignore it since the guy was about to see his dead wife. What had made him nearly trip was that he noticed the light coming from the room was actually brighter than when he'd fallen asleep. It was as brilliant as the first time, which didn't make sense, since he'd stopped passing power to Diana when he fell asleep. He didn't have much time to think about it because Diana called to him, hand outstretched as she sat on the floor facing the wall.

"Can you help me out again, John?" she asked. He took her hand and sat next to her, Michael already on her other side. John sent her his power again, and his chest warmed as he saw Diana's amulet brighten. His chest seemed to warm every time he sent his power her way. He wondered if that was supposed to happen and made a mental note to ask Diana about it later. John watched in wonder, as he saw the Pleovis move and shimmer around them, capturing them in their own little bubble. Then he felt a whiplash come from Diana, and he snatched his hand away.

"What the…" he started.

Diana grabbed his hand back and said, "It's okay. I just made the shield a self-sustaining pattern."

Whatever that meant, John wasn't going to worry about it. He was watching the purple Crystavis in her hand light up, making a three dimensional vision appear in front of them in full Technicolor. It was of a woman. She was so beautiful; it took John's breath away. She had long, thick, black hair and dusty blue eyes. She was wearing a gown from the old days, and her skin was creamy white and … perfect. She looked soft, and warm, and fierce, all at the same time. He also saw an undercurrent of grief that he was getting all too familiar with seeing. It felt like she was staring right at him. It unnerved him and comforted him at the same time. When he looked at her, he was overcome with waves of feeling, each one pure and overwhelming; sensations of softness, warmth, and comfort as he'd noticed right away, but then came a wave of safety, then one of … love.

John looked over at Diana, and she was smiling while tears ran down her cheeks. She whispered, "Miranda!" He couldn't see Michael without leaning around Diana, and he didn't want to be rude. Then the beautiful woman, Miranda, began to speak.

"Oh, my precious Diana, I'm not sure I want you to see this. If you do, it means you are free from your stone cage, but also that I'm not there to rejoice with you. I have tried my very best to break you and my husband out of the statue, but I have failed you both. I have tried every Primary Crystavis in the repository, and nothing has worked. It has been a little over two years since you were trapped. The Founder refuses to release you. The man I knew and loved as my father is gone. In his place is a shell of a man, bitter and uncaring … and I despise him." Miranda paused and looked to the side, biting her lip and trying to compose herself. "I have come to detest this world and see it as my own prison. I refuse to give up on you. I'm leaving New Zigon in search for answers, for a cure. I know it is wrong, but I will be taking all of the Primary Crystavis with me, as well as the Summas Stone when I leave. I need to have them available to me, so I can use them if it turns out I need them to free you. I don't trust my father and fear he will lock them away from everyone out of spite and to keep his control."

Miranda took a deep, cleansing breath before continuing. "I will be hiding them to keep them safe while I go on this journey. However, if something were to happen to me, I want to make sure you are able to retrieve them and use them to protect yourself and Michael." Miranda's voice broke when she said Michael's name, and John heard a reciprocal sound of pain coming from the other side of Diana. Miranda's eyes reddened and her voice started to crack, but she sniffed and forged on.

"I cannot put them all in the same place, should someone stumble upon them by accident. I will not tell you exactly where they are hidden, for even though this message is encoded specifically to your Visity Signature, there's always the chance someone can break through to get the information stored. So, I will give you a clue that will lead you to the first Crystavis I want you to find, the Primary Life Crystavis. I want you to be able to heal yourself and stay young if that is your wish. I will leave a clue with each Crystavis to help you find the next one. The clue will be a small, flattened message Crystavis like this one, stored on the surface of the Primary. The message Crystavis is hidden, camouflaged so that it is not visible to the average Zigonian. The encryption key to these flattened Crystavis is stored on this message Crystavis, and will also be stored with each message Crystavis, to help you not to lose it." Miranda smiled at this, and John guessed there was a private joke in there somewhere. "I have not decided where to put the Summas Stone, so I'm keeping it close for the time being. This will be a great adventure for you, my friend; one that I wish I could enjoy with you. Just know that you are with me now, and on my mind, and in my heart, as I leave this trail of breadcrumbs for you to follow. You are the little sister I never had, and I love you." Tears leaked from Miranda's eyes, but she smiled through them. "You have great potential, Diana, but do not be too hard on yourself. Promise me that you'll live in the moment, instead of always looking to and preparing for the future." Miranda blew a kiss, and then half sobbed, half laughed at herself.

"I want you to share this with Michael. I'm certain you would without asking, but I want to make sure you both see this." Miranda bent down and held her arms out, her face glowing as she sang her words in baby-talk, "Come here my love, come to Mommy! That's right, come give Mommy a big hug!" John felt his heart stop as he watched a toddler skip-walk his way into his mother's embrace and throw his little arms around her neck. She scooped him up and held him close. The child kept one pudgy hand around her neck, and the other he brought to his mouth so he could ardently suck his thumb. He was really cute with white-blond hair and with dusty blue eyes like his mother's. Both sets of eyes looked at the 'camera' or Crystavis, or whatever the recording point was, as Miranda said, "Michael, Diana, I would like you to meet Gianni. He is our son, Michael."

Miranda proceeded to kiss the child all over the face, his hand, and anywhere she could reach. The little boy's face lit up into a smile that showed around the thumb in his mouth. Miranda kept pulling his hand away from his face so they could see him, but the boy brought it right back the moment she let go.

"We have a boy, my love," Miranda beamed through yet another flow of tears. "You have a son! He is everything we hoped for, he is strong, healthy, caring, smart, and has a beautiful laugh. He is also stubborn and demanding. I wonder where he got that from," Miranda narrowed her eyes as she teased. "He is everything to me now that you both are gone. My father hasn't seen him, nor will he. Only my maid, Mirabelle, has seen him. I have kept him hidden from everyone, even Mirabelle's own daughter, Gina. Maybe I'm wrong in doing so, but I want to protect him so badly, and I don't want to share him with people so cruel that they abandoned you and Diana. They will not get near him," Miranda said with steel in her voice. John believed her.

Miranda cleared her throat. "Diana, you will find the Primary Life Crystavis where you put your first bouquet of flowers from our meadow."

Miranda settled her shoulders and straightened her chin in preparation for what she would say next. John guessed she was getting ready to say good-bye.

"Michael, you are part of my soul and are with me always. I think I started loving you that day you saw us walk through the portal. I will never forget the look on your face when I scared you off your horse and you fell on your backside!" Miranda let out a strangled laugh, followed by a sob. "If we don't get to see each other again, I want you to take care of Diana. Diana, you take care of Michael! Do not let the lovable brute bully you around, promise? I want you both to know that I will never give up on you. I will find a way to free you, even if it kills me. I love you." Miranda's lips trembled. She turned to the son in her arms, baby-talking to him to hide her emotions. "Giann, Can you say Da-da? Can you say Di-an-a?" *Giann* was apparently the boy's nickname.

Gianni threw his arm down away from his face and with an ear-splitting smile proclaimed, "ddzha!"

The image froze with Miranda smiling at them with her cheek pressed against the child's, the triumphant smile shining from the little boy's face.

Michael, who John realized was now weeping, stood and reached for the image, his hand moving right through it, as if it were a ghost. Michael dropped to his knees and hid his face in his hands as he sobbed.

Diana stopped the image somehow, and the purple Crystavis went dark. She turned the pretty gem over in her fingers as silent tears flowed down her face. Even John was choked up, and he didn't know Miranda. John had no idea what to do. He knew Michael would probably hate him for seeing him totally break down like this, and he wanted to disappear as fast as possible, yet he wanted to stay and help Diana, but didn't know how. He awkwardly rubbed her arm for a little bit. She gave him a wan smile, then, looking at Michael, seemed to decide something. She crawled forward a few feet and threw her arms around her grieving friend.

John stood up and walked quickly away. He followed the curve of the room and stopped at the entrance chamber. Gina stood in the stairwell just outside the doorway, leaning against the wall with her arms folded, waiting.

Gina sneered at him and said, "What's the matter *boy*, did your new friends send you away?"

"No, they need… a little time alone," John said, looking at his feet.

"Did they like what they saw in Miranda's message? Was it all heart flowers and bird songs? I'll bet she said she would love them forever and never stop trying to break them out of that statue. Am I right?" Gina said wickedly. John didn't answer her; he just walked a few steps into the entrance chamber and leaned against the wall. He tilted his head back and closed his eyes in an attempt to shut out the old witch.

"I thought as much," she gloated. "And where do you fit into this tragic story? Are you the knight in shining armor who blunders his way into a rescue only to find himself in over his head, or are you the outsider want-to-be boyfriend who the overprotective barbarian will soon beat to a pulp and bury in the back yard?" She mercilessly cackled at him. She was feeding his insecurities, and he couldn't let her get to him. Before, it seemed like she wanted to play nice, as long as it was with Michael. With John, she could let her bitterness wash all over him.

"Your girl there, Diana, do you realize how special she is? How *precious*? When I was a child, the Crystavis masters practically kissed the ground she walked on. She was the future of New Zigon, the strongest talent to be born in generations. She could do no wrong. All that praise, all the privileges that came with her talent, Diana didn't appreciate any of it. She just wanted to work and study, work and study. She would deign to talk to me on occasion, but it was the equivalent of feeding scraps to a dog. The whole city mourned her when she was frozen in that statue. But did any of them raise a finger to help her? Not a single one! They all knew she wasn't worth the trouble."

"At least now she is doing something to contribute, even though she has to be dragged and coerced into helping!" Gina scoffed. John felt her staring at him. He opened his eyes and pushed off the wall. Sure enough, Gina's buggy eyes were practically devouring him. It made his skin itch.

"You are a bit of a mystery to me, boy, a puzzle to solve. Something new to consider after centuries of boredom. Yes, you pique my curiosity. A poor little orphan, a nobody, breaks the unbreakable after centuries of others having tried and failed. And what mystical tool do you use to complete this task? Your boots. Ha! And, here you are a descendent of New Zigon. You are all raw power with no talent, no focus. I figured out you were helping Diana block me earlier. How do you think she'll do without you by her side, acting as a walking, talking battery? If I were her, I'd keep you around, keep you close. You are a powerful weapon. She probably doesn't even like you. She's probably just using you to boost her own power."

"Shut up!" John growled at her, finally losing his control. "I know you're just saying these things to hurt me, and it's not going to work. You're just a vicious, mean, ugly old hag waiting to die. You're pathetic!"

"John!"

John should have jumped at the sound of Michael bellowing his name, but his emotions were all over the place, and anger was rising to the top. Fists clenched, he spun to face Michael and demanded harshly, "What?"

"That is no way to speak to your elders! Pull yourself together, it is time to go," Michael commanded. John seethed inside. This man, who moments ago, was weeping like a baby on the floor, was telling *him* to get it together? John turned before he said something he would regret, and used the diversion of retrieving his backpack to settle his nerves.

Gina's attention was on Michael during their way out, so at least John didn't have to worry about her taunting him further. Diana didn't change the reactive projections around the door, despite Gina's complaints. Diana led the way and was the first out of the building. She froze at the entrance, clogging their progress. They poured outside, anxious to see what had made Diana stop so abruptly. The change in the Lacunavim was palpable. The entire dome, not just a small spot, had a brighter, healthier sheen to it. The benches and pillars looked less gray and more white. The entire city was several shades brighter. That one hour had made a marked difference. Gina was certainly happy. She hopped, squealed, and rattled her bones together in a semblance of a clap. Her eyes were so buggy, John feared they would pop right out of her skull. He tried not to look at her; it was too freaky. Even more uncomfortable was the way Gina was laying it on thick with Michael and Diana. Suddenly, Gina was the gracious host, thanking them profusely while trying to get them to commit to a time when they would return. She kept clinging to Michael's arm like a schoolgirl. Before they left, Michael patted Gina's hand as it gripped his arm and told her to hang in there, that they'd be back soon. John just rolled his eyes and followed them home through the black void Diana called a portal.

The three of them sat in silence on the drive back to Mrs. McNeally's house. When they got there, John helped Diana get some leftovers out of the fridge for dinner. When they were nearly done eating, John broke the silence. "Diana, did Miranda's clue make any sense to you? Do you remember where you put that first bouquet of flowers from the meadow?"

"Yes and no," Diana answered, collecting her thoughts. "I lost that first bouquet of flowers. I dropped them in the portal's Void when returning to New Zigon."

"That black, empty space between the waterfalls?" John asked, wanting to understand.

"Yes, they slipped from my hands, and they just drifted off like in outer space. I thought they were lost forever. I didn't know you could intentionally store things there and be able to get them back. I have no idea how to even start going about this. I didn't make it very far in my studies in the Magnetism Avenue, which covers gravity, magnetic forces, and portals. If there are any masters left, I don't know where to find them. We could do some research in the New Zigon library, but then Gina would be on to us for sure."

"Did you say the Magnetism Avenue of Crystavis Study?" John asked.

"Yes, why?"

"Because I just happen to know someone who descended from one of the greatest Crystavis Masters of Magnetism of all time and studied the Magnetism Avenue for a hundred years," John said proudly.

"Really?" Diana asked, getting hopeful. "Where would you have met someone like that?"

"In one of the dementia groups at West Penn Psych institute," John said with a smile. "Her name is Claire."

CHAPTER 23 – MACHINATIONS

Michael made a choking noise. "You want us to go back to that place and talk to some crazy person? That is your suggestion?"

"Do you have a better one?" John spat back.

"Wait!" Diana said, putting a hand on both John and Michael to stop the emerging argument. She turned to John. "You met someone when we were at the institute getting Michael? How did you manage that?"

John felt the flush of embarrassment rising up his neck. He stood up and took their empty plates to the sink. "Remember how I got stuck in the elevator when we first got there?"

"Yes, it took you almost twenty minutes to find me in the cafeteria."

"Well, I rode the elevator for a while but still couldn't get off on the second floor; there were just too many people. Finally, I decided to get out of the elevator as soon as I could and take the stairs. I ended up on the eighth floor."

"Okay," Diana said, following along.

"I must have missed a sign for the stairwell, because I ended up in this room filled with old people in their pajamas." John paused while he ran water over the dishes. "Before I could leave, this little old lady called to me. She said she could see me, even though I hadn't dropped my invisibility projection."

"Really? That means she must be…" Diana said excitedly.

"From New Zigon, yeah," John answered. "She said so herself, and apparently she talks about it all the time, because one of the other patients complained he didn't want to hear about it again. I talked to her for a few minutes, figuring I should find out a little more. She said she was one hundred and eighty-nine years old, and that she was descended from that Crystavis Master, and she'd studied that avenue for a hundred years."

"John!" Diana moved next to him with a towel and started drying the dishes. "Why didn't you say anything about this before?"

"With everything going on, I kind of forgot," John admitted sheepishly.

Michael's chair scraped behind them as he stood up. "Well, I am not going back to that place, and I do not want you going there either. I think it is a bad idea. We should try that library first." He left them with a curt, "I will be in the barn."

Diana moved to run after him, but John stopped her. "Give him some space. He's been hot and cold all day." *Mostly cold, at least to me,* John thought. "I think he is having a hard time keeping it together. He'll probably go throw some things around or cut some more wood to blow off steam."

Diana turned back and leaned against the counter, biting her lip. "What do you think we should do? If Michael won't go to the institute, then we won't be able to."

"What makes you say that?" John asked mischievously.

"How would we get there?"

"I'll drive us."

"Michael has the keys, and he won't let you. Besides, the first cop who sees us will pull us over. It's obvious you're not sixteen," Diana said sensibly.

"Oh," was all John said. He was stumped. In the kitchen he was having flashbacks of Mrs. McNeally bleeding and unconscious, so he moved to the living room. He sat down on the edge of the couch, propping his elbow on his knee so he could brace his chin. His brain felt like sludge.

He looked at his watch. It was barely 12:30 p.m. How was that even possible? That morning's Belgian waffles felt like two days ago. John tried to reason through it. They started their walk around 8:30 a.m. that morning. They heard the gunshots about half an hour later. By 10:00 a.m. they were leaving for the creek, and they were in and out of New Zigon in under two hours. Yep, his watch wasn't broken. This was good though, they had to call Lord Vito by when, about 9:00 a.m. the next day? They still had half the day left to help Mrs. McNeally.

John looked around the room for inspiration. They needed to go see Claire, and they needed to leave now. "Can you make us a portal to get there?" John asked.

Diana had collapsed next to him on the couch, head tilted back, looking at the ceiling. "No, I thought of that. First, we'd have to get to the creek. We could walk, but that would waste time. Second, there'd have to be a waterfall we can travel *to*, and I didn't see any near the institute."

"Mrs. McNeally has some bicycles. They are from before Mr. McNeally died, so they are a bit old and haven't been used in a while, but they could get us to the creek faster," John offered.

"That's good to know," Diana replied, "but it doesn't solve the problem of having a waterfall near the institute."

John started tapping his fingers on the coffee table. He stopped looking for an answer in the room and stared out the window. He could just make out the Cooper's house between the trees that decorated both lawns. Not for the first time, he envied his neighbor Jay. Jay was seventeen and could drive already. He even had his own car, even though it was kind of a piece of junk. Jay and his older brother Joey had saved it from the dump and fixed it up when Joey had been sixteen. *Jay had his own car...*

John stood up and went to the window. He asked himself what Mrs. McNeally would do. She'd find a way to get Jay to drive them downtown and have him thank her for the opportunity. How did Mrs. M get Jay to help with John's chores last week? She had used Annie as bait.

John rushed over to Diana, grabbed her hand, pulled her off the couch and started dragging her to the front door. "Wha... Where are we going?" Diana asked, startled.

"Get your invisibility projection started. We have to sneak over to my house."

* * *

They raced across the bridge and down the road to John's house. When they ran down his driveway between the old maple trees, he noticed they were kicking up dust. He should probably do something about it; with them being invisible it would look weird. John didn't care. They stopped in front of the house to catch their breath. It was Monday just after lunch. According to their home-school schedule, all of the girls should be reading. He looked through the window and saw Beth sitting at the kitchen table, surrounded by books and papers. He couldn't see much of the living room, but he could see the skirt of someone in the rocking chair. He had to get Annie outside. He decided to knock softly on the door. "Drop your projection!" he whispered to Diana. She did so without hesitation. John knocked again. Finally, Beth looked up and saw Diana. Beth did a quick look around her to make sure no one was watching before hurrying out the front door.

"Beth, can you get Annie to come out here?" John whispered. Beth jumped a little and squinted her eyes, as if that would help her see where John was.

"John?" Beth asked softly.

"I'm right here," John said, touching her shoulder. "I'm invisible."

Beth smiled and her face lit up. "You did it! Wow, John, that's amazing!" John didn't want to waste time admitting that he still needed help to get the projection started. Instead, he said, "Can you get Annie to come out here? Tell her Diana wants to talk to her, but don't let anyone else know Diana's here, okay?" While Beth was inside, John told Diana what to say.

A few minutes later, Annie emerged asking, "Diana? Beth said you wanted to see me?"

"Hi, Annie! Yes, I have something to ask you. Will you walk with me?"

"Sure, lead the way," Annie responded immediately. John smiled. Annie was always up for anything that would get her out of doing schoolwork.

Beth had followed Annie outside, and John gently held her elbow as he whispered in her ear, "We're borrowing Annie for the afternoon. Can you cover for her?"

"I'll come up with something, only if you promise to tell me what this is all about later," Beth whispered back.

"Deal!" John said. "You're awesome, Beth!" He gave her elbow a quick squeeze and raced down the steps to catch up with Diana and Annie.

"Say that again?" Annie was saying when John caught up to them. Diana had them walking down the driveway.

"Mrs. McNeally has an errand for us in Pittsburgh. It's kind of last minute. Mrs. M already left doing something different, and she really wants this errand done today," Diana explained.

"And you want me to go with you because…" Annie prompted.

"Because Jay is driving us, but he'll only do it if you come along," Diana smoothly lied. "You can come over to Mrs. M's, and I'll lend you some jeans and everything!" Diana added to sweeten the pot.

John could tell Annie had decided to go before Diana even started explaining. Going to Pittsburgh, no matter the reason, would be too exciting for Annie to pass up. John ran silently ahead on the grass towards the Cooper's house. He could hear the girls' discussion continue. "I'll have to get permission," Annie was hedging.

"Already taken care of," Diana said. "Beth is covering for you. We'll be back before supper, so no one will even know…"

John went behind one of the maple trees and dropped his invisibility projection. He ran across the street and knocked on the Cooper's door. Mrs. Cooper invited him in, puzzled at his unexpected visit. "Is Jay here?" he asked her.

"He just left to go work in the barn. Do you need something?" Mrs. Cooper asked politely.

"Yeah, I mean, yes, Ma'am. We, I mean, Mrs. McNeally, needs him to help us with an errand. She had to go take care of something urgent and is all upset she can't go see her friend in the city. I guess her friend is getting some operation tomorrow or something? Mrs. M made her some cookies to take to her, and wants us to go and cheer her up and distract her for a while. We were wondering, I mean, *she* was wondering, if Jay could drive us. We'd be back by dinner. I know it is inconvenient and last minute, but it would mean a lot to Mrs. M. She was so upset when this other thing came up, and she couldn't go herself." *Ugh*, John thought. He barely got that out without too many mess-ups. Apparently, it was believable though, because Mrs. Cooper's face went all soft and sympathetic.

"Of course he'll take you. Let's go talk to him together. Wait just one minute," Mrs. Cooper said as she turned to her counter. She quickly wrapped up a dozen of her peanut butter cookies. "You take this to her friend, too. What was her name?"

"Claire."

"You give Claire our best wishes for tomorrow," Mrs. Cooper said as they headed to the barn together. John's chest weighed him down. He felt like such a heel using them like this, but Mrs. McNeally's life was on the line. He had to go through with it.

They found Jay in the barn working on some equipment. Mrs. Cooper told him he had to take John into Pittsburgh on an errand. Jay resisted, saying tomorrow would be better. John said, "Annie is coming," and Jay started putting things away, saying that he'd be over in ten minutes. John smiled to himself as he headed back to Mrs. McNeally's house. He couldn't wait to tell Mrs. M about their scheme. His smile dropped and his heart ached as he worried he might never get the chance.

John peeked in on Michael and found him in the barn whipping an old broom handle around like a fighting pole. John left him to it and went inside to clean up. He found the jeans he'd borrowed before, clean and folded on the bed he'd slept in, along with a deep red T-shirt. John gratefully changed, then knocked on Diana's door. The girls were talking and giggling inside. "Diana, I need you downstairs for a sec. Jay's going to be here any minute!"

Diana slipped around the door without letting John see into the room. John just motioned her to follow, and then sped into the kitchen. "We need some food to take to Claire to keep up with our cover story. Do you have any ideas?"

"Did you say what kind of food when you talked to the Coopers?" she asked.

"Yeah, I said cookies."

Diana went over to the cookie jar and found one lonely half-cookie in the bottom. "Lovely," John said, upset.

"Wait, this just might work," Diana said, face tight in concentration. She stared at the cookie intently, then started opening up just about every cupboard door and jar in the kitchen. She got out her amulet, and John watched in amazement, as little bits of what looked like dust pulled from different spots all around the kitchen and concentrated on the table in front of Diana. The dust swirled into several tight balls, then glowed and flashed once. When John's eyes readjusted from the flash, he was looking at a batch of cookies, just like the piece that was in Diana's hand.

Annie's feet sounded on the stairs, and Diana loaded the cookies onto a paper plate and wrapped the pile in foil. She had left several out. "Do you want one?" she asked John, looking very pleased with herself.

The cookie was delicious. They took both Diana's and Mrs. Cooper's cookie offerings and walked all the way out to the road to wait for Jay. Annie had some of the extra cookies in a napkin and made a big fuss over sharing them with Jay when he arrived. Jay had barely put the car in park before they all jumped in. As they drove down the road, John looked back to make sure Michael hadn't come out of the barn. He hadn't. They had gotten away clean.

CHAPTER 24 – THE RIGHT PLACE

"Where are we headed?" Jay asked.

"West Penn Psych," John answered. "Do you know where that is?"

Jay pulled over and got out his phone. "Nope, but I think I've got an app for that," he joked. John's jealousy flared. Jay and his older brother were the most citified farmers he'd ever met; he guessed that was Mrs. Cooper's doing. Jay set up a navigation app on the phone, and they were back on the road in minutes. Jay and Annie talked and flirted the whole way there. John got Diana to explain (quietly) how she did the cookie thing.

"I told you the Pleovis flows through everything, right? It fills up all the gaps between things, down to the tiniest particle. The Design Avenue of study covers manipulating chemical bonds, molecular structures, that sort of thing. It allows you to transform objects and materials. You can't create something out of nothing, however. You can just change the things you have. I pulled the ingredients from the kitchen and bypassed all the manual steps to change the matter into the cookies. If I didn't have the cookie to use as a blueprint, I couldn't have done it. If we get the cookies out, you'll see that they all look exactly the same. They are like little cookie clones." Diana said proudly. Then they discussed what to do once they got to the Institute. After Jay teased them saying they made a cute couple, they didn't talk the rest of the way.

When they approached the institute, Jay asked them, "Do we all have to go in, or can just you two in the back go? Annie and I could find something to do for an hour…" John jumped on that one, asking to be dropped off out front. He had been worried about how to get rid of Jay and Annie so they could ask Claire the real questions.

They had decided there was no reason to sneak around invisibly, so they just walked in, went straight to the elevator banks, and went up to the eighth floor. John led the way into the common room. He couldn't see Claire, but they circled the room just to make sure. When John spotted the large bald guy in the same spot on the couch watching TV, he decided he may as well try asking. He tried to recall what Claire had called the man. She called him an old toad; that, he remembered. He went up to him and asked, "Excuse me, Sir." The guy didn't respond. "Excuse me?" Nothing. John took out Mrs. Cooper's peanut butter cookies and uncovered half the plate. "I've got these homemade peanut butter cookies, and I'm trying to find a family friend…"

"You have cookies you say?" the man said, finally giving them his attention. It was more like he was giving the cookie plate his attention; that's where his eyes were trained.

"Yes, Sir. Maybe you could help us? There's a cookie in it for you…"

"Sure kid, what do ya need?"

"We're here to visit a family friend, but I can't remember her last name. Her name is Claire. She looks to be about eighty-nine?"

"Kid, everyone in here looks that old or older. It just so happens I know the broad you're lookin' for."

John waited. Finally, he prompted, "You do, Sir? Could you tell us where she is?"

"She's down the hall in her room. It's 832 or 834, I forget. Let me have one of those now, won't ya boy?" Before the man could reach the plate with his fleshy paw of a hand, John picked up two cookies and held them out. After the man's first bite, he rolled his eyes and made a satisfied "Hmmmphmmn" noise, then asked, mouth full, "You leavin' all them cookies with Claire?" At John's nod he said, "Me and Claire's real tight. I'll have to stop by and wish her luck for ta'morrow."

"What's tomorrow?" John asked, suddenly worried.

"Oh, she's gettin' an operation." The way he said operation, it came out "awe-pray-tion."

"Thanks," John said, leaving with Diana to find rooms 832 and 834. They didn't have much trouble. The door was halfway open to room 832, and John could see Claire lying in bed, the lights dimmed. He knocked softly at the door. "Hello, Claire? Hello? Can we come in?" John said hesitantly as he pushed the door open further and stepped inside. The room had two beds, the heads touching the right wall. The one close to the door was empty, so Claire had the room to herself. John was startled to see IV and monitoring equipment set up around the frail old lady. He boldly walked into the room and around the far side of her bed to stand next to her. She had her left arm in a splint, from her fingers to above her elbow. She was wearing one of those snap-at-your-shoulder hospital gowns instead of the pajamas she'd been wearing the other day. She blinked up dazedly at him.

"Who are you? Have you come to prick me with more of your nasty needles? Can't you leave a poor woman alone? You tell me to rest, and then you're in here every flipping ten minutes, asking me how I feel. Just go away!"

"Miss Claire, it's your Zigonian friend from last week, John. Do you remember me? You could see me even though I was invisible."

"John?" Claire tried to lift her head off the pillow to see him better. "Be a dear and turn on the light, will you?" Diana went to flip the switch by the door. "Now where did that accursed bed control get to!" Claire said as she fumbled around the blankets. John found it and handed it to her. She hit a button and the head of the bed began to rise to put her in more of a sitting position. "Ah, much better!"

John winced when he saw her face. She had a bandage on her forehead and surgical tape on her cheekbone. The whole left side of her face seemed like one big bruise.

"That bad to look at, am I?" Claire asked forlornly.

"What happened to you?" John asked, pulling a chair up to her bed. Diana dragged a chair from the other side of the room to sit next to John.

"Ahhh, you brought a friend! Two visitors at the same time! How wonderful! You must introduce us!"

"Claire, Ma'am, this is Diana." He leaned forward, putting a hand to his mouth as he stage-whispered, "She's from New Zigon!"

Claire tried to smile, but she stopped, wincing at the pain the movement caused her. "How astonishing! It is my honor to meet you, fellow citizen of New Zigon!"

Diana gave Claire a little wave as John asked, "Claire, Ma'am, what happened to you? How did you get hurt?"

"Diana, would you please close the door so we can have some privacy? That's a good girl," Claire said as the fingers on her good hand played with the blanket. "The hospital's report says that I fell, but that's hogwash. I told them the truth, but they wouldn't believe me. They thought I was hallucinating…" Claire's voice started to catch, the memory upsetting her.

"It's okay, Claire, Ma'am, you're okay now. Please tell us what happened," John said, not knowing why he was pressing this when they had important things to talk about. Diana stayed quiet, letting him take the lead.

"Friday, a couple of days after we met, two men came in here asking questions about your visit. Apparently, we had some chatty Kathy's working that day that wanted to get on TV who spilled the whole story to the news. I didn't feel like going to the common area, so I started keeping to my own room. Everyone kept asking me about how I touched your hand and your face. That's all the rest of the room could see, you know. To them it must have been quite shocking!"

"Sorry about that, Ma'am. I didn't mean to scare everyone," John confessed, embarrassed at the memory.

"Call me Claire. Don't you worry your young head over it! It was my fault for breaking holes in your projection! Anyway, these men didn't have to talk to too many people to find out I was in the center of all the commotion. Then someone, probably that old toad of a man Stuart, *mentioned* that I was always making up stories about New Zigon. They found me in my room, and they… they were not very nice."

"They did this to you?" John asked, his stomach clenching. "Were they tall men wearing business suits?"

"How did you know what they were wearing?" Claire asked, frowning. John felt his anger begin to rise in his gut. He did not like those guys. They had beat up this poor, defenseless woman, and then slapped Diana and Mrs. McNeally around before kidnapping Mrs. M. His chest tightened at his helplessness in both matters, making it hard for him to breathe. "What did they want?" John asked a bit hoarsely.

"They wanted you, silly," Claire said coolly. "But don't you worry; I didn't give you away, even when they broke my arm." Claire motioned towards her splint. "They're operating on it tomorrow to set the bones. Nothing happens around here very quickly I'm afraid."

So that answered one question, John thought. That was the awe-pray-tion the "old toad" had mentioned. John almost laughed as part of the lie he'd told Mrs. Cooper was actually turning out to be true. They *were* visiting a friend who was getting an operation the next day.

"I'm so sorry they did that to you, Claire," John said as he moved to take her good hand. Mrs. McNeally had taught him to always be gentle when shaking an elderly person's hand. That firm handshake that you give to potential employers or girlfriends' fathers could be very painful for someone with arthritis. With that in mind, he was careful with her. He looked down and noticed two things. The first thing he saw was a horrible bruise on her forearm, actually four bruises shaped like the outline of someone's fingers. The second thing he noticed was that her fingers felt small. John gently picked up Claire's hand to examine it and her wrist. The arthritic bumps and contortions were gone. Her joints were … normal. "Claire…"

Claire blushed and looked away towards the door saying, "I'm so sorry I did that, right after meeting you, and without even asking. I'm so ashamed at my weakness. Please forgive me."

"I'm not sure I understa…," John started to say, when the memory came to him of her hands folded on his chest and the burning fire he felt where she touched him. It was sort of like the warm feeling he got when he pushed his power to Diana, but a hundred times hotter. "You… you stole my energy to heal your hands," John concluded aloud. "It burned."

Claire started to cry. "I'm so sorry! I didn't know it would hurt you. I just felt your energy, and there was so much of it! I wanted to see if I could still do it, heal that is, without my Crystavis. All that power, it was just too tempting. I started pulling it before I realized what I was doing. Please don't be mad at me!"

John didn't let go of Claire's hand as he processed what she'd done to him. He gave her hand the gentlest of squeezes. "Don't cry, Claire! There's no harm done, really! And look at your hands now, they're beautiful!" He paused a moment as she sniffed. "Actually, we came here to see if you could help us with something. Then we'd be even, and there'd be no reason to be upset."

Claire pulled her hand back so she could wipe her eyes. "You need *my* help?" she said, incredulous.

"Did you or did you not say that you were descended from one of the greatest Crystavis Masters of Magnetism of all time, and that you studied the science of the Magnetism Avenue for the first one hundred years of your life?" John said with a small smile.

"You remembered all that?" Claire asked, still shocked.

"Well, did you mean it?"

"Of course I did!" Claire said with gusto. "Do you want to become my students?" she asked hopefully.

John nodded at Diana to tell her it was time to join the conversation. Diana began, "I just found out that a dear friend of mine left me something before she died. The thing is, she said she left it in the Void the portals travel through."

"Oh my!" Claire exclaimed. Then she adjusted herself in the bed, trying to sit up straighter. She raised her chin and her eyes danced as she said, "Well, you've come to the right place."

"If you know what you're doing, the Void can be an excellent place to hide things," Claire said, settling into teacher mode. John thought it was cute. "Of course, if you make a mistake, you could lose your item, or yourself, forever."

"What do you mean?" asked Diana.

"Just what I said. The Lacunavim was built by creating a bubble in the Void. The Void is its own dimension that is everywhere and nowhere."

This is making a lot of sense, John thought sarcastically. Diana seemed to be following though, because she was nodding her head like she understood.

"We can travel through the Void using portals. Every portal has three parts, the entrance, the path, and the exit. The entrance and exit are fixed, but the path only exists when the portal is active. If you leave a path when you're in the Void, you'll become lost and not be able to connect to an exit, getting stuck in the Void until you die."

"If you really know what you're doing, you can create a more permanent, one-sided connector, like a tether. You can tether an object to an entrance, and no one will find it unless they know what to look for and where to look. If you *don't* know what you're doing, your tether will likely break and your object will be lost."

"If we know where to look, what do we look for?" asked John.

"There will be a tiny disruption in the Pleovis. You have to be standing on the path after you close the portal entrance to be able to see it."

"And how do we retrieve what is on the tether?"

"Ah, now that part can be tricky. You have to first soften, and then reel the line in, without breaking it. Of course, if you can sense the object itself, you can just call to it."

"How do you do that?" asked Diana.

John's heart sank a little. He was hoping Diana would know some of this stuff already.

"I'd have to demonstrate, and I don't think we can do that here," Claire said with a smile.

Diana bit her lip for a few moments before saying, "It is really important that we learn how to do this. Those men who attacked you? They kidnapped a very dear friend of ours. We have to find something on one of those tethers you described, or they will hurt her." Diana paused as if gathering her courage to ask the next question. "Could I do a knowledge transfer from you to me on the subject, so I have some experience to draw upon?"

By the shocked look on Claire's face, he guessed what Diana asked was not normally done, and maybe was even taboo.

"Please?" Diana asked.

"But, but, … but Diana, do you know what you're asking? If you make one mistake, you could…"

"I know, but I won't."

"And it might not even help you!" Claire protested. "Have you done knowledge transfers before?"

"She did a full language transfer from me to her, then to another guy, as well as some autopilot information," John offered helpfully.

"You what?" Claire gasped. "That kind of transfer hasn't been done since the Summas Stone was lost over six and a half centuries ago!"

"Well, to Diana, that was like a week ago, right?" John said as he elbowed Diana. Diana gave him a dirty look.

"Wait… Diana… you're not *that* Diana are you?" Claire asked waveringly.

"I'm not sure what you mean by *that* Diana, but if you mean Miranda's protégé, then yes, she's *that* Diana," John said proudly. Diana pinched his thigh – hard. "Oww! What was that for?"

Diana didn't get a chance to answer because Claire cut in, "Well then, that's a different situation altogether, isn't it? Go ahead, do the knowledge transfer, but make it fast before I change my mind."

"John, will you go stand by the door, so no one walks in on us?" Diana asked. As he stood guard, Diana pulled out her Crystavis and laid a hand on Claire's good cheek. After only a few minutes Diana pulled back. "Thank you, Claire, I think that will help us."

John checked his watch. "Sorry, Claire, we have to go. We only had an hour, and it's almost up."

"So soon?" Claire said pitifully.

"Oh, I almost forgot. We brought you cookies!" They set the cookies on the bedside tray. "Watch out, toad-face knows they're here," John warned.

Claire gave an uneven cackle, "Toad-face? You mean Stuart, I'm sure. I like that one, a lot!"

John wasn't sure what he should do to say good-bye. Should he give her a hug? *No*, he thought, he barely knew her. He settled for a light squeeze of her hand. "Thank you so much Claire, this means a lot. And thanks for not giving me up to the Suits."

"You're welcome," she said while a few tears leaked from her eyes.

"What is it?" John asked, wondering if he squeezed her hand too hard.

"I didn't tell them about you, but I told them a little about my family. They know I gave my Crystavis to my seventh-great-granddaughter, Rachel. She should be fine though, she's traveling with her parents and will be hard for them to find."

John tucked that news away in the back of his mind to process after they got Mrs. McNeally back. He was beyond capacity with his own worries at the moment, and it didn't sound like an urgent problem, not while the girl and her parents were out of the area. Diana gave the old lady a kiss on the cheek, and they both promised to visit again sometime to tell her how everything went.

Jay and Annie were right on time picking them up. He and Diana were quiet with their own thoughts the whole ride home.

CHAPTER 25 – A BOWLFUL OF JELL-O

John convinced Jay to drive straight to his own house so the three of them would walk from there. At first Jay refused, saying any gentleman dropped ladies off at their doors. When Annie asked him if he would walk her home while John walked Diana home, the battle was won.

They got to the Cooper's around 4:30 p.m. John felt exhausted. This day was a mini-marathon. They had only been gone a little over three hours, and John hoped Michael would buy the excuse that they had been visiting the Coopers. His first go-to story was that he and Diana were hanging out in the loft, but based on the way Michael had been acting, he worried that would get his ears boxed in.

As they walked along the road, John thought it was a good time to ask Diana questions. "Why was Claire so worried about having you do a knowledge transfer?"

Diana turned a deep shade of red. "Well, you have to really trust the person doing it, because they could see things about yourself that you would rather keep private. And… it can be…," Diana murmured the last word so quietly, John didn't catch it.

"It can be what?"

"It can be dangerous," Diana said, flushing even more.

John stopped her on the road. "Wait, what? You didn't say anything about that before! You did them to me and Michael like they were regular things, like going to the store or something! What's dangerous about them?"

"The most common thing is that you can wipe someone's memory by accident, but I've *never* done that, and I've done a lot of them," Diana rushed to reassure him. "It's always been my best skill, and Miranda said I'm better at it than anyone, even The Founder. It's kind of the thing I'm known for."

John looked at her for a few moments. Diana didn't seem the type to brag, and he doubted she would exaggerate something like this. "I guess that's why Claire caved as soon as she found out you were *that* Diana," John thought aloud.

"Thanks for that by the way," Diana said as she resumed walking.

"For what?"

"For giving away my secret."

"I didn't know it was a secret. Why didn't you want her to know?"

"Because… because I was hoping to leave that stuff behind me. You don't understand. Everyone put so much pressure on me back then to succeed, to excel. They treated me like, I don't know, like they put me up on a pedestal all the time. I was more of an asset, a thing, than a person, and definitely not a girl." Diana's voice grew very quiet as she said, "I didn't have very many friends. Kids were either afraid of me or resented me. Miranda understood." Diana sighed and glanced at him with a worried look, like he might not want to be near her after this confession. "With New Zigon as it is, I don't want the existing Zigonians to treat me like that again or use me like Gina is trying to do."

John wrapped an arm around her shoulders, giving her a friendly side hug before playfully shaking her. "So being a Zigonian prodigy isn't all it's cracked up to be, huh? Don't worry. I'll still let you make dinner and wash the dishes if that's what you're worried about." Diana let out a grateful laugh and relaxed as if a weight had been lifted from her shoulders. "I don't think you can hide who you are though, that's not the kind of person you are," John told her. They walked silently for a stretch before John asked, "So, you can do knowledge transfers on how to move the Pleovis?"

"Yes, but it is not encouraged. You have to be able to connect with the Pleovis on your own. It's like how just being told how to do a cartwheel or ride a bike isn't enough; you have to experiment with your own balance to actually do it."

"Can you knowledge transfer some things to me?"

"John, didn't you hear what I just said?"

"Yeah, but if I had more information, like a handbook, I could learn a lot faster, wouldn't I?"

Diana thought for a moment then shrugged. "We can give it a try, I guess. It's not like there's anyone enforcing Zigon rules here."

They had just reached Mrs. McNeally's driveway. John pulled Diana to the side, behind a large oak tree. "Do one now. Give me a copy of what you got from Claire and … and how to start the invisibility projection. Just that." At Diana's reluctance he resorted to begging. "Please! Please, please, please, please, *please*! With everything going on so fast, I don't want to put it off. Do it real quick before Michael sees us and grounds us for the rest of the week."

Diana giggled. "Don't be silly, he wouldn't *ground* us. Okay, I guess we can try just those two things to see how it goes." She pulled out her amulet and touched his cheek, locking their gazes. John's head felt strangely warm and cold at the same time. When she was done, he had that feeling like right after waking from a dream, where you know you dreamt, but the memory is just out of reach, yet there all the same.

"I'm not remembering anything new," he said.

"That's good. That means I put it into your long-term memory successfully. I'll show you after dinner how to access it."

"Okay," John complied as they headed towards the house, even though he wanted her to show him now. He hated waiting.

He didn't have to wait long, however, to find out if Michael noticed their absence. He was in the kitchen, and it looked like he was... cooking. He turned to face them, planting his feet and crossing his muscular arms. John waited for him to ask something or start yelling, but Michael just stared at each of them with a look of irritation and disappointment. Finally, Diana broke the silence. "Hi, Michael! Did you have a nice ... break?" she said with forced energy. Michael didn't answer, so she continued, "In case you were wondering, we were at the neighbor's, the Cooper's. Jay Cooper and John's sister Annie took us for a little drive."

Michael's response was to turn back to the stove and stir something. He was cooking spaghetti noodles to go with some of Mrs. McNeally's canned sauce. The incongruous sight of the big man stirring a steaming pot made John want to chuckle, but he bit his tongue. Diana jumped in to make a salad, and they sat down to an early dinner.

"I've been thinking about the clue Miranda left me, and I think our first step should be to go through the portal from the clearing to New Zigon and check it out," Diana said, broaching the subject they all had on their minds.

"That sounds logical," Michael said. "I do not see any reason to put it off. We shall go right after dinner."

Since John agreed with the plan, he tried not to get upset over Michael making the decision for them. Michael headed to the rooming house to get some things and to bring the truck around while Diana and John did the dishes. This time Diana washed and John dried. Diana went to hand him a clean plate, but as he reached for it, the plate disappeared. He grabbed it anyway, and as soon as Diana let go of it, the plate reappeared.

"Hey," John laughed. He wasn't sure what game she was playing, but she did it with the next two dishes and a bowl.

She handed him another bowl and said, "Your turn. Don't think about it, just do it. Make it invisible." John held out his hand, expecting her to make it invisible like before, but she just handed it straight to him. "Don't think, do it!" Diana ordered.

When he did it, he almost dropped the dish. He made it invisible all on his own! He played with making it disappear and reappear several times, and then he made himself invisible. John whooped over his success. "I did it! I did it all by myself without copying you!" he crowed.

"That's how knowledge transfers are supposed to work," Diana said, smiling. "You don't want to work at remembering something; you just want it to come to you as if it was your own thought to begin with."

"This is so cool! Think of all the stuff I can get away with now!" John said as he flickered in and out, projecting over and over again.

"John!" Diana said aghast, "You are not allowed to use this talent to hurt or trick anyone or do anything illegal, do you hear me? Don't make me clear that knowledge from your brain!"

John laughed and picked her up to spin her once, soapy hands, washcloth, and all. He put her back down saying, "Don't worry about me, Teach! I'll be sure to drink and project responsibly."

"Drink?" Diana squealed, an octave higher than her regular voice.

"I'm teasing," John laughed. "It's just a play on words for one of those sayings; you know, 'drink and drive responsibly'? Get it?"

Apparently, she didn't, or just didn't think it was funny, because she frowned and shook her head at him. "I don't know about you sometimes," she mumbled.

"That's all part of the plan, sweetheart, to keep you guessing," John said with a Texas drawl and a wink.

Michael walked in to hear this and scowled at him. "Truck's ready. Are you two almost done?"

"Before we go… Diana, do you know if Mrs. M has any extra flashlights around?" John asked.

"Oh, good idea!" she said as she hustled around, pulling together a third backpack and making sure the first two were stocked with supplies.

Michael drove them to the creek and they took off their shoes to wade up to the waterfall. Diana made a portal that took them to the hidden cave in New Zigon where they deposited their shoes. Then she turned around and made another portal that took them to a stream edging a pretty meadow. Once again she turned around to make another portal. She repeated the now familiar process of creating a rift in the falling water, leading them through it, and it closing behind them. No matter how many times he stepped through these portals, John thought he never would get used to this part in the middle, the part Claire called "the Void." He clicked on his flashlight, but the emptiness completely swallowed the light, not offering up a surface to bounce it back to his eyes. It reflected off their persons, and that was it.

"Okay," Diana said, "This is where Miranda left the crystal. Look everywhere, but don't move your feet."

"Why can't we move our feet?" John asked.

"Because you don't want to fall off the bridge," Diana said calmly.

"What bridge?"

"The portal's bridge."

"The portal has a bridge? You mean like a *path*?"

"Yes and yes," said Diana, growing irritable.

"And how do you know where it is? I can't feel or see anything in the Pleovis," John said, looking at their feet.

Diana said, "Maybe not today, but someday you will. It's tied to me, since I created the portal."

"Does that mean *you* can't fall off?"

"John!" Diana said in frustration. "It means I have a safety line of sorts. Now will you quit asking questions and start looking?"

"Yes ma'am!"

"Do you know what we are looking for?" asked Michael, finally speaking as he shone his flashlight beam into the nothingness on the other side of Diana.

"Not really," said Diana a little vaguely. John guessed she didn't want to tell him they were looking for a tether, because that would raise questions on where she learned about tethers. He wasn't sure why they brought Michael anyway, since he wasn't able to see or sense disruptions in the Pleovis.

See or sense. Didn't Diana tell him that they didn't really see the disruptions and patterns in the Pleovis in the traditional sense, that they intuited them, and their brains translated the information as images? If that were the case, he really didn't need to use his vision. John closed his eyes, and it wasn't much different from having them open, it being so dark. He had trouble concentrating, because he kept hearing "Feel the Force, Luke" playing over and over again in his head. He had to remind himself that the Pleovis wasn't the same thing as the Force. The Force was supposed to be connected to living things. The Pleovis was everywhere, even in space and this desolate place. "Dancing glue" is what he first had called it. He tried visualizing different things. First he thought of the Pleovis as an ocean of water. The problem with that image was that he pictured currents pushing and pulling at him, making him nervous he would fall off the bridge.

"Find anything yet?" Michael asked in his deep voice, making John nearly jump out of his skin. He decided to ignore him and go back to visualizing. He thought of the Pleovis like air currents whipping around and through things, swirling in complicated patterns. With that image he could almost picture the bridge they were standing on as its own little wind tunnel that fought against the air currents. This image also made him feel like he was about to fall. He was still holding Diana's hand from when they walked into the portal, and he clutched it desperately, trying to ground himself. Quickly, he switched to thinking of the Pleovis like orange Jell-O, like in that one scene in the *Cloudy with a Chance of Meatballs* movie. This made him feel more secure, because in his visualization the Jell-O encased him where he stood. He pushed out his Visity like a small punch and sensed his imaginary Jell-O reverberate in reaction. He did a small push, down in front of his feet, and sensed the ripple in the Jell-O bounce off the surface of the bridge. He started to do wider pushes to see if the ripple he created in the Jell-O would travel straight, or bounce off something, working like radar.

"What are you doing?" Diana asked him.

John held his mental image while answering, "Pretending to be a bat in a bowlful of Jell-O."

"Seriously, John?" Diana said, her voice full of exasperation.

"Shhh! It's working," John whispered without opening his eyes. He systematically pushed his Visity out at different angles to get complete coverage in all directions. Finally, he felt something, a small diversion in one of the ripples he sent out. He pulled his sweaty hand from Diana's and wiped it on his jeans, then turned his back on her to face the direction of the slight disruption. "I think I've got something!" he said excitedly as he used his Jell-O radar to get a better sense of the object, because it definitely was an object.

"Really?" he heard Michael say, just as things started to move in slow motion. He could sense Michael standing with his back to them, checking out his side of the bridge. When Michael spoke, he turned towards them, and it was as if in the dark he forgot how large his body actually was. His upper arm rammed into Diana, who pushed into John. Michael grabbed Diana to steady her, but John had been facing away from them. The only thing he could grab at was imaginary, empty orange Jell-O as he fell off the bridge.

CHAPTER 26 – THE VOID

John heard both Diana and Michael scream his name, but it felt somehow muted, as if he really were submerged in Jell-O. That gelatinous image disintegrated when he opened his eyes and felt the suffocation of nothingness. John shut his eyes again. He felt himself drifting away from Diana and Michael, and he panicked. His heart was pounding, and he was breathing his way towards hyperventilating. He never saw the movie *Gravity* with Sandra Bullock, but he saw the previews where her spacesuit's tether snapped, and she tumbled into space. That's how he felt right now. *Tether.* His shocked mind grabbed ahold of that word. Without really knowing why, he reached out for the object he'd discovered before getting pushed into the Void. He didn't try to imagine Jell-O, or waves, or air, or chocolate pudding; he just *reached*. He felt the object as clearly as if it were under an intense spotlight. He wanted to tug it close to him, but some instinct told him not to tug it to him, but to move *himself* to *it*. John's panic was consuming most of his conscious thought, so his subconscious took over. By some innate, unknown ability, John moved towards the object. When he neared it, he reached out and held onto it as if it were a life preserver. The object wasn't stationary; it was swaying as if it were at the end of an invisible rope, like a kite riding the air currents.

John's blood pounded in his ears as he tried to control his breathing before he passed out. He felt like he couldn't get enough breath, like there wasn't much oxygen in the air. His heart was still racing, and he felt terribly light-headed. He forced himself to hold his breath for short moments in attempt to calm down his breathing. He told himself that he wasn't drifting anymore; he'd grabbed ahold of something solid. He reasoned that if it were "tied" somehow, it could be reeled in, right? He breathed in through his nose and out through his mouth. 'In through your nose, out through your mouth' became his new mantra. When he got his breathing to slow a little and his heart rate to calm down a bit, he opened his eyes to complete blackness. It were as if his eyes were still shut. There was no up or down, no top or bottom, and the sudden vertigo that washed over John almost made him vomit. If he vomited, he wondered crazily, would it fall all over his lap, or spray out and start drifting endlessly in the Void? Maybe it would come up on some random person traveling through a portal. He gave a hysterical laugh at the thought of his puke slamming into some unsuspecting soul, maybe even Michael.

He focused on his hearing. At first he'd heard Diana and Michael screaming his name. He listened for it now. He heard someone sobbing, but it was so faint and muffled, it was hard to tell even what direction it came from. Without thinking, John pulled the sound to him. Suddenly, it was as if he were back standing next to Diana and Michael on the bridge. Diana was screaming and sobbing, and it sounded like she was physically struggling against something.

"Let me go, Michael! Let me go! We have to help John!"

"Diana, I am sorry, I am so sorry. He is gone. We cannot even see him anymore. I will not let you throw yourself out there, it is suicide!" Michael was arguing in a tortured voice. He kept repeating these phrases in different order, pleading with her.

Diana seemed to be calming down somewhat, as she said hiccupping, "Okay, Diana, don't freak out. Stop. Think. There has to be something we can do. Stop crying and start doing!" She was giving herself a pep talk, John realized.

"Diana!" John screamed at the top of his voice. "Diana! I'm here!" John paused to see if she'd heard him. His voice didn't echo; it just dissolved into the blackness of the Void.

"Michael, start shining your flashlight around. Maybe we'll be able to spot him," Diana was instructing.

"Flashlight! Of course!" John said to himself. He had to stop and mentally take inventory. He was barefoot; they all had left their shoes in the small cave in New Zigon. His jeans were rolled up to just below the knee, and his feet and legs were still wet from wading in the creek. The water was slowly evaporating off his skin, leaving his feet cold. He had a belt, a T-shirt, the backpack Diana had given him on his back, and in his hand he had his flashlight. It was between his palm and the object that he'd so desperately grasped. John wrapped one arm around the object, holding it tight like a large football, and lifted the flashlight in the other. He shone it in the direction he felt was towards Diana and Michael.

"Hey! I'm here! Help!" John shouted. He tried waving his flashlight around. Other than Diana making little sniffling sounds, she and Michael were quiet. He called out to them over and over, but they couldn't hear him, and they didn't see his flashlight. John couldn't see them or their flashlights either. He could hear them talk to each other occasionally, one asking the other if they saw or heard anything. John shouted until his voice grew hoarse.

John's heart sank when he heard Michael say, "Diana, honey, I think we should go back. We cannot find anything here. Let us go home where you can rest. I will call Lord Vito and tell him we have a lead, which should buy us more time. First thing tomorrow we can go to that library in New Zigon you mentioned. We might be able to find something to help us."

"But… John!" Diana said miserably.

"We cannot do anything to help him right now. Who knows if…," Michael cut himself off before saying something that would further upset Diana.

"I guess you're right," Diana finally gave in, her voice a bit muffled as if she were crushed in a hug.

John, voice almost gone, pushed a thought towards Diana desperately, "I'm here, you can save me, you just have to find me! I'm okay for now, not drifting away. Please don't leave me!"

John wasn't sure if part or his entire message reached Diana, but he heard her say, "I just know John is out there, closer than we think. We can get him back; we have to get him back!"

"We shall do our best, honey, but do not get your hopes up. We do not know anything about this place. We need a plan, and we cannot research one while we are standing here. Let us go home."

"Noooo!" John croaked as Diana opened a rift back to the cave in New Zigon. The light from the gap nearly blinded him. He put up the hand holding the flashlight to shield his eyes. He found that the brightness from the opening was lighting him up like a Christmas tree as well as the object he was holding onto. It was a green crystal the size of a basketball. He had found the Primary Life Crystavis! Now if Diana and Michael could only find and get to him, they'd be all set. The temporary light vanished as Diana closed the rift, plunging John back into darkness.

John had to wait a few moments for his eyes to adjust. He took the time to give himself a pep talk. He wasn't drifting endlessly; he was in one spot. He had a flashlight. He had his backpack. He had the Primary Crystavis. He was in one piece and wasn't hurt. He had his newfound Zigon talent. Diana was coming back; she hadn't given up on him.

John decided to check out the large Crystavis he was holding onto. He turned his flashlight on it. It was amazing! The light bounced through it in fascinating ways. He had a death grip on the thing. He couldn't see how it was tethered, even though he knew it was. He passed his free hand all around it and encountered nothing. There was no physical line tied to it that he could use to pull himself in; that would be too simple, and he wasn't that lucky. He maneuvered himself so he gripped the Crystavis between his knees, leaving his hands free. He stuck the flashlight in his mouth and pulled his backpack around to check out its contents. He counted two bottles of water, a small bag of peanuts, three granola bars, a little first aid kit, some rope, a trash bag, a small notepad and pen, a jacket, and a tightly wound bundle of cloth with rubber bands holding it together. He took out the coat and the cloth bundle, which turned out to be a thin cotton blanket like you might find at a hospital. He tried to roll it back up again, but he couldn't get it small enough to put the rubber bands around it, so he strung the rubber bands on his wrist and just shoved the blanket into the backpack.

The coat was a thin windbreaker, which didn't provide very much warmth, but he put it on anyway. He left everything else in the backpack for now and slung it over his shoulders again. He was getting cold. It wasn't see-your-breath-fog cold, but it definitely wasn't warm. He rolled down his jeans to cover more of his legs, but he couldn't think of anything to do for his bare feet. He had to figure out a way to make sure he didn't lose his grip on the Crystavis and lose all hope of rescue. He also wanted to examine it some more and experiment with a few things. He thought of the trash bag in his pack. Why would Diana or Mrs. M have packed that? He could stick the Crystavis in the bag, and then tie the bag to himself with the rope, but then he wouldn't be able to see it. He thought for a moment, glad to have something to focus on other than the disorienting feeling of weightlessness. He got the pack out and retrieved the blanket, then put the pack back on. It was thin and wouldn't provide much warmth, just like the jacket. Flashlight between his teeth, he shook it out. It was pretty big. He tried to whip it so it would wrap around him, but without gravity it was near impossible. He grabbed ahold of two opposite corners, and the blanket bloomed out like a parachute. That meant there had to be some kind of current, but John couldn't feel it.

The ballooned blanket gave him an idea. He pulled the blanket back in so he could get his pack out again. This time he retrieved the length of rope. Backpack in place, Crystavis between his knees, the rope stuffed under his belt, and flashlight still between his teeth, John opened up the blanket again. He grabbed all four corners and let the blanket extend like a sail. He thought it might tug at him a little, but it had so little force, it barely pulled against his grip. With two corners in each fist, he did a zero-g forward half-somersault, stopping when the blanket was to his back. He pulled and bunched the ends together until he was in a blanket bubble. He pulled out the rope and awkwardly tied the tassel of blanket ends. It made him think of an inside-out balloon, the knot on the inside.

As a test he let go of the flashlight. It floated in front of him, then drifted over to touch the blanket, where it gently stopped. John let go of the Crystavis next, and it bounced up against his stomach. *He* was the one who probably floated against the Crystavis instead of the other way around, but he couldn't tell. The blanket floated up against his back. John took a big breath and let it out. He felt much more secure in his little blanket bubble illuminated by the flashlight, knowing he couldn't drift away from the Crystavis. As he helped himself to a granola bar and some water, he focused on the Crystavis. The size of it was shocking. It was a captivating green with innumerable facets reflecting the dim light. Holding it in his hands, he closed his eyes and tried to sense it in the Pleovis. He was mentally drained from the long day and the shock of falling into the Void. He thought that fatigue would hinder him, but it seemed to help him instead. Being tired, he didn't over-think things. He just opened his senses, including the new one he discovered for sensing the Pleovis.

An image of the Crystavis appeared behind his eyelids, but the facets that had so beautifully reflected light seemed completely different. They formed pathways through the crystal; it was like a miniature, intricate maze. He instinctively pushed some of his Visity into the Crystavis and sensed how it moved through the object. The passageways molded the Pleovis into specific patterns, which emerged and bathed over him. Suddenly, he felt rejuvenated, all aches and pains from his farm labors gone. *Wow,* he thought, *that was better than an energy drink, coffee, and a good night's sleep all rolled into one!* He suspected he just healed himself, and since there wasn't anything major to heal, it just fixed all the little things, including tired muscles.

He kept his eyes closed and gently wrapped the Crystavis in his Visity. He was amazed at the control he had over his Visity. That knowledge transfer from Diana must have awoken something within him to allow him to project so precisely. He used his projection to map out the Crystavis, learning its structure. He found two abnormalities on the outside surface of the object. He tried poking at them with his Visity as you would scratch something with your fingernail. One was much larger than the other. He focused on the littler one first.

Something familiar clicked in his brain as he inspected the smaller abnormality. He realized he was sensing something that had been flattened. It was as if the outlines of a three dimensional cube had been squashed and drawn on paper. His heart rate sped up as he remembered Miranda saying there would be other messages flattened onto each Primary Crystavis. One of these spots had to be a message Crystavis.

Now he wished he'd asked Diana to explain how she flattened things and, for lack of a better word, unflattened them. Visualization had worked for him several times now, so he pictured different things to try to unflatten the message. First, he thought of a cartoon character getting steamrolled into a pancake, only to have another character put fireplace billows to them or a bike pump and fill the flattened toon with air. He opened his eyes to check the Crystavis, but nothing had happened.

He closed his eyes and after a while came up with a second visualization. He imagined gently picking up an outer edge of the "drawing" and gently shaking it so parts of it would drop/expand. Then, gently blowing Pleovis into it, it would take shape and form. John sensed that he had something, that he'd found a handle of sorts, but it was stuck down. The image of a puzzle box flashed behind his eyelids. Yes, that's how it felt, like he needed some kind of code or sequence to pull the thing free. He projected outward, trying to sense more. He circled the object with his Visity, approaching it from all angles, looking for clues. Upon one angle of approach something clicked, like sliding a key into a lock. His Visity was able to reach through the flattened object and release it. John resumed his visualization of pulling and shaking, gently inflating it with the Pleovis.

He opened his eyes and saw a small, purple crystal floating towards the blanket wall. He grabbed it and examined it first with the flashlight and then with his eyes closed. He didn't get very far when he decided to try to unflatten the second item before he forgot how to do it. He pocketed the purple Crystavis and started plucking at the second abnormality on the large, green Crystavis. This too required him to approach it with his Visity at a certain angle. He had a harder time finding that outer edge, the handle, to pick up and shake out, but eventually he did get it. This one was much harder to bring back to 3D existence. He had to "shake" it longer and "breathe" into it longer. He sensed when it was done and opened his eyes. Slowly rotating in front of him was a jaggedly shaped Crystavis. Shining the flashlight on it, he saw that it looked like several smaller crystals melded together to make a larger one. Different sections were different colors, from light purple like the messenger Crystavis, and green like the Life Crystavis, to brilliant sapphire blue, gold, red, pink, and several other colors.

When his finger brushed the light purple section of the cube, two things happened. The amethyst Crystavis lit up and a moment later a movie started to play in front of his eyes. He wasn't sure if it was inside his head or outside, but his little blanket bubble disappeared and was replaced by an image of Miranda. It looked like she was standing in the cave within New Zigon.

"My dearest Gianni," she said.

John's blood started to pound in his ears as he hung on Miranda's every word.

"It's been over a year since I stole the Primary Crystavis from New Zigon. I've hidden all of the Primary Crystavis and have been looking for a cure for your papa. Now that I've found something, I'm getting worried that it may be too dangerous. This probably isn't the best place to leave you a message, but it was the easiest to get to. You are too young to trust with this now, but if something happens to me, I hope you can find this when you are older. I've encoded it to our family's Signature so you can pass this special Crystavis on to your descendants."

"Oh dear, I'm afraid I'm not making much sense," Miranda said as she finger combed her long dark hair and tucked it behind her ears. She took a deep breath and settled her shoulders as she looked at him. At least it appeared as if she were looking at him.

"I know the message Crystavis I left with Mirabelle for you was very short. I could not leave information where it could be found. Gianni, don't trust anyone in New Zigon. Keep this very special Crystavis hidden. Flatten it on your belly, just like I showed you. Don't let anyone see it or take it. This is very important, Gianni, don't forget! Between this and the Summas Stone, you'll be the most powerful Zigonian on earth. Be careful how you use this power, darling. Remember your servitudes! Be a servant of science, a servant of those in need, a servant of love, and a servant of God. I know you'll make me proud!"

"When you first saw this Crystavis, you called it a Rainbow Rock, and to be honest, I can't think of it as anything else ever since! I built this Rainbow Rock for you, your children, and your children's children. It is all twelve Primary Crystavis rolled into one! I found a way to meld the crystals together and it created synergies I never imagined!" Miranda had laughed at the memory of the Rainbow Rock name, and now her eyes positively glowed with the excitement of new discovery.

"Not only that, but I've added training for each avenue and put it in each Crystavis. You must put your finger on both the Mind Crystavis and the one for which you want information at the same time, and push your Visity through both at the same time as well. We've practiced it, so I know you can do it, honey. Just be patient and let it come to you. The training has both knowledge transfers and messages. I've given Diana several knowledge transfers to get her to advance as fast as she did. It really does help speed up the learning process, but it does not replace learning the lessons and practicing. Keep that in mind, Gianni!" Miranda said this, pointing a warning finger.

"There is one color for each of the Crystavis avenues of study. You know most of them already but in case you forget,

> Diamond is for Mind,
> Light Amethyst is for Encoding,
> Topaz is for Light,
> Ruby is for Energy,
> Turquoise is for Sound,
> Garnet is for Mass,
> Amethyst is for Embedding,
> Sapphire is for Design,
> Emerald green is for Life,
> Peridot is for Motion,
> Rose is for Magnetism,
> and Aquamarine is for Atmosphere.

Even though only you, your children, and your direct descendants will be able to use this Rainbow Rock, Gianni, you must keep it a secret! There are brand new things in it that Diana and I have discovered. I don't want someone hurting you like they did to Grandma Aberlene to get these powers. Trust no one! Your life may depend on it, son." A shiver ran down John's back at Miranda saying 'son.' The message made it seem like she was speaking directly to him. Why did he react so strongly to being called 'son'? He did nearly the same thing when Mr. Cooper called him 'son.' Was he really that pathetic?

"I want you to promise me right now, Gianni, that you'll practice a little every single day! And never, ever try a new projection that could hurt someone until you have mastered it! Remember how to hide things on your tummy?

> *You grab the ends and hold them tight,*
> *Then push them together with all your might.*
> *Squeeze out the space until it is flat,*
> *Then slap it on your tummy and that is that!*
>
> *To get it back out is easy and swift,*
> *You must find the point and gently lift.*
> *Lift and shake, shake it real slow,*
> *Push space back in and there you go!"*

Miranda was doing cute little motions with her hands, pretending to push something between her hands then to slap her tummy. Then she made an OK sign with her hand, pretending to pinch, lift, and shake something fragile between her thumb and forefinger. She gently blew on the imaginary item then held out her hands, palms up, as if presenting something.

Miranda looked to the side and her face broke into a huge smile. She crouched down slightly, arms out saying, "You heard me, didn't you, my smart little boy! Come on, come here and show me!"

A little boy, who looked maybe three years old, ran into Miranda's arms. It was an older Gianni. His hair was thicker and a little more blond than white. Miranda turned him so the boy was looking at John, and John marveled at the two sets of identical smoky blue eyes staring at him.

"Go on, show Mama," Miranda encouraged. The little boy held up a dirty rock. The two said the rhyme together, only Gianni didn't mimic the motions; he actually flattened and unflattened the rock. "Very good, my darling! Very good!" Miranda said as she gently cradled the boy's face in her hands and kissed nearly every inch of it. "That's my smart boy!" John felt a pang of longing to see a mother so affectionate with her child.

Miranda turned Gianni back to face John as she said, "Look, Mama's making a message for you! Say hi to yourself!"

Gianni gave his mother a strange look that to John said, "I love you Mom, but you are crazy!" The little boy seemed to stare right through John as he waved his little hand and gave a very mature, "Hi, Giann!"

Miranda squeezed the young Gianni fiercely as she said, "I love you, Gianni! Perhaps all will go well, and you'll never need to see this message. Perhaps in a few days' time I will have gotten past the Guardians and used the Pleovis Vortex to free Papa and Diana. Pray for me, my love."

The image disappeared, returning John to his blanket bubble.

"What in the world was that?" John said aloud. His voice sounded more normal inside the blanket; it didn't get sucked away by the Void. His mind was overwhelmed, but one truth slapped him in the face. The message appearing for him unequivocally proved that he was a descendent of Miranda and Gianni, which meant that he had original Zigon blood in him, and that he was distantly related, but related all the same, to Michael.

John turned off his flashlight to conserve batteries for a while and replayed the video over again in his mind. He was glad he was alone when he discovered the Rainbow Rock and the message. Should he tell Diana about it? Miranda had been adamant not to tell anyone at all. Did that include Diana? He guessed he had the time to think it over. He ate another granola bar and finished the first bottle of water. He fell asleep for a while, curling his body around both the Crystavis and the Rainbow Rock.

When he woke up he turned on the flashlight and checked his watch to find that it was 8:30 p.m. John ate the bag of peanuts and opened the second water bottle. He figured he should be rationing his supplies, but he didn't intend to be lost in the Void for much longer. He decided to give the Rainbow Rock a go and see if he could learn how to save himself. He remembered Diana saying portals fell under the Magnetism Avenue. He had to replay Miranda's message to find out that the Magnetism Crystavis was rose-colored and the Mind Crystavis was diamond.

John turned the flashlight directly on the Rainbow Rock. The rose color looked pretty close to the two purple colors, but he could tell them apart well enough. The clear crystal was huge. John wondered if it was an actual diamond. He followed Miranda's directions and put one finger on the diamond section and the other finger on the rose-colored one. He felt an instant tingle run through him from finger to finger. He closed his eyes and pushed his Visity towards both sections at the same time. Another mental video popped into his vision. It was Miranda again, but she was outside in a meadow. It seemed to be a recording of a lesson Miranda had given Diana in that little clearing. She talked about how the Magnetism Avenue covered gravity, magnetic forces, and portals. Miranda talked about gravity and magnetic forces for a while, but it was a lot for John to absorb. He learned that gravity was a kind of tether in the Pleovis; a pattern that engaged two objects and brought them together. Magnetism was similar, but it acted more like a coiled spring: compressed, it pushed apart; stretched, it pulled together. When she described portals, she talked about the two ends and the bridge, things John already knew. She went on to talk about the process of creating a new portal, and while John had never heard the words before, it sounded familiar. Miranda was probably explaining things Diana had given him from Claire's knowledge transfer. Listening to the explanation was tremendous because John was able to recall the borrowed knowledge, learn the material this time, and have it stored in his long-term memory as his own thoughts instead of borrowed ones. He knew, however, that learning and doing were still two completely different things. He hoped the lesson would get into tethers, but no such luck. When the lesson ended, John wasn't sure what to do. He broke the connection with the Rainbow Rock for a few seconds, and then reconnected his touch. This time he'd that same feeling he had when receiving the knowledge transfer from Diana; his mind was both hot and cold at the same time, and when it was done there was the feeling of just waking from a dream. He did this several more times, and the Rainbow Rock alternated between knowledge transfers and watching videos. He wasn't sure if the messages had a different name for them, but he just started calling them videos.

He let the training come to him in its own order, but after a while the video messages completely overwhelmed him. He became familiar enough with the Rainbow Rock to seek out what training was available and pick and choose what he wanted. He decided it would be easier to do the knowledge transfers first, and then when he watched the associated video later, he could recall the knowledge transfer at the same time and put it all together like he had with Claire's information on portals. He was also getting to know the layout of the Rainbow Rock and could separate the different sections mentally, so he turned off the flashlight.

He went back to the Magnetism Avenue and plowed through it, absorbing all of the knowledge transfers. It left his head feeling somewhere between dizzy and numb. He was surprised he had enough focus to finish them all, and hadn't passed out somewhere in the middle. That was his last thought before he lost consciousness.

When he woke up, he was starving. He ate the last granola bar and finished his water. His watch said it was 3:00 a.m. His mind felt like sludge, and he had a terrible headache. He was guessing that it was not a good idea to do so many knowledge transfers all at one time. He imagined the look on Diana's face if he told her he'd done one after another for hours. It was probably best if he didn't let her know about his recklessness. But how was he to know he would end up feeling like this? It's not like he was lazing away a Saturday afternoon and decided to have some fun; he was trying to save his own life. That reality sharpened his mind. He had to get himself out of the Void, and soon; he desperately had to go to the bathroom.

He went through some of the videos on the Void, and it worked as expected. He could match what he saw with a buried knowledge transfer. Still, he could barely make his way through three of them before his headache became unbearable. None of the videos covered tethers.

Immensely frustrated, John thought it was time to experiment with trying to find the tether. Before he started though, he wanted to try to flatten the Rainbow Rock onto his skin so he couldn't lose it. Turning on his flashlight, he pulled out the smaller message Crystavis he'd pulled from the surface of the Primary Crystavis, and decided to try to flatten that one first, since it had been much easier to unflatten. He recalled the children's rhyme aloud and tried to do the actions as he chanted,

"You grab the ends and hold them tight,
Then push them together with all your might.
Squeeze out the space until it is flat,
Then slap it on your tummy and that is that!"

To his surprise and utter relief, it worked. He hadn't flattened it onto the Primary Crystavis as he intended, however, but onto his ... shirt? He had slapped his tummy and the flattened message Crystavis was stored on his shirt. *Wonderful*, he thought. He vocalized the second part of the rhyme,

"To get it back out is easy and swift;
You must find the point and gently lift.
Lift and shake, shake it real slow,
Push space back in and there you go!"

The purple Crystavis was back! With the rhyme it was three times easier than the first time he'd unflattened it. He tried to flatten it again but couldn't seem to get it, so he resorted to using the rhyme with a little modification,

"You grab the ends and hold them tight,
Then push them together with all your might.
Squeeze out the space until it is flat,
Then slap it on the emerald Crystavis and that is that!"

And it worked! He thought, *Okay, now to try the Rainbow Rock*. He lifted his T-shirt off his stomach, just in case, as he repeated the original rhyme for flattening. It worked and he wanted to shout in triumph. He realized that no one could hear him, so he shouted, "Yes! I did it!" He felt silly, and it strained his throat a bit because he hadn't spoken in a while, but it was a release he hadn't realized he'd needed.

He tidied up his blanket bubble, tucking wrappers and bottles into his pack. He considered relieving himself into an empty water bottle, but decided to use that as a last resort.

He shut off the flashlight and stowed it in a coat pocket. Now it was just him, the blanket, and the Emerald Crystavis engulfed in total blackness. John could sense the Crystavis in the Pleovis now without even trying. Either it was from being exposed to it for so long, or maybe one of the lessons from the Rainbow Rock was taking hold. Regardless, he had a better feel of the thing. He pushed some of his Visity through it and felt the Crystavis revive him, taking away his headache. He realized he probably should have been using it all along; absorb some knowledge transfers then heal himself, absorb some more, then heal himself again. He wondered if he could use the emerald section of his Rainbow Rock to heal himself. He tried to poke at the Rainbow Rock with his Visity, but all he felt was the two-dimensional outlines. It made sense that a flattened object would not work because you had to be able to move Visity through it, which couldn't be done in that state.

John was tired of these revelations and learning, and just wanted to put his feet on solid ground again. He circled his Visity around the Emerald Crystavis and tried pulsing it out at different angles like sonar. He was about to give up when he finally noticed something. He had passed it over twice already because it was so faint. There was a structure in the Pleovis, but it was all broken up like a dashed line. It immediately made him think of a stretched spring, which he knew meant something but couldn't recall what.

He focused internally and tried to push the memory to the forefront, which only brought his headache back. He decided to relax then and slowly think over the messages he watched from the Rainbow Rock. He started with the very first one. It had gone over Gravity and Magnetism... Magnetism! That was it! Magnetism was like a coiled spring – when stretched it would bring items together. He thought that made absolutely no sense with what he found in the Pleovis. If there was a stretched spring attached to the Primary Crystavis, shouldn't it be pulling him and the Crystavis in? *Unless*, he thought, *there was something keeping that coil extended.*

John reached out with his Visity, this time looking for something very specific. He found it. It was like a thin wire that seemed to be working as a stiff pole, keeping the coil pattern in the Pleovis extended. Before he took any action, John decided to leave the blanket bubble. He pulled the garbage bag from his pack and slipped it over the Emerald Crystavis, using the rubber bands on his wrists to secure the end. Seeing the rubber bands on his wrist made John think of Christie playing with some at church. The thought made his stomach churn and solidified his resolve to get back home. He tied the ends of the garbage bag to his belt, then untied his blanket and stuffed it and the rope back in his pack.

He reached for the thin wire with his Visity and tested it. It was very strong, and he couldn't seem to break it. He decided to try detaching the wire from the Primary Crystavis. This took some doing, but he finally managed it. As soon as the wire of Pleovis was pushed to the side, the Primary Crystavis started moving. John tightened his hold on the thing and went right along with it. John monitored the Pleovis spring and sensed how it collapsed. Finally, it stopped, but John didn't feel any better off than he had before. He was still hanging there in the middle of nothingness! The portal wasn't open, and the bridge didn't exist. John reached out with his Visity, and to his joy he was able to sense the opening to the portal where the coil attached. The connection was very subtle, and John realized they never would have found it without having seen a tether before.

The door to the portal felt like a disc hanging in space. The tether was definitely attached to one side of it. John expanded his projection, and what he found blew his mind. There was an entire wall of portal doors. No, John realized it wasn't a solid wall, more like the doors all aligned on one plane. He threw out his projection perpendicular to the plane of doors and encountered nothing, no matter how far he went. John skimmed his projection along the plane of doors, not sure what he was looking for. He was surprised that he found something, three somethings actually. He recognized one of the doors; it felt like the main waterfall in New Zigon. He also picked up another tether hooked to the same place as the Crystavis tether. The third thing he noticed was that all of the doors seemed to push against his Visity, like he couldn't actually touch them, even though he could sense them. He reached out his hand towards the portal to which the Primary

Crystavis was tethered. His hand met no resistance. It went straight through the door he sensed in the Pleovis. It was weird, his hand felt different on the other side. He pulled it back.

John reached his Visity out to the other object that was tethered. He found the end of the stiff pole pattern that kept the spring pattern extended. He detached the object from the end of the stiff line, and the spring began to collapse, bringing the object towards him. He grabbed it and unhooked it from the rest of the tether. It felt like a bag of rocks. He opened it up and pulled out the first thing he touched. It was a rock. That was helpful. Still, if it was tethered here, it had to be important or special to someone. He flattened it onto the inside of his arm and went back to the problem at hand, the portals.

He moved his head to the other side of the invisible door and experimented with his Visity. This side of the door tried to pull at him. He felt the same from the other doors as he stretched his Visity out further. He pulled his head back and tried to puzzle out his findings. It was as if the doors were magnetically polarized. One side pushed, and the other side pulled. That would make sense if there were two walls facing each other, then you could bridge from one side to the other. How was he supposed to build a bridge from one side of a single wall to the other? Diana's bridge had felt straight, and was only a few feet long. This was way too confusing.

John decided to do a more thorough sweep of the surrounding portal doors. Close to the New Zigon main waterfall door, he found the door that led to the cave in New Zigon. That's where he wanted to go. He tried projecting his Visity between his portal door and the cave's portal door in every way he could imagine. He recalled the pattern Diana's bridge made in the Pleovis and tried to replicate it, but the end kept bouncing off the cave's portal door, like a repelling magnet. John was fed up. Connecting these two portal doors with a bridge seemed impossible. Just for the heck of it, and because he was all out of ideas, John had his Visity reach for the other side of the cave's portal door, the one on the other side of the "wall." His reality changed in a blink of an eye. Now he sensed a bridge coming out of "his" portal and he stepped onto it. The relief of having something solid under his feet was immense. The bridge was only a few feet long and it led to… the cave's portal door, sitting in a plane of doors in front of him.

"What in the…" John said aloud. When he pushed his Visity to find the other side of the portal at his back, it felt the same as it did before, except that he could sense his Visity probe somewhere in front of him, like it was behind him and in front of him at the same time. He couldn't wrap his mind around it. It kind of seemed like one of those cartoon shows where there were two magic hats lying on their sides, openings facing each other. The Magician put his hand through one hat and it came out of the opposite hat. The Magician scratched his own back this way and shook his own hand. It made absolutely no sense, but that's how it was.

John yanked the Primary Crystavis off the end of its tether without even realizing what he was doing. John took a step towards the cave's portal door. Nothing happened. "What am I supposed to do? Arrrgh!" John screamed in frustration. He was so close! Against the odds he'd pulled himself out of the Void, found the correct portal door, and created a bridge. He just needed to open a rift in reality, that's all. Was that too much to ask?

John's heart was thumping loudly, and he was breaking out into a sweat. He needed to calm down and think. He couldn't recall the training video he'd listened to only hours ago. He tried visualizing again, since that seemed to be his link towards making projections work. He imagined taking a sledgehammer to the door and breaking his way through. He thought of unzipping a zipper. He tried an imaginary crowbar. He thought of a knife slicing through the door. That last thought had done something. He sensed a cut in the door. John remembered the first time he saw Diana open a portal. It was like two giant hands were parting a curtain. As he held onto that thought, he was momentarily blinded by the sudden light pouring into the Void from the cave.

He didn't waste any time stepping through the portal door. His feet landed in water, soaking the hems of his jeans. He sloshed out of the water and went to the edge of the cave to relieve himself where the stream disappeared under rock. He took slow, deep breaths to calm himself and to clear his head. The projection he needed to perform to open the portal door came rushing at him from the recesses of his mind. *Of course, now I would remember,* John thought to himself. He looked around and saw there were a couple of old-fashioned kerosene lanterns illuminating the room. It wasn't very bright, but it was much stronger than his single flashlight had been, and at first had seemed to be as brilliant as the sun. John's watch indicated that it was 4:45 a.m.

John considered his options. He could attempt a portal to the creek to head home, but there were a couple of problems with that. First of all, he wasn't sure he was up for creating an entire portal. Second, if he made his way to the creek, he'd have to walk several miles in the dark to get home.

When Diana and Michael returned to try to rescue him, they would likely stop in the cave first, just like they did for the first trip. They'd see he was fine, and he'd show them that he'd found the Primary Life Crystavis. That sounded much easier to John. He decided to wait and let them come to him. He found his boots and gratefully put them on.

He untied the garbage bag from his belt and took out the Primary Crystavis. He lay down on the garbage bag to try to stop the dampness of the ground from reaching him. He cradled the large Crystavis as he covered himself with the thin blanket and used his pack as a pillow. It wasn't very comfortable, but the sound of the small waterfall was soothing, and he was asleep in minutes.

CHAPTER 27 – OUCH

John woke up abruptly, and it took him a moment to realize what was going on. Gina was trying to wrench the Primary Crystavis out of his hands. He jerked it back, but Gina practically threw herself on top of him to keep her tentative hold on the large crystal. Her glowing amulet reflected off her features, lighting her up like a jack-o-lantern. John watched in stunned fascination as Gina's wizened old face began to fill out, smoothing away her wrinkles. Her hair became thicker and darker, turning into a deep brown color. Her eyes no longer seemed to be quite so buggy when she had an actual face to house them. Within a minute she looked to be in her early thirties, and she was continuing to get younger.

"No!" John shouted as he rolled to his stomach, covering the Crystavis with his body. He was able to twist it out of Gina's hands as she rolled off him, trying to stay with the Crystavis. The connection broke and her reverse-aging stopped. As Gina lay on her back staring at her youthful hands, she began to laugh hysterically. John got to his feet, taking the Crystavis with him and quickly moved away from her. His movement snapped Gina out of her laughing fit and she slowly rose to her feet, a malicious smile on her lips.

"Thank you so much for returning our most precious Primary Crystavis to its rightful home. Now hand it over," Gina demanded as she reached again for the Crystavis.

"No!" John shouted, backing away further.

"It doesn't belong to you. It belongs here, in New Zigon, with The Founder. Tell me where you found it, boy. Were there other Primaries with it? Is that where your girlfriend Diana is now, collecting the other Primary Crystavis?" Gina kept advancing towards John, chasing him in a circle around the cave.

"It belongs as much to me as it does to you, maybe even more so," John called out.

"Don't be so impertinent, boy," Gina said with disdain. "Just because you have a little New Zigon blood in you doesn't give you a higher claim than me!"

"But it's not just a little New Zigon blood, it's original Zigon blood!" John bragged, trying to unsettle the crazy woman. "I'm related to Miranda! I have her family Signature!"

"You lie, you little whelp, now hand over the Crystavis!" Gina screamed at him as she made a lunge for him. John felt a movement in the Pleovis, and, without thinking, he threw up a shield. A shield? John was stunned, but he didn't let his expression show how surprised he was. He felt something violent push against his shield, but it couldn't get through.

"Well, well, now," Gina mocked. "Aren't you full of surprises today!" Gina flicked her fingers to make over a dozen stones lift from the cave floor and fly at John. He ducked his head and threw up his arm in reaction, but the stones all bounced harmlessly off his shield.

"So the farm boy learned a new trick," Gina taunted. "How long do you think you can keep it up? You can't outlast me! I've hundreds of years of experience over you, and you don't have an amulet!"

Gina began her onslaught in earnest, throwing wave after wave of attacks in the Pleovis towards him. John wasn't sure what to do, because he'd created the shield in pure reflex, probably using some knowledge transfer he pulled out of the Rainbow Rock. He was afraid to over-think it and lose it altogether. He kept telling himself, "Hold strong, got to hold strong!" The center of his chest warmed, and he felt sweat trickle off his face and down the back of his neck.

Gina was giving herself quite the workout as well. She was breathing heavily, and John could see the veins bulging on her face and neck.

"How did you find this place?" John asked accusingly.

"You led me to it, dear boy. The moment you brought the Primary Crystavis through this portal, I felt it. It took me a while to find my way to you with all the twists and turns of the tunnels."

John noticed her attacks slowed down when she talked, so he prompted her to say more.

"So you didn't know about this place after living here for centuries? I find that hard to believe," John goaded.

"Miranda was clever, much cleverer than I ever gave her credit for. This must have been how she and Diana snuck in and out all the time. Who would ever think to look for this inside what we all believed to be solid rock? Did her message say where she put that Crystavis you're holding? Is that how you found it?"

"Did Mirabelle have a message Crystavis for Miranda's child?" John asked, ignoring Gina's questions.

Gina dropped her hands and stopped in her tracks. In a childlike voice she asked, "How did you know about that?" She quickly snapped out of it, her fury doubling. "What else are you hiding from me, boy? What else do you know?" With the increase of her anger, her projections increased in number and intensity.

John's shield held, and Gina screamed her rage. She stood panting, hunger in her eyes as she stared at the large Crystavis in his hands. Her eyes flared and she raised one hand towards him like she wanted to touch the shield to test it. Quickly, she turned her hand palm up and flicked her fingers, making a come-hither motion. Something crashed into the back of John's head, and he almost blacked out. His shield fell. Gina's next projection lifted him off his feet and slammed him into the cave wall at least six feet behind him. His head banged sickeningly against the rock before he slid to the floor. He curled himself into a ball around the Crystavis, knowing Gina would grab it from him in a few moments. He had to keep it from her; this was Mrs. McNeally's life he was holding. He could make it invisible, but she would still see the outline of it in the Pleovis. Without thinking, he flattened the Crystavis onto his thigh. This time it made it to his skin and not just his pant leg.

Gina was on him, rolling him onto his back as she laughed in triumph. "Where is it?" she screamed as her hands pulled at his arms and searched his person. John could feel a warm, wet sensation on the back of his neck and a coppery taste on his tongue. Was he bleeding? John's thoughts were dulling by the second. He panicked as he remembered she could sense flattened objects, just as he had on the Primary Crystavis. He couldn't let her have the Primary Crystavis, and he couldn't let her find his Rainbow Rock. "Can't let her find them," was the only thought roaring through his head. Running on pure instinct, he projected his Visity to push Gina off him before he put what felt like an invisible patch over each of his two flattened objects. He almost forgot about the bag of rocks flattened on the inside of his arm. He threw a patch over that one, too.

He barely finished when Gina was back on him. She was running her hands all over him, even lifting his shirt to better scan his chest. John grabbed her wrists to stop her. The next second, John was screaming in pain as he heard and felt his forearms crack. His arms fell uselessly to the floor. Gina slapped him hard across the face.

"Where did you hide it, boy? TELL ME!" she screamed inches from his nose. John could barely focus through the pain, but he managed to give Gina a defiant half smirk.

"You'll never see it again, witch!" John spat out. Gina stood up, screaming. She sounded like a wild, rabid animal. She kicked him several times in the side. John felt a rib crack. He couldn't move his arms, but he did roll to his side and pull his knees into his chest in an attempt to protect himself. Gina continued to kick him in the back. She grew tired of this quickly, and John heard a menacing "snick" that sounded metallic. He turned his head to look at the evil woman, and she was holding a deadly-looking switchblade. Her hand holding the knife was shaking wildly as she approached him.

She is truly insane, John thought as she threatened him in a low, almost gleeful voice. "You will tell me where you put the Primary Life Crystavis, or

I will start cutting you apart, piece by piece." She knelt down beside him and scraped a tear from his face with the blade's edge. She licked the salt water from the knife and grinned at him.

"You're crazy! Absolutely nutters, do you know that?" John gritted out through his pain.

"Am I now?" Gina crooned as she shifted closer to him, rolling him onto his back and intentionally ramming her knee into his broken forearm. John clenched his jaw and tried to bite back his scream. Gina floated her knife threateningly over his body, trying to decide where to strike next. "Tell me where it is and this will all end." When John didn't answer, she stopped the knife over his upper thigh and pressed down, the sharp tip cutting through his jeans to his skin, releasing a drop of blood. "Tell me!" She demanded. When John shook his head, Gina pushed the knife at least an inch into his flesh. John let out a ragged scream, his voice starting to crack. "Tell me," Gina sliced through his skin, dragging the knife slowly towards his knee, "where," she kept slicing, "it is!" her knife stopped when it hit his kneecap. John lifted his head and saw his leg filleted wide open. John wondered how she would react if she found out she'd just sliced through the flattened Crystavis. That was his last thought before he passed out.

* * *

John thought he was dreaming. Large calloused hands were smoothing the sweat-dampened hair from his face, and his forearms and one leg felt icy-hot and tingly. He heard someone softly sobbing. His eyelids felt too heavy for him to open.

"Can you not heal him faster?" said a deep, gruff voice.

"We are working as fast as we can, my lord," said a vaguely familiar female voice.

"So you say you found him like this on the cave floor?" asked the man.

"Yes, I heard an explosion, and it took me a while to find my way down here to get to him. I think he was experimenting with the Pleovis on his own, and something went wrong. I healed him the best I could before you two arrived. He was buried under rock. His bones were sticking right out of his skin on both arms, and a jagged shard of rock was buried in his thigh."

"I don't believe you, you're *lying!*" said a voice John knew.

"Diana?" John barely whispered.

"He's awake! Oh, thank God!" Diana breathed in relief. John heard a loud splash from some distance away. He sensed two of the three people around him jump at the noise. During the distraction, John felt something heavy coat his tongue, preventing him from speaking.

"We'd better get him out of here before more of the ceiling comes down on us." John recognized Gina speaking. He desperately tried to voice an objection, but he couldn't get his mouth to cooperate.

"I think he is healed enough to move," Diana said.

John felt strong arms slide under him and easily pick him up. John groaned low in his throat at the pain caused by that small movement. "Gina, I think you should come back with us," Michael said decidedly.

"No Michael, bad idea, we can't trust her!"

"Do not be silly, Diana, she can help heal John. She was already healing him when we got here," Michael said dismissively.

"Yes, but she…" Diana started.

"She probably saved John's life. From the looks of the cave-in, he was probably hurt far worse than when we got here," Michael argued.

"Cave-in? What cave-in?" John wanted so badly to ask.

"She has not even agreed to come yet," Michael continued. "Well, Gina, will you come with us and help us? I can tell you more on the way."

"Um," Gina said hesitantly. "But The Founder… I'm not sure I can leave him." Gina's voice was soft and girlish, nothing like the murderous screams and cackles she made as she'd attacked John.

No, Michael! Don't be fooled! She's evil! John wanted to scream, but he couldn't even open his eyes at that point.

"We will have you back here by this time tomorrow," Michael promised.

"Alright," Gina giggled. "Let me run and get some things and I'll check in on The Founder before we go." John could hear Gina's footsteps nearly tap dancing her retreat.

"Michael, I know you still think of Gina as that little eight-year-old girl, but trust me, she is cruel and unstable. You didn't see her fly off the handle and attack John and me in the repository!"

"She apologized for that, Diana," Michael said in his low, authoritarian voice. "She admitted she overreacted. She has not been around anyone but The Founder for centuries and is a bit rusty on a few things."

"Precisely my point, Michael! She's been alone here with a crazy old man in this dying place, and it's made her completely bonkers! She's acting all sweet and nice around you, but you have to believe me, she has her own agenda and *we can't trust her!* And how about her appearance? Do you believe her story on how she got so young? If The Founder only healed her enough to keep her from dying, why, after hundreds of years, would he return her to her youth? You've never met the man, Michael. You didn't see him after Lady Aberlene died. I totally believe that he is still lurking around here somewhere, waiting to die and edging Gina along with him to keep him company. I don't believe that news of us being freed from the statue, nor the healing we did to the Lacunavim would motivate him to restore Gina so drastically. Before, she made it sound like it was out of his power to heal her that much, not that he purposely refused to make her young. None of it makes sense, Michael! We can't take the chance that she'll undermine us, and Mrs. M will end up getting hurt! It's not worth it!"

Michael was silent for a few moments before saying, "There is truth in your arguments, Diana, but think about John. Can you heal him on your own?"

John felt a cool, soft hand on his cheek as Diana reluctantly said, "No, I mean I can, eventually, but it would take days. When Gina and I work together on it, we seem to heal him three times as fast, like our overlapping efforts amplify each other."

"So, either we stay here where you and Gina can heal him, or we take Gina back with us. Lord Vito demanded an update in a few hours. I do not see we have a choice," Michael said gently.

John was floored by the way Michael was acting towards him. Michael was putting John as a priority. What had happened when he was lost in the Void? John hadn't thought on it much, but it was Michael's fault that he'd fallen off the portal bridge in the first place. Did Michael's guilt finally break through to the man and snap him out of his debilitating grief? Mrs. M's kidnapping hadn't done it; it seemed to have only made Michael more unbalanced, venting much of his unhappiness at John. Michael still scared John. Here he was, holding John like he weighed nothing, throughout this whole conversation. The man's physical strength was intimidating.

John had trouble continuing his train of thought. He hurt everywhere. He knew his arms were still broken as well as several ribs, but it didn't feel like bones were poking through his skin. That thought almost made him vomit. His thigh was on fire, but it no longer felt sliced open. Michael held him gently but firmly, and Michael's chest was emitting heat like a furnace. John realized he was warm for the first time in hours.

"Okay, I'm ready!" Gina giggled as she returned to the cave.

Michael started walking, and the movement sent jolts of pain through John's body. John felt his face twist in agony as he groaned.

"John, hang in there! We'll be home soon," Diana said, seeming to share his pain.

John felt a different hand touch his forehead, and he tried to scream as a white-hot poker of pain traveled around inside his head.

"What are you doing to him?" John heard Diana yell.

"Just putting him to sleep until we get him home," Gina lied soothingly as John once again lost consciousness.

CHAPTER 28 – HANG IN THERE

When John woke up the next time, he was in a bed. His head felt like it had fallen under a steamroller. He barely knew who he was. A girl was sitting next to the bed, holding his hand. The girl smiled at him when she realized he was awake.

"Hi stranger," she said softly.

"Who are you?" John whispered hoarsely. The girl's face blanched, and she immediately scooted closer to him.

"I'm Diana. Don't you remember me?"

Diana, that sounded right. "Diana," John tried out the name.

"Yes, that's me. You broke me out of that statue in the museum. Remember?"

John struggled to think. Diana's words brought up fuzzy memories. "Y..yes. Tell me more."

"Tell you more what?"

"Tell me more about you. It's helping me to remember."

"Oh, John," Diana said, obviously upset. She gently squeezed his hand as she launched into her tale, from John freeing her in the museum, to his getting lost in the Void. She said that on their way back to save him, they found him in a cave practically buried under a pile of rubble with a young Gina healing him.

As she talked, the memories came flooding back to him, but many of them felt incomplete, and he couldn't remember falling into the Void or anything after it. Thinking of it gave him a headache.

John licked his dry lips.

"Are you thirsty? Would you like some water?" Diana asked helpfully.

John nodded, and Diana helped him sit up and adjusted his pillows before handing him a glass of water. The water soothed his throat and helped to wake him up. There was a faint ringing sound in his ears that was very irritating and made it hard to concentrate.

Diana fed him some soup that warmed him from the inside out. He was coming to himself again, and Diana's story helped to unlock his memories. The recollections flooded his thoughts before settling back into place, all the way up until he fell into the Void. He told Diana as much.

"You mean you don't remember how you got yourself out of there?"

"You didn't save me?"

"No, you saved yourself somehow," she beamed at him.

"That's odd, I don't remember it." The more he tried to remember, the worse his headache became. He felt like there was a brick wall in his brain hiding the memories, complete with barbed wire at the top. He pushed at it with all he was worth, eventually causing a respectable crack in the imaginary wall. A breath of memories drifted through the opening.

"Before I fell I had spotted the Primary Life Crystavis. In the Void I somehow made my way to it and grabbed it like a life preserver. It took me a while, but when I sensed the tether I was able to follow it back to where the portal had opened. It was really strange." John tried to explain the plane of possible portal doors and how it had felt after he built the bridge.

"That's fascinating," Diana said. "When I make a portal I don't see what you described. I've never been in the Void without a bridge." Diana was deep in thought for a moment. John guessed she was trying to picture everything he'd described. "Wait!" Diana nearly shouted. John twitched in surprise, and even that small movement made ripples of pain traverse his body. "You actually found the Primary Life Crystavis?"

John would have laughed if it wouldn't hurt his ribs. Trust Diana to be so blown away by the scientific parts of his story that she didn't catch on to the most important part. "Where is it now?" She said as she nearly bounced in her seat.

"I'm… not… sure…," John said hesitantly. He flat-out didn't remember. That blasted brick wall was in the way again. He mentally pushed and shoved at the crack in the wall, trying to rip out a brick, anything to make the gap wider.

"John!" Diana's voice sounded startled. "What's happening? Your nose is bleeding!"

John ceased his assault on his mental brick wall and opened his eyes. He didn't remember closing them. John wanted to lift a hand to his face, but he was afraid to move his arms. Diana held some tissues to his nose to staunch the blood.

"Where did that come from," Diana wondered aloud. She was absently touching his face with her other hand as if assuring herself that nothing else was wrong. "What were you doing just now?"

"I was trying to remember what happened to the Primary Life Crystavis. There is like this big brick wall in my head, with barbed wire and everything. I can't seem to think my way past it."

"A… brick wall?" Diana said, eyes big as if she didn't believe what he was saying.

"Yeah, a brick wall. I wouldn't make that up out of nowhere," John said defensively.

"Oh, sorry, John, I didn't mean to sound like I don't believe you. It's just that it sounds like a mind block... would it be okay if I take a look?"

John only hesitated for a second before he said, "Sure."

Diana moved to sit on his bed to get closer to him. She was still putting pressure on his nose. She checked it and apparently decided that the bleeding had stopped because she set the bloodied tissues aside. With one hand on her glowing amulet, she placed her other hand on the side of his face, her fingertips gently pressing into his forehead. She stared into his eyes, and he couldn't look away. His head pounding and ears ringing, John welcomed Diana's intrusion into his mind; it felt like a calm, cooling breeze.

"Oh, John!" Diana gasped. She didn't elaborate; she just kept up her mental search. John felt her skim along parts of his brain, her mental touch feeling like soft rain on the hot remains of a forest fire. When she came upon the brick wall, she let out another, "Oh, John!" She gently pushed on it and John's head blasted with pain. He jerked away, breaking their connection. Diana sat looking at him with large, pitying eyes, hands held to her mouth in horror.

"What?" John demanded, wondering if his brains had been pureed. "What was all the 'Oh, Johns' for?" He said the 'Oh, Johns' in a girlish falsetto voice.

Diana dropped her hands then slowly curled them into fists as her expression hardened. "Gina!" she hissed between clenched teeth.

"Gina what? John asked, his pitch going higher, unintentionally this time. "What did she do to me? Diana! Don't leave me hanging here!"

Diana forcibly relaxed her face and told him in very teacher-like tones, "Someone has put a mind block in your head to keep you from remembering something. It is a very strong block, and my first attempt to break it apparently hurt a lot. The problem is that whoever did it was not very gentle. That person essentially plowed their way into your head and threw the wall up to hide your most recent memories, in lieu of not really knowing what specific memories to hide. I'm guessing the person who did it wasn't able to recall or read another person's memories. I don't think the damage is permanent, but there's an obvious trail left behind in your mind, like their mere passage caused blisters to your brain. How does your head feel now?"

"A little better," John admitted. "You actually took away some of the pain, like you were putting out fires or something."

"Really?" Diana said with a delighted smile.

"Really!" John said smiling back. "Want to have another go? Bring a fire extinguisher this time?"

Diana got out her amulet and went in his mind again, healing everything in her path. She skirted the wall but didn't try to push it down again. John had a new appreciation for her talent after all those knowledge transfers.

"Knowledge transfers?" Diana said, abruptly stopping.

"Huh?" John responded.

"You were just thinking about knowledge transfers in the Void," Diana said accusingly.

John slightly panicked, feeling somehow like he'd slipped up. Why would he be thinking about knowledge transfers? He mentally pushed against the wall again, and memories of the Rainbow Rock came spilling back to him. He had decided not to tell Diana about it until after they saved Mrs. M. "Yeah, so?" he said defensively.

"So… what knowledge transfers were you thinking about, since the ones I gave you were here on the front lawn?"

"Those were the knowledge transfers I was thinking of," John said, giving a partial truth. "I was trying to recall them to see if Claire had given us anything useful that would help me save myself." This again, while not the complete answer, was true.

"Oh, I'm sorry. Of course, that makes sense. I'm not sure why I made assumptions like that. It's just that knowledge transfers can be really tricky and could hurt you as much as help you."

John wisely kept his mouth shut. His memory of being lost in the Void was almost fully back now, and he recalled predicting what Diana would say about him doing knowledge transfers for hours. Based on her reaction a few minutes ago, he guessed it would not be good. He thought of the Rainbow Rock flattened on his stomach and was itching to cover it with his hand to check if it was still there. "How's my healing going?" he asked instead.

Diana shifted from scolding teacher back into nursing mode. She fluffed his pillows, straightened his blankets, and refilled his water glass as she answered. "It's going smoothly so far. The cut in your thigh is down to just a scar. Gina said you had a jagged rock embedded in your leg from your knee almost to your hip. Your jeans were ruined, sorry." John would mourn the jeans later. He didn't remember anything about a rock falling on him and splitting his leg open.

"You had compound fractures in both of your forearms. We were able to set the bone and project a binding to keep them in place, but we haven't had the chance to heal the actual bone yet. Two of your ribs were cracked, and you had severe bruising all over your back. We healed the broken bones but haven't addressed the bruising yet. You also had some pretty bad knocks to the back of your head. We healed the surface wounds, but you might have a concussion. We were waiting for you to wake up to evaluate you."

"Where's Gina now?" John asked.

"She's downstairs in the kitchen with Michael. We brought her here to help heal you, and she's only done one session with me so far. It's really making me mad," Diana huffed.

"Did Michael contact Lord Vito?" John asked worriedly.

"Yes, he called him after we got back from the creek."

John waited for her to continue. Finally he asked, "And what did he say? Do we have more time? Did Michael get to speak to Mrs. M?"

Diana wrung her hands together. "Lord Vito wants us to go to his private estate just west of Philadelphia. He's sending a helicopter around lunchtime. That's barely three hours from now, and Gina should be up here helping to heal you!" Diana steamed for a few moments. "He didn't get to speak to Mrs. M, but he heard her yelling orders and complaints in the background."

"Three hours? What time is it now?"

"It's almost nine o'clock in the morning."

"What day is it?"

"Tuesday."

Tuesday, John thought. Mrs. M had arranged for John to stay at her house from Monday through to Wednesday morning, so Father wouldn't be looking for him just yet. Had it really only been yesterday that Mrs. M was kidnapped? John forced himself to focus on the subject at hand and asked, "Why does Vito want us to go to his place? Does he expect us to find his Crystavis by then? What if I can't remember where I put it? What does Michael have to say about it?"

"I don't know," Diana said, worried. "Now that you're awake, I'm going to haul Gina up here so we can do another round of healing on you." John knew from the look on her face that Gina would be in his room soon, even if Diana had to drag the evil witch by the hair.

Diana returned a few minutes later followed by a beautiful young woman. She looked to be in about her mid-twenties, had thick, dark brown hair and was average height. Her skin was as pale as Diana's, and her eyes were a very dark brown. When her gaze settled on John, they radiated a deep hatred... for him, he realized. Her eyes reminded him of... "Gina?" he said incredulously.

Gina looked over her shoulder, and at spotting Michael joining them in the crowded room, removed "the crazy" from her face and went all girly by smiling, blushing, and giggling. John thought it was disgusting. What John found to be even worse, was that Michael seemed to be reacting to it, putting on his big, protective, alpha-male persona. Gina's transformation shocked John, but in somehow it felt like he'd seen her before like this. He'd have to ask Diana about it later.

Without any discussion, Diana stood on one side of his bed and Gina on the other. Michael stood at the foot of the bed, arms crossed, watching as the two females gripped glowing amulets while they healed John. For John it was a peculiar sensation. He swore he could tell the difference between Diana's healing and Gina's healing. Gina's was cold and clinical. Diana's was warm and caring. Together they seemed to do the job. The pain and throbbing in his forearms disappeared, and he could breathe now without tightness and pain in his chest. John relaxed back into the pillows, as, one by one, his aches and pains disappeared. When they were done, John opened his eyes to see a very tired Diana and Gina. Michael sent them both down to the kitchen to eat something while he stayed to talk to John.

John adjusted himself uncomfortably. He felt like he should get out of bed now that he was healed, but he was extremely tired and wasn't sure he would have the strength. Michael pulled up the chair Diana had been using and sat next to the bed.

"I owe you an apology," Michael started. John was mute. He couldn't believe what he was hearing. "It was my fault you fell into the Void in the first place. I was careless and made a mistake; a mistake that made us nearly lose you. I am truly sorry."

John locked gazes with Michael, trying to guess the warrior's motives. Was he actually sorry, or was he doing this because he felt it was necessary? John decided to give the warrior the benefit of the doubt and believe it was the former.

"Apology accepted," John said as humbly as possible. He gave Michael a small smile. An almost insubstantial shiver traveled its way down Michael's back, and he abruptly broke the eye contact.

Michael put his forearms on his knees and leaned forward a bit. "I also realize that I have been a bit hard on you," Michael conceded. John was so shocked, his jaw nearly fell on the floor. "In my time, young men are held to a different standard than they are now. I am trying to adjust to this time, and I should not be measuring you against the standards of the past."

Oh, great, John thought miserably. This seemed to be one of those apologies that was really a dig. John wondered why he was being measured at all.

"Diana is all that I have left, and it is my fault that we are here. If I had not tried to trap her to talk to her…" Michael broke off as he inspected his large hands. John hadn't realized Michael was blaming himself for getting Diana trapped in a statue. John felt he had to reassure the man, despite his intimidating size and more mature age.

"You know the whole statue thing was not your fault. There was no way you could've known. It was The Founder's fault for putting such a crazy reactive projection in everyone's amulet, and it was doubly his fault for leaving you to rot in stone instead of breaking you out of there!"

John was getting himself riled up just thinking about it. He was glad he hadn't met The Founder yet. He felt like punching the stupid old man. Suddenly, John remembered that he was a twentieth-something-great-grandchild of Miranda's and was descended from the old coot. That meant Michael was his twentieth-something-great-grandfather, minus one 'great'. John didn't feel like sharing that information at the moment. He wasn't confident Michael's apology was going to change how the warrior treated him.

Michael looked up and actually smiled at him. Before now, John had only seen him smile at Diana. It was amazing how it transformed his face. John had wondered what Miranda saw in him besides the buff He-Man thing. With the smile, Michael looked much more personable. John returned the smile. To his confusion, Michael's face crumpled and he looked at his hands again. John wondered what he did to ruin the moment.

"It is very kind of you to say that. My mind recognizes the truth of your words but my heart is still heavy with guilt. What I was trying to say is that I feel responsible for Diana. She is like a daughter to me, and I am … very protective of her. She did not have many friends in New Zigon. Actually, Miranda is the only friend I knew about. Miranda said Diana was rather isolated by her talents, and she was not very happy. That is partly why Miranda snuck her out to our meadow to practice; to get her away from all of that pressure she was under. She also told me she did not want anyone to know what she was teaching Diana. A lot of it was what she called "unconventional science" and secret bloodline knowledge, whatever that meant. Back to the point, when I saw how close you two had become, I became concerned that you would hurt Diana. That, and I feel Diana is too young to be courted."

"Courted?" John asked, turning beet red. "Do you mean like *dating*? Whoa, hold it right there! Diana and I are just *friends*." John clarified hastily. John questioned if he even thought of Diana in that way. She was a girl after all, and she was brave, smart, pretty, funny, and he felt comfortable talking to her. *Whoa!* John told himself. He couldn't afford to start thinking that way; there was too much at stake and besides, he really liked Diana. If he *liked* liked Diana, he would start acting like an idiot all the time around her, instead of just part of the time.

"I realize that now, and I can see how strong your friendship is," Michael said. John actually felt disappointed in hearing those words. What was wrong with him? John also felt pleased at the same time by the statement. He was so messed up.

"You did not see Diana when you were lost in the Void. I have never seen her so upset. I realized how much she cares for you. You really have saved her, you know. You broke us out of that imprisoning statue, brought her here, and essentially found her a new home with a doting grandmother and female companionship. The way Diana talks about your sisters, they all sound like wonderful young maidens, ehem, girls. Despite the situation, Diana seems to be thriving, and that is all thanks to you."

John was rendered speechless once again. He couldn't even blush this time, he was so stunned. A warm feeling started in his chest and spread all the way to his fingers and toes. He was basking in… approval? Acceptance? Either one or both, it felt like a big deal coming from Michael. Michael had this air about him; maybe it was because the fact that he was a lord was engrained in every fiber of his being. Maybe it was his unquestionable physical strength and presence, or maybe it was just who he was, but Michael was the kind of man you wanted to know, whose approval you sought, and whose word you would follow. John had no trouble at all picturing Michael in the Fourteenth Century, riding a horse, sword and shield in hand, leading his army into battle to defend his land. *It did not mean, however, that Michael was always right*, John thought stubbornly.

"How old are you?" John blurted out.

Michael thankfully wasn't offended and actually smiled again. "I am twenty-six years old."

"How old was Miranda?" John asked before he could stop himself.

Michael's smile faltered a bit. "She was twenty years of age."

"So you were six years older than her? Kind of robbing the cradle, weren't you?" John teased, smiling at Michael again. If he'd said the same thing a few hours ago, it would have come out sounding like an accusation.

Michael's smile returned full force. "That is one of your terms, but in my time it was not uncommon for a man to take a bride half his age."

John suddenly remembered something. "Hey, you lied to me!" he accused Michael, who looked stunned. Before Michael had a chance to say anything, John said, "You told me you dismounted your horse when you saw Miranda come through the waterfall the first time. In Miranda's message she said you *fell* off. So what gives?"

Michael chuckled and looked down at his hands, "Well, I did not actually lie. I did dismount my horse after all. I just got down … a little faster than normal." Michael looked at John during that last admonition with a wry smile.

John laughed and smiled back saying, "Well, I guess that's sort of true, when you put it that way." Once again, Michael broke their eye contact intentionally.

"Why are you doing that?" John asked, all reservation gone for the moment.

"Doing what?"

"Nearly every time I smile at you, you look away. Do I have food stuck in my teeth or something?"

"Nay, I mean no, you do not have food stuck in your teeth," Michael said with a hoarse chuckle. "It is just that, for some reason, your eyes remind me painfully of someone."

John's mind immediately went to the memory of two pairs of smoky blue eyes staring at him out of a mental video. He rarely paid attention to his eyes, but the next time he was in front of a mirror he would compare them to his ancestors.' John guessed that was one more thing beyond his Visity Signature that was evidence he was descended from Miranda.

John wanted to tell Michael that they were related, but for some reason he hesitated. What if Michael rejected him? John wanted to enjoy being taken off Michael's bad guy list for a while before he said or did anything to mess it up. For the first time since he met the warrior, John felt connected to him. Michael's approval suddenly meant more to John than he cared to admit.

"Diana said that Lord Vito is sending a helicopter for us," John said to change the subject. They *were* guys after all, and there was a definite limit to how much gushy stuff could enter a conversation.

"Yes, that is correct."

"Are we all going?" John asked even though he was afraid of the answer.

"Yes, Gina convinced me it was better to have you close at hand than to leave you here undefended."

"She did?"

"Why does that surprise you?"

"Because she is an evil witch!"

Michael's brow furrowed. John was afraid he'd just lost some of that newfound approval. "That is an uncharitable thing to say. She is a little odd, I admit, but she did save your life."

"But I don't remember anything about what happened in the cave, and Diana said she found a memory block in my mind. For all we know, Gina might have caused the collapse in the cave to hurt me, or even worse, she caused the collapse to cover up what she'd already done to me."

Michael mulled over his words and seemed to take them seriously for once. John could get used to this Michael. He hoped he didn't disappear and get replaced by heart-broken, unfriendly Michael. "She found a memory block in your head?" When John nodded, Michael said, "Have you run into any other New Zigonians?" John shook his head 'no'. "Then we have to assume it was Gina who put it there. I do not like this. She seems superficial and harmless to me, but obviously she is trying to hide something. I will try and be more observant of her behavior and be on guard, as should you."

John solemnly said, "Yes, Sir. So, does Gina know all about Lord Vito kidnapping Mrs. M, and that we were after the Primary Life Crystavis?"

"Yes."

"And?"

"And what?"

John wasn't sure if Michael was playing dumb on purpose or didn't fully understand his concern over Gina yet. "And, how did she take it? She couldn't have been happy that we intend to just give Lord Vito the Crystavis."

"You are right; she did not like that part and argued against it. But she could not come up with an alternative plan to rescue Mrs. McNeally, so she has accepted it."

"At least she wants you to *think* she has accepted it, and she'll turn on us at the last minute," John grumbled.

When Michael didn't speak, John asked, "Do you know why Lord Vito wants us to come to him? Does he know that four of us will be coming? Is he okay with Gina coming?"

"Actually, Lord Vito practically insisted that Gina attend. Lord Vito does not know about you yet, and I would like to use that to our advantage. I want you to make yourself invisible for the trip. You can be our 'ace up the sleeve' as you might say."

John wanted to correct him saying that he probably would never utter that phrase himself; just because the expression was in his memory didn't mean he would actually use it. Then the meaning of the words soaked in, and John started to grow excited. "Cool! I can do the invisibility projection on my own now, too," John said proudly, demonstrating his new skill for Michael.

"Excellent," Michael said, building John's confidence. He stood up. "I will send Diana up with some food, and then get some sleep. We are all going to need to be rested and alert for this journey."

John suddenly felt overwhelmed with everything that had happened in such a short period of time and with what still lay ahead of them.

"Hang in there, Mrs. M, we're coming for you," John said to the empty room.

CHAPTER 29 – HELICOPTER RIDE

Diana brought up some ham sandwiches, and John devoured them. Diana headed across the hall to her room to get some rest, and John barely finished chewing his last bite before he fell asleep himself. It seemed like it was only seconds later when Diana was waking him, saying it was time to leave. John moved to get out of bed when he realized he wasn't wearing any pants. He knew he hadn't been wearing a shirt earlier, and while that was slightly embarrassing, that was how he usually slept, and he didn't question it. The sheet had been pulled up high the whole time as far as he knew. Diana was still in the room, looking at him funny.

"You need to get up, the helicopter will be here soon," she said.

John flushed and said, "Um, I'm not wearing any pants."

"I know that silly! Your clothes were torn and covered in blood. We couldn't just leave you in them."

The blood drained from John's face. "Who… who…" he stuttered.

"Who undressed you?" Diana asked innocently. "Michael did, of course. He was very insistent that Gina and I both leave the room."

John let out a tremendous sigh of relief. Diana still didn't leave. "Um, can you shut the door on the way out, so I can change?" John prompted.

"Oh, I'm sorry," Diana said, seeming to wake herself up from some kind of trance. "There are clothes in the dresser. Mrs. M and I went through a bunch of Bobby's old things and put what we thought might fit you into the dresser and closet. See you in a few minutes," she said as she closed the door after herself.

John leapt out of bed to check out the clothes. There were two more pairs of jeans, plenty of T-shirts, and the closet held some polo shirts and a coat. He even found underwear. Wearing someone else's old underwear grossed John out, but his were bloodstained and over a day old. He really wanted to take a shower. He found a washcloth next to a water basin and a pitcher of water. John guessed they had to clean him up a little when he was still unconscious. He washed himself the best he could and threw on jeans and the first T-shirt he touched. He found his belt on a chair and his boots were next to the door. His socks, however, were missing. John knew from experience that you did not wear boots without socks, or else your ankles would be rubbed raw. Going through the drawers again, he found some socks. Putting on a pair, he noticed one sock was bumpy on the heel, and the other bumpy under his big toe. Upon further examination he saw that someone had darned the socks, apparently to fix holes. John knew that it had to have been Mrs. McNeally's handiwork, and instead of bothering him, the rough spots gave him comfort. He went downstairs, and saw that Diana had their three backpacks ready to go. "You never know what you'll need," Diana explained.

"No, I think it's excellent. The food you put in my pack last time really saved my stomach!"

Diana smiled and maybe even blushed a little as she gave a pack to John and one to Michael. She took the last one for herself. She did not have one for Gina. "Sorry, Gina, we didn't have any more bags. You are welcome to take some food and flatten it if you wish."

"No, thank you. I'm sure Lord Vito will take good care of us, and I don't want to haul one of those nasty things on my back all day," Gina griped.

John studied Michael's reaction. Michael had been watching Gina as she spoke, and now he wore a small furrow in his brow. John guessed it was the first time Michael had heard Gina complain.

"Time to go invisible!" Diana said to John. He complied, and they all went outside to wait for the helicopter.

John was surprised when they started walking out through the fields. "Where are we going?"

"We're going far enough away that the neighbors won't see the helicopter land," Diana explained.

John was so nervous and excited that he could barely contain himself. "I've never flown in anything before," John commented as they walked.

"Neither have we," Diana said with a shaky smile.

John hadn't thought about it, but he was the only one who had actually seen a helicopter. He looked over at Gina, and she appeared slightly green.

"Did you explain what helicopters are to Gina?"

"Yes, I did," Diana said mischievously. "I only gave her language in the knowledge transfer, so every piece of new technology is freaking her out," Diana laughed.

Diana was lucky she didn't see John's expression through his invisibility projection. "You gave her a knowledge transfer? With stuff that came from *me*? You and Michael were bad enough, but *her*? How could you?"

"Oh, sorry," Diana apologized. "I didn't think you would get upset over it. We're not in the Lacunavim now, and she couldn't speak English. I had to do it so Michael could communicate with her."

John didn't answer, and they all walked in silence for a few minutes. Finally, they arrived, at least John assumed they did, because they stopped and rested under some trees bordering a field that had been left fallow this year. The cows had been to it a few times so the brush wasn't too high. They didn't have to wait long.

The helicopter flew in and executed a perfect landing. There were two people inside, the pilot and a copilot, John guessed. The pilot stayed seated while the other man got out and approached them. He looked a lot like the thugs who had kidnapped Mrs. McNeally.

"I'm here to take you to Lord Vito. Follow me, please," the man said formally before he turned his back on them and returned to the helicopter.

They had prearranged for John to walk just behind Michael and to get on the helicopter immediately following him. There were four bucket seats in the back of the helicopter. John said a silent prayer of thanks. He had been worried he would have to sit on Michael's lap, which was their backup plan.

Michael and Gina sat in the first two seats, and Diana and John in the back two. After John buckled up, Diana hissed at him, "Seatbelt!" John looked down and saw how funny it looked with the seatbelt hanging in the air over nothing. John really didn't want to ride without being buckled in and was starting to panic, when Diana saved him by saying, "Make it invisible, too."

John extended his projection over the seat belt just in time. The co-pilot leaned back to check that everyone was buckled in. They were airborne in under a minute. John and Diana were glued to their windows, checking out the view. John noticed Michael doing the same, but Gina looked even greener than before. He tapped Michael on the shoulder whispering, "I think Gina is going to puke." Michael asked the co-pilot something, then sat back, handing Gina an airline barf bag. Michael patted Gina politely on the arm, and she reached down and grabbed his hand. John could see Gina's knuckles turn white and knew she had a death grip on Michael, who did not look pleased. Eventually, Michael returned to looking out the window, allowing his hand to remain in Gina's clutches.

When the helicopter came in for its landing, Gina dropped Michael's hand to better manage the bag into which she was emptying her stomach. John snickered as he saw Michael discreetly try to shake out his fingers. When they got out of the helicopter, John was shocked to see Gina hand her bloated barf bag to the copilot. *Oh, Gina is so good at making friends*, John thought. The look on the man's face was hilarious.

John picked up his step to walk next to Diana and whispered in her ear, "That trip just *flew* by, didn't it?" Diana just rolled her eyes, but she looked like she was trying to hold back a smile.

John made sure to walk in the middle of the group. Michael had asked that John hold onto his elbow so he knew he was still with them. John felt a little silly holding onto the big man's arm like a child, but once he took in his surroundings, he actually stepped a little closer to Michael.

They had set down on a landing pad next to a mansion. The huge yard was professionally landscaped and perfectly maintained. Early summer flowers were everywhere, accentuating strategically-placed water fountains. They were taken into the house through a side entrance and walked past some utilitarian rooms before entering the main living quarters. Looking around, John wondered why one person would need so much space. They were crossing what looked to be a ballroom, complete with a gently curving grand staircase, crystal chandeliers, and marble floor.

The marble flooring continued into the next room, which reminded John of a museum. The space was painted all white with soaring columns sprinkled along the wall, connected by intricate molding. A large oriental carpet defined a conversation area in the middle of the room, with comfortable looking leather chairs, a couch, and several end tables. There were statues *everywhere*. John had a sudden flashback to one of his nightmares right after the museum trip, where statues just like this got down off their pedestals and came after him. He physically shook himself to clear the memory, but the feeling of unease lingered.

They were led to the sitting area and told to wait. Gina and Diana sat on the couch, but John and Michael remained standing, positioning themselves close to Diana.

Something was bugging John about the statues. He looked at them more closely. There had to be over fifty of them. It looked almost like a small army. Some of the statues were of a single person, and some had two people depicted, like in Michael's and Diana's statue. *Like Michael's and Diana's statue,* John thought. Suddenly, it came to him, and his stomach turned sour. Every single statue was of a scene where someone was being captured. Looking at the style of clothing in the statues, they ranged from Diana's and Michael's time up until now. John saw one girl with earbuds hanging out of her jeans' pocket. The older statues were the ones that mostly had two people. The method of capture varied. One woman was being roughly gripped about the arms by a man. Another showed a man with his wrists being tied by someone. Another showed a teenage boy being lassoed. Another showed a man putting one of those poles with a loop at the end of it, like a dogcatcher uses, around another man's neck. In each statue that held two people, the attacker seemed to be doing the capturing further and further from the victim, as if testing the boundaries of what triggered the reactive projection. John recognized a weird tugging feeling in his chest that had started when he entered the room. It was similar to how he felt when he first saw Diana's statue, although not as strong, and this one pulled him in multiple directions.

John thought back to Diana saying how the kidnappers seemed to know how to walk the line between trapping her and physically capturing her. Now John knew how they got that knowledge. Lord Vito had experimented with capturing Zigonians to learn where that particular distinction lay. John was disgusted and enraged at the same time. Lord Vito had sent his men, employees, hired help, someone, to capture a Zigonian, knowing that the person was likely to be part of the resulting statue. John wondered if Lord Vito's lackeys knew the risk they had faced when they carried out their lord's orders.

Michael shook his elbow. John realized he was squeezing it so hard that you could actually see his finger marks on Michael's skin. John immediately let up. "What's wrong," Michael asked behind gritted teeth.

"Look at the statues," John whispered. Michael was looking, and the frown on his face told John that Michael realized something was wrong, but hadn't arrived at the same conclusion yet. "They are captured Zigonians, just like you and Diana were."

Michael's already fierce face turned deadly. John made the sign of the cross as he said a fervent prayer that all of them get out of there safely. Normally, he was too embarrassed to make the sign when he prayed in public, but he was invisible at that moment, so who really cared anyway?

Looking over at Diana, he could tell by the mixed look of horror and rage on her face that she'd figured it out, too. Only Gina sat placidly, apparently just happy to be on solid ground again. Diana leaned over and whispered into Gina's ear. Gina sat up a little straighter and scanned the room, her eyes wide with disbelief. John couldn't quite figure out Gina's next expression. There definitely was anger in it, but there was also… respect?

A door opened on the far side of the room and five men entered. The one in the center was obviously Lord Vito, and the other four spread out as if in formation, two to each side.

Lord Vito looked like a CEO. He had thick, black hair perfectly parted to the side and swept back away from his face. It was movie-star-worthy hair. He had olive-colored skin, a bit darker than Michael's golden coloring. John couldn't make out his eye color, just that his eyes were dark and conniving. Yes, they were conniving; if eyes could ever emulate that characteristic, Lord Vito's did. He was around six feet tall and skinny. He wore an impeccably tailored suit that must have cost a fortune, bearing jeweled cufflinks at his wrists and heavy rings on his fingers. His face was long and pointed. His cheekbones were high and sharp. His nose was large with a narrow bridge, and his chin, which, despite it prominently jutting out to compete with his nose, appeared weak. John had expected him to be a slightly smaller, slightly less athletic version of Michael, not a tall weasel hiding behind designer clothing. Still, he looked darn good for someone coming up on seven hundred years old.

John had slid behind Michael when the men entered, which was silly since he was invisible. He felt better keeping Michael's muscles between him and Lord Vito's entourage, who, while not matching Michael's dimensions, were big in their own right.

Lord Vito wisely did not get too close to Michael as he said, "Ah, cousin! At last we see each other again. Six and a half centuries is much too long for families to stay apart, don't you agree?"

CHAPTER 30 – LORD VITO

Michael simply said, "Lord Vito," as his greeting.

Lord Vito quickly moved on. "And dear Diana, New Zigon's brightest star in generations. I'm so glad you could come and visit." Lord Vito walked over to Gina and held out his hand to her. "This lovely woman must be Angelina, daughter of Mirabelle."

Gina placed her newly youthful hand in Lord Vito's. "I go by Gina now," she said shyly.

He gallantly bent over and kissed her knuckles saying, "Welcome, Gina." Gina actually blushed.

Lord Vito retreated to sit in a large leather high-backed chair that closely resembled a throne. John was sure the impression was intentional. He wondered what Lord Vito would have done if one of them had chosen to sit there when they arrived. Would he have asked them to move? Lord Vito said, "Now that the introductions are over, let us get down to business. We have an exchange to make; one special Crystavis for one special Grand-mama."

John thought Lord Vito came across as oily. Every word slid out of his mouth almost lazily. His English was perfect with no trace of an accent, and he spoke with the assurance that his wishes were always met, his orders followed without question. John knew Lord Vito was a powerful businessman, but meeting him in person brought that reality to bear. John imagined an evil aura radiating from the 'lord'. John had no trouble picturing this man capturing and torturing Lady Aberlene to get what he wanted.

Michael stepped forward, not intimidated in the slightest. "I need to see Mrs. McNeally, to know that she is unharmed."

"Oh, of course, I'm sure you're concerned with her welfare. We may as well bring her in now, so you'll be able to focus on our business dealings," Lord Vito said, drawing out the "s's" like a snake. Lord Vito nodded to a guard on his right, and the man went back out the door through which they had entered moments before.

"This may take a few minutes. Your Mrs. McNeally has proved herself to be... very uncooperative."

John shuddered at what that had meant for Mrs. McNeally, and what she'd suffered. Lord Vito rang a small bell John had not noticed on an end table next to the throne-like chair. A maid walked in carrying a large silver platter laden with a variety of small sandwiches, fruits, desserts, a pitcher of what looked like lemonade, and glasses. The servant laid the tray on the coffee table in front of the couch, curtsied, and quickly left the room without a sound. John wondered if Lord Vito still lived in the Fourteenth Century to have the help curtsy to him like that.

Diana and Michael barely gave the tray a glance, but Gina's face lit up like a small child's as she scooted to the edge of her seat to better inspect the offerings. She helped herself to a drink and made up a small plate of food before she sank back contentedly into her seat. John could not figure out her game. Where was the steeled cruelty in her eyes? Where was her unwavering purpose to save New Zigon? This transformed younger Gina seemed happy to be along for the ride, the whole trip an adventure for her.

John forgot all about Gina's strange behavior, as he could hear Mrs. McNeally's voice well in advance of her arrival.

"Watch your hands, you big oaf! Didn't your mother teach you any manners? You push me like that again, and you'll make me fall, probably breaking my hip. Then where will you and your goons be? In the hospital, pushing me around in a wheelchair, that's where." John thought he heard the guard mumble something about how Mrs. M being in a wheelchair would make life easier, and maybe he should just put her in one now.

Mrs. McNeally was pulled through the door and into the room by the same man who went to fetch her. She looked a little worse for wear, but John's heart leapt when he realized she was still all in one piece. Mrs. McNeally was still wearing the blue plaid cotton button-down shirt and the faded jeans she'd been wearing when she was kidnapped. Her hair was majorly falling out of her standard bun; the gray and black strands frizzed about her face and hung messily over her shoulders. John's blood raged when he saw the bruises. The entire left side of Mrs. McNeally's face was a kaleidoscope of blues, greens, yellows, and purples. She had a cut lip, and a cut on her forehead was being held closed by Steri-Strips. Her hands were handcuffed in front of her, and John could see the skin was rubbed raw around her wrists, and there was more bruising on her forearms. John wanted to punch something, he was so mad.

Apparently, Diana and Michael had similar responses, because Diana jumped to her feet, and Michael made a low menacing noise deep within his throat as his body tensed all over. John gave Michael's elbow a couple of squeezes, hoping to remind him they had to see how this played out. They were outnumbered, and John was sure Lord Vito anticipated Michael going all fourteenth-century-warrior on him, because that's who Michael was.

Luckily, they hadn't been searched when they arrived. John knew Michael had several of his knives stashed away in different places on his person, and he was wearing his sword and scabbard at his waist. Diana had put a sustaining invisibility projection on the large weapon, and John could just make out the outline of the distortion in the Pleovis.

Since John had been focusing on Michael, he initially missed Diana running towards Mrs. McNeally. By the time he saw her, she was more than halfway across the room. Lord Vito held up a hand to his guards, notifying them to allow the impending reunion.

"Mrs. M!" Diana cried as she raced up to the battered woman and gently pulled her into her arms. Mrs. McNeally tried to awkwardly pat Diana's head as she said, "There, there, child, I'm fine, everything is going to be all right." Diana pulled back just long enough to focus on Mrs. McNeally's handcuffs until they opened as if by magic, the metal chiming as it hit the marble floor. John was shocked to see that Diana didn't even use her amulet to unlock the cuffs. Mrs. McNeally wrapped her arms around Diana at that point and kissed the top of her blond head. "I was so worried about you," Diana said, voice muffled from the hug. John wanted desperately to join them, to hug Mrs. M and reassure himself that she was okay. He also wouldn't mind being the one who was being held and rocked as Diana was at that moment. Michael pulled his elbow close to his body, signaling John to stay put.

Lord Vito said in his slimy voice, "How touching. Now, both of you sit down on the couch. And Diana… no more projecting or there will be consequences." At Lord Vito's words, all four guards pulled out their guns and released the safeties. This is what John had been expecting. If Michael pulled out his sword and rushed Lord Vito, he would be shot before he ever got near him. Diana and Mrs. McNeally walked over and sat down on the couch, arm in arm.

"Now that your curiosity has been satisfied," Lord Vito said as he rubbed his hands together excitedly. "Let's talk about your progress on obtaining the Primary Life Crystavis."

"Why do you want it?" Diana asked boldly, apparently recovered from her momentary lapse of control at seeing Mrs. McNeally. "We all know you forced Lady Aberlene to make you your own Life Crystavis and give you the means to use it. Apparently, it has been working," Diana said as she swept her eyes up and down over Lord Vito's body to emphasize her point.

"I have my reasons," was all Lord Vito would say as he crossed his legs and laced his fingers together over his lap like he was relaxing at a country club.

"How do you power it anyway?" Diana couldn't resist asking. "Lady Aberlene wouldn't have been able to change your DNA to make you Zigonian. Only The Founder can do that."

"That is true, she could not change me," Lord Vito said as he started tapping his thumbs together, keeping the rest of his fingers laced. Lord Vito tilted his head to the side as if contemplating whether or not to answer the second part of Diana's question. John saw Lord Vito's Adam's apple bob, slow and relaxed, up and down his skinny neck. He didn't seem to be annoyed by the questions, thankfully.

"After six and a half centuries, you learn a thing or two about being immortal," Vito continued. John suspected Michael's cousin was answering not only to brag, but to hear himself talk. *What a piece of work*, he thought.

"People notice if you don't age, even the slow, uneducated ones. You either have to move from place to place every few years, or actually allow yourself to grow old with your neighbors."

John was fascinated. He never thought it through before, but it made sense. He had watched an old movie about a highlander cursed with immortality who had stolen social security numbers and fake identities every so many years.

"And I'm the kind of person who likes to grow roots and nest in one place," Lord Vito said, gesturing to the grandeur around them. "So, I decided to let myself age… to a point. Once the gray hair started coming, I would have an unfortunate *accident*, and my son, the spitting image of me at that age, would inherit everything."

John couldn't help but admire his strategy. Out of the corner of his eye he caught Gina shifting and noticed that she was impressed as well. He thought he saw a flash of her evil focus wash over her countenance, but it was gone so quickly, he wasn't sure if he actually had seen it in the first place.

"But I digress, the point that I was trying to make, is that I only need to use the Crystavis once every twenty, thirty, or forty years, depending on what kind of run I'm having at the time, and, of course, for sudden illnesses. I always have at least one Zigonian on staff at any given moment that can do the job for me."

Diana gasped, "So Lady Aberlene must have made you your own Primary Life Crystavis; it's the only kind of Crystavis that doesn't have any restrictions on Visity Signatures without impacting the result."

"Living up to your reputation, I see," Lord Vito oozed. "Did you also know that Crystavis can be designed so the output can be received by only one Visity Signature as well?"

"Theoretically, yes, but I've never seen it done before. That rather limits the usefulness of a Crystavis, don't you think?" Diana contemplated.

"Limiting who can benefit from the Crystavis means it is only valuable to those predetermined few. It makes it less desirable to potential thieves," Michael said.

John desperately wanted to ask if it was programmed to just Lord Vito's Signature or his family's Signature, like his Rainbow Rock. He wanted to whisper the question in Michael's ear, but he couldn't reach that high.

"Yes, cousin, I knew you would understand. Unfortunately, that means I cannot grant immortality to anyone but myself."

"You have someone you don't want to die," Michael reasoned bluntly.

"Enough of skipping around the main subject. Where is the Primary Life

Crystavis?" Lord Vito commanded, ignoring Michael's statement.

"I told you on the phone, *cousin*, that we know where it is but have not figured out a way to retrieve it yet," Michael said with calm confidence. John thought Michael's restraint was impressive, especially given how volatile he'd been up until now.

"With the time I gave you since our last conversation, I expected you would have the Crystavis in your possession by now!" Lord Vito said angrily. Since John hadn't heard the phone conversation, he didn't know what to think about the accusation. "Gina in particular seemed supremely confident you would have met your goal by now. Knowing how you prefer to use brawn over brain, dear cousin, I insisted she come along to help balance you out. Was I wrong?" Lord Vito directed the last question directly at Gina.

Gina stood saying, "No, my lord. I'm here to help you attain your goal. I only ask for one small thing in return."

John shouldn't have been surprised Gina was trying to strike her own bargain with Lord Vito. He tried to head towards her, to do what exactly, he didn't know, just something to keep her from talking. To his horror, he discovered he couldn't move. Gina had her hand over her glowing amulet as she glanced triumphantly at Michael and him, her gaze back to the sharp and more-than-just-a-little-bit crazy Gina they all knew and hated.

Lord Vito jumped to his feet as his men trained their guns on Gina, hammers cocked. "I said, 'No projecting!" Lord Vito roared, highly incensed. A fifth guard John didn't know was there, stepped up from behind them and aimed his gun at Diana, only inches from her head.

"Stop immediately, or I will have the girl shot!" Lord Vito ordered.

Seeing Diana at gunpoint, Gina's face lifted in a slow, devilish smile. "Go ahead, my lord; you'd be doing me a favor. Nearly the exact same favor I referred to."

"In return for helping me, you want me to kill one of your own people?" Lord Vito asked, intrigued.

"You can kill her if you want," Gina waved her hand dismissively. "I just want her amulet."

"Her amulet for getting me the Primary Life Crystavis?" Lord Vito summarized. "Stop projecting and we can discuss this."

"I don't think you want me to do that, my lord," Gina said sweetly. "Unless you want me to let your barbarian of a cousin loose as well as that insipid boy."

"Boy? What boy?" Lord Vito demanded, looking a little shocked. John guessed he wasn't shocked very often.

"The boy who released Michael and Diana from their statue, the boy who knows where the Primary Life Crystavis is and may even have it flattened on his person, the boy who is standing behind Michael this very moment, hiding behind an invisibility projection," Gina said, betraying them in nearly every way she could when it suited her, just as John had predicted.

Cattails! John thought lamely, hating that he'd been right.

"Gina, No!" Diana shouted and made to lunge for the traitor. When the gun aimed at Diana's head clicked its precursor to firing, Mrs. McNeally forcefully pinned Diana so she couldn't move.

"It's not going to help anyone if you get yourself shot," Mrs. McNeally was saying, as she looked right through the space John occupied, a worried expression on her face.

One of the guards flanking Lord Vito came towards them and looked behind Michael. "She's telling the truth, my lord; there's someone definitely back here. I can see his outline through the Pleovis distortion," the guard said. John cringed internally as the guard felt around until he found and gripped John's upper arms. "I've got him," the guard said. Gina must have dropped whatever she was doing to him because he could now move. The guard hauled John away, as another guard moved closer to Michael and trained his gun on him.

"Behave now, Michael," Lord Vito drawled. "I'd hate to have my own flesh and blood killed, but I will not hesitate; you know that."

Lord Vito waved at Gina and she dropped the projection on Michael. Michael shifted his weight on his feet, clenching and unclenching his fists, clearing itching to pummel someone. "Get away if you can, son," Michael said. John wasn't sure if Michael was trying to keep his name from Lord Vito or just naturally called him 'son'. Either way, it gave him a little boost of courage.

"Drop the invisibility," ordered Lord Vito as John was dragged before him.

John remained silent. Lord Vito nodded at the closest guard, who immediately strode over to John and, ewe, felt him up. When the fist rammed into his stomach, John figured the guy had just been trying to find his mark. John wanted to say something, but all the air had left his lungs. He managed somehow to hold onto his invisibility projection. His punisher straightened John up, getting him ready for another hit. John extended his projection and made both of the man's arms invisible. It only bought him a couple of seconds. The guard gave his invisible arms a funny look, and then shrugged before he landed another punch, this time to the side of John's head.

John would have fallen if the guard behind him hadn't been holding onto him. The world went black for a few dizzying seconds, and John lost his grip on his invisibility projections. He forced himself to stand despite the pain. He stared straight into Lord Vito's beetle-black eyes defiantly.

"Ah… so this is?" Lord Vito said.

"John," Gina supplied.

"John. So, you are a Zigonian, and you are the first one in nearly seven hundred years to figure out how to break The Founder's curse. What is your secret?" Lord Vito asked, totally diverted from his Crystavis obsession for the moment.

John stubbornly stuck out his chin and remained quiet. Lord Vito nodded his head again at the guard, who punched him hard in the gut. John bent over in pain, but still refused to speak.

"Stop it! Don't hurt him!" Diana screamed.

John straightened again and stared back at Lord Vito who walked pensively towards him. John struggled against the guy holding him, but wow, the guy was strong. Lord Vito stopped a few inches away from John, his gaze sweeping all over him, sizing him up. Lord Vito reached out and roughly grabbed John's chin, tilting his head up to look at him. Lord Vito turned John's head from side to side, inspecting him closely. "Interesting . . . what a unique shade of blue," Lord Vito murmured, only loud enough for John to hear. John assumed he was talking about his eyes.

"Smoky blue?" John asked, just as quietly. John wanted to scream at himself! What in the world had possessed him to say that? If there was a brick wall nearby, John would use it to bang some sense into his own head.

Lord Vito's eyes widened slightly at John's words. He squeezed John's chin harder as he looked straight into his eyes. "Yes…," Lord Vito said almost absently, "definitely a smoky blue." Lord Vito pushed John's chin hard to the side before letting go and backing up.

"Who are you, boy? Where do you come from?" Lord Vito resumed his interrogation. "You obviously don't have a Crystavis or else you'd be part of the décor by now. Answer me!" he shouted.

Gina stepped closer and said, "His name is John Brown. He comes from a little hick town in Western Pennsylvania. He's an orphan and doesn't know who his parents are, poor thing," she finished mockingly.

"I appreciate the information, but I need *him* to start talking," Lord Vito admonished. John thought Lord Vito was uncharacteristically patient with Gina. "Gina, why don't you tell me now what you meant when you said this boy knows where the Primary Life Crystavis is."

"So, you agree to get the girl's amulet for me?" Gina said hopefully.

"Yes, yes, that is a small thing for me to grant. You may have it."

Gina just about bounced on her toes in excitement as she softly brought her hands together twice in a silent clap.

"He knows where it is, because I saw him with it," Gina said, her eyes nearly glowing. A massive headache descended upon John as he tried to process Gina's words. John couldn't remember anything after following the tether back to the portal. Did he get the Crystavis off the tether?

"You're lying!" John accused. "I don't remember having it!"

"Of course you don't, silly boy," Gina said gleefully. "I put up a mental block in your head to keep you from remembering. Once I remove it, you're going to tell us where you put it, isn't that right, John?"

"I'll never tell you!" John shouted out. "I don't care if you beat me to a bloody pulp!"

When Lord Vito said, "That can be arranged," and nodded at his guard again, Gina boldly stepped up to him and put a tentative hand on his arm.

"I think there's a faster way to motivate the boy," she said coyly. "Have them bring the girl over here."

Lord Vito looked approvingly down at Gina, a devilish smile creeping over his face. "I like the way you think." Lord Vito kept his gaze on Gina, taking it one step further as he ordered, "Bring Diana *and* dear Grand-mama"

"No!" John and Michael roared together. John fought his captor furiously but froze when the sound of a gunshot reverberated through the large room. The sweat on the back of John's neck felt icy as his stomach dropped to the floor. He thought, *Oh no! Who...?*

Then the gravelly voice of one of the guards said, "That's your only warning shot!"

John looked over his shoulder to assess the room. There were five guards. One was holding him, one was staying close to Lord Vito, one had his gun trained on Michael, one was manhandling Mrs. McNeally towards them and the last one had his gun pointed at Diana urging her along. John stared at Michael, looking for direction. Michael stared back, his gaze packed with meaning. John wished he knew what Michael was trying to tell him. He needed help. He needed someone to tell him what to do. He needed... John suddenly heard something. He cocked his head, trying to find out where it was coming from. It seemed like it was coming from inside his own skull. It sounded like Michael's voice, but Michael's lips were not moving. The voice said, "Stay strong, John! Don't fight back if it means Diana gets hurt. Just give them what they want. Nothing is more important than Diana's and Mrs. McNeally's lives and your own. Cooperate. Don't give them a reason to hurt you. If you go along with them, there's a chance they will let us go."

"Hey, no projecting!" yelled the guard holding him. John remembered that this guard was a Zigonian.

"Sorry, I had no idea I was," John said honestly.

"You sure you don't have a Crystavis on you, kid?" the guard asked suspiciously.

John shook his head and reveled in the thought that he'd just read Michael's mind... from across the room! And without a Crystavis! It must have been something from those hours of knowledge transfers he'd done. John steadied himself with Michael's thoughts. He tried to calm down, bite back his anger, and do what he had to do in order to get his friends out of there.

Suddenly, John nearly fell to his knees as a white-hot pain ripped through his mind. Gina was touching his head, doing something to him. Despite his best efforts, he cried out in pain. His guard had to hold him up, as his legs wouldn't support him anymore. John thought he heard his name being shouted, but the pain was overriding everything. It felt like someone was slicing out a part of his brain. The guard apparently got tired of holding him up, because he let John sag to the floor.

"There! Give him a few moments to remember," Gina was saying from somewhere above him. John blacked out, escaping from the pain for a few precious moments.

John was roughly awakened and dragged back to his feet. Once again his guard stood behind him, maintaining a vice-like grip on his arms.

John's eye had begun to swell from the punch to the head earlier, and he tasted blood on his lips. He suspected his nose was bleeding, and badly wanted to wipe it, but wasn't able to lift a hand with his arms pinned to his sides. Gina's face swam in front of him. His head kept flipping her image between new, young Gina and old, skeletal, buggy-eyed Gina. He almost preferred the old version; at least then her outside matched her inside.

Gina started patronizingly patting his face. "Time to remember now, boy. You found the Primary Life Crystavis. You somehow brought it back to the cave, because I found you there holding it while you were sleeping. We played tug of war with it, and then it disappeared. Where did you put it?"

The memories came flooding back to John, harsher in their recall than in their making. He felt like his brain was being caressed by an extra-sharp cheese grater. He said as much. "I... I can't think. I feel like my head is being shredded by a cheese grater. I'll tell you, just give me a minute. Can I... May I have something to drink, please?"

"Well, at least you remembered your manners," Gina mumbled. "I guess I *was* a little rough yanking that wall out of your head." John wondered if he heard right. Did Gina just apologize for hurting him? Michael had said Gina saved his life in the cave, but he couldn't remember ... yet. Someone pressed a glass to his lips, and he drank greedily. It was the lemonade from the tray. "Delicious, isn't it? Hand-squeezed, I'm guessing. I told you Lord Vito would take care of us."

John wondered who was the person talking to him, because the voice sounded like Gina, but the words didn't. John had decided to cooperate, so he started to sift through the painful memories.

"I had put up a shield," John started.

"Yes, that's right! It was a surprisingly good one, too," Gina admitted. "You just forgot one very important thing."

"I forgot to watch my back," John remembered with a grimace. Gina had made a rock fly at him from behind his shield, and it had broken his concentration. "You threw me across the room..."

"Yes, I did, didn't I? And you made such a delightful sound when you hit the wall..."

"And I flattened the Crystavis onto my..." John paused, pulling hard at the memory.

"Onto your what, boy, where did you put it?" Gina demanded, all softness gone from her voice.

"On my ... leg," John finally remembered. "The one you sliced open with your knife."

"WHAT?" Gina screeched. She started groping his thigh, looking for the flattened object. "I checked, I know I checked! It wasn't there! I was trying to make you get out the Crystavis to use on yourself, but your friends showed up. There wasn't anything there, I'm sure of it!" Gina was panicking now. "Is it still there? Why can't I sense it?" she wailed.

John was confused by Gina's reaction. Then he remembered, he himself had wondered what would happen to a flattened object stored on skin when that skin was sliced right down the middle of the thing. It gave him an idea. He gently pushed out with his Visity along his body until he got to the flattened Crystavis. It was still there, and amazingly, the patch was still covering it, although it felt like a gap almost an inch wide cut right through the middle of both. He now essentially had two flattened objects and two patches.

"It's there," John reassured her, "I just need to sit down for this. May I sit down? Here on the floor?" Gina hastily motioned to the guard to lower him down. John wondered where Lord Vito went in all of this. John wasn't sure how much longer his extra-polite behavior would work on Gina, seeing that she was near hysterics. While he was sitting down, John removed his patch from one side of his leg injury, hoping the action would go unnoticed as he changed positions. Once he got to the floor, he stretched his legs out in front of him.

He rubbed his hand over the uncovered half of the flattened Crystavis. This is the side that had the "handle" as John was calling it, i.e. the end that he mentally picked up and shook out. He was embarrassed that he had to use his hand to simulate the unflattening, pretending to pinch something, lift it and gently shake it. He even recited Miranda's rhyme silently in his head. He had a hard time pushing the Pleovis back into it; it was like the ends were frayed. He instinctively put a binding on the torn edge to hold the Pleovis in place. The Crystavis appeared in his hands. John opened his eyes to look at it and saw only half of the glorious crystal, like part of it had been sheared off with something incredibly sharp. The cut surface was as smooth as glass.

Gina ripped it out of his hands, crying and screaming, "Noooooooooo! I didn't know! This is not my fault! This is not my fault!"

John dropped his head into his hands to hide his grin. He wasn't sure if he would be able to get the other half of the Crystavis out of his leg, or if he would be able to put the two parts back together again. He just knew that he'd denied Gina something she wanted, and it sounded like she was blaming herself instead of him. He knew she'd soon question him over the other half, and he bit the inside of his mouth to stop himself from laughing. He had just mastered his expression when Gina grabbed him by a fistful of his hair and yanked his head back, hard. Okay, he was no longer at risk for laughing at least.

"Where is the other half of it, boy? Where did it go?" She screeched in his face.

"I... I don't know," he lied, hopefully convincingly. "It's not there anymore. What's supposed to happen when you slice through a flattened object in somebody's skin? I thought I was pulling out the whole thing. If something's wrong, it's your fault, Gina, not mine."

Gina resumed groping his upper thigh, mumbling to herself.

"Gina, explain what is going on! I've never seen a Crystavis shaped like this. Aren't they usually rounded? This one, while larger than I expected, looks like it was cut in half," Lord Vito said, irritation plain in his voice.

"Maybe it still works," John suggested to Gina. He wasn't sure if he just helped her or hurt her. It would depend on whether or not the half of a Crystavis could do anything.

Gina rushed to Lord Vito to give him the Crystavis, but kept her hands on it like she didn't want to let it go. John noticed she was sweating, and strands of her dark hair were sticking to her face and neck.

Gina looked up into Lord Vito's aggravated face and said, "I didn't notice this before, my lord, but this Crystavis got damaged while it was hidden in the Void. Part of it was destroyed, but I think it will still work, just maybe not as effectively as before."

John was amazed at the story that Gina had just spun. He guessed she believed him that the other half was gone, and that it was her fault. That was the only reason he could think of that would cause her to risk lying like that to Lord Vito.

"Well, what are you standing there for, try it out!" ordered Lord Vito. Gina took one glance at John and his injured face and decidedly passed him over, marching directly up to Mrs. McNeally.

"Can I look at it first?" Diana asked Gina. "Just for a moment, please? To make sure it doesn't backfire on you?"

"Make it quick," Gina growled, pushing the Crystavis at Diana without letting go of it. Diana had obviously picked up that a little please-and-thank-you seemed to go a long way with Gina. Diana got out her amulet and looked up quickly to make sure they weren't going to stop her. One hand on the broken Crystavis and the other on her glowing amulet, Diana closed her eyes in concentration. John tried to sense what she was doing and was amazed that he could feel something. It didn't seem like she was just checking out the Crystavis, it felt like she was reforming it, maybe fixing it. John guessed she wanted to make sure the Crystavis wouldn't end up hurting Mrs. McNeally.

Diana dropped her hands and said, "The generic receptor is missing. This portion of the Crystavis wholly contains the healing capabilities but the age reversal capabilities are mostly gone."

"What does that mean?" demanded Lord Vito.

"It means that with the generic receptor gone, the Crystavis will not be as effective for anyone other than the person or persons who created it. In this case, Lady Aberlene and The Founder made this Crystavis together. You have seen to it that Lady Aberlene is no longer with us, and The Founder is holed up somewhere in New Zigon, wasting away. It can still be used, and for healing it will work, it just will be much slower and take a lot more energy than if the Crystavis were whole. If you want this for age reversal, most of that functionality is missing. I can't predict what will happen if you try it," Diana explained. John was proud at how calm and brave she was while she gave her explanation with Lord Vito breathing down her neck.

"I'm not concerned about the age reversal at this time; tell me more about the healing. Why will it be slow-working?" Lord Vito asked.

"Because," Gina said jumping in, "the part that makes this a Primary Crystavis, the part that allows anyone to use it, is missing. Every Crystavis will always accept the Visity Signature of the people who created it. If a Crystavis does not have a receptor built into it, and you're not one of its creators, you can still push your Visity through the Crystavis, but it is like trying to blow a yolk out of a pinprick in an eggshell. You have to push a lot at it for a long time to get any to go through." Gina thought for a moment then said, "Families all have a similar Visity Signature. The Signature of the more powerful parent gets passed on to the children."

Gina stared at John. "Make the boy try it," she said.

Lord Vito told her, "You try it on the old lady *right now.*" Surprisingly, Gina didn't argue. She just turned to Mrs. McNeally, holding the broken Crystavis between them, and closed her eyes. John couldn't tell what was happening, but Lord Vito's disgusted grunt told him it wasn't much.

"Bring the boy here," Lord Vito commanded before Gina had stopped. John was hauled to his feet and dragged over to Mrs. McNeally.

Gina placed the Crystavis in his hands and warned, "I'll know if you aren't doing your best, so no tricks!"

John sent out his Visity to sense the piece of Crystavis in his hands. The part he held was perfect, just missing its other half. He could even tell where Diana had made some changes. There were flows that went straight out of this half with a flow waiting for something to come back in. Diana hotwired these together to keep the Pleovis flow contained within the Crystavis until its ultimate pattern had been reached. When he'd first used this Crystavis in the Void, he only had to nudge his Visity at it, and it nearly sucked it in to do his bidding. Now he felt like he was fumbling around for a door lock, roughly trying to jam in a key he wasn't sure would fit. He eased back a bit and approached the Crystavis again, slowly and cautiously. He felt there needed to be an alignment, but he couldn't describe it. Finally, it clicked into place and he found the right angle in which to push his Visity. It was like when he'd first unflattened the message Crystavis and the Rainbow Rock. At the right angle his Visity slid in like a key into a lock. He felt the Pleovis move and dance through the formations in the crystal. John directed the Pleovis exiting the Crystavis at Mrs. McNeally. Within seconds her bruises disappeared, and her cuts and scraped wrists healed. John pushed a little more, and the Pleovis continued on to heal some arthritis, removed the beginnings of a kidney stone, cleaned out some of her arteries, fixed some damaged tissue in her lungs and spine; basically giving her a full body tune-up. This only took moments. When he was done, he directed some of the Pleovis at himself to heal the places where he'd been punched and to heal the damage Gina had done to his brain when she removed the mind block. He let out a relieved sigh.

"Excellent!" Lord Vito declared. "Why did it work for him, but not for you?" he grilled Gina.

"Because, he has true Zigon blood. He told me so himself. That means he is descended from The Founder and likely your ape of a cousin over there," Gina expounded, "which means he is distantly related to you as well, Lord Vito."

John saw that Mrs. McNeally was examining her healed arms, not paying attention, but Diana was looking at him with wide eyes. He gave her a half smile as if to say, "Yeah, that's me." Then John nervously turned to look at Michael as Lord Vito said, "Michael, you sly old dog, you! You and Miranda had a kid? But I never saw Miranda with child… and I'm guessing you didn't either, did you! You were trussed up in granite or whatever stone that devil Founder used, ha! Poor Miranda had to raise a baby all on her own. Funny how none of my Zigonian guests knew about it or even mentioned it. You'd think they would've kept careful track of something like that, wouldn't you?" Lord Vito seemed to have fun taunting his cousin, but John doubted Michael was listening. Michael was looking at John from the other side of the room. John's neck and face heated, afraid of what the warrior would think. They had just started trusting each other, and now Michael found out from *Gina* of all people, that John had been hiding this from him. John couldn't see Michael's expression from this distance, which worried him further.

Lord Vito grabbed the Crystavis from John and pushed John at the nearest guard. "Bring him now, there's not a moment to lose. The rest of you stay here," Lord Vito ordered as he raced out of the room through the door he and his guards had used. John stared at Michael the whole way out. As he got closer, he was better able to see Michael's face, and he seemed… gob-smacked. All feeling was stunned off his face. John didn't know what to think about that as he was pulled from the room down a well-decorated hallway. They took an elevator to the fourth floor. John wondered what kind of house had an *elevator*. This one, apparently. They followed Lord Vito into a room that looked like it belonged more in a hospital than in a mansion. There were two hospital beds surrounded by beeping equipment. All kinds of tubes reached from the machines to the patients in the beds. There was a thin, well-dressed woman sitting between the beds, her eyes bloodshot from crying, a fancy handkerchief clutched in her hands. Lord Vito took John to the first bed. It held a girl John's age. She had white-blond hair, the same as the crying woman, and her skin looked nearly transparent, stretched over her skeleton with very little muscle. She was almost bonier than old Gina.

Lord Vito thrust the crystal into John's hands and commanded, "Heal her!"

John pushed out his Visity, quickly finding the right approach angle to the Crystavis. He directed the outpouring of Pleovis to the sick girl in the bed. Nothing happened right away.

"I said HEAL HER!" Lord Vito shouted, making the crying woman jump.

John ignored him and closed his eyes, sending out some of his Visity towards the girl to see what was wrong. She was near death; that was the problem. Her kidneys had failed, and her other organs seemed to be almost disintegrating. John helped to guide the healing Pleovis, repairing what he could. He found that there wasn't enough "stuff" to fix everything though. He remembered Diana making the cookies. She had taken all the ingredients out of the cupboards to make them, and John supposed this was the same kind of principle. He couldn't rebuild tissue from nothing. He did everything he could. When he opened his eyes, the girl's skin wasn't as transparent and had a soft pink glow. Before, she seemed to be in unbearable pain, but now she seemed relaxed and much more comfortable.

Before being asked, John moved to the other bed. There was a boy in this bed, almost the spitting image of the girl. They both were so pale and gaunt; John had to guess their gender by the length of their hair. He went straight to work, and not a moment too soon. The boy's heart was barely functioning when he started. Again, he did all he could, then turned to Lord Vito. The woman was hanging on Vito's arm, crying in earnest, but her tears seemed to be hopeful, not sad.

"I did what I could, but they are so thin there's not much for me to work with. What's wrong with them? Their organs were dying, and this boy's heart was about to stop…" John faltered. The woman let out a large sob and hid her face in Lord Vito's chest.

"That's none of your concern," Lord Vito said coldly. "You need to do more for them. This will not be enough."

"Then you need to get Diana up here. She will know what to do, and I can execute it."

At a nod from Lord Vito, a guard set off running and soon was back using his gun to push Diana into the room. John noticed he did not seem to want to touch Diana. *Smart man*, John thought. Diana went right up to John and put an arm around his waist. John soaked up the comfort and support she offered. She looked at the boy and girl patients. With compassion in her eyes, she turned to John and asked, "What's going on?"

"We need to help these kids. I did what I could, but they don't have much inside for me to work with. I figured it was like the cookies, and asked them to get you."

"The cookies?"

"The ones you made for Claire. You said you couldn't make something out of nothing. I'm guessing I'm facing the same problem here."

Diana smiled at John like a proud parent. "Excellent logic. Can you use the Crystavis on them and let me sense what's happening?" In answer, John focused on the Crystavis and sent the healing Pleovis back towards the boy. He let it travel through the boy's body, not finding anything it was able to heal. "I see," said Diana. At some point she had put both of her hands over his on the Crystavis. "You are exactly right, John." She turned to Lord Vito and said, "We need food to make these kids better. They do not need to actually eat anything; we just need the substance to convert to tissue to make them healthier. If I make a list, can you have those things brought here immediately?"

Lord Vito snapped his fingers at a nurse John had not noticed in the corner. "Give the girl a pen and some paper, quickly." To one of the guards, he said, "Go, alert the kitchen staff that we will be putting in an urgent request. GO!" he shouted when the guard didn't move fast enough.

Diana had wandered over to a dresser, scribbling madly onto a piece of paper, which she handed directly to Lord Vito. Then she took John aside and started giving him instructions. "We are going to have to work closely on this. I can extract the material and bring it to the skin. You are going to have to take it from the skin and move it to the correct cells. To create new cells, you'll basically have to double the organic matter within a cell, and then give it a nudge to split, creating two new cells. It will be hard at first, but once you get a pattern established, it will go much faster. We will need to start with the central organs then work our way to bones and muscles. Do you follow me?"

Diana looked up at John with so much faith and trust in him, that he couldn't say anything but, "Sure." After a moment, he asked her shyly, "Any chance you could give me a knowledge transfer on this to help?" John worried he was going to turn into a knowledge transfer junkie. "It really helped me with the invisibility projection, and I swear, some of the things I did in the Void to save myself had to have come from the knowledge transfer." He intentionally didn't mention *which* knowledge transfer had actually helped.

Diana bit her lip, worrying. "I guess it can't hurt," she finally said as she reached for her amulet.

Within minutes the house staff was pushing in carts of raw food. There were steaks with the bone in them, a variety of other meats, some fish, milk, cheese, vegetables, salt, some cooking oils, and large containers of water.

Lord Vito and his staff stood back and watched. Diana took John's hand and guided it over to the boy's hand, making him grasp it. Diana laid one hand over John's and the boy's joined hands, and put her other on her amulet. John was cradling the Crystavis in his free arm. "Just follow along for now, and when I squeeze your hand, employ the Crystavis, okay?" John solemnly nodded his head then closed his eyes in concentration. The sensation was foreign but amazing. He felt like he glued his Visity to Diana's and just went along for the ride. She started with the heart. He felt her make a snapshot, like a molecular map, of the heart muscle. Then she reached her senses out towards the food trays and called for what she needed. She didn't have to go to each thing individually; it was more like she had an empty puzzle board, which attracted its missing pieces. She directed the collected matter over to the boy's chest, and then squeezed John's hand. John used the Crystavis, focusing on the heart. This time, he included the matter just outside the boy's chest into the equation. The Pleovis did most of the work, pulling the materials it needed to divide cells, making new ones. The process started to accelerate, just as Diana had said it would.

Diana squeezed his hand again and John could feel her Visity on the move. He followed it to the lungs. They repeated the process over and over again. By the time they were done, almost an hour had gone by. The tray of foods looked horrible. It looked like gnats had gotten to it and other parts had been freeze-dried. The boy, however, looked like a new person. He was three times the size he'd been before they started. He had strong muscles covered by thick, healthy skin. All the monitors were whirring quietly, displaying normal readings.

As soon as Diana and John stepped back, Lord Vito and the blond woman rushed to the boy, touching his face and calling to him.

"He's probably not going to wake up for a while. The healing process is just as exhausting for him as it is for us," Diana said.

"Now her, heal her!" Lord Vito said excitedly, pushing John to the girl's bed. John was so tired he wasn't sure he could stand much longer.

"We need something to eat before we can start again, or we are likely to make mistakes," Diana said tiredly. John admired Diana's choice of words; she craftily wove a small threat into her request. They were soon sitting at a folding table on the other side of the room, drinking orange juice and eating toast, which was followed by the most delicious steak John had ever had in his life. When he was done, he was even sleepier than before. He whispered his concern to Diana. She gave him a conspiratorial smile. "Now, you heal us before we start again on her," she said. John did and it was as if the food disappeared completely from his stomach. It was like the Crystavis sped up his digestive track and reset his brain better than a good eight hours of sleep. They repeated the healing process with the girl. When they were done, John stared in wonder at the new person now lying in the hospital bed. She was beautiful.

Diana politely asked if they could have more food, and Lord Vito absently agreed, his focus concentrated on the healed girl. They ate, and John managed to surreptitiously heal them again before the Crystavis was taken away from them. It was a good thing, too, because the day was far from over.

CHAPTER 31 – MORE DUST

John and Diana were led back to the room with the statues. Michael and Mrs. McNeally were resting comfortably on the couch, and Gina was weaving her way through the statues, examining each one. There were four guards, one in each corner of the room. Michael and Mrs. McNeally jumped up at the sight of them. The guards didn't seem to care, so John and Diana rushed over to their friends. Mrs. McNeally grabbed John first and gave him a huge, grandmotherly hug. Even though John was an inch or two taller than Mrs. McNeally, he sank into the hug like a little boy.

"Oh, my dear child, Michael here has been filling me in on your adventures. You have been so brave! I'm so proud of you! I love you so much!"

John tried not to cry at her words and mumbled into her shoulder, "I love you, too, Mrs. M!"

Michael had pulled Diana into a hug, but now he laid a huge hand on John's shoulder. John immediately stiffened, afraid of Michael's reaction. To his complete and utter surprise, Michael tugged John into a hug. John remained stiff, not knowing what to do. He never had a man hug him before, and he didn't know how to react. He hesitantly patted his hand on Michael's broad back. The big man's torso began to shake. John wondered in shock... was Michael *crying*? No, it had to be something else, John convinced himself. Michael gave John a large, rib-cracking squeeze before releasing him, only to hold him at arm's length. Michael's smile was brilliant as he looked at John. This was *not* what John had expected. He was so uncomfortable; he almost wished Michael had been mad at him instead.

"You are of my blood," Michael choked out. Mrs. McNeally and Diana stood on either side of John, each putting a supportive hand on his back. "Some of my dear Miranda remains in you. I cannot tell you the joy that brings to me!"

"You know this doesn't mean you are my dad or anything," John said stupidly. "You are my great-great-great-about-twenty-more-great's-grandfather."

Michael laughed, and the sound filled the room. "That does not matter, son, you are of my blood," Michael repeated, "and we are family."

A slow, loud clapping bounced through the room. "How touching," Gina mocked. "Are you one big happy family now? That's probably a good thing, since Diana won't have her amulet for much longer. She'll need you to protect her," Gina taunted as she lazily circled them like a vulture.

"And what do you think is going to happen to you, Gina?" John asked, trying to push the witch's buttons. "First, you flirt disgustingly with Michael, even when you were old and repulsive. Now you're throwing yourself at Lord Vito, expecting what, that he'll take you in to cherish and honor you? Not likely! Your fate is to spend the rest of your life in that dying Lacunavim, with only a crazy old man for company. New Zigon is dead, no matter how much you try to heal it," John spat. "You'll be lucky if you make it out of here in the flesh and not in stone!"

"So cheeky!" Gina said delightedly. *What was she so happy about*, John wondered suspiciously. "I like that about you, John, no matter how pathetic you are, you're never boring." Gina laughed madly as she continued circling them. "You think I will not make it out of here? I, who handed Lord Vito what he wanted? Look around you, boy, do you think Lord Vito will just let *you* walk out of here? He is obsessed with The Founder's curse. Do you think he is going to fly you home first class, thanking you for your good deeds? He needs you to use what is left of the Primary Life Crystavis, which we probably can't call a Primary any more. Maybe he'll keep you on retainer. Or maybe he will cut you up into little pieces to find out how you broke The Founder's curse. Oh, how I would love to see that!" she giggled.

"Not a bad idea, Gina, my dear," Lord Vito said as he strode into the room.

"Did the kids wake up? Are they okay?" Diana asked, always the kindhearted one.

"Yes, they are awake and well," Lord Vito said in a clipped voice.

"Don't bother thanking us or anything," John muttered.

"Ah, my manners. I do believe some thanks are in order." Lord Vito walked over to Gina, picked up her hand and placed a kiss on her knuckles as Gina blushed. "Thank you, lovely Angelina, for helping me attain the Primary Life Crystavis." With that, Lord Vito walked over to his high-backed chair and sat down.

"That was it?" John spluttered. "Diana and I just spent two hours saving those kids' lives, and you're thanking *her*?"

Lord Vito just templed his fingers and gave them a smug smile. Michael, who had shifted to stand between John and Diana, had a powerful arm around each of them. He squeezed John's shoulder, probably trying to tell him to keep quiet.

"I do have to admit, you two make a stellar medical team, but you complied only under duress, whereas Gina decided to help without coercion," Lord Vito said calmly.

"Speaking of coercion," Lord Vito continued, "will any be necessary in getting you to tell me how you freed Diana and my dear cousin from The Founder's curse?"

"It is a lovely story," Gina cackled, moving to stand by Lord Vito, placing a hand on the back of his chair. "Amazing, really," Gina was preening, enjoying herself immensely as she reveled in John's embarrassing story. "Miranda tried to break the curse for *years*, and this marvelous boy broke it with his *boots*, if you can believe it."

"His boots, you say?" asked Lord Vito, entertained.

"Yes, I believe he tripped and broke part of the statue," Gina gloated.

"Fascinating," Lord Vito said as he stared at John and assessed his large, steel-toed work boots.

"Can I have her amulet now?" Gina pouted. John wanted to gag. He kept imagining Gina as her old bony self, and picturing her trying to puff out non-existent lips and cock a skeletal hip was nauseating.

John gathered his Visity and pushed a mental, "You're pathetic!" at Gina. She visibly recoiled, and John pressed his lips together to stop the smile that wanted to surface.

"Yes, I believe you have earned it. I am very satisfied with the results," Lord Vito said coolly. He nodded at the two guards who had entered the room with him, and, as if it was prearranged, one targeted his gun at Diana and the other grabbed Mrs. McNeally and put a knife to her throat.

Gina strutted over to Diana and held her hand out, palm up.

"Better cough it up, dear, or Grandma over here is going to get a little bloody," Gina purred. *Goodness gracious,* John thought. The witch was alternating back and forth between crazy psycho and evil sidekick. The way she was swinging her hips, he wondered if she'd seen the Jessica Rabbit comic rendering in *Who Framed Roger Rabbit?* It certainly was over the top. John nearly gagged again as he noticed Lord Vito literally ogle Gina.

John didn't know what to say. He didn't want to see Diana hand over her amulet, but he didn't want Mrs. McNeally to get hurt either. The guard holding Mrs. McNeally pressed the knife into her throat just enough to make a trickle of blood appear, which ran down her neck and soaked into her shirt collar. Mrs. McNeally didn't make a sound, but Diana gasped, "Okay, okay! Don't hurt her! I'm handing it over, see? Don't hurt her!" She made her amulet appear then hastily dragged it over her head and held it out to Gina. With the tiniest of sobs, she dropped her amulet into Gina's waiting palm.

"There now, that wasn't so hard, was it?" Gina crooned as she smoothed her fingers over Diana's cheek. Michael shot his hand out and grabbed Gina's wrist.

"That's enough, Gina, you got what you want, now leave her alone!" Michael said in a controlled growl.

"Better watch it, muscle man, you don't want to trigger The Founder's Curse, now do you?" Gina said flippantly as she pulled her wrist away and sauntered back to Lord Vito. She placed Diana's amulet around her neck and flattened it into her chest. John was ready to burst, he was so angry.

"We have given you what you asked for, it is time for us to leave," Michael declared as he started to move to the door and out the way they had come. One of the guards blocked his way, gun raised.

"I just need a little more from John before you go," Lord Vito said as he stood. "As you probably have noticed, I have a special interest in The Founder's curse," he said as he gestured to the statues around them. "I cannot let the opportunity pass to perform some experiments."

Lord Vito strolled around his gallery of prisoners, bragging about his morbid accomplishments. "Michael and Diana were the first to get caught by The Founder's curse. After Michael didn't come home for over a week, his men sent out a search party. They came across your statue in a pleasant little clearing on the edge of our lands. It took four teams of horses to bring you back to the keep. You were my favorite courtyard decoration for nearly fifty years. When my business interests led me abroad, I spent less and less time at the family castle. We were attacked by a nearby city-state, and without dear cousin here, our army just wasn't up for the match. The keep was overrun, and your statue was taken as a trophy of sorts. I lost track of you after that. I had enjoyed your statue so much, that I decided to acquire a new one. Zigonians started to pop up everywhere. As I said, I had some in my employ at all times, and they helped me identify their fellow citizens. I sent servants out to catch them, expendable servants mind you, and I began to experiment with the curse's trigger. I was curious; did proximity play into it? Physical contact? And do you know what I found?"

Lord Vito continued without waiting for an answer. "The curse was triggered only by a capture with physical contact. Place someone in a cage? They were fine until they touched the bars. Hold someone at gunpoint? Nothing happens. Tie someone's hands? You'll barely finish your first knot before triggering the curse. Now, if a Zigonian ties their own hands, they are still free. If someone picks up the other end of the rope, BAM! Statue!" Lord Vito walked up to the statue of a man grabbing a woman by the arms. "And as for person to person physical contact, the intent is just as important as the touch. Affectionate touching does not work, even if the participants are playing a game. Grabbing someone to ward them off does not affect the trigger. There has to be intent to take and restrain, attaining control of a person against his or her will." Lord Vito stopped and faced them, adding a bit of the dramatic to his little speech. "Such intent will carry through a master to his servants." Lord Vito motioned to several of the two-person statues. "Even if my servants didn't like what they were doing and had no wish to detain a Zigonian, my intent carried through to their actions and triggered the curse."

Lord Vito sauntered back to their little group. "I've never really cared to try and break the curse, but you have raised my curiosity." Lord Vito signaled to a guard who hurried to his side. After some whispered instructions, the guard disappeared and returned with a large hammer.

"So, you just smashed part of their statue with your boots?" Lord Vito asked.

"I smashed the rope connecting them. I didn't smash their bodies," John said hastily, afraid Lord Vito would randomly start smashing legs and arms.

Lord Vito approached the statue with the man caught by a dogcatcher's pole. He raised the hammer and smashed it down on the pole part of the statue. The stone didn't break, and John could almost feel the sting of reverberation that had to be traveling up Lord Vito's arm. After a few choice swear words, Lord Vito composed himself and said, "Fascinating. I always wondered why these statues never lost their clarity, never disintegrated in the sun or harsh weather. There must be a protective barrier around them. Come here, boy," he said to John.

The one guard still had his knife out, and while he no longer had it poised at Mrs. McNeally's throat, he was still standing dangerously close to her. Lord Vito handed John the hammer. "You try it."

John complied. What was the worst that could happen by hitting the pole on this statue anyway? It shouldn't hurt either captive. John swung the hammer hard, and it, too, bounced off the statue, painfully vibrating John's arm. He *had* made a crack in the stone, however, even though it was small. Lord Vito stepped forward to inspect the result. "Try it again," he ordered as he stepped back. John really didn't want to rattle his arm out of his socket, so he shook out his sore arm trying to buy some thinking time. When he'd freed Diana and Michael, it had been with a part of his body, not a tool like this hammer. Technically it had been his boots, but still, it was his feet. He wondered if the business end of the hammer was too far away from his hand. It was worth a try. He choked up his hold on the handle so his grip was just below the metal head. This time when he swung, the hammer bounced back, but not nearly as much. He also made some respectable-sized cracks in the statue.

Lord Vito stepped up once again and discussed what John had done differently. "Again," he ordered. This time John tried one more thing. He used the same choked grip on the hammer as last time, but he also projected his Visity around the hammer. Since his awareness over his Visity had greatly improved during his time in the Void, John had noticed that without consciously trying, his Visity tended to run through his body and was always there, ready at the surface. If his Visity had been projecting subconsciously over his boots, that might have been what broke through the stone.

When John swung the hammer, it went clear through the stone, and a puff of smoke and dust burst out of the broken pieces. It was déjà vu as John watched cracks travel over the captured man. He backed up and covered his face just in time for the stone to shatter and fly in all directions with a considerable amount of dust. A man stumbled and fell from the low pedestal, covered head to toe in grayish-white, plaster-like powder. The end of the dogcatcher's pole was dangling from his neck. John looked about the room. His friends were still grouped together, the guard with the knife standing close to them. Gina had slid to Lord Vito's side, and they both were totally enraptured with the phenomenon occurring before them. The other guards in the room held their posts, but several of them were wiping the dust out of their eyes, and one of them coughed.

John had been playing along with Lord Vito's experiment, just as curious to see what happened. In the back of his mind, he'd continued to mull over Gina's taunt that Lord Vito would never let them go. After this display, he was certain that she was right. Looking around though, he came up with an idea. Not just an idea, a great idea! John sensed the Pleovis around him. There were all kinds of shock waves moving through it. He couldn't tell which guard was the Zigonian, but he felt safe in projecting undetected with everything going on. He launched his Visity at Michael and Diana, sharing his plan. "Nod if you receive this," he added at the end. They both nodded. They all waited.

John couldn't remember how long it took between Diana's release and Michael's. In the museum they seemed to be barely a minute apart. Now it seemed like years. John sent out his Visity to map out the room in preparation. No one was helping the poor dusty man coughing on the floor. That made John hesitate; he hadn't thought everything through.

"Isn't the other man going to break free?" asked Lord Vito. As if on cue, the cracks in the statue began to radiate towards the remaining figure, pieces of rock breaking off. John took a few more steps back and tensed. Just as before, there was an explosion of rock fragments and dust. John headed to the closest two-person statue and swung his hammer at the victim's bindings. His Visity-encased hammer broke straight through. The noise was barely recognizable in the midst of rock shards falling throughout the room. He quickly moved onto the next statue and smashed through the tool of capture in it as well. By the time he hit the third, the first one shattered, adding even more dust and confusion to the room.

"Now!" John punched his Visity in Michael's direction. He strained to hear some shuffling of feet as Michael disarmed the guy with the knife. He thought he heard a strangled cry and a thud. John made his way through several more statues as he warned Michael and Diana there was a guard still in front of the door they had to exit through. John was on his sixth or seventh statue, and the dust was so thick, he couldn't see his hand in front of his face. He was completely dependent upon his Visity for navigation. With his Visity, he could see the room as clear as day. The drawing in his chest deepened as he felt an answering tug from the waiting statues. He moved through them as quickly as he could, shattering through a new set of stony bonds every ten seconds. New stone explosions were going off like clockwork. John sensed one of the guards drag Lord Vito out of the room and into cleaner air, thankfully in the opposite direction from where Michael, Diana and Mrs. McNeally had gone. Gina had ahold of Lord Vito's arm and left with him. John thought he could feel that the guard leading them out was the Zigonian one. The others still standing in the room were desperately coughing. Michael had felled two of the guards with barely a sound. One guard shot a bullet that ricocheted terrifyingly around the room. Luckily, he'd aimed high and didn't seem to hit anyone.

John continued his destructive path through the gallery of statues. He had run out of two-person statues, and the single statues were a little harder to figure out. John wasn't sure if he actually had to strike the capturing element or not, but he wasn't about to chance it and hurt someone by mistake. As a result, he had to take a few extra moments to find the correct strike point. He located, evaluated, smashed, moved on, and repeated. The room was a war zone of explosions and falling shards of rock. John paused for a moment to search for the guards. They all had left the room. In his moment of stillness, John realized he wasn't coughing and hadn't been for some time. Looking down, he sensed a bubble of clean air floating around his nose and mouth. He had done some kind of defensive projection without even knowing it. *Hurray for knowledge transfers!* John thought. He continued around the room until the last statue had its bondage point shattered. He had been so intent on completing his task, that he hadn't noticed that the air in the room had cleared.

John stood up, shook some dust and rock bits from his hair, rolled his shoulders and looked around. The room was filled with grayish-white people, all shapes, sizes, and manners of dress represented. Many looked like they could barely stand and were leaning heavily on each other. Almost every one of them had hands over glowing amulets, and were either patiently waiting in a semi-circle around him or were helping the newly emerged Zigonians. It was a veritable army. There were about a dozen men huddled in a corner, looking scared out of their britches. John guessed they were the captors. He felt bad for them. They had been duped and were victims just like the Zigonians. Several of the waiting Zigonians noticed where he was looking. As if reading his mind, for all John knew they had, they went over to the group of dissatisfied ex-Vito-lackeys and held out welcoming hands to guide them into joining the larger group of dusty people.

John didn't say anything. Time seemed to freeze as he just stood there staring blankly at what had to be over fifty people, as they all waited for the final statues to shatter and release their prisoners. All dust and other debris generated by the remaining mini-explosions was swept up into the air to join a thick gray cloud covering the ceiling. John guessed the glowing amulets were responsible for their clean air. It was only moments between John's last swing of the hammer and the statue's subsequent eruption. The last statue to crumble was the one of a girl John had noticed earlier who had earbuds hanging from her jeans' pocket. As soon as she was able to stand on her own and stopped coughing, the earbuds girl said loud enough for everyone to hear, "Well, that was horrible!" Some of the dusty people chuckled, and some nodded their heads in total seriousness.

John cleared his throat and said in what he hoped was a commanding voice, "My name is John. I'm sure you have lots of questions, but they will have to wait. We have to get out of here, fast. It would be best if we project invisibility. Help those around you if there are some who can't do that. Please, follow me."

He stood there nervously for a moment, wondering if they understood English, when the earbud girl said, "You heard him, let's get out of this dump!"

John sighed appreciatively as he turned and made his way towards the door that would lead them out of the mansion. He could feel that strange bond with these people that he'd experienced with Diana after he'd freed her. He felt responsible for the group, and he had to get them to safety. He looked back and saw that at least half of the people appeared crippled. They seemed stoned (*Ha! Get it, stoned?* John chuckled to himself) and exhausted. The Zigonians wearing modern clothing didn't appear to have any problems at all. He remembered how dazed and sleepy Diana was when she got out of her statue. It looked like the longer you were encased in stone, the more dramatic those side effects.

John made himself invisible just before he walked into the adjoining ballroom. No guards seemed to be coming after them. It looked like the path was clear to get out of the house. He had no idea what to do once they reached the lawn. At least he had a minute or two to figure it out, as he led the invisible parade through the elegant room. He nearly laughed when he looked back and saw a stampede of dusty footprints dirtying the marble floor in the wake of his invisible charges.

John called out to Michael and Diana using his Visity, asking them to meet him on the lawn. They all couldn't ride in the helicopter, obviously, and none of them knew how to fly the thing anyway. The Zigonians were about halfway out of the house when John sensed Michael, Diana, and Mrs. McNeally approaching, Diana hiding them in an invisibility projection. John wished he could see their faces when they saw all the Zigonians following him, before he realized that only Diana would be able to see the Pleovis disruptions.

They moved further onto the lawn to make room for the rest of their crowd to get outside. John had just opened his mouth to ask his friends for ideas on where they should go from here, when the answer was figured out for them. They were standing by the largest fountain in the yard, the focal point of the decorative landscaping. The fountain was nearly fifteen feet tall. One of the Zigonians had created a portal in the falling water, and John could see the blackness of the Void in the parting rift. One by one, the Zigonians and the handful of refugee humans stepped through the portal into the Void.

259

John and his friends went last. John didn't know where the portal would take them, and he didn't care. He just wanted to get away from this place. The late afternoon sun felt wonderful on John's face as he waited. John was the last one to step through the rift, and he was shocked that he couldn't see a portal opening at the other end. The rift closed at his back, and once again, he was in the Void in total darkness. Thankfully, he had his Visity to sense his surroundings. He found himself at the end of a long line of people, all standing on the bridge, patiently waiting. At least most of them were patiently waiting.

"Will you open up the second door already? What's the hold-up?" yelled someone who John was pretty sure was earbud girl.

Light filtered over the line of grayish-white heads as the other end of the portal was opened. Apparently, everyone had dropped their invisibility projections and John followed suit. John had to wait several minutes for all fifty-plus people to shuffle their way across the bridge and through the portal. Once again, John was the last to step through the portal door. He emerged through a raging waterfall onto the platform in New Zigon. John looked around. Michael and Mrs. McNeally were at the railing checking out the view. Diana was facing him, a smile on her face. She held her hand out to him, and he took it. The small platform was overloaded with people, as were the cliff-side steps. None of them seemed too surprised by the state of the Lacunavim. He realized they all had been captured after New Zigon had started to decline. John was happy to see that the healing he and Diana had done to the Lacunavim had not regressed. John kept ahold of Diana's hand during the long march up the steps to the top of the waterfall. He filled her in on what happened in the room of statues after she'd left.

When they reached the top, they found all the Zigonians waiting for them in the circular courtyard Diana had called the Scholars' Circle. They looked like a wild jungle tribe with wet tracks of statue dust running in patterns down their bodies; water splashes from the waterfall, John guessed. They crowded the benches, and some were lined up along the wall. Michael and Mrs. McNeally were waiting for them just inside the archway at the top of the steps. The Zigonians were all looking at him and Diana. It weirded John out. The four friends stood together in silence, staring back at the awaiting crowd.

"What do they want?" John whispered.

"Are you going to talk to us or what?" shouted the earbud girl. John wasn't sure he liked her anymore.

"How about we start by taking questions," Diana suggested.

"Excellent idea," approved Michael. "John, I think you should talk first. They are probably expecting you to, since you freed them and led them out of that mansion."

John's mind agreed with Michael, but his stomach didn't. John just swallowed, and then nodded his head, accepting the task. Michael put a strong, steadying hand on the back of John's neck and walked with him over to the tile design in the center of the space. John wished there was a podium, so he could hide behind it. No such luck.

Michael dropped his hand and stood to John's right. Diana and Mrs. McNeally joined him on his left. John nervously cleared his throat and said, "Hello everyone. My name is John Brown. This is Michael, Diana, and Mrs. McNeally." John didn't know Diana's last name, and he didn't want to share that Michael's last name matched Lord Vito's. "Welcome back to New Zigon." John internally cringed. That came out sounding pompous. John took a deep breath. "I'm sure you have lots of questions. We will answer them the best we can." John paused, facing the staring crowd. "We can answer them now..." John prompted.

"What century is it?" someone shouted.

"The twenty-first century," John answered. Several people gasped and began talking in low voices.

"Duh, of course it is," said none other than earbud girl, standing. "What's the *year*?" After John told her she slumped back down on her seat saying, "Thank God, my family hasn't aged and died on me yet." Several of the Zigonians around her sent her horrified looks, but she didn't seem to notice.

An older, dignified man leaned heavily on the wall in the back. "John, are you the one who freed us all?"

John humbly nodded, saying, "Yes, sir."

"Then we are all in your debt. Thank you for saving us."

John turned beet red and thought his skin would burn from his face as the Zigonians began to applaud him. In moments they were all on their feet, clapping to show him their appreciation. Diana wrapped her arm around his waist to hug him. Mrs. McNeally reached behind Diana's head to give his shoulder an affectionate squeeze. Michael proudly patted his shoulder. John wanted to crawl into a hole and hide, he was so uncomfortable. At the same time, a ripple of pleasure started in his stomach and traveled through him, calming his blush. He soaked in the love from his friends and the support being offered to him from the Zigonians. John would remember that moment for the rest of his life.

CHAPTER 32 – DECISIONS

After a time, the Zigonians sat back down and the questions began to flow. John answered them the best he could, often with Diana's help. He refrained from mentioning that he was a descendent of The Founder, and Diana followed his lead and didn't say anything about it either. Unfortunately, they couldn't keep Diana's and Michael's story a secret. Several in the crowd had already guessed the truth and called them on it. None of the Zigonians had seen the severed Life Crystavis, and John and Diana didn't bring it up. John knew they would talk about it eventually, but it would open up a whole new set of questions he wasn't prepared to answer.

It was getting late, and John felt like he'd lived a lifetime in the last thirty-six hours. It was only yesterday morning when Lord Vito's goons kidnapped Mrs. McNeally. Now it was nearly 6:30 p.m. They had been answering questions for almost two hours. The longer they had been answering questions, the more comfortable John had become speaking to the group. Finally, he said, "Look, it's getting late and it's been kind of a long day for us. If you feel anything like Diana felt after getting out of her statue, I'm guessing you're about ready to fall asleep on me, and you probably want to wash up a bit."

John turned his back to the Zigonians and asked his friends, "What do you think we should do now? Where should they all go? Diana, do you think they can stay here?"

"They can stay in the capitol building in the master's quarters. There are at least twenty-four rooms, and I think they all have big beds. If they can double up, they should be fine. Everything they need they can get here with their amulets. Why don't we all break and call an assembly sometime tomorrow?"

"Great idea! Go for it!" he said, giving Diana a little push towards the crowd. She passed the information along to the group, asking the older, more experienced Zigonians to help the younger ones and Vito's former employees.

"Let's assemble here in twenty-four hours. We'll not make any decisions until everyone is well-rested and fortified," Diana concluded.

The Zigonians slowly dissembled, many of them reaching out to touch John and/or Diana as they passed. "Are we ready to go home, children?" asked Mrs. McNeally. "These old bones aren't used to standing in one place for so long, and it has been too long since I've seen my own bed."

Diana's face tensed, and she looked down at her feet. "I didn't realize until now... without my amulet I can't make a portal to get us home."

"Don't be silly," John told her, taking her hand. "We can do it together. I did half of the stuff already to get out of the Void. It'll be a piece of cake."

Diana gave him a weak smile saying, "I hope you're right."

Their group wearily made their way down the long staircase to the platform in front of the waterfall. John and Diana stood together before the rushing water, still holding hands. "Let's join our Visity like we did when we started healing that boy," John suggested. Diana nodded and closed her eyes. John followed suit and began to project. Their Visity joined like old friends. Diana directed them to begin the portal projection. Somewhere between her guidance and the knowledge transfer information in his head, everything suddenly clicked for John. The portal opened in front of them, and they stepped through. In a few moments, they were all standing in the creek, getting their shoes and pant legs soaked. John was confident that he would be able to make portals from now on. Selecting the destination was the one thing he was unsure of, but he could have Diana help him with that. They started the long walk to Mrs. McNeally's house. Michael offered to run ahead and get the truck to come pick them up. *He must be a super-fast runner,* John thought, because he was there picking them up in under ten minutes.

They arrived at Mrs. McNeally's house a little after 7:00 p.m. John had already missed supper at his house, and his stomach had been growling embarrassingly on the truck ride home. He had sat in the truck bed, so he doubted anyone heard. Mrs. McNeally let out a grateful sigh as she stepped into her house. "Home sweet home!" She patted John on the arm saying, "Get upstairs. You're the first one in the shower. By the time you're done, I'll have some dinner ready for you."

"But... but Mrs. M!" John spluttered. "You don't need to cook for me after all you've been through!" John allowed Mrs. McNeally to push him to the bottom of the staircase.

"Don't you worry about me! Whatever you did with that green crystal made me feel twenty years younger, I swear! My arthritis is gone, my back doesn't ache, my legs don't creak... I'm a whole new me! If I could stand for two hours with nothing to do but listen to people talk, I can certainly stay on my feet a few more minutes in my favorite room making vittles for the people I love. Now, go on, get!" she said, giving John a swat on his butt for good measure.

The hot shower was heavenly, and John was tempted to take longer than he actually needed, but he resisted. He reluctantly changed back into his overalls and T-shirt. He had really liked wearing jeans these last two days.

John felt tired and hungry and longed for his own bed. Even though he'd healed himself several times in the past few days, the human spirit still has its limits.

Mrs. McNeally had some hot soup and ham sandwiches waiting for him in the kitchen. She sat down and ate with him.

"Are you okay, Mrs. M? What did they do to you to cause all those bruises I saw before I healed you?"

Mrs. McNeally tutted at him. "I've told you before, don't you worry about me; I'm a tough old bird. Believe me when I say I gave as good as I got," she said with a devilish smile.

John contemplated how Mrs. M's devilish smile was a couple dashes of naughty on top of mischievous, whereas Lord Vito's devilish smile was cold and mean. "Good for you! I was really worried about you," he admitted.

Mrs. McNeally reached over and patted his hand. "You've got a good heart. Make sure you hang onto it for me."

"Mrs. M? What do you think they'll do, the Zigonians?"

Mrs. McNeally sighed and pulled off the kitchen towel that she'd flung over her shoulder, only to start playing with it on the table. "Those that have family waiting for them will likely return to them. Those that don't, will have to make a new life for themselves. They may choose to stay in New Zigon or come back to earth. I guess we'll find out."

"Do you think…?" John said having trouble getting the words out, "that Diana will want to go back and live in New Zigon to help them rebuild?"

"I don't know, John," Mrs. McNeally said seriously. "She'll have to figure that out on her own. Selfishly, I want her to stay with me. I think she is going to have a hard time adjusting without her amulet if we can't get it back for her."

"Yeah, I know," John said. Impulsively he asked, "Hey, Mrs. M, do you have an old necklace I can have, like a gold chain? I want to make something for Diana."

Mrs. McNeally gave him a slow, knowing smile that made John wonder if she knew something he didn't. She disappeared and returned with a gold locket on a chain. "You can do whatever you want with this. It belonged to a cranky great aunt of mine. It's high quality gold, mind you. I never really liked that aunt and don't have any use for it. You know that I rarely wear jewelry anyway. Take it, do what you want with it; pound it into dust and sprinkle it on a cupcake, for all I care. If you bring a smile to my girl's face, it will be worth it."

John pocketed the locket and gave Mrs. McNeally a grateful hug. Diana walked in on them. "Did I miss anything?" she asked.

"Not really," John replied. "Mrs. M is just awesome, that's all."

"That she is," Diana said, giving the widow a kiss on the cheek as she passed by to help herself to a bowl of soup. John watched in amusement as Mrs. McNeally actually blushed.

They tried to talk John into sleeping at Mrs. McNeally's, but he wanted to get back home and back to "normal" as quickly as possible. Michael came in and gave him an awkward hug good-bye.

Once John was in bed, he couldn't get to sleep. He pulled out the locket Mrs. McNeally had given him. He had nearly forgotten about the bag of rocks he'd found in the Void. He unflattened them from his arm. Turning on the light, he dumped them on his bed. It was a mix of jewels and rocks. There were twelve different small, colored jewels and over a dozen rocks of different shapes and sizes. The smallest rock was almost as big as a half dollar, and the largest was slightly bigger than an egg. John was pretty sure what he was looking at. This was more than he'd hoped for. He had guessed that the bag contained Pollampium, but not the gems. Miranda must have collected these to make an amulet for her son. Well, they were his now, and he could do what he wanted with them. He arranged all of the crystals in a circle, and then started looking through the rocks. They were all polished and smooth like river rocks, but each one was fascinating. They were rich with earthen colors, and little pinpoints sparkled when caught in the light. John examined each one with his Visity. Some of the stones felt like the one in Diana's amulet. He guessed those were Zigonite. How Miranda had gotten her hands on so much of it was amazing. The other half of the stones had to be quartz, since Diana had said that was the only other stone that could be used as Pollampium. John compared the largest quartz rock to the largest piece of Zigonite. He pushed a little Visity into each and gauged how much was returned. The Zigonite won hands-down.

John got up and wedged his chair under the door handle as a means of locking the door. He sat back down on the bed and unflattened his Rainbow Rock. He scoured it for information on metal. He found something in the Sapphire Design section. He did knowledge transfers from that area until his head hurt. He listened to a couple of lessons and learned the basics for what he wanted to do. He hid the Rainbow Rock on his stomach, covering it again with the patch for safekeeping. He decided to put the largest Zigonite piece in the necklace, and use the second largest piece to help him build it. Looking over the crystals, he confirmed they were all Crystavis. He picked up the Sapphire Crystavis and his chosen Pollampium and held them in his fist. He laid out the locket in front of him and held the largest piece of Zigonite on top of it. Projecting his Visity through the Sapphire, John was able to reshape the gold in the locket. He slid it into a band around the Zigonite, holding it in place. The sapphire Crystavis was shining blue through his fingers. John took a breath before reaching for another Crystavis, grabbing the ruby one. When he held it to the locket, he involuntarily shook his head. He put it down and deliberately picked up the diamond. He held it in the twelve o'clock position on the gold band. He made some of the gold stream away from the band to wrap around the diamond, securing it to the piece he was creating. He did that for the other ten Crystavis, leaving the sapphire for last. He allowed his instincts to choose which color Crystavis went where. When there was one space left, he held the sapphire Crystavis between his fingers and carefully maneuvered it into place, securing it with gold. It was hard to add it while he was still using it, but he managed.

When he was done, John sat back and admired his work. He thought it looked awesome, maybe even better than Diana's first amulet. He took the Zigonite he'd been using to reshape the gold and flattened it onto the back of the amulet's Pollampium, applying a patch to hide its presence. John knew it wouldn't work as long as it was flattened, but it was always good to have a backup "just in case." John put the rest of the stones back into the bag and flattened it onto the inside of his arm, like before. He was about to do the same thing with the amulet when he decided to try it on. It made his chest nearly hum with power. He flattened it into his skin and the hum disappeared. Excited for the next day, John turned off his light and fell asleep.

* * *

John got up the next morning and went about his normal chores. Going through the familiar tasks gave him a sense of peace and accomplishment. Father had a ton of work lined up for him. John's earlier calm quickly evaporated as the day wore on, and he worried what was going on in New Zigon. Diana, dressed as Miss Invisible, visited him just before lunch. She was disappointed John had to work all day. She said the meeting wasn't until after dinner, and they wouldn't be going to New Zigon until then. She said they'd have to wait for him, so he could help with the portal. John wanted to give her his present right away, but he was dirty and smelly from working all morning, and decided to wait until after dinner.

Diana came back after lunch and was his invisible shadow for a while. They talked over the events of the last few days. Diana kept making a big deal about all the things he'd been able to do with the Pleovis, like getting himself out of the Void, healing the kids, and sending and receiving mental messages from across the room. "I'm surprised Michael could hear you," Diana commented. "Normally, humans have a hard time receiving mental messages because one usually needs to use the Pleovis to interpret them. You two must be more alike than you thought. Your thought processes must be very similar for him to interpret them on his own." John told her about how he'd picked up Michael's thoughts, then immediately regretted it. Diana got all excited over it, and nearly everything she said embarrassed John. "You're kidding! You read Michael's thoughts from across the room? Wow! And without any training? That's amazing, John, you have no idea how special you are! Of course, if your thoughts are similar, it would explain a lot of it. I wonder if Miranda gave Michael some training! Some humans are able to do some things with their Visity, but it is rare. I can't wait to ask Michael! He's going to be so pleased to find out your brain patterns are alike. Michael is like a whole new man now that he knows you are family, like he has found a purpose." That last part worried John.

"What does he expect from me?" John asked, upset. "I told him he's not my dad, and I've got a family. It might not be a *normal* family, and it has its faults, but it's mine!"

Diana sympathized, "Just spend some time with him; get to know each other. I think that's all he is hoping for right now."

They talked some more. Diana didn't mention her missing amulet, and John didn't bring it up. Eventually, Diana went home, and left John to finish his work.

John took extra care cleaning up for dinner. Dinner itself seemed never-ending. Father was in a talkative mood. When he asked John how his time at Mrs. McNeally's went, John hedged and just said that Mrs. McNeally had worked him from sunup to sundown, that a lot of it was dirty and smelly, and that she fed him well. He had forgotten their cover story and didn't want to contradict anything Mrs. McNeally had told Father in church. Father seemed to accept the vague answer. Father was always more interested in how *much* he worked when he helped Mrs. McNeally versus what he actually worked *on*.

When dinner finally ended, John ran to the barn, went in the front door, turned invisible, and slipped out the back. He was out of breath by the time he reached Mrs. McNeally's house. They were all waiting by the truck for him. John had hoped to run upstairs and change into some of Bobby's old clothes, but everyone was obviously eager to go. John rode in the back again, and when they got to the creek, they took off their shoes and waded up to the waterfall. John was surprised Mrs. McNeally was going with them. She had used portals twice now, so maybe it wasn't a big deal anymore. John was a little uncomfortable around Michael, not knowing what to expect. There wasn't time for much talking as it turned out. John and Diana made the portal together, and they arrived on the platform in New Zigon. A Zigonian was waiting for them and walked with them up the stairs. John thought that was impractical. He certainly wouldn't want to take those stairs any more than he had to.

The group was waiting for them in the scholar's circle, mingling and talking in hushed voices. They had all cleaned up pretty well. They sat down when they saw John and company. John and Diana answered questions for about half an hour before the conversation turned towards the future. Someone actually asked John and Diana, "What should we do now?"

John squirmed uncomfortably, then remembered what Mrs. McNeally had told him the night before. "You have a choice in front of you. You can return to your families, for those that have them. For others, you can choose to make yourself a life on earth, or you can choose to live here in New Zigon.

It's a bit of a fixer-upper I have to say, but it could work." No one commented. "I would like to hand it over to you now. Pick someone to manage your… talking. Unfortunately, I can't stay. Good luck." Before anyone could comment, John took Diana's hand, walked over to the entrance, and leaned against the wall where Michael and Mrs. McNeally were standing.

Michael patted him on the shoulder, "Good job, John. Very well said, simple, and to the point."

Michael and Mrs. McNeally were ready to go, but Diana didn't want to leave yet. John said he was confident he could create the portal on his own to get them home, so Diana could stay and watch the proceedings. One of the older Zigonians had taken center stage, and they were deep in discussion over their options. Diana was listening intently and barely waved goodbye to them as they left. John looked back to see her move to join the group.

John made the portal home without any trouble. He chose to ride in the back of the truck again instead of trying to squeeze between the two adults on the bench seat. Mrs. McNeally insisted they all go inside for milk and cookies. They didn't talk much. When John stood to go, Michael also got up and asked to walk with him a ways. John couldn't think of a polite way to decline, so he soon found himself walking outside next to the large warrior. It was a cool summer night. There was a light breeze, and the nighttime animals and insects were out and about, making their familiar noises.

"John," Michael started, "I want you to know how happy I am to find out that we are family. Family is everything in my time. But, I do not want you to feel uncomfortable around me."

Wow, John thought. Was he that obvious that Michael had noticed his feelings?

"I know I was a bit of a grizzly bear towards you at first, and for that I am sorry," Michael continued. "I felt we had come to an understanding before this news, and I do not want to ruin that. Diana told me that you are afraid I will interfere with your current family."

Traitor! John thought towards Diana.

"I just want to get to know you. It is enough for me to know you live, are doing well, and are nearby. I would like to be your friend if that is possible."

They walked in silence for a while before John said, "I think that'll be cool."

Michael gave John a side hug and gruffly said, "Thank you."

Michael left John off at the end of his driveway. John turned invisible and started down the drive between the maple trees. The conversation with Michael had been awkward, but it left John feeling relieved. He would like to be friends with Michael. He seemed like a cool guy. His over-exuberance at discovering they were related had scared him, but Michael seemed to have calmed down, and things would be okay. John liked the idea of having an ancient, deadly warrior as his backup, especially when he started high school in the fall.

John fell asleep easily that night, one burden lifted from his chest. Worry over whether Diana was going to stay or go, unfortunately, played heavily in his dreams.

He was awoken by someone jiggling his bed. He groggily rubbed his eyes and saw Diana sitting on his bed facing him. She must have shaken the mattress, waking him up.

"Hi," she said softly.

"Hi," he returned. He glanced at his clock. It was only a few minutes before sunrise. His alarm would ring soon; he'd decided he deserved to sleep in a little. "Good Morning," he added.

When she didn't say anything, he pulled himself up to a sitting position and tucked the sheet up under his arms to cover himself. "What are you doing here, Diana?"

"I need to talk to you," she said, not meeting his eyes. John's heart sank. He knew what was coming. She was leaving them to go live in New Zigon. John sat, quietly waiting for her to continue.

"Most of the Zigonians decided to try and rebuild New Zigon. Some of the younger ones with families have already left to return to them. The rest are staying. They are taking turns putting their amulets on the podium in the repository to heal the Lacunavim, but it is very slow, nothing like when you helped me. I had to work with someone to take the reactive projection off the door to the repository. The Founder has disappeared. They located the chamber where he'd been living, and it looked like he'd been gone for several days. I think that had a lot to do with people staying. The Founder isn't very popular among his people." Diana fiddled with John's bedspread and wouldn't look at him as she said, "They asked me to stay with them." After a few moments she looked up and searched his eyes. John was about to say something mushy to convince her to stay with him and Mrs. McNeally, when his alarm clock rang, saving him from embarrassing himself.

After he shut off the alarm, he turned to look at her. "What are you going to do?" he asked quietly.

"I decided to stay here, with you and Mrs. M, that is, if you want me to," Diana said, looking vulnerable. John remembered wiping the statue dust off her face at the museum and how far they had come since then.

"Are you an idiot?"

Diana was instantly offended, "Wh-what?" she huffed.

John was so relieved, that he grabbed her by the arms and pulled her against him into a tight hug. "Of course we want you to stay, you nincompoop!"

Diana wrapped her arms around his neck and started to cry. John wondered why she was crying. *Girls are weird*, he concluded. John held her tight, so thankful that he wouldn't be losing his closest friend. It was odd that he should find such a great friend in a girl. A girl ... A GIRL! He was hugging a girl, in his room, on his bed, and he was only wearing sleeping shorts under the blankets. *Yes!* Part of him wanted to cheer and do a victory dance. John didn't recognize that part of him; it was new. The other part, the normal part thought... *No! Not good!*

Diana had stopped crying and seemed just to be enjoying the hug. He pushed her away from him as gently and as quickly as he could, then he tucked his sheet tighter under his armpits to keep himself covered. "I'm... uh...glad you're staying."

"Thanks," she said smiling through her tears. She dried her eyes, and they just stared at each other for a few minutes.

"Well, I'd better get back. Stop over when you can, okay?" Diana said as she moved to leave. John shot out his arm to stop her, and his sheet fell a few inches.

"Wait!" he said, quickly pulling his hand back and retucking his only cover. "Do you think you could hand me that T-shirt on the chair over there?"

"No problem," she said as she retrieved the shirt.

He quickly put it on and relaxed. "I have something for you."

Diana sat back down on the bed. "You have something, for me?" she said eagerly.

John unflattened the bag of Pollampium from his arm and gave it to her. "I found these in the Void on another tether. I thought it was just some rock collection and nearly forgot about it."

"You could loan these to the Zigonians to help repair the Lacunavim." Diana poured the stones out onto John's bed. "John! These are fabulous! Oh, these should really help, thank you!"

As she was distracted putting the rocks back in the bag, John unflattened the amulet he made for her and lifted the chain over his head. Face beet-red and burning, he dangled it in front of her. "I, um, I... made this for you," he managed to choke out. Diana glanced up and her eyes locked onto the amulet. She slowly lifted her face to catch up with her eyes. Her mouth was hanging open, and her face was blank. *Oh perfect*, John thought. *She hates it. It's all wrong. It was a stupid thing to do.* John wanted to dive under the covers and hide.

Diana lifted her hand and reverently accepted the gift. "John, this is the most beautiful amulet I've ever seen! How in the world did you manage this?"

John no longer wanted to hide under the covers as he said, "All the pieces were in the bag with the Pollampium. The chain came from Mrs. M."

Diana held it up in the soft morning light beginning to come through his window. "It's gorgeous!" she said as she watched the amulet spin and sway on its chain, sparkling like a Christmas tree as it caught the light. Suddenly, she grabbed it in her fist and closed her eyes. A second later she was thrusting the amulet back at John. "It was a nice thought, but I don't want it."

John sat even straighter as he tried to push the amulet back at Diana. "What's wrong with it? You just said it was beautiful!"

"You made it, you should keep it," she pushed back.

"I made it for you, you dope," he returned, pushing it to her again.

"Don't call me a dope, you're the dope," she said, upset as she pushed it once again towards him.

"Why don't you want it?" John almost yelled as he tried to hide his hurt feelings. He held it out to her one more time.

Diana closed John's fingers over the amulet and pushed his fist away gently saying, "It won't work for me."

"Why not? Did I make it wrong?"

"No, it's perfect; it's just that the Crystavis don't have any receptors, meaning they won't work for me. I made all the Crystavis in my amulet, so they didn't need receptors, they just accepted my Visity Signature automatically," Diana said, near to tears. "That's the way most of them are."

"Awe, don't cry," John said, triggering two tears to leak out of Diana's eyes. "They worked for me, so that means I can change them, right? You can help me change them, add your Signature to them."

"If they worked for you, that means they belong to your family!" Diana cried out. "Family Signatures are similar, remember? That's how amulets can be passed down through generations. I definitely can't take it now!"

"I insist, and I won't take no for an answer. Come here," John ordered, trying to emulate Michael's authoritative tone. It must have worked because Diana scooted closer to him on the bed. "Which color covers Crystavis modification? Isn't there one called coding?"

"It's called encoding, and it is the light amethyst one. That's light purple for those who are gemstone illiterate," Diana answered, shifting into her teacher mode.

John gave her a crooked smile. She was giving in, and it looked like she was no longer at risk for crying.

"Great!" John said, adjusting the amulet in his hand. He placed it in his right palm and held it out to her. "Now you cover it with your hand, then we'll close our fingers, like we're shaking on it." She did as he said. "Perfect. Let's start with the diamond, since that was the first one I put in, then we'll do the rest going around clockwise. The only thing is, we'll have to end with the sapphire because I put that in last."

"Do you think the order matters?"

"I don't know; it just feels right." In his head he was cheering, *Knowledge transfers, Rah! Rah! Rah!*

"Okay, now join our Visity's just like before. I'll get us into the Crystavis, and then you guide us to add the receptor parts, alright?" Diana nodded. "Let's do it then," John said as he closed his eyes and reached for Diana's Visity. The whole process went smoothly and only took a few minutes.

When it was over, John opened his eyes. They looked at each other. "Well, try it," he encouraged. Diana tightened their handshake, and he felt her Visity whistle through the Diamond Crystavis, then each of the other Crystavis in turn.

"There now, that wasn't so hard, was it?" John said as he lifted the amulet from their hands and hung it over Diana's head. As he settled it around her neck, he said, "Now you're all set with a brand-new amulet. Gina can go rot in… some bad place. And I can borrow it whenever I need it, right? Since you and I can both use it now?"

Diana gently held up the amulet to see it sparkle in the morning sunlight once more. She stared at it for a long moment. John wondered if she was ever going to say anything, when she flung herself at him, wrapping her arms around his neck and nearly banging his head against the wall in the process. "Thank you! Thank you, thank you, thank you!" Diana repeated.

John returned the hug, saying with much satisfaction, "You are welcome."

"You are the best-est, best friend ever!"

"Same to you," John said, smiling widely. Mrs. McNeally was back safely, the Zigonians were taking care of themselves, things were cool with Michael, and now Diana was staying. John thought that this was going to be the best summer ever.

Then Diana broke into tears, and, once again, John thought, *Girls are weird.*

THE END

GLOSSARY

Crystavis   [**kris**-t*uh*-vis] *n.* A crystal that has been engineered to create patterns in the Pleovis. A person can push their Visity into a Crystavis to mold it into a specific pattern. (Similar in concept to how pushing air through a flute or other wind instrument makes music.) A Crystavis only works for the person who created it, unless it is altered to accept more than one Visity Signature. *(see Generic Receptors)*

Crystavis Amulet   [**kris**-t*uh*-vis **am**-y*uh*-lit] *n.* Each Zigonian makes their own amulet once they possess the skills to create a Crystavis. Pollampium is in the center, and it is surrounded by up to twelve Crystavis, one for each Pleovis avenue. Amulets can be passed down through families.

Crystavis Master   [**kris**-t*uh*-vis **mah**-ster] *n.* A Zigonian who has attained the level of master in a particular Pleovis Avenue (line of study.)

Encoding   [en-**kohd**-ing] *v.* The act of storing information in a Crystavis. Examples of encoded information include knowledge transfers and 3D recordings (mental videos.) *n.* One of the twelve Pleovis Avenues of Study.

Embedding   [em-**bed**-ing] *v.* The act of putting one item atomically into another; the two objects share the same space without impacting each other. Most often, one object is completely embedded in another and is not visible. *n.* One of the twelve Pleovis Avenues of Study.

Flatten, Unflatten   [**flat**-en], [**uhn**-flat-en] *v.* To flatten an object is to remove its mass, leaving a molecular diagram that has to be stored on another object. Zigonians often flatten their amulets and store them on their dermis, like an unseen tattoo. An item is flattened by removing the Pleovis within it.
To unflatten an object is to return its mass by "inflating" it with Pleovis.

Founder, The   [**foun**-der] *n.* Son of the first Zigonian to reach earth. (*see Zigon*) He altered the DNA of a group of people to better match his own, turning them into Zigonians, just as his father had done to his mother. He founded the New Zigon community.

Founder's Curse, The   [**foun**-ders kurs] *n.* A Reactive Projection The Founder managed to place on every Zigonian that reacts when a Zigonian is captured, turning both the Zigonian and his/her captor to impenetrable stone.

Generic Receptor   [juh-**ner**-ik ri-**sep**-ter] *n.* A Crystavis will always accept the Visity Signature of the person who made it. A generic receptor can be built into a Crystavis so that any Zigonian can use it. This is extremely difficult to do successfully, i.e. it is hard to create a Generic Receptor without compromising the Crystavis's output. Very few Zigonians can build them. A Crystavis with a Generic Receptor is called a Primary Crystavis.

Knowledge transfer   [**nol**-ij **trans**-fer] *n.* The process of sending information directly into your long-term memory. The transfer can occur from one person to another, or from an encoded Crystavis to a person. Person-to-person transfers can be dangerous, and not many Zigonians attempt it. If not done correctly, the person whose knowledge is being pulled may experience memory loss.

Lacunavim   [luh-**kyoo**-nuh-vim] *n.* The Lacunavim is a pocket of space within the Void. It is where New Zigon is built. Diana describes it as, "A Lacunavim isn't another world; it is more like an in-between place. It is a contained space, encircled, like under a dome. It is really pretty. The 'dome' is partly luminescent and shimmers in pinks, blues, and reds. My mother said it is like being inside the womb of the universe." Claire describes it as, "The Lacunavim was built by creating a bubble in the Void. The Void is its own dimension that is everywhere and nowhere."

New Zigon   [nyoo **zahy**-gawn] *n.* The community of people whose DNA has been altered, in a way that allows them to control their Visity. Also refers to the city built in a Lacunavim where those people live.

Pleovis [plee-**o**-vis] *n*. The substance that is in between all particles. The Pleovis is fluid like water or air and moves in patterns around and through objects. It is what gives an item mass. It holds things together, pulls them apart, moves them and stops them. It is constantly changing. Sometimes it circles around molecules binding them together, and sometimes it vibrates like when it supports an electric current or hums like when it transmits light energy. Sometimes it stays still and acts like both a filler and a glue. It has a song of its own, dancing around and through everything in the universe.

Pleovis Avenue [plee-**o**-vis **av**-*uh*-nyoo] *n*. Pleovis functions are divided into twelve lines of study, each called a Pleovis Avenue. A different colored Crystavis is associated with each avenue.

Pollampium [puh-**lam**-pee-uhm] *n*. A substance that can amplify a pattern in the Pleovis. A rock from Zigon (Zigonite) works best. Quartz can also be used.

Pottitude [**po**-ti-tood] *n*. A person's aptitude towards projecting. It defines a person's raw projection strength as well as the person's potential ability to master projecting in a particular Pleovis Avenue.

Primary Crystavis [**prahy**-mer-ee **kris**-*tuh*-vis] *n*. A Crystavis with a generic receptor. Usually, the largest and best Crystavis within a Pleovis Avenue of Study had a generic receptor added to it by The Founder, Miranda, or Lady Aberlene, and was stored in the repository. *(see also generic receptor)*

Project [pro-**jekt**] *v*. The act of controlling the pattern one's Visity makes in the Pleovis. This is called projecting. The pattern itself is called a projection. Uses: A person can *project*. A person is *projecting*. A person made a *projection*.

Reactive Projection [ree-**ak**-tiv pro-**jekt**-sh*un*] *n*. Diana describes it as "It's when the Pleovis moves in a type of holding pattern, waiting for a certain pattern to initiate the desired Pleovis manipulation. It's like encasing one pattern inside another. Once the one on the outside recognizes its trigger, it releases the pattern on the inside. The more complex projections use this concept over and over just like an 'If...then' statement in programming. The Founder's Curse is a Reactive Projection.

Repository   [ri-**poz**-i-tawr-ee] *n.* A circular room at the top of the capital building in New Zigon. It is where the Primary Crystavis and the Summas Stone were stored. The Lacunavim uses the platform within this room to power itself.

Scholar's Circle   [**skol**-ers **sur**-k*uh*l] *n.* A tiered pit at the top of the cliff within New Zigon. It is in front of the capital building. Each tier has stone seating, like an outdoor ampitheater.

Summas Stone   [**suhm**-*uh*s stohn] *n.* The Summas Stone is the largest piece of Zigonite brought to earth. It is the size of an ostrich's egg; it is oval and approximately 10 inches long and six inches high. It sat in the repository in New Zigon and helped maintain the Lacunavim. Miranda stole the Summas Stone during the fourteenth century and it hasn't been seen since.

Visity   [**viz**-it-ee] *n.* The waves in the Pleovis caused by a person's brain activity. Some people call it an aura. A Zigonian can control the pattern their Visity makes in the Pleovis. This is called Projecting.

Visity Signature   [**viz**-it-ee **sig**-n*uh*-cher] *n.* Each person's Visity has its own format, called its Signature. Signatures are unique like fingerprints, but there are common components that are tied to genetics. These common components are passed down through families, allowing families to share Crystavis Amulets.

Void, The   [void] *n.* An undefined space between portals. It is much like outer space in that it has no light nor gravity. It does have the same air as Earth. There is a gentle, almost imperceptible current of Pleovis moving throughout the Void.

Zigon   [**zahy**-gawn] *n.* Another planet, somewhere in the universe.

Zigonian   [**zahy**-gawn-ee-*uh*n] *n.* A person from Zigon or New Zigon. A Zigonian's DNA is different from regular human DNA. This altered DNA allows a person to control their Visity.

Zigonite   [zahy-gaw-nahyt] n. A rock from the planet Zigon. It makes the best Pollampium, and it is highly valued by the Zigonians.

ACKNOWLEDGMENTS

A special thanks to my dad, Paul, my sister, Lisa, my nephew, Jared, and my friend, Susan, for reading along with me; their enthusiasm wouldn't let me give up. Thanks to my mom, Deanna, for her love and never-ending faith in me, and to my mother-in-law, Nancy, for supporting me in all I do.

Thanks to all my honorary editors: Aunt Ruth, Brenda, and particularly my godmother, Aunt Rose, to whom I think I owe a new case of red pens.

ABOUT THE AUTHOR

Danelle O'Donnell lives with her husband and three sons in Western Pennsylvania. She wrote, edited, and published her debut novel, "New Zigon - The Founder's Curse" in 2014, at age 44. She has 20 years' experience in Information Technology, and owns her own arts and crafts business. She is still trying to figure out what she wants to be when she grows up! Danelle had been working on the science fiction and back story for New Zigon for over ten years before finally sitting down to write. Once putting 'pen to paper' or 'fingers to keyboard,' the story quickly came together and was finished in six weeks. Editing, of course, took much longer.

You can find more about New Zigon on
    Danelle's blog: www.newzigon.blogspot.com
    Facebook: www.facebook.com/New Zigon

27845452R00175

Made in the USA
San Bernardino, CA
19 December 2015